'There is nobody else like Mona Awad, daring enough to plunge her hands – rings and all – into the viscera of story and discover an unsettling beauty within. *Rouge* is her most magnetic work yet, a thrilling dystopian romp that knows that beneath the glossy, aspirational veneer of self-care lurks the same old gothic abyss.' **Alexandra Kleeman, author of *Something New Under the Sun***

'A brilliant, biting critique of western beauty standards as well as a soaring, phantasmagoric, Angela Carter-esque fairy tale about trauma and the loss of self. *Rouge* is deeply unsettling, funny, obsessive, and unlike anything I've read. A truly mesmerizing read.' **Paul Tremblay, author of *The Cabin at the End of the World* and *A Head Full of Ghosts***

'Unsettling, whimsical, and moving, *Rouge* is an authentic, innovative kind of narrative magic that's both surreal and absolute. A striking novel of incandescence and heart.' **Iain Reid, author of *I'm Thinking of Ending Things***

Rouge

—a novel—

Mona Awad

SCRIBNER

LONDON NEW YORK SYDNEY TORONTO NEW DELHI

First published in the United States by Marysue Ricci Books,
an imprint of Simon & Schuster, Inc., 2023

First published in Great Britain by Scribner,
an imprint of Simon & Schuster UK Ltd, 2023

1 3 5 7 9 10 8 6 4 2

Simon & Schuster UK Ltd
1st Floor
222 Gray's Inn Road
London WC1X 8HB

Simon & Schuster Australia, Sydney
Simon & Schuster India, New Delhi

www.simonandschuster.co.uk
www.simonandschuster.com.au
www.simonandschuster.co.in

A CIP catalogue record for this book
is available from the British Library

HB ISBN: 978-1-3985-0493-6
TPB ISBN: 978-1-3985-0494-3
EBOOK ISBN: 978-1-3985-0495-0
AUDIO ISBN: 978-1-3985-2745-4

Printed and Bound in the UK using 100% Renewable
Electricity at CPI Group (UK) Ltd

MIX
Paper | Supporting
responsible forestry
FSC
www.fsc.org
FSC® C171272

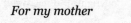

For my mother

Because what is the face, what, finally, is the skin over the flesh,
a cover, a disguise, rouge for the insupportable horror
of our living nature.

—*Elena Ferrante*, The Days of Abandonment

Prologue

She used to tell you fairy tales at night, remember? Once upon a time. When you were a sad, dreamy little girl. Each night you lay in your princess bed, surrounded by your glassy-eyed dolls, waiting for her like a wish. *Tick, tick* went the seconds on your Snow White clock. The moon rose whitely from the black clouds. And then . . .

"Knock, knock," Mother whispered from your bedroom door.

"Come in," you called in your child's voice.

And she did. She came and sat right on the edge of your bed like a queen, didn't she? Cigarette between her white fingers. Exuding her scent of violets and smoke.

"All right," Mother said. "Which story do you want to hear tonight, Belle?"

Belle. French for "beautiful." It's what she called you, even though you were a beastly little thing. Not at all like Mother. She was fair, slim, and smooth, remember? Like something out of a fairy tale. Like the dolls that lined the walls of your room. It was Mother who'd bought you those dolls. Positioned them in every corner, every nook, so no matter where you looked, you saw their glossy hair, their fair skin, those lips of red that were always sort of smiling at you. Like they all had a secret between them.

"Well, Belle?" And she smiled at you just like the dolls, remember?

She was wearing the red silk robe, the one you loved best. Sometimes you tried it on when she wasn't home, breathing in her violets and smoke. She had a pair of red shoes that matched. Satin, heeled, with puffs of red feathers on the toes—your favorites. You tried those on too, but it never went well. Two teetering steps and you were on the floor, weren't you?

"Which story?" Mother prompted now. Beginning to get impatient with you, your dreaminess. How you were staring at her like a little psychopath.

"The one about the beautiful maiden," you said.

Again? And she looked a little like she was sorry for you, like you were damned. Definitely. Because there were other stories, weren't there? There was the one about the rabbit and the turtle, for instance. There was the one about three pigs and a wolf. There was one about a girl who turned into a seal, that was a sweet one. But you didn't give a fuck about the other stories. You never did. You'd already chosen, hadn't you?

You nodded. "The beautiful maiden," you said. "Again."

And Mother sighed. Or did she smile? She didn't take the familiar book off the shelf with its very cracked spine. Didn't need to. Thanks to you, Mother knew this story by heart.

"Once upon a time," she began, "in a land far away, there lived a beautiful maiden in a castle by the sea . . ."

That's how it always started. You sighed too. A land far away. A beautiful maiden. A castle, the sea. You closed your eyes the better to see it all shimmering in your mind.

"How beautiful?" you asked Mother, your eyes shut tight.

"So incredibly beautiful," Mother said, "that all admired her from near and far." She sounded bored. A familiar digression. You sought this embellishment every night, didn't you?

"Yes." You nodded. "From near and far." Of course they would.

"From near and far," Mother confirmed.

"And many envied her too," she added in a low voice. The night it all began. Your once upon a time. Remember the wolf moon in the window? Two gray-bodied spiders dangling from webs on the pink walls. A red-haired doll with a crack in her face staring at you from a satin pillow.

"Envied her?" you repeated, opening your eyes. You saw Mother had moved away from your bed. She was now sitting at the little white vanity table she bought you last Christmas, the one with the three-way mirror. She was so pleased to give you this gift that you acted pleased too. But you didn't like this mirror. It was enough to have to see yourself once, let alone three times, remember? It was enough to have to open your eyes and see yourself at all. But Mother loved this mirror. She was looking at her three selves right now, brushing her hair with your long-handled brush. The brush was painted gold to match the gold trim of the vanity, another gift from Mother. The back was encrusted with bright-colored bits of plastic that you thought were precious stones. The bristles didn't work on your kind of hair, so thick and coarse. But it worked wonderfully on Mother's. Now you watched her brush her dark red hair with long, slow strokes.

"What's envy, Mother?" you asked her.

"Envy is when you hate someone because they have something you want," she said simply.

You stared at her reflection in the three-way glass.

"Like being pretty," you said.

"Exactly," she yawned. A glimpse of her red throat. "Like being pretty. Or young," she added, looking back at you in the glass. Her glossy dark red hair tumbling over one white shoulder. Her red robe brought out the bright blue of her eyes. The robe was a gift from the faraway country where your father was born. He bought her one in nearly every color, each jewel-bright and threaded with gold. You'd never met your father, but you'd seen pictures. He reminded you a little of the ogres in your fairy-tale books. Swarthy and stout, like you. You could see your eyes in his eyes. Your skin in his skin. There was a time when you even feared you might be part ogre, remember?

When you told Mother this once, she'd laughed hysterically. She'd thrown her head back and laughed until she'd cried. And then you cried too, you couldn't help it. So it was true. You were definitely part ogre, just as you'd feared. *Stop it*, she said, and then she slapped you. Right across the face. Tears instantly stung your eyes. *Listen to me*, she hissed. *Listen*. And the world grew very still while she assured you with the softest voice that of course your father was not an ogre, *of course not.* He was a lovely man, *god rest his soul.* Handsome, even, many women thought so. He was just from a place where there happened to be more sun, that was all. And people in that place were darker and they were hairier. So you were darker and you were hairier. You were *lovely.* You were *lucky,* she'd said, putting her white hands on your shoulders. Shaking them a little. *Lucky, do you hear me?* She *wished* she had your skin and your hair, absolutely. *Definitely.* And then she petted you like a dog. Smiled at you in the three-way glass. And you knew then that she was lying. She didn't wish that. Not at all.

Now you looked at her in the mirror until she looked away. Took a drag of her cigarette. Went back to brushing her hair with your gold toy brush.

"Anyway," Mother said. "The beautiful maiden. She had this mirror. And the mirror talked to her."

Yes, yes. This was your favorite part of the story. That the maiden talked to a mirror. That she had a friend in the glass who told her things. You were such a lonely little girl, weren't you? Whispering to grass. Befriending sticks. Dreaming yourself into movies and books. Every screen, every page, like a door to another world, remember?

"What did it tell her?" you asked like you didn't know. Like Mother hadn't already told you this part a thousand times.

"That she was beautiful," Mother said as if it was obvious. "The most beautiful in all the land."

You nodded. An ache opened up inside you. Deep, deep. For what? Some other life, some other self, some other body. In a land far away. In a castle by the sea.

"But then one day," Mother said, and her tone shifted. "One day, the mirror didn't say that." She was staring at her three selves in the glass when she said this.

"It didn't?"

"No."

And in the mirror, you saw a shimmer. A sparkling something that wasn't there before.

"Mother?" you whispered, your eyes on the shimmer.

Not just a shimmer now, a shape. A darkly glimmering shape hovering in the mirror behind Mother's reflection. Mother shook her head at the mirror. She took another drag of her cigarette. She was staring at the shape too. Like she wasn't at all surprised to see it there.

"It said something else," Mother whispered, her eyes on the shape. What sort of shape? Something or someone?

Someone.

A figure. Staring at Mother. You could feel it staring though it had no eyes you could see. Just a silhouette, remember?

"What did it say?"

"Something terrible," Mother said, staring at the figure who stared back. "Something inevitable. Something true."

Like what? Like what?

Mother shook her head again and again. She looked in the mirror like she was about to cry. The figure was looking at Mother sorrowfully. Fake sorrowfully, you felt, you didn't know why. And that's when it looked up. Lifted its eyes from Mother to you. Yes, it had eyes, though you couldn't see them. You could feel them on you. A coldness. It stared at you and smiled. You knew it was smiling, though it had no mouth you could see either. Just a man-shaped shadow. Just that shimmering silhouette.

You should've been afraid. You really should've been. Definitely. But you weren't, were you? When you felt his eyes on you, all of you was suddenly lit up. Like the glow-in-the dark stars on your bedroom ceiling. Like your grandmother's chandelier. You were smiling now.

"And then what happened, Mother?" Your eyes were staring right into his eyes, you could sort of see them now. He had eyes that saw your soul, you knew this. It was a he, you knew that, too, didn't you?

Mother wasn't looking at the figure anymore. She was looking at you.

"Mother?" you pressed, feeling the figure's eyes on you. "What happened?"

But Mother just smiled darkly in the glass.

"And then all hell broke loose."

Part I

1

2016

La Jolla, California

After the funeral. I'm hiding in Mother's bathroom watching a skin-care video about necks. Cheap black dress that chafes. Illicit cigarette. Sitting on the toilet amid her decorative baskets, her red jellyfish soaps, her black towel sets. Smoke comes tumbling out of my mouth in amorphous gray clouds. I blow it out the window where the palm trees still sway and the alien sun still shines and the sky is a blue that hurts my eyes. There's a Kleenex box made entirely of jagged seashells at my back—probably she never once filled it with Kleenex. There's her mirror over the sink, a crack running right down the middle of the glass. Whenever I look at myself in that mirror, I look broken. Cleaved. There's the perfume she wore every day of her life on the marble counter, the Chanel Rouge Allure lipstick in its gold-and-black case. A little cluster of red jars and vials on a silver tray. *For the face, dear. For the face*, I can hear Mother saying to me. *Need all the help we can get, am I right?* Cynical smile of the beautiful who know they're on the downhill slope.

Yes, Mother, I'd say. *But not you. You don't need any help at all.*

I don't look closely at any of it.

Instead I stare at my phone, where the skin video plays. My eyes are dry and they are focused. Focused on Dr. Marva, who is telling me in her reassuring English accent all about my poor, poor neck. The video is actually called "How to Save Your Own Neck." I've watched it before. It's one of my favorites.

Dr. Marva's soft yet firm words fill my mother's bathroom.

"We don't take care of our necks," Dr. Marva is saying sadly. And she looks quite sad in her white silk blouse. As if she is grieving for us and our poor necks. "They often get neglected, don't they?"

She looks right at me with her golden eyes. I find myself nodding as I always do.

"Yes, Marva," I whisper along. Yes, they do get neglected.

"Which is quite a tragedy," Marva observes. "Because the skin there is already so thin."

Didn't Mother always tell me this? *The neck never lies, Belle. The neck is truthful, deeply cruel. Like a mirror of the soul. It reveals all, you see?* And she'd point at her own throat. I'd look at Mother's throat and see nothing. Just an expanse of whiteness shot through with blue veins.

I see, Mother, I always said.

On my phone screen, Marva shakes her head as if this truth about necks is one she cannot bear to speak. "What atrocities," she whispers, stroking her own neck, "might bloom here? Redness, of course," she intones. "A brown pigment, perhaps. Thinning, atrophied patches. Essentially," she adds with a laugh, "a triumvirate of horror."

As Marva says this, she tilts her head back to reveal an impossibly smooth white column of flesh. Untainted, unmarred. She strokes the skin softly with her red-nailed hands.

As I watch her do this, I begin to stroke my own neck. I can't help it.

A flash of Mother's throat appears again in my mind's eye. Smooth and pale just like Marva's. Always some pendant to show off the hollows. Then toward the end, this sudden fondness for jewel-toned glass, stones cut in the strangest shapes. An obsidian dagger. A warped, dark red heart. The way she'd clutch that heart with her fingers. Look at me on video calls like she was lost and my face was a dark forest, a mirror in which she barely recognized herself.

Dread fills my stomach now as I stroke my own neck. Not at the memory of Mother, I'm ashamed to say. But because I feel the skin tags, the unsightly bands here and here and here.

"Your poor, poor neck," Marva whispers, shaking her head again as if she can actually see me. "It could really use some tightening and brightening, couldn't it?"

Yes, Marva. It really could.

Knock, knock.

Sylvia. I can feel it. Her little knuckles rapping on the door. Then the saccharine tone I hear in my teeth roots. "Mirabelle?" she says. "Mira, are you in there?"

Terrible to hear my name spoken by that voice. I think of Mother's voice. Rich, deep, accented with French. I was only ever *Mirabelle* when she was angry. She never once dignified *Mira*, though it's what I mostly go by these days. *Belle*, she always called me. Toward the end, though, she just stared at me confused. *Who are you?* she'd whisper. *Who are you?*

Now I close my eyes as though I've been struck. The cigarette is ash in my hands.

Another, more persistent knock from Sylvia. "Hello? Are we in there?"

I can't ignore Sylvia. She'll try the door. I'll watch the crystal knob rattle. When she finds it locked, she'll take a screwdriver to the handle. A credit card to the lock. She might even kick it down with her little Gucci-soled foot. All under the smiling guise of concern.

I open the door. Step back and smooth my little black dress down. Is it a dress? More like a strangely cut sack. It hangs on me like it's deeply depressed. Maybe it is. It was Sylvia who loaned me this dress, of course. Brought it in from her and Mother's dress shop, Belle of the Ball, where I myself used to work years ago. Before I left California and went back to Montreal. Left Mother's dress shop to work in another dress shop. *Left me*, Mother might say.

Here you are, my dear, Sylvia said yesterday, handing me the sad black shroud on its wooden hanger. *My dear*, she called me, and I felt my soul shudder.

In case you need something to wear for the . . . party. That's what they call funerals here in California now, apparently. *Parties.* I looked at the black shapeless shift and I thought, *Since when did Mother start selling such grim fare in her shop?* I wanted to boldly refuse. My firmest, coldest *No thank you.* But I actually did need something to wear. I'd brought nothing with me on this trip. Ever since last week, I've been in a haze. That was when I got the phone call from the policeman at work. *Mirabelle Nour?* he said.

Yes?

Are you the daughter of Noelle De . . . De . . .

Des Jardins, I told him. *It's French. For "of the gardens."* And as I said those words, *of the gardens*, I knew. I knew exactly what the cop had called to tell me. An accident, apparently. Out for a walk late at night. By the ocean, by the cliff's edge. Fell onto the rocks below. Found dead on the beach this morning by a man walking his Saint Bernard.

Well, Mother loved Saint Bernards, I said. I don't know why I said that. I have no idea how Mother felt about Saint Bernards. Silence for a long time. My throat was like a fist tightening. I could feel the hydrating mist I'd just applied to my face drying tackily.

No foul play, the cop said at last.

Of course not, I said. *How could there be?* I felt my body become another substance. I looked at the mirror on the wall. There I was in my black vintage dress, standing stiffly behind the shop counter, gripping the phone in my fist. I could have been talking to a customer.

I'm so sorry, the cop said.

I stared at my reflection. Watched it mouth the words I must have also spoken. *Yes. Me too. Thank you for telling me, Officer. I appreciate your taking the time to call.*

He seemed hesitant to hang up. Maybe he was waiting for me to cry, but I didn't. I was at work, for one thing. My boss, Persephone, was right beside me, for another.

Mira, Persephone said after I put the phone down. *Everything all right?* She was dressed, as always, like she was about to go to a gothic sock hop. Her powdered, too-pale face turned to me with something like concern. I stared at her foundation, cracking under the shop lights.

My mother died, I said, like I was reporting the weather. *She fell onto some rocks. She was found by a Saint Bernard.*

And then what? There was a chair placed behind me into which I fell. There was a bottle of Russian liqueur brought to my lips. It tasted like cold, bitter plums. A semicircle of saleswomen in vintage dresses, my co-workers, surrounded me, whispering to me in French that it was terrible, just terrible. So sorry, they were. Shaking their beehives and French-twisted heads. All those sad, cat-lined eyes on me, I could feel them. Waiting for me to cry. Afraid that I might. Right there in the middle of the dress shop. "It's My Party" was playing on the radio. Almost giving me a kind of terrible permission. I apologized for their trouble. *So sorry about all this,* I said to them, avoiding their eyes.

Mon Dieu, Mira, don't apologize to us, they murmured. A customer appeared in the shop doorway just then, looking nervously at our little huddle. *Can I help you find something?* I called out to them. *Anything? Please,* I said, walking toward this customer like they were a light at the end of a very long tunnel. *Please tell me what you're looking for.*

On the Uber ride back to my apartment, I bought the plane ticket for San Diego between swigs of the liqueur Persephone pressed into my hands. By the time I got home, I was out of it. Could barely make my way down the hall to drop off my cat, Lucifer, with my neighbor, Monsieur Lam, whom he preferred to me anyway. Lucifer literally jumped from my arms and disappeared into Monsieur Lam's hallway the moment Monsieur Lam opened his door. *My mother died,* I told him as he stood in the doorway, blinking. *Oh dear,* he said, and scratched his face. Monsieur Lam has excellent skin. Quite the glisten, I envy it. I often wonder about his secrets—do they involve a fermented essence, some sort of mushroom root elixir?—though I've never dared to ask. *Would you like to come in for tea?* he offered. I could tell by his eyes that he would die inside if I said *sure.* Monsieur Lam, like me, has manners, in spite of himself. *Oh no,* I said. *Thank you. I should get ready for tomorrow, pack.* He nodded. Of course I should. We both knew I would do no such thing. I would be watching Marva all night while I double cleansed in the dark, then exfoliated, then applied my many skins of essence and serum, pressing each skin into my burning face with the palms of both hands. Monsieur Lam would hear the videos, as he did every night. Only a thin wall separated our bedrooms, after all.

The next day, when I opened my suitcase in the hotel in La Jolla, all I found in there was a French mystery novel, some underwear, and seven ziplock bags full of skin products. Apparently, I remembered the Botanical Resurrection Serum and the Diamond-Infused Revitalizing Eye Formula and my three current favorite exfoliating acids. I remembered the collagen-boosting Orpheus Flower Peptide Complex and the green tea–and–chokeberry plumping essence and the Liquid Gold. I remembered the Dewy Bio-Radiance Snow Mushroom Mist and the Advanced Luminosité snail slime, among many other MARs—*Marva Adamantly Recommends.* But not a single dress. Hence Sylvia to the rescue.

Now here she is in the open doorframe, her face full of terrible sympathy.

"Are you all right, dear?" she says. *Dear* again. And again, my soul shudders. Her voice is as spiky-sweet as the lilies and birds-of-paradise perfuming the living room. She looks at me like I'm crying. I'm not, of course. Just the bright sky hurting my eyes probably. Or my Diamond-Infused Revitalizing Eye Formula. It's a potent powerhouse that lifts, firms, and lightens and is sometimes known to run into the eyes, appearing to make them tear. So I could look like I'm crying. I might even feel actual tears slipping down my cheeks, leaving rivulets of dryness in their salty wake. I could look so much like I'm crying to the average person unfamiliar with the Formula that they might feel compelled to say to me, *Are you okay?* But I never explain about the Formula to such people. I always just say, *I'm fine.*

"I'm fine," I tell Sylvia.

"Are you sure?" I know she's judging me for my escape from the funeral, the dining room full of her prim flower arrangements and sandwich triangles, full of people I've never seen before who all claim to know Mother. All of them offering platitudes of sympathy.

So sorry for your loss.

Well, she's in a better place now, isn't she?

The soul lives on forever, doesn't it?

Does it? I asked. I really wanted to know. Silent blinking from these people. I should've just nodded my head gratefully and said, *She is. It does. Thank you for that.* Instead I just stared at them. *Does it?* I whispered again. And I took a sip of what I thought was champagne. It was apple cider. It was in a flute like it was champagne. *This isn't champagne*, I heard myself say.

Appletiser, someone said. *Isn't it lovely? Sylvia thinks of just about everything.*

She does, I agreed. And then I said, *I need a minute. Excuse me.*

And this is what I say to Sylvia now in the door. I say, "I needed a minute. Excuse me."

I can feel her staring at me in that searching way I've always shied away from like a too-bright light. Like she's hunting for some key to the closed door of my face. She looks at my phone on the counter. On the screen, Marva is paused in mid-stroke of her white throat. I quickly grab the phone and tuck it into my pocket.

"I hope the party is all right?" she says.

"Wonderful, Sylvia," I lie, nodding. "Thank you. Thank you for putting it together."

"We could have had it at my apartment, of course, but your mother's view is just so much better than mine." And then she looks over my shoulder at the ocean view through the bathroom window. The ocean I haven't been able to look at since I arrived, though each night the sound of the waves keeps me thrashing in bed until I black out. Then it seeps into my dreams.

I look at Sylvia smiling serenely at this ocean in which Mother met her end. Seeing nothing but pretty waves, a beautiful view, her view if she plays her cards right. Possibly her own reflection beaming back at her. Suddenly an urge to throttle her thin little neck throbs in my fingers. It's a mottled neck, I notice. Not a serum or SPF user, is Sylvia.

"A beautiful view, don't you agree?" She looks at Mother's perfume on the counter, the lipstick, her red jars and vials *for the face.* "She really loved her products, didn't she?"

"She did."

"Well, we all have our little pleasures. Mine are shoes." She beams at me, then down at her own small feet encased in their boring designer flats. "Of course, your mother loved those too."

"Yes." I light another cigarette in front of Sylvia. I can feel her judge me for it. She looks at me through the smoke, saying nothing. I'm the bereaved, after all. I have certain allowances, don't I? I'm tempted to exhale the smoke in her face, but of course I wave it away, apologizing. She smiles thinly.

"So. How long will you be here?"

I think of the transcontinental flight I took only three days ago— was it only three days ago? How the pills and the airport wine and then the plane wine kept me slumped deep in the window seat. How the beauty videos I was trying to watch kept freezing on my phone so I had no choice but to look at the sky. I kept my sunglasses on even after it grew dark. Even when there was nothing left of the view but one red light on the tip of the wing, flashing in the black night.

"I took a week or so off from work," I tell her.

"Work?" She looks surprised that I do anything at all. After I left La Jolla, didn't I just sink into oblivion? "Oh, that dress shop, right? What's it called? Damsels in Something?"

"Damsels in This Dress."

"*In Distress.* How fun. Like mother, like daughter." Smiling at the thought of her and Mother's shop. *Our little shop*, Sylvia likes to call it. She never calls it *Belle of the Ball*. Doesn't like the name's affiliation with me or that it predates her. Sylvia took more of a role after I left, but she was insinuating herself long before. Her crisp white shirt and pearls forever in my periphery, unnecessarily straightening the side merchandise. *So organized*, Mother always said of Sylvia. *The yin to my yang, so to speak.* And Sylvia's smile would tighten. *Sylvia, what would I do without you?* Mother would ask. *Perish*, Sylvia said. And only I knew she was half-serious.

"*Montreal*," Sylvia sighs now, attempting the French pronunciation. Massacring it, of course. She looks wistful for this place where she's never once been. "So chic. Where Noelle got her style, no doubt. Your mother had such style." Little sweep of her gaze around the bathroom. "You'll probably need help packing up, don't you think?"

"I can manage, Sylvia. Really." I say this evenly. Calmly. With infinite politesse.

"I'm happy to drop by," she insists. "Just say the word."

"I'll be sure to. Thank you. In the meantime, I think I might go back to the hotel. Get some rest. Didn't sleep well last night."

Didn't sleep at all. Tossed and turned in the perfumed dark. One eye kept open, always. When I'd checked in, the man at the front desk had said he was giving me an ocean view, like it was a gift. The waves, he said, would put me right to sleep. *They always do*, he said, and smiled. *Trust.* They didn't. The crashing waves made a crashing sound, not lulling at all. And there was the image I couldn't unsee even in the dark. Mother in her robe of red-and-white silk. Falling into the black water, onto the sharp rocks.

"Of course," Sylvia says. "You must be tired." Magnanimous smile. So very sad for me. "Well, be sure to come by our little shop before you fly back home. You mother left some things there. There are also some things . . . you and I should discuss. When you're ready, of course."

Things? Discuss? "What things, Sylvia?" There's an edge to my voice now.

"There's a time and a place, my dear. Isn't there?" She says it very carefully, almost reprimanding, as if I'm the one being hideously inappropriate.

"A time and a place. Absolutely. Excuse me." I squeeze past Sylvia and duck out into the hallway. A mirror there all along the length of the corridor. A crack in this one too, just like in the bathroom. Another mirror, another crack. Like Mother took a sharp diamond to it and just swiped as she walked. Strange. A coldness whenever I look at these mirrors. More of them in the living room—so many shapes and sizes. A wall of cracked glass, each one in its own heavy black frame.

The living room is more crowded now, and the mirrors make it look like her mourners are infinite. Did she really know all these people? Most of them are strangers to me. They are saying, "Such a shame, such a shame. So young. Fell into the water? Jumped? So terrible." And then they turn to look at the ocean and shiver. Or they're talking about other things. Upcoming vacations. Traffic on the 805. What Trump said yesterday on Fox, he'll never get elected. "If only we could keep Obama forever." Everyone's holding glasses of Sylvia's fake champagne like it isn't fake at all. They smile sympathetically as I enter the living room. Whispers and soft words fill the air. "The daughter, I think. It's hard, isn't it? Oh, life. A mystery, a mystery." Shaking their heads insufferably. I need to get away from all their piteous eyes and soft words that do nothing, mean nothing. I put on my sunglasses, keep my mouth a straight line. Make a beeline through the living room, eyes fixed on the front door. I have a plan. I'll get in Mother's dark silver Jaguar. Drive to the pink hotel. Take the elevator to my room, bolt the door. Get in the bed and lie there. Hear the clock tick and the waves crash, and then the sun will sink eventually, mercifully, on this day. And night will come, won't it? That's a promise.

Are you sure you won't stay? their faces seem to say as they watch me escape. *Going already?* They look at the cigarette in my hand, the shades covering my eyes, as I push past, murmuring, "So sorry, excuse me," in spite of myself.

When I leave the apartment, something quiets. A roaring in my heart. The heaviness lifts a little and I can breathe. I stand there on the veranda and breathe. Palm trees. That bright blue sky stretching on endlessly. Not so alien anymore. But there are a few people outside too, I see, milling. Can't get away from them. All I want to do is get away from them. These people who don't know. Who never knew.

Knew what? says a voice inside me.

And then I see there's someone else there too, standing away from the small, murmuring clusters, staring out at the water. Staring out and smiling. Her hands gripping the rail of the veranda like she's on a cruise. A woman in a red dress. Red at a funeral? Am I seeing right? Yes. A dark red dress of flowing silk. Beautiful, I can't deny that. Mother would have approved. Something else about her sticks out, but what is it? Something about her face so sharply cut, her skin smooth as glass. Have I seen her somewhere before? She looks happy. So happy, I can almost hear the singing inside her. She has red hair, too, like Mother. Red hair, red dress, red lips. It makes her look like a fire. A fire right there on Mother's veranda. As I notice her, she turns to me and her face darkens, then brightens. I feel her look deep into the pit of me with her pale blue eyes. Inside me, something opens its jaws. She is staring at me so curiously. Like I'm a ghost. Or a dream.

"She went the way of roses," this woman says to me. And smiles. Like that's so lovely. When she says the word *roses*, I see a flash of red. It fills my vision briefly like a fog. Then it's gone. And there's the woman in red standing in front of me against the bright blue sky.

"The way of roses," I repeat. I'm entranced, even as I feel a coldness inside me, spreading. "What's the way of roses?"

She just smiles.

"What's the way of roses?" I ask again. "Who are you?"

But someone pulls me away. A sweaty man I don't recognize. His grim wife. They want to tell me all about how sorry they are for my loss. The man has his hand on my shoulder. It's a heavy hand and it's squeezing my arm flesh. "We saw your mother in a play once," he's saying. "And we never forgot, did we?" he asks his wife, who says nothing. Well, *he* never forgot, anyway. The wife nods grimly. "She shone," this man says, his eyes all watery and red. *So there* is *alcohol at this party somewhere,* I think. "Like a star on the stage," the man insists. And she was so nice to them afterward. That's what he'll never forget. How nice Mother was. So gracious and humble. No airs, despite her great beauty, her great talent. So down-to-earth. I can imagine her feigning interest in their lives. Sucking his admiration like marrow from the veal bones she used to enjoy with parsley and salt.

I want to laugh in their faces. My mother, down-to-earth? And then I think of what's left of Mother. Soon to be in the literal earth. Suddenly I can't breathe again. "Excuse me," I say, and push past them.

But she's gone, the woman in red by the railing. Where that woman was standing is just empty space. I stare at the rosebushes planted along the other side of the railing. A red so bright, it hurts my eyes. Petals shivering in the blue breeze. Shining so vividly in the light.

2

At the pink hotel by the sea, there's a bar right on the water. Don't know why I came here. Can't afford this place, not at all. And if the lawyer's tone on the phone is anything to go by, that isn't going to change. *We'll talk tomorrow morning*, Chaz said when I asked him to tell me the worst of it. *Please tell me*, I said. *Tomorrow*, he said. I've been staying at the hotel ever since I landed. Of course I'm afraid of the bill. But I'm more afraid of being alone in Mother's apartment. Have to face it tomorrow, of course. Pack up the place. But not now, not yet.

"Table for one, please," I tell the waiter at the bar. Because I may as well go down in style. You would have approved, wouldn't you, Mother?

"Of course," the waiter says. He looks a little like Tom Cruise, which is funny. Funny, too, how I suddenly feel a little dizzy looking into his face. Maybe it's just how intensely he's smiling at me. He brings me to a table with an ocean view but looks puzzled when I sit with my back to the water. I just smile. "Glass of champagne, please."

He stares at me. Still that smile, that puzzled look. *What?* I want to say. He looks up at my forehead. Is he noticing the faint scar there? Shaped like a warped star. Faded now but never gone, despite my regimen of acids and lightening agents. *Barely there, really*, Mother always assured me. *No one can see it but you.* But this man sees it. Does he see it? *Very rude to stare*, I want to tell him. I think he's going to ask me about it, but instead he says: "Do you have ID?"

My turn to stare now. Is he serious?

He doesn't flinch. Oh yes, he's serious.

I forgot this about America. How they card the very obviously over thirty. I give him my driver's license, and he stares at it forever, squinting. *My mother's dead, you know*, I want to tell him. *I just left her funeral. This drink, it's deeply important to me.* My fingers begin to twitch to show him the birthdate on the license. It's a Canadian license, so he probably has no idea where to look, and I should be patient, I should help. But I'm a little mesmerized by how long this is taking. How many times he looks at me, then at the license.

Finally, he hands it back. "Miss?"

Miss? "Yes?" I steel myself for his words. That he can't take this kind of international ID, sorry. He'll need to see my passport, please.

But he just looks at my face, sort of dreamily. "Whatever you're doing?" he says in a low voice. "It's working."

A smile in spite of myself. A vile flush of shallow happiness. "It is?"

"Definitely," he says. *"Definitely."*

Shouldn't matter at all. What this stranger makes of my skin. But there's my hand on my cheek, there's me looking up at his well-meaning expression.

"Thank you," I whisper, thinking of my bathroom counter cluttered with Marva-recommended jars and bottles and vials. My purse full of sunscreens and rejuvenating mists. "I have a whole thing that I do," I tell him, surprising myself. I never speak of what I do, with anyone. *Because it's for you, isn't it?* Marva says. *A secret between you and the mirror.*

He smiles. "Let me get you that champagne."

It comes in a chilled glass, bubbling like a cauldron. *Like drinking stars, Belle*, Mother would have said. I always rolled my eyes when she said that, but now look at me with my glass. Marva says alcohol is a collagen destroyer. Dries you up, dries you out. *If you want good skin, you must stop drinking immediately*, she says sternly. And when I watch Marva say this, I usually have a coffee cup full of champagne in my hand. Sometimes a cigarette in the other, also verboten by Marva. And I feel scolded, hideous, guilty. But Marva also says, *We are human, aren't we? We all have our little fixes, our little indulgences, balms to this mortal coil, don't we?*

We do, I agree. And there are tears in my eyes at Marva's compassion. Her understanding of the paradoxes. *You should be kinder to yourself*, she says to me softly, her eyes staring right into my eyes. Like they know. They know exactly how cruel I can be.

First one glass, then another. Not going back up to the hotel room to start my evening routine, though I can feel the grit and dust and debris on my face. The many free radicals that are burrowing their way through my skin barrier, oxidizing my flesh as we speak. I'm in desperate need of a clarifying cleanse, followed by a regenerating cleanse, followed by a triple exfoliation, after which I'll likely baste my face in some barrier-repairing zinc. But not just yet. The sky is an unholy pink fire, the palm trees blackening. I feel the waves roaring at my back. Not too many people at the bar tonight. Just a man nearby staring hard at his laptop, clicking away. Working late, I guess. A breeze blows through the terrace. Warm. Gentle. I forgot that about California. How even the breeze is a dream. Where would I be right now if I were back in Montreal? Working late too, probably. Staring at the checkered black-and-white store floor. Avoiding the mirrors on the walls. Not wanting to see my face ravaged by a day of smiling falsely under bright lights. Smiling still, just in case anyone should push through the doors at the last minute. That ring of the little silver bell. I hear it in my dreams. I hear it now. People coming into the dress shop so hopeful. Wanting what? Never just a dress. Mother taught me that. What they want, she said, is an experience. A transformation. A touch of magic.

Can't happen, I want to say to them. *You are who you are who you are. Trust me, I know. There's no escape.* In my dreams, I tell them this. I tell them all the awful truth. But in reality, I just smile. I say *it looks wonderful* even when it looks hideous. *Wow*, I say. *And if you paired it with this blazer, it would really finish the look.* And I'm lying. There is no look. The blazer will finish nothing. But they always believe me. They thank me, still frowning at themselves in the mirror. And I stand beside it, another mirror, smiling. My hands folded over my crotch. Waiting for them to look at me instead.

At this time of night, in the empty shop, the mask that is my face would be coming off. My smile would be slipping. I'd be playing music for myself and not the customers. Something dreamy and dark, with distortion. Something I could close my eyes and drown in beautifully. Mother used to describe my music taste as Otherworldly Funeral. Or Bleakest Party. *Can you please turn down Bleakest Party, darling? Some of us have chosen to embrace life.* It's the hour when all the shop mannequins conspire to look menacing. When they all appear to be smirking a little. Reminding me, with their flawless whiteness, of Mother. I might even have called her out of guilt. Or because I missed her. Those last times we talked, she'd sounded strange. *Hello? Hello?* she'd call into the phone. Like she was calling out into a dark night with no idea where she was.

Mother, I said, staring at a mannequin.

Who is this?

Your daughter.

Pause. *Who?*

Belle? Your daughter? Mother, what's—

Oh, Belle of the Ball. Sunshine, yes of course. Sunshine was her nickname for me. Sunshine because I was such a rain cloud according to her, a *glum drop.* Sunshine to spite me.

You know it's seventy-two degrees and sunny here. The sky is so blue and lonely, Belle. You should see it.

Lonely?

Did I say "lonely"? I meant lovely, of course. You should see it.

I've seen it, Mother. Are you okay? You seem a little—

I'm roses. I'm wearing a dread—a dress made of stars. The question is how are you, Sunshine? Are you still exfoliating your face off?

No, I said, though of course I was. I had seven different kinds of acid on rotation, each one for what Marva called a different *skin predicament*. I had the Universal Brightening Peel Pads and the Overnight Glycolic Resurfacing Matrix and of course, the triple-exfoliating Lotion Magique, a cult French elixir that's still illegal in some countries—the one with the banned ingredient that reeks of sulfur and numbs your face. I also had the infamous blood-colored Eradikating Ambrosia, which smells like turpentine and looks like fresh goat placenta. Each night I rub one or more on my face with a cotton pad, and my skin screams beautifully. Goes an unholy red. I watch it burn in the mirror while an animal scent, a smell of sacrifice, fills the bathroom like smoke.

I'm not, I lied to Mother.

And Mother tsked. *You know those cells turn over all by themselves, Belle. Your sin's beautiful on its own.*

My sin?

Skin, of course, why would I say "sin"? So funny. Anyway, the point is, Mother Nature is a fucking wonder.

Is she? And I stared at the mannequin. Little sideways smirk. Little slant of her gleaming eye. Mother said nothing. Silence filled the connection as it often did between us. I could hear the waves crashing on her end of the line. Chiding me. That I should have stayed in California. Been happy. Sunnier of soul and mind. But no, I had to choose darkness, didn't I? I had to skulk back to our bleak homeland of snow and ice. *To look after Grand-Maman*, I always interjected. But then Grand-Maman died, didn't she, and I still didn't come back. No, I felt compelled to stay and brood in the Montreal shadows, working in a dress shop, no less. Talk about a slap. When she herself had a dress shop in paradise where I could work right alongside her, didn't she?

And then there was our last phone call a couple of weeks ago. An evening shift at Damsels. No customers. I could see snow falling outside through the window, slow and fat. I remember the way the mannequins shone under the track lights. How they seemed to smile more broadly that night. Mother was speaking so quickly, so breathlessly. She kept slipping into French the way she did only when she was extremely distraught.

Mother, please, I said. *What are you saying?*

I'm wearing a dread of liquid gold that burns like the sun. I'm wearing shoes of reddest blood. The mirrors are cracking all around me. The waves are saying, entrée, entrée.

What? Mother, you're scaring me.

Belle, do you ever look in the mirror and see . . . ? She trailed off. I could hear her breath quickening on the line. I thought I could hear her heart beating. Or was it my own heart I was hearing pounding in my ear?

Mother, what are you seeing?

I'm going the way of roses, Belle, she said at last, dreamily. *Remember the roses? Te souviens-tu?*

And my vision filled briefly with a red fog. *Mother, you hate roses.*

And click went the phone on her end of the line.

I sat there on my cashier stool with the phone in my hand, wondering, *What the fuck?* How she had answered the phone like a torrent. How like a torrent she was gone. And I was left. Left even though I was thousands of miles away, in another country. I could feel the slam of her door in my face. The wind blowing my hair back. The cloud of violets and smoke she'd trail in her wake. What the hell was she on, anyway? Drugs? Not drugs, surely, I told myself, trudging home through the snowy dark. Not Mother. Just her usual romanticism and joie de vivre gone awry, that was all. Getting stranger in her older age. A little more lost in her own world, her own reflection. (I'd have to be careful about that. Wasn't I going down the same road? I was, I was.) Or god, could it be early-onset dementia? I made a mental note to call Sylvia about it. To check in with Mother again the next day. If not the next day, I told myself, then soon. I'd go and visit soon too. I'd take her to a doctor myself.

It was the last time I'd ever talk to her.

Now I stare at my phone, its blank face. For a moment I glimpse the void. I see it gaping, black, bottomless. *She went the way of roses,* that woman at the funeral said, and smiled. Like that was so wonderful. Her blue eyes lit up.

"What's the way of roses?" I ask aloud.

Just then, my phone buzzes. I brace myself. Some vapid sympathy note from a co-worker, maybe. Or Sylvia *just dropping a line* to remind me to come by *our little shop* tomorrow. Or Persephone checking in to see when I'd be coming back to Damsels. *Take all the time you need*, she lied, patting my hand. But I could hear the clock already ticking in her voice.

When I look, I see a notification from a name I don't recognize. *ROUGE*. Who's Rouge? There's an icon of a wide-open eye inside an oval mirror. Staring at me.

Is Grief Afflicting Your Skin Barrier? Tap to Go Live, it reads beside the eye.

Something about this eye . . . I shiver as though I'm being watched. I look around the terrace. Just the sun sinking bloodily over the waves. Just the palm trees still blackening, swaying in the warm breeze. Just Tom Cruise making napkin swans at his station and whistling. An unease, cold and slippery, moves through me. I see the man sitting a few tables away, still clicking at his laptop. I look back at the eye in the mirror. *Fuck you*, I think. Fuck you and fuck the eavesdropping algorithms of the internet. Can they hear even our thoughts now? I'm about to turn off my phone, when I catch a glimpse of my own face reflected in the tabletop glass. What I see makes me colder still. Wretched. I look wretched. *Is Grief Afflicting Your Skin Barrier?*

"Yes," says a voice. My voice. I click on the link.

On my screen is a smiling woman in red. *The* woman in red from the funeral. She's standing on a stage, flanked by red curtains. What is she doing on a stage? What is she doing in my phone? She's staring right at the camera. Right at me the way Marva does. She actually looks a little like Marva. Same bright eyes. Same knowing look. Like she can see me sitting here on the terrace, my ravaged face and emptied champagne glass in hand. She's looking at me sympathetically.

"Bonsoir," she says. "Are you, at this very moment, in the grips of grief?"

She shakes her head like she knows. "Lacrimosa" from Mozart's Requiem plays softly in the background. I hear the applause of an invisible audience. The word *LIVE* is flashing in the corner of my screen in red. "Of course you are. We all are, aren't we? And it shows up, doesn't it? Even when we don't want it to. It shows up in the mirror."

Now the camera switches to another woman, this one in a bleak-looking bathroom. This woman looks ravaged, sick, around my age. She's also staring directly into the camera, at me, like I'm a mirror reflecting back her misery. Frowning at herself. Shaking her head slowly in time with the Mozart swells, as if she can't believe her own face. I hear the woman in red, in voice-over: "Here at Rouge, we believe the secret goes far beyond exfoliation. The true secret? That lies somewhere else."

Here at Rouge? The true secret? What is this, a fucking ad? *Turn it off*, I tell myself. But I'm still staring at my screen. The scene has shifted. Now there's a red jellyfish undulating in a pool of dark water. I watch it pulse redly in a sea of black. My heart quickens. *What the fuck?* And then it's gone. There's the woman in the bathroom again, except now the room is bright white and she herself is glowing. Bouquets of red roses bloom beautifully on either side of her in tall black vases. She's still staring at me like I'm a mirror, her reflection. But now she's smiling at what she sees. Her skin is like glass, shining with a light all its own.

"Jesus Christ," I whisper.

And her lips curl up on one side like she heard me. She holds up a red jar of cream. Right beside her glowing face, like it's an apple. Didn't I see jars just like that in Mother's bathroom this afternoon?

"Where does the secret lie?" It's the woman in red talking again. A voice-over that sounds not like it's coming from my phone's speaker, but whispering right in my ear. "Do you want to know?"

Yes.

"The inside," whispers this voice. The red jellyfish in black water fills my screen again. And then like a flash, it's gone. The glowing woman in the video smiles wide. She brings the red jar closer to her lips like she's about to take a bite. Something about the look in her shining eyes. As if she, too, can actually see me sitting here with my back to the water. The future a void and I'm standing at the black mouth looking down. She sees all that. Sees and knows. Not just the truth of my face, but what lies beneath. "The human soul, of course," says the voice.

I turn off the video, put my phone down. But it continues to play, because I hear: "And if you choose the way of roses, you'll see for yourself."

What? Where's the sound still coming from? My eyes rest on that man with the laptop sitting a few tables away. Dark blue suit. Red handkerchief blooming from his pocket. He's staring at his screen like I was just a moment ago, transfixed. This man? Watching the same skin video? He must be, I still hear the Mozart. He looks up now. The sound changed for him, too, of course, when I turned my video off. *Why did it change?* is a question all over his face. A handsome face, I can't help but notice. Tan, angular, sharp. Very well hydrated. His brimmed hat and his suit remind me of old movies. The sort Mother liked us to watch together, mostly French New Wave and Hollywood noirs. A certain kind of man in those movies she loved. Mysteriously broken. Beautiful, but something off. Forever moving to a minor key. Always in the process of lighting a cigarette. Always half smiling through the smoke, sort of like this man is now. *That's Monty Clift*, Mother might sigh, pointing at the screen. *That's Alain*, she'd whisper reverently, meaning Alain Delon. *Ooh, Paul Newman. Love Paul*, she murmured. *So much.* She talked about these men like they were her personal friends. Now this man suddenly locks eyes with me, my phone hot in my hand. I feel myself instantly redden, blotches blooming hideously all over my face. *Look away*, I tell myself, but I can't look away. My eyes are locked with his, cold and pale against his olive skin. He looks angry, maybe. Like he's been caught at something or like he caught me at something. Something shameful. But then he sort of softens. Smiles, almost. Snaps his laptop shut. Raises his champagne glass to me, then drains it in one gulp, eyes on me the whole time. *That's Monty*, Mother might say. *That's Alain. That's Paul.* He drops some money on the table and gets up, tipping his hat to me. Whether he's greeting me or simply adjusting the brim is hard to say. He saunters away whistling Mozart, and I sit there watching him go, my skin prickling at the sound, my phone still hot in my hand.

3

Dreaded breakfast with Mother's lawyer. When I get to the hotel dining room the next morning, Chaz is waving at me from a table by the window.

"Mirabelle," Chaz says. "Been a long time."

"It has," I agree. Yet Chaz hasn't changed. Pale violet suit of wrinkled linen. Tanned and emanating a musky cologne. Still standing on ceremony like someone in a French court, which I suppose he sort of is, being Mother's lawyer. When I was younger, he reminded me a little of a perverted Rumpelstiltskin. I'd watch him ogle Mother. Take her in with a twinkly-eyed delight I found obscene, like she was a bowl of bright, erotic candy. *Hi*, Chaz would say to me. And I'd grip her hand tighter. *Shy*, Mother would say. And he'd nod sympathetically, though he was obviously annoyed. What did Chaz always say?

I'm your mother's gentleman friend.

Now he looks me up and down as he used to when I was a teenager. Takes me in, so to speak. His face says I've made an impression on him. On his dick. *Good for you*. He nods a little. *Good work. Impressive*. Though of course I'm not Mother.

"So good to see you again," he says, giving me what he believes to be the gift of his grin. "Got us a table by the water." He gestures graciously to the seat facing the waves. I take the seat with my back to the ocean and stare at Chaz. I don't say it's good to see him. Mother would have smacked me for this. *Manners!* she would have snapped, probably even now. But it isn't good to see Chaz. At all. If he looked troll-like to my young eyes, he looks more so now. A hobgoblin with a fake tan, conspicuously brown glossy hair. Though he does seem to be exfoliating.

"I ordered coffee," Chaz says, as if offering condolences. "There's a basket of pastries coming too. Croissants." He tries for a wink. Because I'm from Montreal. And being from Montreal, I love croissants, don't I?

Most mornings, I have what Mother called my *skin sludge*. A blueberry and spirulina smoothie into which I pour a copious amount of collagen. The smoothie is really just a vessel for the collagen, but I enjoy the ritual, watching the powder dissolve into the blue-green mulch. *You drink that?* Mother said the last time I visited. I was making one in her kitchen. She watched, looking disgusted but also curious. *What's all that white powder you're putting into it there?*

Just a little cocaine.

Well, now I'm interested.

"I'm not hungry, thanks," I tell Chaz.

And then his face changes to a performance of recognition, grief. Ah yes, of course I'm not hungry. How could I be? He watches me pour myself some coffee.

"How are you holding up?" Trying for softness. Though I know he doesn't care, his tone does something to me in spite of myself. I feel I could crack like an egg. But I won't. This morning, I applied three layers of an antioxidant serum enriched with Firma-Cell, followed by seven skins of a roaring water kelp essence, followed by the Iso-Placenta Shield to smooth and tighten. Then the White Pearl Pigment Perfector mixed with the Brightening Caviar for Radiance. Then of course the Diamond-Infused Revitalizing Eye Formula, the Super-defense Multi-Correxion Moisturizing Cloud Jelly, and two layers of broad-spectrum Glowscreen, physical and chemical. I did this in the half-dark of the hotel bathroom, while Marva played on the counter, talking softly to me about the benefits of moisturizing cloud jellies. I think about the many layers, the many ingredients, the many sophisticated formulas right now shielding me from oxidizing free radicals while also keeping me hydrated. I shrug and stare at Chaz through Mother's sunglasses. They're huge and dark, that Jackie O style she loved. For those days, she said, when the truth is laid bare. Or for when the Revitalizing Eye Formula goes rogue and bleeds, creating a teary effect. I won't lay the truth bare before Chaz.

"It's hard," Chaz offers.

"I'm fine," I say.

And then he smiles at me with something like understanding. Reaches out and puts his hand on mine. "There, there," he says awkwardly. I look down at his Apple Watch. Nestled there in his hairy wrist. Two fat gold rings on his pudgy fingers, one of which has an insignia of an *S*. His hand feels heavy on mine. Smothering.

A waiter arrives bearing a tray. "Eggs Benedict with smoked salmon? Pastries?"

"Perfect," Chaz says.

I watch him ravage his eggs, making vapid observations about Mother's death as he chews. "Sho shudden," he says, shaking his head. "I'm as shocked as you must be, honestly." Respectful silence or is he just swallowing? "And so young, too. Well, maybe not *so* young. She looked it though, that's for sure. Younger looking every time I saw her. Almost like she was moving *backward* in time rather than forward, you know? Not like us mere mortals, right?"

"I guess so."

You're a fucking freak of nature, I told her once. And Mother just looked at me, touched. I watch Chaz take a knife to the wobbly egg.

"So. You're back in Montreal now, huh?" he asks. Because we have to make a little conversation before he gives me the terrible news, right? Makes it more human. *I'm human*, says his face.

"Yes."

"No more playing Mulan for you." He smiles. See how he remembers that I used to work at Disney while I was in college? He got the princess wrong, of course, but he remembered she was ethnic. Because I'm ethnic, aren't I? Something other than Mother, anyway. He forgets what exactly. Somewhere from the south and the east. *I was Princess Jasmine*, I could tell him. *The Arab one*. Like the father I barely knew. Died of a heart attack when I was five, before I could form a memory beyond the smallest fragments. The closest I ever got to him was lining my eyes with kohl, talking to little kids about how I flew here on my magic carpet. But I just smile at Chaz.

"No more Mulan for me."

"And how is Montreal, anyway?" he asks, like he wants to know. How much did Mother tell him, I wonder, about my leaving here? *My daughter deserted me, didn't you know? Barely visits her poor mother except when I beg.* Chaz would shake his head at Mother with infinite pity. *How terrible.* I could tell Chaz that this was only a distorted sliver of the story, that Mother deserted me too once. But he'd never hear me over the fact of his undying lust.

"Well, you know me, Chaz. I love the cold."

He smiles. Of course I would love the cold. "I haven't visited Montreal since the eighties, you know. The old days."

A shiver runs through me. *The old days.* My childhood days in Montreal. So many I can't remember. So many behind a veil. Fragments until I was nine, and then at the age of ten, a blank. And then? Suddenly I don't live with Mother anymore. I'm living in Grand-Maman's place and Mother's moved away to California. *Soon you'll join her there*, Grand-Maman said, *but not now, not yet.* Five years go by in the flash of an eye. Then I'm fifteen and on a plane out west. I'm blinking under an alien sun, beneath a bright blue sky. There are palm trees swaying in my peripheral vision. *Aren't they pretty?* Mother said, taking my hand, her hair now short and dyed a Hitchcock blond. *Isn't this just the life?*

"Who needs the dark and the cold when you have all this, am I right?" And here, Chaz gestures to the view of the sea Mother drowned in. "You know they shot *Top Gun* here? Tom Cruise and all that." Trying to smile. Make this a bit of a nice breakfast. Not just about Mother's finances. We're old friends too, aren't we? Catching up.

I stare at him.

"Look," he says. And I know what's coming. Know what he's going to say. It was when the eggs came that I knew. Hearing him talk is like having déjà vu. "She had some serious debt." Braiding his hairy hands together. Rings gleaming in the light.

"What do you mean?" I say, though of course I know what he means. I think of Mother's voice on the phone lately. Giddy like a leg jiggling under the table.

"She took out three loans over the past year," Chaz says, pouring himself more coffee.

"*Three?* For how much?"

Chaz takes out a gold pen and dramatically clicks. I watch him scrawl a number onto the back of a bone-white business card and slide it over to me with a somber expression. I look down at the number. All those zeros stopping my heart.

"In total?"

"Each."

My stomach sinks. Heart pounding now. I stare at Chaz, who stares back at me impassively. *Just the messenger here. Don't shoot.* But I do want to shoot. I want to take aim at something and fire. I have a memory of Mother from about three months ago, the last time I visited. Waiting for her to pick me up at the San Diego airport. Staring at the palm trees swaying in the dark and thinking, *Shouldn't have come.* The night air was warm like a bath. I was smoking to the performed disapproval of all the people nearby. And then Mother rolled up in a silver Jaguar. The new car didn't surprise me too much—she'd always had her patrons, men who bought toys for their toy. It was her face that struck me. Unsmiling. So pale, it seemed to glow like another moon in the dark. As I approached the car, I noticed her skin was eerily smooth. She looked like she belonged in one of those old Hollywood films she loved, where the actresses' faces are made preternaturally flawless by Vaseline smeared on the camera lens. But more than her face, it was her eyes. Shining and blank. How they looked at me like they didn't know me. *Mother*, I felt compelled to say, *it's me.*

And Mother just stared at me through the passenger-side window. *Of course it is*, she said in a voice I didn't recognize. *Get in.*

But I just stood there staring at her through the window. *Mother, you look—*

What? And her tone was suddenly terribly eager. Hungry.

Strange, I should have said. *Empty. What's with your face? Your eyes?* But I said, *Beautiful.* As I always had. All my life. She seemed to smile then. Some warmth or recognition bloomed in her face. Like her soul had risen to the surface of her skin and made a light shine there briefly. Her eyes filled with tears. She looked into the ever kind and gentle mirror of me.

I'm so happy you're here, she said. And then we roared off into the dark. I never asked about the car.

"What were the loans for?" I ask Chaz now.

"Window renovation, apparently."

Window renovation? "Well, how much could that cost?"

"Can't say," Chaz says. "But it does look like she spent it all." He shrugs, stirs his coffee. It happens. People take out a loan for one thing, then spend it on other stuff.

Suddenly I can't breathe. I need a cigarette. A shot of something. Anything. Chaz keeps stirring his coffee with a little spoon. He's loving this, I can feel it. My helplessness. My sudden breathlessness, my flushed face, all of it is giving him a hard-on.

"I'd advise you to sell the condo. Use the equity to pay off the loans. You might barely break even if you do that."

"I *might* break even?" I shout this. Everyone's looking at us now. The waiters, the rich couple at the next table roused from their passion fruit and champagne brunch. I think of my studio apartment in Montreal. Barely decorated but for the skin products lining the walls of my single room. Closet bursting with dresses from work that I never wear. Every day the same black shift. Yet I was content in this little life, I was. In the back of my mind, did I think Mother would somehow save me?

"Well, there's the Jaguar," Chaz offers. "You could sell it, although it's unlikely to be worth much since she dinged it up a bit."

"Dinged it up?"

"Just in a few places. A few little fender kisses here and there. Some scratches." He grins as if recalling some past intimacy. "You know your mother."

Do I? I think of Mother behind the wheel in her dark glasses. Staring at me through the windshield, neither grinning nor frowning because she didn't want to disrupt the planes of her face.

"Fixing it is going to cost a pretty penny, of course. Vintage Jaguars don't grow on trees." He looks at me sadly. "But you might get a buyer as is. Men do love their toys. Especially fixer-uppers."

I think of her entourage of rich, smiling ghouls.

"As for the condo, I can put you in touch with a real estate agent," Chaz is saying. "But you'll want to fix the place up a bit too so you can sell it. It seemed a bit . . . run-down . . . last time I visited." He laughs a little. I picture Chaz visiting Mother. Rolling up in his Rolls. Rocking on his elevated heels at her front door. Mother answering with a cigarette between her fingers. Donning a black silk shift or maybe one of her white suits. That pendant of a warped red heart shimmering darkly on her chest. Smilingly entreating, *Entrée, entrée.*

She'd never let him fuck her, would she?

"Anyway"—he signals to the waiter—"a lot to think about." He looks at his watch and smiles. He's so sorry he doesn't have better news. I hear the rich couple toast each other with a clink of their flutes. Their easy laughter. What am I doing here in this place I can't afford? In my borrowed sack dress? *From our little shop,* Sylvia said when she handed it to me. *I'll always think of it as ours, Belle.* Then I remember. The shop.

"Wait! What about her dress shop, Belle of the Ball?" *Named after my daughter,* Mother would say, gripping the back of my neck. That shop was her consolation prize after her acting career failed spectacularly. Got one of her many gentleman friends to foot the bill. *I'll consider it an investment,* I imagine he said, winking. Probably dead now.

"I could sell her share of the dress shop, right?"

Chaz looks at me. "She already sold it, Belle."

Inside me, something shatters like glass. "Sold it?"

"A couple of months ago. To her partner. Sylvia Holmes?"

I drop my coffee cup. It makes a crashing sound like the world ending. We watch the spilled coffee gush to the ends of the table and drip, drip to the floor.

"You know the name, of course," Chaz says quietly.

"I know the name."

Another respectful silence. Or maybe he just doesn't know what else to say. Doesn't want to call attention to how little I know about Mother's life. Maybe out of sensitivity or maybe because he doesn't want another scene. The check comes. "All on me," he says magnanimously, though all I had was the coffee. And then I remember that Mother owes him money too.

"Your mother," he says wistfully. I watch the rings gleam on his hairy fingers as he signs the bill. "Bit of a mystery, wasn't she?"

4

Belle of the Ball is in the heart of the village. Mother made sure you couldn't miss it. How it gleamed there redly on the street full of shops, flanked by palm trees. Display window full of diabolically beautiful women. The sign featured a girl in a ball gown reclined in the crescent of a silver moon, swinging from an iron hook over the door. The shops nearby couldn't really hold a candle to it. You'd walk right past their windows full of Turkish rugs and Chihuly glass, ignoring the salesmen lurking in the doorways.

Hello, they'd whisper, grinning desperately in the shadows.

Welcome, said the bolder ones, bowing their heads.

Mother never did that. She never lurked in her own doorway, grinning. The mannequins in the window did all the luring for her. The way they'd stare at you, through you, from behind the glass. Pointy white faces. Red lips curved in slight smiles. That strange color of eye—topaz—that glittered. All of them had Mother's dark red hair. She'd put them in whimsical, sometimes sinister configurations. *To catch the eye. Have a little fun.* One day they might be waltzing. Another day they might be throttling one another. Or sitting for afternoon tea. They wore fanciful dresses, vintage-looking and shimmery as dreams. They oozed a formidable glamor. You'd become afraid, looking at the mannequins in their finery, even as desire filled you like darkness. *Bitches*, you'd think. Yet you'd want to buy whatever they were wearing. You'd go in and hand Mother all your money, the little shop bell jangling softly when you finally figured out the scissor-shaped door handle and pushed open the door. She had that handle installed just to make it that much harder for people to come in. But inside, oh inside, the air would be bright and sweet with her violets and smoke. Music played, too, something French or classical usually. Beautiful but intimidating. You'd be intimidated. You'd wonder if you made a mistake, coming through the scissor door. But you'd gather yourself. Remember the dress you saw, the dream of yourself it gave you. *I want that*, you'd say, pointing at the mannequin's swanlike back clad in whatever dress. And Mother would size you up with her shop woman's eyes. She was like a living mannequin behind the counter, oozing her own glamour. Looking so bored by you. Everything from her half-buttoned silk shirt to her loose curls to her lips red like a perfect stain said, *I only give the very slightest of fucks.* And maybe she'd oblige you or maybe she wouldn't. *Sorry*, she might say, though she never once looked sorry. *Last one*, even if it wasn't. Even if there were a row of these very dresses hanging right behind her. Shrug of her silk shoulders. Can't be helped. A question of destiny.

I used to feel so much envy for the window mannequins. I'd imagine that they were Mother's true children, that they tortured me like Cinderella's evil sisters. Their whiteness glowed beneath the moon of my dreams. In these dreams, Mother also loved them more.

After I check out of the hotel, I drive over to the shop, bracing myself. A little afraid to see it all again. But when I pull up, there are no sinister sisters in the window. No scissor door handle anymore. No girl on a crescent moon above the door, either. The storefront is all chrome and glass. Behind the window, there's a row of gray torsos under track lighting. Drab dresses hang from their headless bodies like sacks. Dark gray columns of fabric that show no shape at all. There are the odd embellishments at the collar and cuffs. Some absurd rhinestone swirls—are they meant to be galaxies? *Eye-catching!* I can picture Sylvia thinking. *Eclectic.* I see my own face reflected back in the window, between the torsos. My own face looming over my black sack, looking punched. There's a furrow in my brow. The scar on my forehead's throbbing darkly. The one I've been trying to lighten and brighten, exfoliate away. The one I barely noticed when I used to live here. Back now with a vengeance.

Tsk, Belle, Mother would say, patting my shoulder. *Don't frown or your face will freeze that way. You'll thank me later.*

When?

And Mother smiled. *When your soul starts showing, of course. Sooner than you think.* I remember she looked excited by this.

The sun goes behind a cloud, and I see Sylvia through the glass. Standing behind the counter. Mother's counter. Once artfully arranged with scarves and brooches and a few choice perfumes. Filled now with what appears to be shitty costume jewelry. Sylvia's talking to a customer. The customer's back is to me, but I know the type, I can see her face in my mind's eye, hear her awful voice in my head. Sylvia's palms are pressed into the counter, so at ease in her terrain. Ingratiating smile. I feel my furrow deepen, my scar darken. My heart beating more quickly now.

When I burst through the shop door, ready to scream, ready to shout, Sylvia just looks at me out of the corner of her eye. Smiles with one side of her face, a saleswoman trick. *I see you, I'm with someone, I'll be with you in just a bit.* Then she goes back to talking with the customer. "Oh yes. Hahaha. Absolutely. And with a blazer, you'll be all set."

I stand there, feeling like a ghoul, waiting for her to finish. Michael Bublé's playing softly. Hideously. Gone is the scent of Mother's perfume from the air. The customer turns around to look at me. A woman in capris and Nine West flats. Coral lip gloss. Chunky jewelry. Smiling tersely. She would never have come in here if Mother were behind the counter. Driven away by the pointy-faced mannequins, Mother's beauty, the sex-and-death scent of the room atomizer. *Bonjour*, Mother would have said, smiling coldly. *And what brings you here today?* Meaning well, possibly, but she still would also have scared the living shit out of this sort of woman.

Sylvia isn't like that. Hers is the wily face of the sycophant. Greasily beaming. Doesn't mind being walked all over. *Walk over me*, her face says. *I love it.*

"I *was* going to go to J.Crew," this woman is telling her, telling us both, "but then I thought I'd come *here* instead." And then she looks around with a proprietary smile. So pleased with herself for shopping local.

"Well. We're so *very* glad you dropped in." Sylvia smiles, folding up the woman's purchase. Some sort of brown sack dress. Wrapping it in tissue paper like it's worth something. Winking at me. *See? Customer service. Something your mother didn't understand.*

"Please come see us again sometime," she urges the woman. She slips the turd-colored dress into a plain brown bag. Mother used to use glossy red paper bags, I remember. *Belle of the Ball* embossed on them in loopy gold. Some gold stars swirling around the words. *Belle, like my daughter*, she might explain, her hand on my neck, softly throttling me. I could feel her red nails sinking into my nape flesh as she beamed at me. And the customer would smile. *How sweet*, they'd think. *What a beautiful example of mother-daughter love.*

"Now, Mirabelle," Sylvia says softly. "What can I do for you?"

I look around the place, at the headless torsos in their sacks, the swell of soft hits like an aural lobotomy.

"You stole Mother's shop," I hear myself say. My voice is calm, flat, polite, though I'm trembling. Did I really just come out and say it like that?

Sylvia looks at me, horrified. "*Excuse* me?"

The customer who bought the turd dress turns around on her way out. Looks at us. Oh, now this is interesting. Some drama!

Sylvia turns pink. Something like anger flashes in her dark eyes.

"I didn't steal anything, Mira." Now it's Mira. "She sold it to me."

"That's impossible. If she'd sold it, she would have told me. I know she would have." I can hear the crack in my voice. The Formula stings my eyes. I'm thankful for Mother's dark glasses. But Sylvia sees through them. That searching gaze of hers.

"Esther," she says softly to a joyless-looking clerk hovering nearby. The clerk, Esther, is clutching a few hangers heavy with sack dresses to her chest like a shield. She observes my grief wordlessly, through thick glasses with whimsical red frames. The glasses are attached to a red chain around her neck. "Mind the register for a minute, will you?" Sylvia says to her.

Esther just blinks.

Sylvia leads me to the back room, *Come along with me, dear.* More shitty, shapeless dresses back here hanging in sad rows. A few of Mother's old mannequins are in here too. The white, red-lipped ones from my nightmares. One is standing up, two are lying down. The standing one beams at me with her golden eyes. She's naked. A purse hangs absurdly from her shoulder, shaped like a glittery black swan. *A bit of fun*, Mother would have said of the purse. *A reminder to fuck function. Embrace form.*

"I can't tell you how sorry I am, Mira," Sylvia begins. "I really thought you knew. I thought surely she would have told you."

How's the shop, Mother?

The shop? What are you talking about?

Belle of the Ball? Your shop?

Oh right. The shop. Fine, fine. Ça marche.

"To be honest, she left me in a bit of a lurch, too, doing that," Sylvia says. "But I wanted to help. I wanted to be a friend. I'm honestly very surprised she didn't share her decision with you." There's an accusation in there. *Estranged from each other toward the end, weren't you? Not so terribly close after you moved away. If you ever were. Whose fault is that?*

Behind Mother's glasses, my vision goes swimmy. The Formula has gone rogue, I guess. I find myself telling Sylvia everything about the meeting with Chaz. Mother's multiple loans to repair god knows what. It all comes gushing out of me like the tears I don't shed. I can't stop the tide of words.

"All that money," I whisper, sinking to my knees. "Where did she spend it? Where did it go?" As I say this, I flash to her bathroom full of red bottles and jars. Mother's unlined face behind the wheel of her Jaguar, expressionless. Pale, empty eyes fixed on the windshield.

"Well, your mother never really thought too much about things like money." She crouches down beside me, pats my back.

"Was she in her right mind?"

"Right *mind*?" Sylvia looks confused. "What do you mean?"

"Was she . . . going crazy?"

"*Crazy?* No. No, no, no, not crazy. *Eclectic*, maybe. And of course . . ."

"What?"

"Well, you know your mother. She never had much of a filter." Embarrassed laughter. "Not with me. Certainly not with the customers. You know she *was* French," she adds, lowering her voice.

"What does that mean?"

"Just that maybe she was getting a little more . . . French. In her old age is all."

"*More* French?"

Sylvia shakes her head. "Look, Mirabelle, I really wouldn't worry yourself about this now. We all get more eclectic in our old age, don't we? Although sixty-one's not so old. She wasn't even a senior citizen yet, right? Too young to get a discounted bus pass! Not that your mother would ever ride a *bus*."

I stare at the naked mannequin. Shorn of all but her little swan handbag. Her topaz eyes staring at me sadly. "Why did you move the mannequins back here?"

"No one liked these but your mother. And you know," she says, lowering her voice again, "I never found them to be very . . . *inclusive*." She looks at me meaningfully. Surely this word, *inclusive*, will get me on her side. I stare at her.

"So pale," she insists. "And those red lips. Those weird eyes." She looks up at the mannequin and makes a face. "They always creeped me out, to be honest. I don't know where the hell she found them. Anyway, you really mustn't work yourself up like this, my dear. You're already dealing with *so* much."

I look at her pleading face. So very dehydrated. In desperate need of glycerin. Same age as Mother, but you'd never know. Sylvia looks her age. Older maybe, from a life in the California sun. No sunscreen regimen—probably sees it as vanity. I could send her some Marva videos. She might benefit from a replenishing miracle seed essence or a regenerating human stem cell serum. Marva tells us self-care is telling yourself you matter every morning in the mirror. *You should talk to it. Become friends with what you see there.* And when she says this, I feel my neck skin prickle. Nervous suddenly to look in the glass. Whom will I see there? Can I really befriend them?

"You'll sell the condo," Sylvia is urging. "The car, too, I'm sure. Surely someone will want to buy the place. Such a beautiful property. And with that view, that view!" I see the mouth of her soul water a little.

"But the debt. *The debt*," I whisper. "What am I going to do?"

"We'll sort it all out," she whispers back. "You'll see," she says, squeezing my hand. "Someone will come and snatch that place right up. Save you from all this. It's too perfect. Just like your mother. Which reminds me," she says. "She left some things here."

"What things?"

"A few boxes in the basement. She sort of treated this place as her own personal storage, even after she left. I never said anything, of course. You know your mother."

Why do people keep saying that to me? *I don't know*, I want to tell them. Even as a voice inside me hisses, *You do*.

"I'll just go down and grab them and meet you out front, okay? Esther, can you grab the dolly? Oh good, you've got it."

I turn and there's Esther standing behind me, staring blankly. She's gripping a dolly with both hands. How long was she standing there? She wheels the dolly around my kneeling body and follows Sylvia through a door I always thought was locked, that Mother said led to nothing but boilers. *You don't want to go down there,* she'd said, *trust me.*

I look back up at the mannequin. Smiling at me mysteriously, cruel sister. "Why didn't she tell me about the basement?" I whisper.

"Excuse me." A woman standing in the doorway, holding one of the sack dresses limply in her arms. "Sorry, I was just looking for someone to help me, but there's no one out front."

"They're in the basement," I tell her.

"Oh." She stares at me kneeling on the floor before the mannequin like I'm praying. "Well, if now's not a good time . . ."

"No, it's fine. I can help you. You wanted to try on that dress, right?" She looks at me hesitantly. Even a little afraid. "Yes."

"The dressing rooms are just out and to the left. I can take you."

Her face brightens. "Oh. That would be lovely, thank you."

"No problem," I say, smiling a little as I stand up, wipe the shop floor dust off my knees. "This way, follow me." Behind me, I can feel the mannequin gazing coyly at me. Like Mother used to whenever I handled a customer for her. *My best saleswoman,* she always said. Making up for her coldness. The good cop to her bad.

"Any particular occasion?" I find myself asking, slipping into the mode. Like I'm interested. It's a throwaway question. I can intuit the needs of the customer with one look in their stranger's eyes. Guess the event, the existential crisis behind the potential purchase.

The woman smiles. She enjoys this question of an occasion, though there is none. "Oh, just this and that."

"Of course," I say. I picture what *this and that* might look like for this woman. A three-hour prosecco lunch on a patio with her fellow blonds. Long drunken nights on rooftop terraces overlooking a roaring ocean they ignore. Lots of loud talk about personal journeys. When we get to the dressing rooms, she asks me would I mind terribly waiting here? She'd love to get my take. Of course I mind. Now that I'm back in

the shop, I want to get the hell out of here. But I just smile at her plac-
idly. "Not at all." And I stand outside the door with my smile still on
my face. I stare at the dress forms in their sacks. Watch a few women
paw through the racks. Still the swell of soft hits all around. *I bought
this place for both of us, you know. Besides, what else are you going
to do, Belle? A French literature degree is all well and good but come
on. And you can't be Princess Jasmine forever. I mean, can you? You
tell me.*

"Well," the woman says, emerging at last from the changing room
door. "What do you think?"

It's hideous. A taupe halter-neck dress that bells out straight from
the clavicle in a strange, asymmetrical triangle. It hangs on her like a
poorly pitched tent. The taupe washes her out.

"Tell me," she says, a little pleading.

But she doesn't want me to tell her. Not truly. I can tell by the
twitch in her lip, the hopeful shine in her eyes. She's brimming with
it: a longing for delusion. She's not looking at the giant gilt-trimmed
mirror Mother nailed to the wall, though it's right beside her. She's
looking at me. An entity capable of reflecting back exactly what she
desires to see. Like how Mother used to look at me instead of a mirror
sometimes. Slavering for just the right adjective. *Well, Belle? What do
we think?*

"It's a little too, I don't know . . . *look at me*, isn't it?" the woman
says, and then laughs, embarrassed.

I smile. "Is that such a bad thing?"

"What do you think?"

"Honestly?"

"Honestly."

I can feel her holding her breath. For a moment, I savor the power,
the true words right on my tongue. *Unflattering. Unfortunate.* I could
speak them and crush her.

"I think it's wonderful."

"Really?"

"Sophisticated," I offer. "*Avant-garde*, even," I add, over-enunciating the French.

"*Avant-garde*," she repeats dreamily. Another language. She likes that. "You really think so?"

"Never hide your light," I tell her. She smiles. She's prone to hiding her light, her eyes say. She looks at herself in the mirror. Now it's safe. Her face brightens at what she sees.

"It *is* sort of elegant, isn't it? Cutting edge, even."

I nod. Absolutely. It could be those things if she likes. "And versatile," I add. "A daytime sharpness that could translate easily into a nighttime chic."

Where are these words coming from? My lips, apparently. It always comes so easily. Telling people what they want to hear. Divining the perfect words with one look at their waiting faces. Giving them their dream of themselves. I did it in a spangled bra for ten years beneath the arch of Sleeping Beauty Castle. *Aren't you as pretty as a princess?* I'd say, even to the homely ones. Especially to the homely ones. I do it now at Damsels in my dark, high-necked dress. And, of course, I did it for Mother. In this shop and all my life, I'd have my slew of words ready to hand out like candy. *You always have the magic words*, Mother said, grateful but also suspicious. *How do you always know exactly what to say?*

The woman smiles more broadly. "I should take you with me everywhere. Normally I shop with my daughter. She's very cruel. She calls it *being honest*, of course." Laughter.

I smile. "Of course."

"And how are we doing here?" Sylvia says, suddenly appearing at my side out of nowhere. "Oh my, that looks *fantastic*. Aren't these halter necks *just* the cutest things? Just got them in from Sweden." It has the ring of falsehood. Of too much.

The woman smiles tightly. "Your saleswoman was just helping me."

"Was she?" And Sylvia's face darkens, looking at me. "I see. How wonderful. Thanks so much, Mira. I'll take it from here." She pats my shoulder and leans in. I catch the scent of her: an insidious freshness spiked with citrus. She whispers hotly, "We left the box by the car. Just the one in the end." Prim smile. "I'll come by and visit later, okay? See how you're getting on."

She turns her attention to the woman in the taupe tent. Time to reel her in. "Now, are you looking for a little bolero or blazer to go with or . . . ?"

I walk quickly away toward the door, the sound of Sylvia's voice, a pitch too high, ringing in my ears along with the insipid adult contemporary. The store is an alien landscape, nothing of Mother remaining. Just the mannequins alone in the dusty back room. Smiling mysteriously in the dark.

5

Afternoon. A reapplication of sunscreen, physical and chemical, which I can already feel melting in the light. I'm standing outside Mother's apartment, gripping the basement box. Staring at her doormat, which reads *Wipe Your Paws*. On either side of her front door, pots of spiky plants and flowers assail my eyes with their bright shades. Don't want to go in. Want to check back into the pink hotel. Lie down in a dark room watching Marva videos until I fly back to Montreal. Three days from now. But the flowers need to be watered, don't they? And her cat, Anjelica, needs to be fed. Her things need to be sorted through, packed. The place needs to be cleaned up, fixed up, Chaz said. Before I can sell it and get out of here. Never come back again to this sunny place she loved despite her enmity for the sun.

Took me a while to get out of the Jaguar. Stared through the windshield at the chrome cat on the hood in mid-pounce, practically ablaze in the light. *What happened to you, Mother?* I asked the cat. *Did you fall down some well of madness? Am I following you now into the dark?* The cat just shone there quietly like a sphinx.

From outside, the apartment looks impeccable, like Mother herself. Windows sparkling. Flowers bright. The place seems alive, awake, even. Like she might still be in there, she never fell from the cliff. Can't I picture her inside, singing to herself right now? At her vanity table, maybe, before her three-paneled mirror. Smiling as she powders her face with her little white puff. Strangely, I hear music then. Coming from inside Mother's place. Doesn't sound like Mother's music though. Not the Édith Piaf variety. This is heavy, loud, psychedelic-sounding. And then I notice that the plants have already been watered. The soil in which the roses grow is black and damp and slick. The pots are going drip, drip onto the concrete floor of the veranda. I put down the box and grab one of them—a heavy pot, just in case—and open the door, already unlocked. Oh, I'm awake now. Heart beginning to pound. Potted plant raised.

Inside, the music's so loud, Mother's windows seem to tremble. No one in the bright living room apart from Anjelica on the couch, licking her paws.

When I get to the kitchen, I scream.

There by the sink stands a man with his shirt off. Bopping his head to the earthquake of sound.

For a minute I watch him, transfixed. The pot must have slipped from my hands, because there is a crashing sound. He sees me standing there in the shattered clay. He smiles. Lowers the volume on a little speaker on the table. "Hey," he says. "You must be Belle. Nice to meet you."

I just stare at him.

"I'm sorry for your loss," this man says. He reaches out his hand. I stare at that, too. On his wrist is some sort of braided leather bracelet. Two black twisting cords. A feeling in my body. Coursing through it. Not the first time I've encountered a half-naked man in Mother's kitchen. Not the first time they've known my name, said it's nice to meet me while I just stood there like a psychopath. I almost expect Mother to come sauntering in now in one of her silk robes, glowing from sex and reeking of smoky violets. *Oh good, looks like you two have met.*

The man reaches forward and hugs me. Suddenly I'm enveloped in hard, beach-scented flesh. I can feel him patting my back with a large, friendly hand. *There, there.* He really wants me to feel this, but I'm rigid in his embrace.

"I'm sorry," I say. "Who are you?"

He pulls back, still gripping my shoulders with his very warm hands. "I'm Tad," this man says softly.

Tad, I think. *Of course he is.* Did Mother ever mention a Tad?

"I clean your mother's windows," Tad says. "I water the plants and things too. Do a bit of landscaping." He waves a hand vaguely at the rosebushes outside. I stare at tall, broad, shirtless Tad. Leonine hair. Tanned torso. Impossible biceps covered in oceanic tattoos. Apart from the tattoos, all of Mother's favorite man-traits.

"My mother's dead," I say, a little shocked at myself.

But Tad just nods somberly. "I know," he says. "I'm so sorry." He's got a beer in his hand now. "How are you holding up?"

"Fine, thank you." I nod. But there's a crack in my voice. My lip twitches. I look away.

"Cool," Tad says. "I lost my father a while ago. And that really knocked me out." He shakes his head. Dirty-blond hair. Sandy, really. "So I get it. You can just tell me to fuck off if you want to."

He pauses here. I should say, *Of course not. Thank you though. Sorry about your father.* "Don't fuck off," I say.

"Honestly?" Tad says. "I just came over today because I didn't know what else to do with myself, you know?"

On the table, I notice two roses floating in a martini glass filled with water. Tad must have done this. Clipped the flowers and set them afloat in the glass. There's a bowl full of floating roses on the coffee table, too. Also Tad's handiwork. *Mother hated roses*, I could tell him. For as long as I can remember. She even used to be allergic. *I'm still allergic to cheap apologies, easy bribes*, she always said. But shouldn't Tad know that? I try to imagine him clipping the roses, whispering to them, perhaps. Cupping them in his hands like baby birds. Setting them afloat in a bowl to die. *I'm going the way of roses, Belle.*

"And I didn't know if anyone else was going to water the plants and the bushes," Tad is saying. "And I didn't want them to . . . you know . . ." He lets the word *die* hang in the air, unspoken.

"I appreciate it, thank you. I was actually coming by to start packing up." *Your cue to leave, Tad*, but Tad just looks at me. He puts a hand on my shoulder again. Squeezes meaningfully without breaking eye contact.

"That fucking sucks," he says. He walks over to Mother's fridge and opens it. Reaches down to the bottom shelf where there are a row of beer bottles gleaming. When did Mother start drinking beer? *Beer*, she'd mutter if it was offered, making a face. *I just don't get it.*

He opens a kitchen drawer—he knows which drawer, I notice—and grabs the bottle opener. I watch his biceps come into relief as he cracks open the bottle. Some faint stirring of lust visits me briefly like a ghost. He hands me the beer. Clinks his bottle against mine. "To Noelle," he says. The sound of Mother's name in his mouth conjures her up briefly again. Silk-robed and smiling in a light that loved her. I watch him take a long sip. I take one too. It's surprisingly refreshing. Crisp. I gasp in spite of myself.

"I didn't come to the party," Tad says. "No disrespect to your mom or anything."

What party? I think, then realize he must mean the funeral.

"I'm just not really a *death* person, you know."

"Right."

"Also, I don't really dig her crowd." He frowns as if recalling something deeply unpleasant. I think of Mother's crowd. Mostly wolfish gentlemen of a certain age and their wives. Sylvia, of course. That strange woman in red outside.

"But I paid my respects, in my way," Tad says. "I want you to know that."

"Thank you," I say. I wonder what this looks like, Tad paying his respects. Tad on his knees in a room decorated with conch shells, maybe a framed poster of white stones on tilled sand, lighting some sort of scented candle. Tad at an outdoor tiki bar, raising a beer to the bloody sunset. Taking a somber sip. It tastes bittersweet.

"Did a one-man paddle-out just yesterday," Tad tells me.

"Really?" A surfer. Of course.

"It was amazing. I could feel her energy out there, you know? All around. Big-time. There was a seagull flying around and around over my head." He raises his index finger, making it spin. "A dolphin even came up out of the waves and sort of smiled." Now his hand is a dolphin's beak rising out of the imaginary waves. "And the waves were just . . . perfect." He drops his hand and sips his beer. "Pretty sure that was all your mom saying *hey*."

"You think so?"

"Oh yeah. I could feel it. Right here." He pumps a fist gently against his left pec and I immediately drop my eyes to the shattered pot at my feet.

"That's nice," I murmur. When I look back up, I see he's now seated on my mother's red velvet sofa. Reclined. At ease. His feet on the glass table. One foot jittering like it's on speed.

"Sorry, do you mind?" he says. "I'm just a bit wiped out from all the landscaping." He pats his taut, bare stomach. Anjelica, Mother's very white cat, immediately leaps into his lap and settles herself on his crotch. "It was a hot one today. I'll finish this and be on my way, okay?"

"Okay," I say. I'm just standing there staring at him, at Anjelica purring on his crotch. She looks fiercely content. Her blue eyes, just like Mother's, half closing with ecstasy.

"I'll just roll this here and smoke it outside." I watch him pull a tin of tobacco from his pocket, careful not to disturb Anjelica. Clearly they've done this dance before.

"So what's your plan, anyway?" he asks me.

"My plan?" I watch his tongue lick the white rolling paper. So tenderly.

"For the place. Are you selling? Are you staying, you think? Going back to Canadia?"

"Canada," I correct.

He smiles. He knows it's Canada, he just made a little joke, see? Lighten the mood a bit. How old is Tad? I wonder. He looks a little younger than me, but definitely in his thirties too. Very Jesus-y.

"I'm selling," I tell Tad.

"Why sell? If it were mine, I'd hang on to it." He grins at me.

"Because my mother spent all her money on bullshit," I say. I look right at Tad when I say this. "I have to sell the place if I want to crawl out of the black hole she dug for herself."

Tad looks unfazed. He nods philosophically. "You could also Airbnb it. That's what a lot of people in Eden are doing these days."

"Eden?"

"That's the name of this complex—you didn't know? I guess your mom bought it after you left. Yeah, Eden. Not a lot of people *live* here anymore. They rent out their places. It's an old building, you know? Run-down. Shitty pipes and appliances and fixtures. Things not really working the way they used to. But." He gives me another sly grin. "The view's spectacular. That's the thing."

Then he looks out the windows. Freshly wiped down by him, by Tad. He's inviting me with his glance to look at his handiwork. *Window renovation*, I remember Chaz said.

I don't look out the window. I just keep staring at him manspreading on Mother's couch, her cat rubbing whorishly against his crotch. He's slung an arm around the cushion like he's holding her ghost.

"If you fixed it up a bit," he says, "you could really cash in. You have to fix it up anyway, right? To sell it, I mean."

"Yeah."

"Pretty big job to fix it up. You have any help? I'd be happy to—"

"I don't need help," I blurt out. "I mean, I appreciate it. Thank you, Tad." Even his name on my tongue sounds like it's mocking me. "But I can manage." I hate the way I sound. Prim as my borrowed sack dress. A theme park princess talking to a troublesome guest. A shopgirl dealing with the FedEx guy. There's a little curtsy in my voice. A clicking shut of a door. A drawing down of a shade over my life, my soul.

He smiles at me slowly.

"What?"

"Nothing. Just that you look like her. In some ways. In a lot of ways, actually. I didn't really see it at first." I can picture Mother smiling at this. *She's more exotic-looking, of course. That dark hair. That golden skin, so jealous. But we have the same bones, don't we, Belle?* And she'd pat my shoulder, squeeze my chin between her fingers. And whoever we were with, usually a man, would be forced to agree. *The same bones. Oh yes. I see it.*

Tad sees it. He's grinning widely. What does he see exactly?

"We're very different," I say to Tad.

His placid gaze offers no response. He finishes the rest of his beer, sets it on the table. "Well, I'll leave you to it." He rises from the couch to the great consternation of Anjelica, who jumps away from his lap with a screech.

"If you change your mind about needing help." He pulls a card from his pocket and hands it to me. *Tad Olsen. Landscaper. Window Washer. General Handyman.* In the corner of the card, there's a little illustration of a smiling merman. He's holding a squeegee in one hand and a pair of gardening shears in another. The merman has chin-length hair like Tad.

I watch him walk to the front door. Suddenly, I feel afraid. I don't want to be alone in Mother's place. "Tad?" I say. And again, I hate the way my voice sounds. This time like a hand reaching out. Grasping for something solid in the dark.

"Yeah?" He stands at the door and looks at me questioningly. Waiting.

Ridiculous to ask him to stay. This man I don't even know. But something about his eyes, the way he's looking at me. It takes me back to my nine-year-old body. Standing in the dark hallway of our old Montreal apartment. Watching from the shadows as Mother entertained whatever man in the living room. Men who looked like Tad. Sometimes they'd notice me standing there in the hall. Their eyes would meet mine and my body would freeze, I'd catch fire. Usually they'd turn right back to Mother after that. But sometimes they'd keep looking at me curiously, even kindly. Some might even wave. *That your daughter?* they'd ask Mother. And Mother would frown. *Belle, go back to bed.*

Don't be silly, the man might say. *Let her come out and say hello.* And he'd smile at me standing there in the dark. *Hi.*

And I'd fill with warmth. My heart would open stupidly, only to be broken later. *Hi.*

Tad will be one of those. He'll be a waver. He'll be a smiler. He's smiling at me now. "Yes, Belle?"

Then I notice the mirror behind Tad, on the wall above Mother's couch. A crack right down the middle. Just like the one in the bathroom. Just like the one down the hall. And in this mirror above the couch, I see the wall of them behind me. Each one with a crack in its face.

"What's up with the mirrors?" I ask.

"What do you mean?"

"The cracks? The cracks all down the middle?" And for a second, I feel crazy. Like maybe I'm the only one who sees them.

"Oh, those," Tad says. "Yeah, I kept trying to replace them. But your mother said it was no use. I still tried one time when she was away. But the crack was back the next time I came. Like I hadn't done anything. Weird. Something to do with the air? The building settling, maybe?"

"The building settling?"

"Sure. All buildings have energies, you know. This one has some energy, let me tell you. In fact, I think it was having a bit of an effect on her. Your mother."

My heart skips. "An effect on her? What do you mean?"

"It's hard to verbalize it. Language feels so meager, you know? In the face of certain things?"

For a moment, I picture him gripping a tambourine. "Can you try?"

He shakes his head. "Oh man, listen to me talking my shit. *Energy.* What do I know, right? About life or death? About anything, really?" He tucks the rolled cigarette behind his ear and smiles. "I'll get out of your hair now." And in spite of myself, I picture Tad's fingers combing through Mother's dark red hair.

"Oh hey," he says in the open front doorway, "thought you were moving out?"

"I am."

He points to the box outside. I forgot about it when I heard the noise, which I thought was an intruder. Which turned out to be Tad. Grinning at me now.

"Looks like you're moving in."

6

After Tad goes, taking his music and his beachy scent with him, the place is quiet. Just me on the floor with Tad's beer in my hand, watching the sky darken through Mother's immense windows. Tad offered to stay, but I said, *I'm fine, thank you, Tad*, and again his name mocked me. I am fine. Really. Just an apartment. Just Mother's apartment. Filled with her furniture, all of it sharp-edged and winking in the light. Shouldn't be afraid, it's silly. If Mother knew I was afraid, she'd laugh and laugh. She'd say, *Ridiculous*. I stare at the wall of cracked mirrors in their heavy frames. Were there always this many, Mother?

Angelica has disappeared, slithered whitely away. A clock somewhere ticks and ticks. Didn't know Mother had a clock like that. *Tick, tick*, telling me I should move along. All I've done so far is unpack the box Sylvia gave me from the shop basement. Disappointing. Mostly old dolls—my childhood dolls, I guess. They all looked exactly alike, like Mother, in fact. Pale skin. Blue eyes of glass that stared up at me unblinking. There was an old clock in there too, with a picture of Snow White and the Seven Dwarves on the face. Funny, I don't remember owning a clock like that. There was a red diary, locked, no key. A picture book of what looked like a Snow White story. *The Beautiful Maiden*, it was called. Very worn. Spine cracked. I must have loved that story once.

The shoebox was a little curious, I guess. I thought it was just the dolls, the clock, and the books in the box at first, but something told me, *Put your hand in deeper*. And there was the shoebox at the very bottom. Taped up just like the box itself had been. Taped tighter than the box. Someone had wrapped the tape around and around. I had to

take a knife to all sides to get it open. Then what? I held my breath a little. Maybe this would be . . . something. What was I looking for? But it
was nothing, really. Just an old torn poster of Tom Cruise in *Top Gun*.
Some magazine clippings, mostly of Tom Cruise too, it looked like. All
of Tom Cruise, it turned out. Each one carefully folded. I stared at page
after torn page of his glossy face, the cracked mirrors shining in my eye
corners. Dizzy, I felt then. Cold suddenly in the very white room. *Who
ripped these out?* I wondered. But I knew. I knew before I even saw
the childish handwriting scrawled across one of the clippings—Tom
smiling in his sunglasses in *Risky Business*. *I'm yours*, I'd written in
tiny red letters. How funny. I'd even drawn a heart, how very funny.
Right around Tom's face in red ink. I looked back at the torn *Top Gun*
poster. Half was missing. Kelly McGillis, his co-star, torn out so it was
just Tom alone on his motorcycle. I looked at Tom's face, the mirrors
nearly blinding me now with the light of the dying sun. His eyes were
in shadow, so they looked like black holes. I must have had a crush or
something at some point.

Now I stare at the open box brimming with dolls, the clippings,
that worn little picture book. Just more shit to pack up, really. *Are you
moving in or moving out?* Tad joked again as he was leaving.

Moving out, Tad. Moving out.

So get going, I tell myself. *At least now you have a box.* Her
books, her clothes, dishes, just fucking pick something. Beer in hand,
I wander the apartment, my footsteps clicking along the floor. *Belle*,
Mother would snap, *shoes!*—but I keep them on. As I go from room to
room, my heart sinks like a stone. Because her hobgoblin lawyer was
right. Her place is in terrible shape. The more closely I look, the more
I see. Cracks in the white walls. Water stains on the ceilings like ink
blots. Paint peeling everywhere. In the bathroom, where I hid away
yesterday watching Marva, I notice chips in the sink now, decaying
grout around the rim. When I pull back the flowery shower curtain,
I see the tub's filled with cracks. The shower head yields nothing but
a thin stream of rusty water. I try to turn off the tap, but it comes off

in my hand. The kitchen is a disaster. Ancient stove, I can't see the numbers around the dials anymore. Fridge that hums, that's the humming noise I was hearing during the memorial. I thought it was Sylvia playing some Gregorian chants. I take a long swig of beer. This is bad. *Mother, did you really live like this?*

And the jars. Red jars and bottles in every room, how did I not notice them all before? Lining the walls of her bedroom. Cluttering her countertops. *She really loved her products, didn't she?* Sylvia said. I think of the video, the glowing girl in the bright bathroom, holding a jar up to her face like an apple. Red glass just like this. It feels heavy in my hand. Gold, slanted characters like runes are etched across it. *ROUGE*, it reads, and nothing else. No ingredients list. No instructions. *Oh, I have my secrets, Belle. We all have our beauty secrets, don't we?*

I open the jar. More than empty. Like it's been licked clean by the cat. There's a faint scent of ocean and roses that rises up like a ghost.

I look in the cracked mirror. "Mother," I whisper. "What the fuck is all of this?"

Belle, do you ever look in the mirror and hate? she asked me once on the phone.

Hate? I stared at the silhouette of my reflection in the dark. Yes, I thought. Of course. All the fucking time. But I said, *Hate what, Mother?*

I could picture her sitting alone in the dark like I was, staring at herself in the mirror.

Ce que tu vois, Mother whispered. A crack in her voice. She sounded lost and sad and afraid. What were you afraid of, Mother?

Now in the mirror I see a shimmer of something. A shape. My heart pounds. *Oh god, what*—but it's just the cat sitting by the front door. Staring at me with her eyes pale and sharp as Mother's. She blinks at me slowly and slinks away.

A pair of red shoes come winking into focus. Shining by the open box behind me.

I turn around and there they are for real. Gleaming between the dolls and the shoebox full of Tom Cruise clippings. Like they were always there. Like they could have come out of the box. Maybe they did and I just didn't notice them in the sea of dolls. *Pretty*, I think, walking over to them. *So very red*. Mother's, they have to be. Funny, I don't remember her having a pair like this. And yet there's something familiar about the worn, thin heel, the sharply pointed toe with the feathers, this red web of straps. The clock, that clock I didn't know she had, ticks louder somewhere. Quicker? Maybe quicker, too. *Try me, try me*, the red shoes seem to say. Almost like they're speaking to me. I shake my head. Mother's shoes would never fit me. I think of her little white feet with their painted red toes. Nothing at all like my freak shows. *What are we going to do with you?* she used to say when she took me shoe shopping as a teenager. Shaking her head at my huge, misshapen feet in their scuffed black Doc Martens, the only shoes we could find that fit. *I don't know, Mother*, I said. *Put me in a sack. Drown me. I'm hopeless*. And she'd frown as I smiled.

Holding the shoes, I feel a strange charge in my hands. Light as feathers. Giving off a faint scent of flesh, her flesh. I close my eyes. It's funny how Mother's shoes make me feel silly, sort of ashamed. Like a stupid, sad child again. Just then a memory hits like a cold, crashing wave. My childish feet in red shoes. I'm looking in a mirror, but it isn't myself I see there. Someone else is in the glass. A man. I can't see his face, but I feel him smiling at me. I'm smiling too. Then all goes black.

I open my eyes. I'm a grown woman again. Lying on the floor of my dead mother's living room. Anjelica's licking my face with her rough little tongue. I thought she hated me. Maybe she still does and just wants food.

It's dark now. No more blood-colored sun. No more blackening trees. Now a moon shines whitely through the curtains, which lift in the black breeze. How did it become night? Clock's ticking quick.

Fridge humming its Gregorian chant. I'm wearing one of Mother's dresses, I see. The silk silver one that falls like such luxe water. Pretty, but how did that happen? When did I take off my plain black dress and put this one on? The red shoes are on my feet now too, gleaming in the dark. I was about to try them on when I went down some sort of memory hole. When something unbidden just floated up and sucked me in. What? Can't remember now. I stare at the red shoes shining on my feet. They fit, look at that. Suddenly I feel like going for a walk, why not? On a night like this, so black and windy and warm, why not? The air is calling to me. There's a song in it, it sounds like. I feed the cat, then hurry out the door. I'll pack later.

Outside, the roses are swaying in the breeze. So alive, they seem to be breathing, like each one has a little gulping mouth. Can't see the ocean, but I can hear it. The roar, the crash against the sharp black rocks. So long as I can't see the water, it's pleasant, the sound. A kind of music. I'm walking the coastline, snaking right along the winding path beside the beach, the same one I used to walk late at night as a teenager. It's black as pitch but I'm not afraid, just like I wasn't afraid then. Back then, we lived farther from the beach, but I'd come here all the time. Knew every turn and groove in the path. Still do, it seems. I guess feet never forget.

I'm walking quickly like I'm late for something, like I'm going somewhere. Funny, because how could I be late for anything? How could I be going anywhere? Nowhere to go at this hour. Just a night stroll I'm taking along the beach in these pretty red shoes. So surprisingly comfortable, despite the high, narrow heel. Feels like I'm wearing nothing at all, really, like I'm floating. And yet there's a pull to my steps as though something's carrying me. The click of my heels gets faster, though in my mind I'm walking slowly. Maybe just the wind. Yes. That has to be all it is.

I've reached the other side of the cove now. Where the seals congregate on the rocks and stink up the air. I used to visit them, talk to them. Funny to think of myself back then. Lonely teen in black with buds in her ears blasting dark wave. Sunglasses forever over my eyes, even at night just like Corey Hart. Speaking to seals only. Whispering the secrets of my heart to them like they actually heard me. Wearing dresses that hurt Mother's eyes, they were so black and mournful. *Are you in mourning?* she'd ask me.

Always, I'd say.

The path beneath my feet is dirt now, not sidewalk. I'm on the dirt path that rims the cliff; I'm on the cliff's edge. On one side of me are trees, shrubs, tall grass, flowers; on the other side, nothing at all. Just air, and at the very bottom, the dark, whirling ocean. Where Mother must have walked, must have fallen. Don't think about Mother falling. Keep walking. One foot in front of the other, though it's so dark, I can't see a thing. Just black. And yet my feet still seem to know where to go. My feet, or my shoes?

As I turn a corner, something lights up the dark. Houses on the side of the cliff, nested deep into the greenery. Not houses, mansions, really. Glowing with money and architecture. I used to wonder about these places. Who was rich enough to live here? There's a house I've never seen before on the very edge of the cliff. All curved glass and extravagant geometry. Black polished concrete that shines in the dark. What I really notice is the red light. Glowing from the dramatically contoured floor-to-ceiling windows. I'm heading for this house like I was heading there all along. A soft, airy music's coming from the place like an exhalation. Filling my ears so pleasantly. I'm smiling in the dark in my red shoes as I walk toward the light and the sound.

As I approach the iron gates, they open, look at that. Like they knew I was coming. Knew I would walk the tree-lined path to this front door. The eucalyptus trees look red from the red light of the house. There are roses growing on either side of the path, tall and red too. So pretty. *What a very impressive structure this is all around*, I think. Which is a strange thought. Why am I walking toward this opulent monstrosity gleaming redly in the dark with such a smile? But even as I wonder, I walk on. Just a night stroll to a strange house I've never seen before. Just walking right up to its sleek front doors of obsidian glass. LA MAISON DE MÉDUSE, it says on a small black plaque beside the doors in red looping letters. *Méduse.* Huh. Next to it there's a symbol. Some kind of squid, it looks like. Or maybe a flower?

The doors open. A woman's standing there in the doorway, smiling like she expected me. "Bonsoir," she says.

Bonsoir? But I say "Bonsoir" to her too.

She's beautiful in a way that destroys me a little. It's a lot of things about her. Little things that add up. Hair sheen. Eye gleam. Mostly it's her skin. Not a hair or a line or a blemish. Like actual glass. So very white. She glows, moonlike, Mother-like, against the tall black doors. Wearing a long silver dress like I am, though hers falls like a literal dream. Eyes clouded in glittering smoke. The reddest, ripest lips I've ever seen. She could be wearing a very rich lipstick. She could have eaten a bowl of overripe cherries.

"Bonsoir et bienvenue," she says, in a voice that could only come from that kind of mouth. Impeccable accent. I'm wondering if she's actually French when she says, "You're just in time." American accent. Equally flawless.

"Just in time," I hear myself repeat. "Oh good." *In time for what exactly?* But something about how this woman's smiling at me keeps my mouth shut tight. I smile too, like I know what she's talking about.

She looks me up and down, her eyes lingering on my face. I become painfully aware of my own abominations, my many layers of corrective, protective product suddenly sitting so heavily on my skin. Yet she looks delighted by what she sees. When her eyes meet mine again, she beams brightly. Opens the door wider and says, "Entrée."

And I go right in, don't I?

Is there a moment where I wonder if I should enter this stranger's house on the edge of the cliff? No. When I look back at this moment, this moment of going through the spiked black gates, down the path flanked by roses, through the wide-open doors of La Maison de Méduse, everything awash in red light, I'll remember no hesitation at all.

7

Music. Laughter. Soft voices. Where am I—some sort of living room? No, too grand for that. More like a hall. Giant, coiling staircase. Tall, curving walls of glass all around. No actual ceiling I can see, though there must be one, because a massive red chandelier's dangling down. A million tiny red lights burning. Beneath it, people in the most elegant suits and dresses swan around in shimmering clusters. A party, must be. A party for the very beautiful and very rich. Not the typical California rich, looks like. No rumpled linen or slapping sandals. No jumpsuits or zombie eyes. This is what Mother would call *another fucking level*. What she might even call *style*. Everyone seems to be dressed in black or red or white. All quite pale-faced. That woman at the door probably mistook me for someone else. There's a drink in my hand now, where did that come from? It looks like champagne, except red. *La Maison de Méduse* etched on the flute in gold. I take a very long sip. Cold, bright bubbles go singing down my throat. Wow. *Like drinking stars, Mother*, I think.

"Like drinking stars," I hear someone behind me whisper dreamily.

I freeze. Turn around. *Mother?* A young-looking couple. Both luminous, both decadently dressed. They stare at me with eyes like the sky, dripping their dark silks.

"Sorry," I say. "Thought I recognized someone."

"A side effect of the Journey, perhaps," one of them offers in a zen voice.

"Perhaps," I echo. I have no idea what they're talking about.

They smile slightly. "Bon voyage," they murmur, raising their fizzing flutes and sauntering away.

"Bon voyage," I agree. *Bon voyage?*

"Aux recommencements," another woman says to me mysteriously as she passes. Also exquisitely dressed, also radiant.

"I'm sorry?"

"'To new beginnings,'" she mutters over her white shoulder, like I've ruined something.

"Oh yes. New beginnings." I raise my glass to her. "Thank you. *Merci.*" What the hell is this place? The music is louder now, a celestial drone full of airy chimes. Sort of like what you might hear in a spa. Just then I notice the signs in the arches above each corridor flanking the grand staircase: SIGNATURE RITUALS, reads one. VOYAGES MERVEILLEUX, reads the other. Up on the wall, there's a screen playing a video of a very white woman with her eyes closed. She has small black discs on either side of her head. She looks to be in absolute bliss. Superimposed over her pale face are lapping ocean waves. *A Rendez-Vous with Yourself*, it reads in red looping letters by her high, plump cheek. I smile. A spa. Of course. There's even what looks like a little boutique in that corner over there. Tall glass cabinets full of red bottles and jars. Each cabinet backlit like the products within are works of art. The red jars are just like the ones in Mother's apartment. She must have come here for treatments. Now I'm really smiling. So this was it, Mother. Your secret place. Probably you loved the little French touches, the old-Hollywood fashion. Sipping red stars. I take a long sip from my flute.

In the boutique, I see an older woman in a white suit—a customer, must be—ransacking one of the cabinets. I watch her greedily gather all the bottles and jars she can into her arms, then dump them into her large, glittery purse. She catches me watching her and frowns. Marches over to me briskly, her purse brimming with jars.

"So," she says, looking me up and down. "You've done it." She smiles a little warily. Probably around Mother's age. Unlike Mother, this woman looks it. Her skin has that preserved, almost pickled quality, suggesting a complex system, a rigid methodology that might be failing her. Still beautiful, though.

"Done it?" I ask her.

She laughs like I've just said something funny. Funny and painful.

"All right, then. Good for you," she says dryly. "*Bravo.*" She doesn't look like it's good for me at all. I notice she's wearing a thick ruby choker around her neck. It makes her look like she's bleeding from the throat. "Did you get a tan or something?" she asks me.

"Excuse me?"

"Shouldn't do that on your Journey, they said. Compromises the result."

"I'm sorry, have we even met before?"

She smiles with a kind of pity. "Was it painful?"

"Painful?"

"Or was it beautiful? I've heard it's a little of both." She looks wistful. Then suddenly, she reaches out and grips my shoulder, drawing me close to her. Her face, I see now, looks very old. Her eyes are wild, yellowed in the corners. "Tell me," she says.

"I'm sorry, I really don't understand what you're—"

"You found the place," someone shouts from above. I turn and look up. The woman in red. From the funeral. From the video. Standing over us, on the first landing of the staircase. Smiling down at me like we're old friends. She's flanked by two people dressed in black. She waves at me to join them on the landing.

I look back at the woman in the white suit who's bleeding rubies from the throat. She's gone pale, looks even older than she did a minute ago. "I envy," she hisses at me in a low voice, then disappears from my side into the shimmering crowd.

I envy? Envy whom? Surely not—

"Join us," sings the woman in red from above. Waving her hand and smiling.

I take a step forward and trip spectacularly. Fall right on the red carpeted stair, my god. I get back up, apologizing, flustered. I try to climb the stairs once more, but it's the funniest thing: I fall again. You know when you're in a dream and you're trying to run and suddenly you can't

run right or you can only run slowly? When what was solid ground suddenly feels like sucking mud beneath your feet? That's how it feels to go
up these stairs. I keep tripping on my feet, which keep feeling like they're
sinking beneath me. I have to grip the banister with all my might, like I'm
climbing a rope. From above, they watch me wrestle with myself. They
wait patiently. Sip their drinks. "So wonderful," says the woman in red.

At last when I reach the landing, frazzled and out of breath, they
smile. The woman in red does, anyway. The strangers on either side of
her do not. They're both wearing black veils over their faces. I can only
just see their solemn expressions through the black netting. They look
like they might be twins.

"So glad you could join us," the woman in red says. The veiled people on either side of her nod slightly.

"Me too," I say, even as I think, *Who are these people? What is
this place?* But it's true, I am glad to be here. I'm very glad to be here
instead of Mother's apartment, among the long shadows. To be at a
party—when was the last time I was at a party? To be at a spa—is this
a spa? Of course it is. Mother's secret spa, no less. What else could it
possibly be? I watch the woman pour me some more of the red stars.

"Sorry," I say. "For my clumsiness just now. On the stairs."

"Sometimes the first steps in our Journey are the most trying, are
they not?" She lets out a laugh like a bark. The veiled people say nothing. "The most trying and yet the most crucial." I look up at her face.
Beaming so brightly at me. "Aren't they, Mirabelle?"

It strikes me again that she really does look like Marva. Same
dreamy smile. Same ageless white skin. Same pale knowing eyes that
seem to look through me, right into my twisted, palpitating heart. "You
remember me?" I ask her.

"Remember," she repeats, and smiles, like she's amused by the
word. "How could I forget?" The way she says it has an air of tragedy,
of knowledge. Perhaps she was a friend of Mother's. Maybe that's why
I was drawn here. Somehow I knew that.

"Did you have any trouble finding us?" she asks me now, Mother's friend. She looks so deeply concerned for my well-being.

I shake my head. "No," I say. "No trouble at all. In fact, this is going to sound funny but—" They all laugh now in anticipation. I wait for them to quiet, and say: "I was actually led here by my shoes."

They look down at my shoes. The veiled people hiss. Do they hiss? No, impossible. Surely I'm imagining that. What kind of person hisses? The woman in red smiles. "Interesting." A light in her eyes like the girl at the door. "I'm glad there was no trouble. There's already enough trouble out there, isn't there? In the world?"

"Yes." I nod. Why am I nodding?

"Tragedy likes to leave its mark, doesn't it?" Her eyes flit up to my forehead scar. Immediately, I flush. *Accident*, Mother said whenever I asked her about it. *You fell.*

How did I fall?

You were a kid. Kids fall. End of story, okay?

She's still staring at my forehead. "Quite the mark it likes to leave." She reaches out with a hand and strokes my cheek. Shocking, her sudden touch, but I don't pull away. Maybe she's the spa manager or something. She's assessing my skin to divine the depth of my need for self-care. I close my eyes. Her touch feels strange. Soft and slightly sticky. My heart begins to beat more quickly. I feel her reach up and trace my scar. My eyes fly open. She's smiling at me, and so are the people in black. Their black veils have been pulled aside like curtains so I see their twin faces. One male, one female. Both impossibly exquisite. I remember the childhood dolls I found in the basement box. Staring at me with their glassy eyes.

"Quite the mark," the male twin agrees.

"Quite," the female twin murmurs. Their voices are low and deep and rich.

They gaze reverentially at my forehead, which feels like it's on fire now. I swallow more red stars. I should say something. *What are you staring at?* But I'm speechless before their luminous faces. Dazzled by how fucking beautiful they are. Maybe they're managers too. They seem more like owners than managers somehow with their black veils. They look, in fact, a little like the goth twins I slept with in college. Christine and Sebastian Whyte. I met them one afternoon when I was skipping my French literature class, trying to have a cigarette in the campus shade. They were smoking and reading Kafka side by side. Christine, the letters; Sebastian, *The Trial*. As I tried to spark up my lighter, they watched me with their black-lined green eyes. *Hi*, they said. *Hi*, I said. They were my first loves, my best friends. It was Christine who got me the Disney job. She worked there playing Snow White, for whom she was a dead ringer. Not because she loved it. No, she was doing it to fuck shit up, she said. Mess with the Mouse from the inside. *You're pretty*, Christine said to me, as if it were a curse. *In that Disney-does-exotic way, isn't she, Brother?* That's what she called Sebastian: *Brother*. He worked at Disney too, playing all the princes. Also supposedly to *fuck shit up*. I slept with Christine first, and then later, Sebastian, and then Christine again, but then she found she just couldn't anymore after she'd learned I'd been with Sebastian. *You're tainted now*, she told me, confronting me in the park in her Snow White costume. *You're tainted in my eyes forever.* I stood there contrite and sweating in my Jasmine costume, feeling like a whore in a cheap, spangled bra. I looked into her eyes where I was tainted. They were a green I'd never seen before and have never seen since. Sebastian's were like that too. These twins in black, they have eyes just like that.

"Fortuitous, isn't it?" they whisper to me now. "Your coming here tonight." Still staring in a way that makes me burn with shame. That makes me almost whisper, *Am I really tainted, Christine? Am I tainted forever?*

"Definitely." The woman in red smiles. "After all, self-care is really our only escape from the Abyss, is it not? I know your mother would agree."

"You really knew my mother?"

"Oh, intimately," she says. "Very intimately."

The twins smile now too. Did they know her? Can I imagine my mother having a cigarette with these doll people who so resemble my teen lovers? Clinking flutes with the woman in red?

"And you. We know so much about you, Daughter of Noelle," offers the male twin. I feel his voice in my vertebrae. He reaches out and strokes my cheek.

"So much," echoes the female twin, reaching out to stroke my other cheek. I stare at the woman in red, while these two gloved hands caress either side of my face. Cold silk against my burning skin. Inside me, a black box, locked tight, rattles.

"She told you about me?" I whisper.

They look at each other. "You could say that, couldn't you?" the female twin asks the male.

"Oh, you absolutely could." He smiles. "In a manner of speaking, yes." *What did she tell you?*

"We're very happy to have you, Daughter," the male twin says, eyes still on my forehead. Gloved hand still stroking my face.

"Très heureux," the female twin agrees, also still stroking my face. So many soft silk fingers. Must be a communal assessment of some kind. They must take assessments very seriously here. I should probably tell them I can't afford this sort of spa. Can't afford any spa ever again, thanks to Mother. But their pale eyes and silk hands on me are like a bit of a dreamy drug.

"I'm happy too," I murmur.

"And we hope you'll come back," the woman in red says. "There's someone whom we'd like you to meet."

"Who?"

"Someone important. Very important to your mother," the woman in red says. "You'd like that, wouldn't you, Daughter? In this time of grieving?"

I picture another pale stranger stroking my face with a gloved hand. "Yes," I whisper. What am I saying? "I mean no."

Their smiles fade.

"I mean, I'd love to, of course," I say. "But sadly, I have to get back."

They look like they don't understand my words.

"*Get*?"

"*Back*?"

"I actually live in Canada. Montreal. I'm really just here for the next few days. To settle her affairs. Then I fly home." *Home*. When I say it, it feels like such an empty word. What does it signify? A one-room apartment, the walls lined with bottles and jars. A narrow bed where I lie each night curled around my laptop like it's a fire, like it could actually warm me. Watching Marva's face talk to me about my own face until my eyes close. And then? A dreamless sleep until my eyes open to the sight of her white face once more. Smiling kindly. Patiently. Like she was waiting for me the whole time.

I glance down at all the beautiful people glowing redly under the chandelier. There's a man in a hat standing a little apart from the crowd. Staring up at me, it looks like. Do I know him?

"Home," the woman in red repeats, calling me back. A flash of something like anger in her face. Anger or hunger? But it quickly retreats. "Of course. Daughter has her worldly obligations." The twins drop their cool silk hands from my face. Terrible. It feels terrible.

"I really wish I could stay," I say. "This seems like such a lovely . . ." Is it a spa? Suddenly, looking into their pale eyes, I'm not so sure anymore. They smile widely.

"Well. It'll all work out, I'm sure."

"Sure it will," the twins say at the same time.

"Although you know, Daughter," the woman in red says, suddenly stepping in closer to me. Suddenly inches from my face. "*Sometimes you gotta say what the fuck. Make your move.*"

"I'm sorry?"

"*Risky Business*, isn't it?"

I flash to the shoebox full of Tom Cruise clippings. The torn movie poster. "What?" My skin grows cold under her smiling eyes.

"I must say you're looking a little pale, Daughter," she murmurs, still inches from my face.

"Am I?" I do feel very funny suddenly. Perhaps those red stars are really beginning to hit.

"In need of some rejuvenation. Perhaps a visit to the Depths is called for."

"Oh yes, you must see the Depths," the female twin says.

"The Depths?"

"I'll take you down," the male twin says.

"I'll take you down," says the female twin.

I notice the lights have dimmed. They're leading me down the stairs, each taking an arm. Such a gentle grip. I can feel their finger pads through the silk gloves, caressing my arms. "We hope you'll come back and see us, Daughter," they're whispering into my ears as we glide down the hall. Are they whispering that? The words are only a bit louder than silence. We move quickly across the hall, through the glittering crowd, like we're floating. They stay close to me, whispering to me. Causing a chill down the sides of my neck. "We really hope you will," they say.

And then? They've left me. Their lips no longer at my ear. Their scent of bergamot and rose and oud hovering faintly in the air. I'm standing in a large crowd before some ceiling-to-floor red curtains. They surround what looks like a grand circular stage in the middle of the hall. Was this here before? The curtains are lovely. Heavy, velvety. So red. What's behind them, the Depths? Must be the Depths, because all around me people murmur excitedly, like they're waiting for a show. Like I used to when I was a child watching Mother perform onstage. Little independent theaters. Experimental plays. Mother bowing before a small audience of mostly men. All of them clapping fiercely when she came out from behind the curtain, as though their hands might break. To my child's ear it sounded like a roar. It would ring in my ears hours later in my bedroom full of spiders. But I clapped too in the audience, surrounded by those violently applauding men. I clapped slowly, quietly, my little rebellion. Mother didn't see me though. She could see only the light on her own face. She could hear only the roaring approval of the dark. I watched her bow humbly as bouquet after bouquet was thrown at her feet. Beaming in the spotlight like she was a plant performing photosynthesis, all the petals of her unfurling. Now I look at the red curtains, almost waiting for Mother to emerge from behind them. I hold my breath, afraid. But when the curtains are pulled back, no Mother. Not even a stage. A vast aquarium tank, ceiling to floor like the curtains. Bell-shaped, like a downward-facing flower. The glass walls aren't smooth, they're warped and convoluted, causing distortions. A dancing golden light like sunlight through the blue-green water. The tank is filled with what looks like giant red jellyfish. They glow redly in the water, swelling and undulating as they pass the uneven magnification of the glass. Everyone around me claps and makes sounds of delight.

"Merveilleux!" I hear under someone's breath.

"Bigger than last time!"

"Too beautiful," someone whispers right beside me.

I stare at the red jellyfish, their bell-shaped heads pulsing in the bright aqua water. It looks like another time, another world, behind the glass. Mesmerizing to watch them undulate and float, trailing all those tangly tentacles. I can't seem to stop staring. Beautiful up close, I'm up close now. Somehow I've walked myself right up to the tank without realizing. I'm inches from the glass, staring deeply into the blue-green of this small sea. The light is what draws me. How it reflects me back to myself in the warped glass. And what I see there. Me as I've never seen myself before. Glowing skin. My features sharp as Mother's. I'm smiling. I don't feel like I'm smiling, but there I am, smiling in the glass. Gone are the folds around my mouth; the scar on my forehead; my misery lines; the sad, slack jaw and the puffy, dark-ringed eyes. All is sharp and taut. All sparkles. Brightly. Whitely. *Beautiful.* I look beautiful. Like a film heroine from the forties. Better than even my dream of myself. A red jellyfish swims through my reflection, but I still appear to smile as the tentacles move across my face. Wider, like it pleases me. Tears glisten behind my shining eyes.

And then I hear a gasping sound. Coming from the left and the right of me. Coming from all around. I see everyone's gathered around the tank. Everyone's gazing at themselves in the aquarium glass, transfixed. I can't see what they see. Only their gasping faces, the tears in their eyes. A woman covers her mouth and laughs into her hands. I look back at myself. She's still there, the other me. Still smiling at me with her red lips. *This could all be yours*, she seems to say. Like the twins' mouths whispering right in my ear. I could watch the play of light across her face forever. A jellyfish swims past her, through her, and then through her I see another figure. At the opposite end of the tank, on the other side of the glass. Standing there like I am. Gazing into the water. That man in the hat who was staring up at me earlier. He's got a black, pointed beard. Circular eyeglasses that make him look vaguely Victorian. He's familiar too, why?

I stare at his face through the glass. He's also looking at me, I see. A jellyfish swims between us in the blue-green water. It hovers there, blocking my view. Yet I can still see this man right through the red jellyfish. Like the creature is suddenly translucent, nearly transparent. In that instant, I see something I didn't before. Through the jellyfish, the man loses his black beard, his ostentatious mustache, his strange eyeglasses. For a flash, it's all stripped away and I know why his face is familiar. He's the man I saw at the hotel bar last night. The one who looked like old movies, with his dark suit and hat. Under the brim, his watchful eyes are locked with mine through the water. Looking deep into me. The water makes him look blurry around the edges, like he could dissolve any moment. Is he smiling at me? The jellyfish swims away. And then the man from the hotel looks the strange Victorian way he did before: His black beard comes back. His mustache. His glasses. It all looks like a disguise now. It is a disguise, I realize. "What the fuck?" I whisper.

And then he's gone.

My reflection's gone too. Just a tank full of red jellyfish and people with their faces inches from the glass, marveling at their reflections. A woman's laughing with such violent delight right beside me. She's clapping her old face with her old hands.

"Oh my," she murmurs. "Oh my, oh my, oh my."

The chime music is still playing, louder now. People are swaying with their reflections like they're slow dancing. One man's cheek is pressed against the glass, cheek to cheek with his other self. His eyes are closed so painfully, I have to look away. Suddenly, the red curtains close all around the tank. There's a collective sigh. People stumble away. I hear cries of anguish. The man beside me drops to his knees, clutching the curtains. The old woman is hugging her chest, caved into herself, like she's clutching a dagger someone stabbed into her heart.

Mother, what sort of spa is this? Did you really come here?

Get out of here, I think. *Leave, leave, leave.* But where and how? No exits that I can see. Only the grand hall that seems to extend into black. Only bodies hovering by the red curtain as if awaiting a second act. Only the spiraling staircase where the woman in red stands alone now on the landing, sipping her cold stars, watching the tumult below. Though I can't see her face, I sense she's smiling. The twins are gone from her side.

Then I see him again. Disappearing down the dark hall that gapes blackly like a maw. I follow him. Or I realize I'm following him. My shoes lead me down the hall, in spite of myself. I'm walking right behind him, my footsteps trailing his. He looks over his shoulder and, seeing me behind him, frowns. Quickens his steps. And though I'm angry about this, though I think, *Fine, fuck you*, I quicken my steps too. I reach out and grab him by his collar, surprising myself. He turns to look at me. Sort of smiling now. Like he's surprised that I grabbed him, but not entirely. Not unpleasantly. It's actually a very good disguise, I see. Much better than it seemed through the jellyfish.

"Can I help you?" he says in a low voice. Rough. Deep. Almost like it's wearing a disguise too.

"I don't know." I realize it's true. I have no idea what I want from this man. "I just . . . thought I recognized you. From last night. You were—"

He puts his finger to his lips, as if to say *shhh*. Glances both ways down the dark hall. Then he smiles. Looks at me through his spectacles, spectacles I suspect he doesn't need. Eyes a slate-gray that reminds me of river water. "Not here," he says quietly. "Not now."

"I'm sorry?"

He leans forward, puts his hands on my shoulders. As he leans in, I smell forest botanicals, something bittersweet like green tea. His skin's very smooth, what I can see that's not covered in fake facial hair. Could the green tea scent be from a hydrating essence?

"*À bientôt,* as they say," he whispers, as if people might be listening. "For now, just walk away."

"Walk away?"

"Don't follow me."

"I wasn't," I whisper back.

He lets go of me and straightens his suit jacket. Looks all around as though there are eyes in the walls. Then he smiles at me with one side of his mouth. A full mouth in that fake black beard. "Of course you weren't," he says.

He turns away and starts walking farther down the hall.

Don't follow him, I tell myself as I watch him walk away. But I'm following him again. My shoes moving more quickly as he moves more quickly. *What the fuck am I doing?* I think, my feet literally racing down the dark hall that seems to go on forever, lit now and then with a candle on a sconce. He speeds up and I speed up until we're both walking nearly side by side. He reaches out and grips my arm.

"What the fuck?" But there's still a smile in his voice. His grip is so different from the male twin's. Not silky and cool. It's warm and bold. Unmistakably of this world. "Didn't I just say *Don't follow me*?"

"I'm not," I lie. "I'm just going the same way. This is where I'm heading too."

"Is that so?"

I nod.

"And where are you heading exactly?"

"Home," I say. The word rips in my throat. Rips like a torn page. It's nothing. I know it's nothing when I say it. It's cracked mirrors. Rooms violently empty of all but her scent's ghost. A counter cluttered with bottles and jars.

He shakes his head. "Home, huh?" he says. Strangely, I hear the rip there, too. He pulls a cigarette from behind his ear. Sparks a silver lighter. In the light of the bright flame, I see three people gliding toward us in the hall. Dressed head to foot in black, veils over their faces just like the twins. They're carrying black umbrellas as though it's raining inside. *How odd*, I think. Although odd compared to what? The red jellyfish in their great tank? This house of curved glass, full of rich, beautiful eccentrics? *Who are they?* I wonder as they glide closer.

Just then he presses me against the wall and kisses me. His mouth on my mouth, lips crushing mine gently. The fake beard is surprisingly soft. I taste Altoids and cigarettes. A lip balm that gives off the faintest scent of roses. His scent, his mouth, his grip, it's all a shock to my body, which has been holding itself tight and away. Now opening, melting under this stranger's kiss. How long since I've kissed anyone? Months. The last time was a woman in a bird mask. Halloween party at Damsels. A friend of a co-worker. Lonely. We both were. Outside the shop, my back against a wall of bricks. Clear, cold night. A Montreal quarter moon like a scimitar above us. *Come home with me*, she whispered into my neck. *Home*, I repeated. But I knew I couldn't go back with her. It would have been like fucking my own loneliness. Also, it was Resurfacing Night, the night I apply my Radiance Rescue Exfoliating Dewtopia and follow it up with my NuuFace. Then, after administering various brightening, tightening, and refining serums, I slug my face with Vaseline and sleep on my back, emanating a vague scent of sulfur.

But of course I couldn't explain all this. So I just said, *I'm sorry. I have to go.*

He pulls away suddenly. The black-clad figures have floated past us down the hall. He watches them go, then looks back at me and grins. His beard is slightly askew now. In his gray eyes, I see the Saint Lawrence River rushing darkly beneath the bridges of my city.

"Home," he repeats dreamily, tracing my cheek with his incredibly soft hands. "You're going the wrong way."

When he walks away this time, I don't follow. I just stand there, panting from the kiss, watching him disappear down the dark hall.

Part II

8

Light from a bright sun. Burning my closed eyes. I open them. See myself in the ceiling mirror. I'm lying in a bed the color of blood. There's a squeaking sound somewhere. *Squeak, squeak,* what the hell is that? Where am I? I look around. Blood-colored curtains. Black vanity with a three-paneled mirror. I'm in a vast four-poster bed that sags dangerously in the middle. The red silk sheets bearing the ghost of violets and smoke, a scent of flesh and sweat. Achingly familiar. And then I remember. Mother's bedroom. Must have slept here. Must have found my way home somehow. How did I leave that house? How did I even leave that hall? Didn't it seem to be stretching infinitely into darkness? And yet I'm back here, smelling ocean and roses, the stink of the seals on the cove. Still wearing the silk silver dress, the train now covered in dirt and ripped at the hem. The red shoes are still shining on my feet. I kick them off. Who were those people last night? Those strange people (proprietors?) who claimed to know Mother. To know me, too, didn't they say so? *We hope you'll come back, Daughter.* And then the man in the fake black beard. His kiss in the dark hall. And those red jellyfish . . .

The squeaking sound feels closer, why am I hearing this sound? And then I realize it's coming from inside not outside. In the house. Oh god, Mother's ghost. Here, now, in the middle of the day? Impossible. Get yourself together. There's her red silk robe hanging on the back of the bedroom door. Get up and put it on, that's it. A little light-headed, a little shaky, that's all. That champagne, I remember. Those red bubbles I sipped and sipped. Cold, bittersweet, bright as forgetting. That's all I wanted was to forget. Squeaking getting louder.

Does a ghost squeak? Of course not, I'm being silly. Only a living intruder. They know Mother's dead and now they're breaking in. I make my way into the hall, looking for a weapon, any weapon at all. In the bathroom, a curling iron. Not much, but it's something to grip, *get a grip*. Living room just like I left it. Couch. Table. Roses floating in a bowlful of water and black, slick stones. Roses seem redder, how is that possible?

"Hey there," says a voice.

I scream.

And there he is standing by the windows. Long blond hair. Shirtless, as yesterday. More shirtless somehow. Tad, the merman handyman. Squeegee in his fist. The wet sponge dripping onto Mother's floor. Her cat, Anjelica, slithering around his golden ankles, licking the drops at his feet like a whore.

"Belle," Tad says. "Good morning. Whoa, wait." He looks at his watch. "Afternoon now." He grins. Looks down at the red robe that I'm pulling tighter around my body (does he recognize it?), the curling iron clutched in my fist. "Uh-oh," he says. "I scared you again. Did I scare you again?"

"No." The curling iron slips from my fingers, clattering at my feet. Anjelica runs away, shrieking. "I mean yes, Tad. You did scare me a little. A lot. I thought someone was breaking in."

"Oh no, I'd never break in. No, no. I have a key, see?" He points to it, one of several attached to his tool belt. I look at my mother's key just hanging there on his hook.

"I see." I try to smile. "I just didn't expect to see you again. So soon."

Tad nods. Waves a hand at the glass behind him. "Just here to do the windows."

Though I don't look directly at them, though I keep my eyes on Tad, I can see that the glass has indeed been cleaned again. So clear, it doesn't even look like glass. It looks like there's nothing at all between me and the palm tree–lined shore, the pelicans and cormorants flying through the blue sky. "Hope you don't mind," he says. "Tried to be quiet."

"Didn't you just do the windows yesterday?"

"Oh, I like to do them every day. Your mother liked it that way too."

"Why?"

"Because they get dirty, Belle. All that spray. It may look faraway, but it finds its way here, trust me." I look at Tad. His beautiful face so earnest, so shadowless. He reminds me of a golden retriever. I picture my mother patting his golden head. Tad barking happily.

"I see."

I walk over to the breakfast table by the window but I don't look out, won't look out. I sit with my back to the glass, staring down at the table. I can feel Tad staring at me, and heat floods my cheeks like I'm a child again. As a child, I'd always find men in the kitchen in the morning. Making her coffee. Breakfast in bed. *Well, hello there, kiddo*, they'd say when they saw me staring up at them from the kitchen doorway. *Mirabelle, am I right?* I remember I said nothing. Neither confirmed nor denied this. Just stood there in my dumb little night-gown patterned with pink bunnies, clutching my stuffed white rabbit by its foot.

Sometimes the men were wearing just boxers, which embarrassed me. All that visible, sculpted flesh. All that hair on their legs, sometimes chests and backs. Some of them were ugly. Little hedgehog men. Some were old and withered, reminding me of toads. Their liver-spotted skin lifting ghoulishly upward whenever they smiled. Mostly, though, they looked like men from the soap operas Grand-Maman watched in her rocking chair in the dark while eating religieuse. The men had those kinds of chiseled bones, those penetrating eyes. I would watch the soaps on Grand-Maman's beige bed, lying on my back and hanging off the bed's edge, looking at the television screen upside down, my head filling with blood. *That looks like Jake*, I might say, pointing at the screen.

Jake, c'est qui? Grand-Maman would ask. Speaking to me in French like Mother never did.

Un ami de Maman, I'd say, staring at the screen.

And Grand-Maman would snort. Wolf down another pastry. *Un ami*, she said. Shaking her head of undyed white hair. She'd disapproved of my father, too, of course. But at least my father had manners, Grand-Maman said. Even if he hadn't been a Catholic. Always so very polite, respectful. Brought her what she called *those oriental pastries* and gold trinkets whenever he visited. The pastries were far too sweet for her taste and the trinkets were tawdry, of course, but the gesture was something. Whenever Grand-Maman talked about my father, I'd have a dim flash of a tall, dark man with an afro standing in her front doorway, sweating and smiling and bowing his head. A hairy hand engulfing mine, the cave of it hot and dry. How our skins, side by side, looked like different gradients on a single scale, his fingers ringed with the same gold that encircled my wrist in a slim chain. A soft male voice speaking a broken, heavily accented French to an unsmiling woman dressed head to toe in crackling black lace. *No*, Grand-Maman always conceded, my father, god rest his soul, was nothing like Mother's gentleman friends.

Sometimes the men I met in Mother's kitchen were fully dressed in suits or polo shirts and jeans. Wearing whatever they'd worn the night before when they knocked on our front door. One morning I found one of them wearing her red silk robe as he made her espresso, the robe I'm wearing now, in fact.

My father bought her that, I screamed at him from the doorway of the kitchen. *You can't wear that.* And I burst into tears.

What's going on here? Mother said, coming into the kitchen. Clip-clopping into my nightmare like she was walking on air. Looking lazy and oblivious. So beautiful, she hurt my eyes. Everything seemed like it belonged to her. The morning light, the blue sky. *Everything okay, Sunshine? Why the long face?*

Oh, we're fine, the man said, winking at me like we were in on something together. *We were just getting acquainted, weren't we, my dear?*

And he smiled at me like he hated me. I didn't know what to do. I nodded *yes* though I hated him, whoever he was. I was rewarded with a flash of his white teeth. And Mother smiled like how lovely it had all worked itself out in her favor. *Oh good. Chin up, then, Sunshine.* Patting my cheek. *No more long face. What do we always say?* And she did an impression of me. Folded her arms tightly in front of her chest. Stuck out her lower lip in a pout. *My face will freeze that way*, I said. *That's ri-ight*, she'd sing, lighting a cigarette and winking at the man. I remember I hated her, too, in that moment. I recall the hate coursing through my little body. And then? Black after that. I've reached the edge of this memory. Can't go any further into its dark wood.

"How about some coffee?" Tad says softly now.

Though I don't nod, Tad pours some from a French press. Tears threaten to fill my eyes as I sip. At what? The kindness of Tad? The richness of the coffee? The absurdity of being a grown woman tended to by my mother's lover? Or perhaps just the remnants of the Revitalizing Eye Formula that can cause watering long after applied, and no matter how carefully applied. It happens, Marva says, even with the most sophisticated formulas. It is their nature to run.

I watch Tad pad into the kitchen and start to make what I presume is breakfast. "You really don't—"

"Happy to," Tad says. "You're exhausted, I'm sure. After a long night of packing."

I look at the opened basement box from the shop sitting in the middle of the living room, which is as far as I got yesterday before I put on those red shoes. Now Anjelica is sitting on top of the mound of dolls, yawning.

"And you've got another big day today, I'm sure. Need your protein."

I watch his back for a while, stupefied. He pulls a frying pan from the cupboard. Spatula from a drawer. Eggs, berries, and greens from the fridge. He tips the fruits and greens into Mother's Vitamix like he's done it a thousand times before. It roars to life with the push of a button.

"You really know your way around," I say to his back, over the roar.

He goes still. Then he turns and grins. "Yup," he shouts at me. Winks. I drink the coffee. It's in a bowl that says *café au lait* on it in five hundred different fonts. I remember Mother's look of hurt the last time I visited, when I refused the café au lait she'd made for me in this very bowl. *Since when did you switch to black coffee?*

Since now, I said. And she gaped at me like I'd slapped her.

I don't understand why you're freaking out, I said. *It's just coffee.* I looked at her over the untouched bowl. She'd given it a mountain of foam, shaved chocolate curls into it just like I'd loved as a teenager.

Just tell me it isn't some SKIN thing, she muttered at last, clearing the bowl away.

It's not, I lied.

Never mind, she said, holding a hand up. *What else should I expect, right?*

Now Tad sets a plate proudly before me. Two sunny-side up eggs that regard me like eyes. A vegan bacon strip for a mouth. Strawberry nose. Beside it, a smoothie so blue-green it looks radioactive.

"That's the spirulina and blueberries," Tad says. It's the exact smoothie I made for myself when I was here, the one Mother mocked and called my *skin sludge.*

"Where did you learn to make this?" I say, pointing to the smoothie.

"Oh, your mother taught me a while ago. This was her favorite."

"Her *favorite*?"

"She had it every morning when she remembered. With two scoops of this stuff too." And he holds out the blue tub of collagen powder that I left here, that she wrinkled her nose at. *You're drinking BONE gelatin now?*

"What's wrong?" Tad asks me.

"Nothing," I murmur at the eggs. He pats me on the back gently like he's my father. This shirtless man who is at least five years younger than I am. I stare at the eggy eyes, the leering bacon mouth. One of the yolks is oozing now like it's weeping.

"Tad? What would you say my mother's mental state was?"

"That's a good question," Tad says. He thinks for a while, scratches his neck. "Overall, I'd say it was . . . great."

"Great. Really?"

"Sure. I mean, she was really upbeat. Sunny-side up," he says, looking at my weeping eggs. "Always."

"Upbeat?"

"Oh yeah. She loved looking out of windows. She loved looking at flowers."

He grins and stares out of the windows. "Sometimes she'd look over there." I watch him point happily through the glass at a row of carefully clipped shrubs outside.

"And sometimes she'd look that way," he says, pointing straight ahead at a row of palm trees near the shore. "Sometimes"—he looks at me in wonderment—"a pelican would fly by. Or a dolphin would jump up from the water. Leap right out of the waves. She loved that." He smiles at me. "So much."

"Really."

"Sure." He moves in closer to me. "But do you know what I think she loved most?" I look at Tad in his cutoff jeans. He's wearing a necklace made of seashells. There's a tattoo of a grinning dolphin leaping from green waves on his upper arm. The green waves are the exact same color of the waves outside and the exact same shade as Tad's eyes.

"What?"

"That she never knew what she might see."

I catch a whiff of his sunscreen. And Mother's own perfume, could he be wearing it? Tad's eyes, Tad's cheekbones, Tad's exceedingly white teeth. Framed by his sun-bleached straggly hair. I think of Mother walking along the beach at midnight. Falling onto the rocks. For a moment, I have a dark thought. A very dark thought.

"There were just so many surprises, you know?" Tad says.

"Yeah."

"Every day. It gave her such joy."

"Joy every day. Really?"

"I mean, we all have our dark days. Very dark days, sometimes. When our demons come out to play. No one lives entirely in the light, right?"

"Right."

"But your mother . . ." He trails off, looking at the window. Then he turns to me, smiling. "So. What's your day like today, Belle?"

"My day?" I look around Mother's apartment. So pristine on the surface, but I know I'm standing on a sinking pit. *My day is fucked, Tad,* I want to say. I have to pack this place up. Hire someone with money I don't have, to fix all the broken shit. Sell it. Then get the hell out of here and go back to work. All in a few days. It's impossible. It may as well be a tower full of straw that I'm supposed to spin into gold. I may as well be waiting for a goblin to show up with his dark promise to help me. In the wall of cracked mirrors, I see that my skin is in desperate need of mushroom mist.

"This and that," I tell him, trying to smile.

"Look," Tad says. "You can't do this by yourself, Belle. This place. It's old. Run-down. Things not working like they used to, you know?"

"I know."

"So let me help you, please. I'll help you pack and fix up the place. I can even bring some buddies to help me. I want to. I'd love to." Now he grips my hands.

"But aren't you busy? Don't you have a . . . job or something?" His business card flashes in my head. The merman wielding the shears and the squeegee.

"I manage," he says. "I'm well taken care of." And just then he waves out the window. I look out and see an older woman in shorts and a visor holding a pair of gardening shears. She's in the midst of clipping her bushes. When she sees Tad, her face visibly brightens. She waves enthusiastically, then turns and looks at me darkly. She keeps her eyes on me as she clips the bushes now. A snip of the shears that I feel at my throat.

"Gloria's great," Tad says, looking at me.

"Is she?"

"You know your mother has a ton of antiques. Sometimes old stuff is worth more than you think just looking at it. Not me, I like to look closely. I see its value. Like this right here." He walks over to a chest of dark wood in the living room. He runs his hands lovingly over the wood.

"We could sell this. I know a guy downtown we could take it to. Get a good price on it, you know? Buy you some time."

"Time?"

"To fix the place up. Sell it for what it's *worth*, Belle. Do it right." He puts his hands on my shoulders. That warm, large grip. His beachy, benevolent eyes imploring me.

A knock at the door. Sylvia. Wearing dark glasses. Peering into the windows and waving at me. Tad sees her, and for the first time he frowns. His hands drop quickly from my shoulders.

"Mirabelle," Sylvia says, coming in. She takes one look at me in my red robe, at Tad in his cutoff shorts, and visibly bristles. Oh, she knows him. All too well. But she doesn't share Gloria's or Mother's enthusiasm. "I was just checking in." She tries to be sunny, pleasant, but her judgment is all over her face. *Like mother, like daughter.*

"Just packing up," I say.

"I see." She glares at Tad, who mumbles that he'll get started on the bedroom. But that isn't enough for Sylvia.

"Why don't we go outside," she entreats, "and sit in the sun?"

I'm reminded that my face is bereft of mist. Bereft too of the moisturizing cloud jelly that seals in the mist. Not to mention the Glowscreen, physical and chemical, that shields it from all. "Do you mind if we stay in here?" I say. "Not quite ready to face the world yet."

She frowns at the hall down which Tad disappeared. "Of course, dear. Only if you're absolutely sure you don't need some . . . air."

"I'm good. Coffee?"

She looks at the French press as though it were something obscene. Shakes her head of crisp little blond spikes. "Let's just sit," she whispers. She walks over to the red couch. Perches lightly on the very edge of it. Her manicured hands folded in her little lap. Thin lips pressed together in a smile. Drawn-in eyebrows furrowed. She's attempting sympathy, I think.

"Mirabelle," she says softly, staring at the bowl of roses when she speaks. "I've been giving it some thought."

"Yes?"

"Your situation. This whole terrible thing. Your mother dying the way she did. Leaving you with this mess, this debt. Everything you told me yesterday when you came into our little shop. Just devastated." Yesterday. It seems like a year ago. I picture myself on my knees in the stockroom before the old mannequins.

"I haven't been able to stop thinking about it. And I've decided I want to help you."

"You do?"

She sighs. "I think you're in a real bind here. I don't just think it, I know it. You need to go back to Montreal, don't you? And this place is really just a burden. I mean, I know you'll do what you can to get her things in order but . . ." She looks at the basement box sitting open in the middle of the floor. Anjelica the cat slinks by, batting around one of the red jars. "It's a big job. Bottom line. I think you need help." Sylvia turns to look at me meaningfully. "How about I take it off your hands?"

"Off my hands?"

"The apartment. You'd be selling it to a friend. You could come back and visit whenever you like. I'll help you pack and sort through everything this week. I could get some girls from the shop to help. Between us, we'll get it done lickety-split. And you could go home when you planned. In—what is it again? Two days?"

Did I tell her my flight plans?

"Go back to work. Go back to your *life*. Begin to put all of this . . ." She shakes her head at the roses. "*Horribleness*," she spits. And then her lip jerks to one side.

I stare at her.

"Such horribleness," she insists, tears filling her eyes. "Put it behind you."

Put it behind me. Isn't that what Mother used to always say to me about the past?

"That's very generous of you, Sylvia."

She smiles greasily through her tears. *Yes. It is.*

"Well"—she wipes her eyes—"you know your mother and I were friends, of course."

I think of visits with Mother over the last years. Always awkward whenever it was just the two of us. Always the radio way up in the car, even if it was a song she hated. Always a movie on full volume in the house. Always a restaurant where she knew a waiter and could banter with them instead of me. Usually she'd recruit Sylvia to join us for at least one lunch or early dinner. Mother would silently sip champagne from under the vast brim of a black hat that shadowed her pale face. Sylvia, hatless, melasmic, beaming with toadyism, would have a salad and sparkling water. Fill the silence with light, boring chatter. Inane comments about her book club. What she'd heard on NPR the other day that was so true. What she'd read in *O* magazine that she was internalizing—*that Oprah just gets it, doesn't she?* And this restaurant—*such a cute place.* Just look at those cocktails going by! Of course she much prefers to eat her calories, hahaha. Mother would just nod absently. As if she'd left her body just as I'd left mine. And our souls were both floating elsewhere, this silly woman's voice the only thing holding us down.

"I want to help where I can," Sylvia says softly. "I really do."

We both watch Anjelica bat at the red jar with her white fluffy paws. *Sylvia, was my mother crazy? Did she ever bring you to a spa on the other end of the cove? An opulent glass house, right on the*

*cliff's edge? Did she ever introduce you to two beautiful twins clad in
the most elegant jet? Who could be thirty, who could be teenagers?
How about to a lady in red?*

I look at Sylvia in her tan capris and Breton top—a *marinière*,
Mother would have called it. She would've approved of this outfit, I
know—*a classic*—but to my eye, Sylvia just looks like she's going sailing
on a very dull boat. Diamonds like little pinpricks of rich in either ear.

"You know," she says, "I was thinking about what you asked me the
other day. About your mother getting a little . . ."

"French?" I offer.

Sylvia nods. "Toward the end of her . . . toward the end. And there
was something else."

"What?"

"Well"—Sylvia laughs—"it's a little embarrassing. But she kept
coming into our little shop. After she sold it to me. It was like she'd forgotten she'd sold it or something. I'd catch her behind the counter or
with the customers. Being her usual self. Maybe *more* than her usual
self." She laughs again. "I'd catch her staring at herself in the mirror.
You know your mother and her mirrors. Forget about her five million
boyfriends," she says loudly, no doubt for the benefit of Tad in the bedroom. "That mirror was the affair of a lifetime." She smiles at Mother's
wall of cracked glass. "Anyway. We sorted it all out in the end."

"I don't understand. How could she forget she'd sold it to you?"

"I'm sure she didn't *actually* forget, Mirabelle. Probably just
seller's remorse. Not that she had anything to be remorseful for. Your
mother was never much of a saleswoman, as you know, and the shop
was in excellent hands. She knew that, of course. She just had to learn
to *let go.*"

She looks at me meaningfully. "So what do you say? Do we have
a . . . *deal*?" When she says this, she glances over at Mother's windows.
I keep calling them windows, but they aren't really. They're a wall. A
ceiling-to-floor wall of glass wrapping around the living room and the
dining room and the kitchen. I see a hunger in her eyes at the sight

of all that ocean, which I know she can't see from her own apartment facing the street. I hear the scraping sound of some kind of tool in the bedroom. Tad most likely. I look at the red shoes gleaming by the front door. Didn't I kick them off in the bedroom?

"I don't know, Sylvia."

"What?"

"I'll need to think about it."

"Well, forgive me for saying this, but you don't have much time, do you?"

The red shoes wink at me by the door.

"You're right," I say. "I don't."

9

Evening. I'm in the living room, staring at the red shoes by Mother's front door. Just sitting there. Shining there. Almost like I never wore them last night. Never walked along the shoreline, then along a dirt road to the house on the cliff's edge. *We hope you'll come back*, they said. A visitor would be coming, they said. Someone important. Very important to my mother. *Who?* I think of those strange jellyfish swimming in that massive tank. The woman in red waving at me from the landing of the grand stair, beneath the blazing chandelier. Shouldn't go back to that house. Was it a spa? Some cult or pyramid scheme too, probably. Rich eccentrics peddling red jars. *For the face, dear, for the face. Unlike you, I need all the help I can get.* Mother was such a sucker. Probably they were going to try and sell them to me. Mother knew some very strange people, it's true. People who wore gloves in the summer. People who owned rare exotic pets. People who always smiled at me with far too many teeth. Pointed and white and shimmering.

We know so much about you, the twins said. And that shudder I felt. Deep in the pit of me. *What do you know?*

All a scam, surely.

Sylvia's long gone. Left in a huff after I told her I'd think about her offer. From the door, I told her again. I told her *thank you*, and she waved back at me like she was batting away a fly. Tad's just left too, after a day of handymanning around the apartment. *This is so satisfying*, I heard him whisper to the walls, running his hands over them lightly.

Today, I did some things myself. Didn't I?

No. There's still just the open box sitting there in the middle of the room. Anjelica's sleeping in a sea of dolls, eyes opening and closing. All day I ignored the endless ringing of my phone. First, Chaz wondering if I'd made a decision about selling the house, if he could bring in a real estate agent later today or tomorrow? Then my boss, Persephone from Damsels, checking in. She was looking forward to seeing me for my Sunday-afternoon shift, to hearing how I was doing, too, of course. *We're all here for you,* she lied. Then the funeral director called. Mother's ashes were ready to be picked up. Whenever I was ready.

I did an extended version of my morning skin routine to make up for the fact that I had somehow, unbelievably, missed my evening routine the night before. The morning ritual is all about protection. Each morning we must arm ourselves, Marva says, against the many free radicals and pollutants that assail the air, leaving their unsightly oxidizing marks on our epidermis, that most porous of membranes between our souls and the world. After Sylvia left, I went into Mother's bathroom and triple cleansed, then doused myself with a copious amount of snail slime. I then used my NuuFace followed by my MasknGLO. Then ten skins of a green tea, algae, and rice essence for much-needed hydration and luminosity. Then an antioxidant serum specifically targeted toward my free radicals, followed by the Lumière Pigment Lightening Correxion Concentrate because *an even skin tone is next to godliness.* Then the Alchemie Liquid Lift followed by the Brightening Caviar for Radiance, followed (of course) by the Diamond-Infused Revitalizing Eye Formula. I misted diligently between skins with the rosewater and birch milk Moon Juice to create what Marva calls *a moisture mille-feuille.* I then anointed myself with the Marine Collagen Regenerating Day Soufflé using her patented seventeen-dot technique. The Day Soufflé not only brightens, firms, and plumps, but seals in the hydrating Moon Juice skins, preventing any transepidermal water loss. I patted it in with the recommended upward, counterclockwise strokes. *Like an overcoat for the skin,* Marva says of the Day Soufflé, and I have always loved this idea. And then of course the most crucial step, *an overcoat for the overcoat*: Glowscreen, physical and chemical. I applied both in Mother's unlit bathroom, staring at the dark outline of my reflection, repeating the seventeen-dot technique, which works so well for the Day Soufflé. *Why don't you turn on the fucking light at least*, Mother might have said if she'd caught me. *So you can see what you're doing to yourself?* I'd turn to find her standing there in the doorway. Morning cigarette in hand, flawless face watching me as if to say, *This is my daughter? This is mine?*

I can see fine, Mother, I'd say.

And Mother would look at the jar clutched tightly in my hand. *I'm not so sure about that*. She'd walk up to me then. Place her hands on either side of my overcoated face, drenched and sticky with skins. Her cigarette smoke coiled around both of our heads like a gray fog. *You know you don't need any of this shit. You do know that, right? I've told you*. Her voice was soft and hard at the same time, like it was gently shaking me. It made a dark shame unfurl. Anger rose like a wave. Were we not, after all, surrounded by her own sea of skin products? Her many jars and vials? Was she not the pot calling the kettle black? But I just stared past her at my own reflection. *You've told me*.

She was leaving the bathroom when I called out. *What about you, Mother?*

Me? she said, like the word was a dark joke. *I'm another story*.

Later, I'd find a jar of the Day Soufflé on her bathroom counter, of course.

By the time I finished my morning routine, it was early evening. I sat on Mother's red couch and watched Marva until my eyes watered. Her *Come to Bed with Me* series, where she sits in a silk teddy talking about skincare ingredients like lovers. I watched "Acids Part One," and then "Acids Part Two." I watched "What I'm Doing about My Hyperpigmentation," where Marva solemnly points to various "dark" spots on her forehead and cheeks that I can't see, that just look like more expanses of white cream. *Staying on top of it is key,* she says. *A multipronged approach is always best.* I watched "My Tretinoin Journey." "After One Year." "After Two Years." "After Five." I watched a hand vigorously rubbing cream into a cheek. Finger pads dotting oil over eyelids fluttery with hope. Marva sniffing rapturously from an open vial of marula oil. Then a voice was calling my name. Again and again. *Belle. Belle?*

I looked up from my screen. Tad. Standing in the darkened living room in his biker jacket. Holding a hammer in his fist like Thor. Behind him the sky was black. *Done for the day,* he said.

Great, I heard myself say. *Thank you.*

He looked down at the open box full of dolls on which the cat was sleeping. *Tomorrow I can get some more people in. Help you pack.*

I can manage, I said.

For a while he just stood there looking at the box. Then he glanced at me, café au lait bowl full of prosecco gripped tightly in my hand.

Thank you though, I said. *For the offer.*

I'll still need more time. To do the foundational stuff.

How long?

A few weeks, maybe. If not more. I'd really think about selling some of this stuff. I could take you to that antiques man downtown tomorrow. Buy you a month.

A month, I thought. I have to be back at work Sunday. Three days from now.

I'll think about it, I said.

I thought he would leave, but he just kept standing there, so I said, *What?* It was rude. I heard the rudeness and winced at how Mother would have frowned. Tad didn't notice.

I was just going to grab some dinner, he said. *Did you, uh, want to join?*

I looked at Tad's face in the dark. Sandy hair. Eyes like the Pacific on the clearest day. Looking like he belonged on the screen of Grand-Maman's old box television, her world of daytime soaps. More beautiful than any of my lovers apart from the twins. And can I tell you I saw it all? Saw it all, saw it all. The levity he would make me feel, briefly, over shared tacos at some outside hut. The beers we would sip in the palm tree–filled dark. The coolness bubbling crisply down my throat. The sense of rebellion. The brief escape from my own pain. Maybe I would cry. Actual tears, not Formula runoff. Maybe Tad would comfort me with some Zen philosophy quote. About how we are all drops in the river of time. How that river flows backward and forward. The sex we would likely have later in his apartment in Pacific Beach, on his futon. Surely he had a futon. The smell of Tad would be thick in the air, would be lovely. Beachy and young. How many times had Mother breathed it in greedily? From his neck. From his chest. The dolphin winking at her from his arm with each thrust. Hands gripping her white waist, her red hair. Hands that stroked her perfect face with such wonder at its—

No, I said. *Not hungry. Thanks.*

And Tad half smiled.

He left, closing the door so quietly it felt like a stroke of my hair.

And now here I am. Alone. Sitting in the dark, hands clutching Mother's bowl. Staring at the red shoes glowing by the door. Which I won't put on. Of course not.

One foot then the other on the dark path along the shore. First the path by the water, then the dirt path along the cliff's edge. Tonight, it feels like the path I've walked all my life. The blackness is like an old friend. Lovely to hear the ocean roar, the grass hum and twitch. I'm whistling to myself as I click along. I'm at the spiked gates before I know it. They open for me again like they knew I was coming.

As I walk up the path to the house, the roses sway gently in the black breeze, seeming to nod their red heads in welcome. I feel such welcome. It's good I came, I think. They were expecting me. Then I see the front doors are closed. No woman in a silver dress with eyes of smoke waiting there. Smiling at me and my red shoes.

I stare at the closed doors and my heart suddenly sinks. Someone important to Mother. Even if it is just a scheme, I need to meet
this person. I knock. Nothing. Knock again. Nothing. I notice there's a
peephole in one of the doors. I try to look through. Black. But I feel an
eye looking right back at me. An eye I don't see so much as sense. And
then the door opens.

Tonight, the hall is shimmering grandly. Empty. No radiant rich people
in red, silver, or black. No one there behind the door. Just the sound
of my own footsteps clicking along the marble floor. Just that chime-y
music, that airy spa drone. The boutique in the corner is dark, all the
glass cabinets unlit. I look at the great coiling staircase where the
woman in red stood on the landing, waving. No one on the landing tonight, though on the wall, a screen still plays the video of that blissed-
out white woman with the black discs on her temples, ocean waves
lapping endlessly over her face. Tonight her eyes are open. Smiling at
me, it seems.

Above my head, the red chandelier blazes brilliantly. Though I
crane my neck, there's still no sign of a ceiling. In my mind's eye, I see
myself as a child, Mother reading me a story in the dark. About a beautiful maiden. A castle by the sea. *This castle by the sea*, I asked Mother.
What did it look like inside?

Oh, you wouldn't believe this place, Mother said. *Great halls like
labyrinths. A ceiling so high, you could look up, up, up and never find
it. Only the chandelier blazing down. The grandest chandelier you
ever saw. Dripping with honest-to-god crystals.*

"Hello?" I call now. Nothing, no one emerges. I walk a little farther
down the hall, toward the Depths. Tonight, the red curtains are drawn
around the tank. Behind them, I feel the jellyfish float. I notice there's
a single champagne flute on a small silver tray on a lacquered black
table. Filled to the brim with that red champagne. It's bubbling in a
way I've never seen before. Like it's excited. There's a little black card

beside the flute that reads *Santé*, in elegant red scroll. I lift the glass to my lips. Cold bubbles course down my throat, sweet and sharp. In my head, I can almost hear the house applauding me. So many silk hands clapping. I look up at the video of the woman with the black discs, still smiling at me through the waves. Why do I feel as though I'm being watched tonight? As though the house is watching? Not just watching, but holding its breath. A particular person is holding their breath.

I take another sip and sigh. The whole hall seems to sigh with me. It's strange but pleasant. The red curtains are drawn suddenly, quickly, in one velvety swish. And there are the red jellyfish in the great glass tank. Pulsing in the blue-green water. I'm surprised that I'm delighted at the sight of them. Delighted or horrified? I drink more of the excited champagne. Walk up to the tank, though I don't want to come any closer to those creatures, beautiful as they are. So red. Bigger than they were last night. Do jellyfish grow that quickly? My face is right up against the glass now. The water's cloudy tonight. A little darker, though still blue-green. I'm noticing one jellyfish in particular. Floating away from the cluster of floating spheres. Drifting toward me, close to the glass now. Like it can see me.

"Hi," I say to the big jellyfish. And feel stupid. I even blush.

But it moves in closer still. It has some sort of pattern on its body, can't quite make it out. And eyes. Do jellyfish have eyes? These ones do. Red and jellylike just like their bodies. Ghostly so it almost looks like a trick of the light. As I'm looking into its eyes, I smile. The eyes are looking back at me. Tense. Could the eyes of a jellyfish be tense? My heart begins to beat very strangely. I feel it fluttering in my chest like a panicked bird. Someone's here. Watching me from one of the black mouths of the corridors. I hear a clicking sound. A breath drawn in. In the corner of my eye, a figure appears. The woman in red? No. A stranger clad in black silk. Clearing her throat. About to call to me in greeting.

But instead of walking toward her, my shoes walk me away, around the tank. *Away? Why away?* I think.

We're circling each other now. She's walking toward me and I'm walking away. We go around and around the tank slowly. Every time she takes a step forward, *click, click* go my shoes around the tank. *Stop*, I tell my shoes. *Please.*

And then they do. I turn around and look at the young woman standing a few feet away. She's looking right at me as if she was waiting patiently for me to turn toward her all this time.

"Daughter of Noelle," she says.

For a moment, my breath catches. I'm struck. A beautiful young girl. Maybe thirteen or fourteen. Translucent skin. Pale glowing eyes. A fountain of golden curls like a living doll. Long black dress, a grown person's dress, on her child's body. And yet there's something about the way she's looking at me. Cold, knowing. She doesn't seem at all like a child. Familiar-looking, too. I've seen her heart-shaped face before. Felt those eyes on me. Was she Mother's friend?

"I'm Mother's friend," she says. "Exactly. And Daughter of Noelle's friend too, I hope."

She smiles at me with her red bow of a mouth. The childhood memory comes flashing back again: me sitting on a princess bed clutching a doll I hated, watching Mother brush her red hair in my three-sided mirror. She's telling me that fairy tale about the beautiful maiden. *So beautiful*, Mother said, *that all admired her from near and far*. I remember I thought *ridiculous*, even as I ached to be so beautiful. I thought *what a lie*, even as a picture began to form in my mind of a young girl. This young girl, in fact. Standing before me now. Same golden hair, same face of glass, same cold eyes. Same dress falling from her lithe white body like liquid jet. On her shoulder, a pinned red rose.

"You," I whisper.

She smiles like she knows my child's dream, though how could she possibly know it? Just a dream.

"No dream is ever just a dream," she says.

My skin begins to crawl a little. When she smiles, I'm devastated by the awful symmetry of her face. "Excuse me?"

"*Eyes Wide Shut*. One of my favorites. So mysterious and full of fucking. Lots of skin. Have you seen it?"

I look at her heart-shaped face that is a child's and not a child's. The word *fucking* so comfortable in her little mouth. "No," I lie.

"You like skin, don't you, Daughter of Noelle? Like your mother."

"You really knew my mother?" *Why would this child know my mother?*

She looks up at my forehead scar. But unlike the woman in red, she keeps looking at it. Smiling at it, like it's telling her a joke.

"Oh yes," she says. "And I know you, too, Daughter of Noelle."

"Through my mother?"

"Perfect," she says. "Yes, exactly. Through your mother."

"You were important to her." I say it like a question. Desperate to know all the things I don't. To be out of the dark.

She stares at me, looking sadly amused. "Yes. And she was dear to me, too. To all of us here." She smiles dreamily. "At Rouge."

"Rouge?"

She holds up her excited red drink in a toast.

"A way of being. A way of becoming one's Most Magnificent Self. Your mother was among our most prized members."

She moves toward me. But as she does so, my shoes walk me backward, away from her. I can't believe I'm doing this. Surely she'll be disgusted at this rudeness. But she just smiles and catches up to me easily. Cups my cheek with her gloved hand. She's tall for such a young girl. Tall as I am.

Now I'm walking backward and she's walking forward at the same pace. We're moving like this around the tank, with her hands on my cheeks like we're a couple in the strangest slow dance.

"Dear Daughter of Noelle," she sighs into my face. And her breath is cool and crisp as smoke. "This has been a very trying time for you. I imagine it must be."

I look into her eyes, bright like stars. I first saw them with my child's mind. They dazzled me then, and they dazzle me still. I nod. A tear falls from my eye. The first I've truly shed since I learned about Mother. Not the Formula this time. She looks pleased that she has this effect on me.

"Death," she says, "is just another door, Daughter, we must remember. Your mother," she sighs, "was making such progress. A shame to lose her. But she did go the way of roses." She smiles sadly. "Surely that's a consolation."

"I don't understand," I say, as the two of us sway slowly around the tank, her hands on my face, my hands on her silk shoulders. Soft music plays from somewhere, a kind of waltz. "My mother fell off a cliff. What does that have to do with roses?"

She just keeps smiling at me. So sadly.

"Was Mother okay?" I ask. "Was she losing her mind? My last conversations with her were . . ."

"What?" For a moment, she looks at me curiously.

I'm wearing a dread of liquid gold that burns like the sun.

"Strange," I whisper. "I felt like something was happening to her."

"What was happening to her was that she was becoming her Most Magnificent Self." She sighs like *isn't that the loveliest thing?*

"Her Most Magnificent Self," I repeat.

"Definitely. Perhaps you saw."

A flash of the last time I saw Mother. A FaceTime call about a month ago. *Hey there, stranger*, she said slowly, her voice terribly dreamy and serene. *So nice to see your face.* But I could tell by her eyes that she was staring at her own face. Lost in the dream of it. I was too. She looked shockingly pale. So smooth and flawless, she took my breath away. And empty. *Empty* was the other word her face was.

What's your secret these days, Mother? I asked her, though I told myself I didn't want to know, didn't want to go down this road, whatever it was.

If I told you, it wouldn't be secret, now, would it?

A feeling crept into me then. Dark and sharp. Bitter as poison. Terribly familiar. I hadn't felt it in a long time. Mother saw it in my eyes and smiled a little.

You don't need my secrets, Sunshine. You never did.

Now I nod, and the impossible girl-woman meets my eye and nods too.

"She'd peeled away all the regrets, all the mind shadows from the past. Such persistent wounds, don't you agree?"

"Yes." We're still gliding around the tank in this strange dance, me moving backward, her moving forward.

"To become one's Most Magnificent Self. To strip away the dark cobwebs in the mind. Basement boxes full of moldy memories. Chests under lock and key." She stares at me. "Get rid of all that, right?" Her hands are still on my face, grazing my forehead scar now. I feel a shiver in the pit of me. Something opening in spite of myself.

"You'd like that, wouldn't you, Daughter of Noelle?" she whispers. Coming close.

"Yes." Even as a voice says, *No. You wouldn't. You shouldn't.*

She looks deep into my eyes and smiles. And inside, I feel myself opening, opening. An electricity singing along my skin. The scar on my forehead tingling beneath her fingertips.

"I fly back home in a couple of days," I say.

"Do you? What a shame." She looks amused. Amused by my feet still walking myself backward, even as I'm so transfixed by her touch, her face. I can't stop staring at her eyes, her cheeks, her forehead, her lips, the fucking glow of her. Glowing just like Mother did. Tears, real tears, gather behind my eyes. She looks tenderly at me.

"I want to show you something."

She leads me away from the tank, and I follow her. I can follow her now. We walk hand in hand toward a small black pool in the corner of the room. She takes a seat on the pool's black marble edge, patting the space next to her. When I sit, she reaches out for my hand. I give it to her and she smiles. That awful symmetry again. She turns my hand, palm up, then lowers it into the black water. All the while looking at me with her cold, knowing eyes. The water is cool, opaque, velvety against my hand.

"What is this?" I ask, my hand in the water. "What are we doing?"

She puts a finger to her lips. *Shhh*. Her eyes are on my face.

And then I feel something in my palm. Light and slippery as a wish. Almost weightless.

She raises my arm from the pool. And there it is. Beating like a heart in my hand. A small white jellyfish. Translucent as a ghost. A whisper of a creature.

"Look at that," she says. She's smiling widely now. "It found you."

"It found me."

"It loves you."

"It loves me?"

"Can't you tell?"

I look at the creature undulating softly in my palm.

"You're going to go on quite a journey together," she says.

"We are?"

"Oh yes. A marvelous journey. *Un voyage merveilleux*. I can feel it."

Whenever I hear the word *journey*, I think of Marva. Her many skin journeys that I follow on her vlogs, step-by-step. Her brightening journey. Her retinoid journey. Her post-inflammatory hyperpigmentation journey. Her skin barrier recovery journey. So many journeys I've been on with her in my bedroom dark. I stare at the tiny white creature in my hand. "What sort of journey?" I ask.

She looks at me like *what a question*. "The only journey that matters in the end, Daughter of Noelle."

"Retinol?" I whisper.

"The soul. A journey of the soul, of course."

And the white jellyfish in my palm quivers.

10

Afternoon the next day. I'm in Mother's car with Tad driving to the antiques dealer downtown. Tad's driving because I seem . . . a little out of it, he says, looking concerned. Well, it's understandable. Grief is a journey, isn't it? Winding, unexpected dips and turns and circles. He keeps the Beach Boys at a respectful volume. "God Only Knows" filling the dark jaguar with so much splotchy sunshine.

"Shouldn't take long. You'll like this guy. Buddy of mine. He'll give you a great deal."

That's right. This is what this is all about. Selling Mother's things. Mother's antique chest, now in the back seat. Her lamp shaped like a lady in a red dress. Her statue of a British butler holding out a tray. *Le petit homme*, she used to call him. A painting I always loved that is just a dirt road to a dark house in the woods. All about to be sold by Tad. Handsome young Tad, who has no idea of death or loss.

I stare out the windshield. How did it become afternoon? Did I do my morning ritual? I touch my face. I did not. Pretty sure I didn't do my night ritual, either. Marva says if you must skip the morning, so be it, but the night ritual is crucial for barrier repair. How could I fail to restore and replenish? Am I sitting here now, without my overcoat for the face, my skin dirty and exposed and unprotected from the light of day? The last thing I remember is sitting across from the girl-woman in black, the small white jellyfish pulsing in my palm. She took it from me, tipped it into a tiny glass box of water. And then her hands were on my forehead. I was shivering at her cool, soft touch, a tear dripping down my cheek inexplicably. She watched it like it was miraculous. *Would Daughter of Noelle like to go on a journey?*

And what did I say again? What words did I splutter nervously into her beautiful, waiting face? *I'll think about it*, I said. I feared she might be angry. She wasn't at all. She was still smiling. Maybe just a slight crack in that. A hair of a hair of a hair.

And then she walked away from me, around the aquarium tank. It felt terrible, her walking away from me, my face suddenly untouched. I wanted to follow but I couldn't because my shoes kept me nailed in place. Instead I looked at her through the tank, standing on the opposite side. She was looking at me, too, right through the blue-green water. Still smiling like all was well, like my thinking about it was fine. Then a red jellyfish darted between the two of us and hovered there. I could still see the girl-woman through its translucent, pulsating head. What I saw made me gasp. Suddenly she looked very old. Much older than Mother. Maybe Grand-Maman's age before she died. Maybe even older. *Gnarled* was the word that came blazing into my mind. My nightmare of age and death in one face. I couldn't stop staring at her thin mouth, her eyes like black pits, the sunken, shriveled cheeks etched with so many folds and lines, like she was melting right before my eyes. I could see the skull behind her sagging flesh, beaming at me. Then the jellyfish drifted away and she was herself again. The beautiful maiden once more from my child's dream. Smiling just like she was before. Maybe more widely now. All those white teeth.

Think about it, she said through the tank, repeating my words. *You do that.*

"Well, here we are," Tad says.

I see we're parked on a street in front of a crooked-looking house. A weathered sign out front reads ANTIQUES in an antique-y font.

"It looks closed," I say. It really does. All the windows are dark.

"Oh, it's open," Tad says, grinning. He already looks like he's having a ball. An old man's face appears in the shopwindow above the sign. Tad waves, and the man frowns and disappears. "That's Al," Tad says. "Good guy. Super knowledgeable." Such magic in the world of Tad. Such faith. His eyes are literally shining with it. I wonder if this is how I look when I watch Marva. A flush creeps into my neck, my cheeks.

"Tad, did my mother ever talk to you about Rouge?"

He looks at me. Just for a second something flashes darkly in his eyes. Like a cloud passing quickly over the sun. It's there and then it's gone. And then: "Rouge," he repeats like a question. Too much of a question. He squinches up his face like he's confused. "No? Never heard of that. Rouge, huh? Is that French or something?"

"It's French for 'red.'" I look carefully at Tad.

He's turned away from me now, staring at the windshield strangely. Like he sees something there. Something terrible or lovely, I can't tell. But then he just smiles and turns to me again. "Well, how about that? You learn something new every day, don't you?"

The shop is a labyrinth of old things collecting dust. Aisles of glass animals in mid-roar. Dreary paintings of dreary landscapes in heavy gilt frames. End tables. So many little end tables fit for only one vase. And the vases themselves, of course. Urns patterned with carnivorous-looking flowers and white-eyed maidens in diaphanous gowns. The air in here is full of death. Everything still and sad. A decadent scent rises up from the furniture that reminds me of Grand-Maman's place. Her dark, creaking rooms full of crap. The way she glided through them in one of her long nightgowns of cheap, Easter egg–colored lace. Carrying a small gold-rimmed plate full of pastries she would eat in the dark. The way she'd sit on her rose-gold chaise and watch soap operas or else read Nostradamus and talk to me about the end of the world. The Four Horsemen on their black horses. Did I know they were coming soon? I shook my head. Their eyes were black as pits, Grand-Maman said, and she looked at me with her own eyes black as pits. She was very excited about the horsemen. And the black horses with their foaming mouths galloping through a world full of fire. She'd smile and lean back in her chaise as though she were picturing it all burning in her mind. Her white arms, hairless like Mother's, covered in gold bangles my father had brought back from Egypt. Then she'd turn on the television, a giant black box. I watched her soul close its eyes inside her body as she stared at the screen.

At last, Mother would appear in the doorway to pick me up. *Belle, are you all right? Why do you look so pale?*

Mother, are the Four Horsemen really coming?

And Mother would frown. Whisper something to her mother in rapid French, something I wouldn't quite catch. About filling my head. About religion. And Grand-Maman would hiss back. *My granddaughter. The truth. Deserves. What did I say?*

"Belle," Tad says. And then I'm back in the shop, standing still in the aisle full of glass animals and urns and end tables. Tad's looking at me worriedly. "You coming? It's just back here."

At the very back of the shop stands Al, behind a tiny antique register. He's wearing a sailor's cap and a sky-blue Hawaiian shirt patterned with obscenely red flowers that look like vulvas. He does not look up at me and Tad. Instead, he eyes the items that Tad has just set on the floor. He picks up the lady lamp. Lifts the hem of her dress in a bored way, exposing her coils and wires.

Don't fucking touch her, I want to scream. But I just stand there letting him fondle Mother. Mother's lamp, I mean. His fat fingers. Assessing eyes. He picks up the butler statue and puts him back down. Strokes the gilt frame of the painting. *Hundred already like it in the shop*, says his face. Then he turns to the black antique chest. My heart starts to pound as he grips the lid. But it won't open. Al looks at Tad, raises an eyebrow.

"Belle," Tad whispers. "Do you have a key?"

I look at the chest, Al's hands on the lid. I shake my head. "No key."

"Well maybe a screwdriver could—"

"No screwdriver!" I shout. They both look at me. "It could damage the wood," I add quietly. "Or the lock. Best to leave it locked."

Al and Tad exchange another look. "Well, maybe we could—"

"Look, I'm very sorry, but if it's locked, it's locked, okay?" I bend down, tugging on the lid. And it comes right open.

I can feel Al looking at me with new interest. Tad beaming like he knew this would happen. "Magic touch."

I look in the chest. Empty, of course. Just a blackness. What was I expecting to find?

"Oh hey," Tad says, reaching down into the chest. He holds up a key. Tiny and golden. The size of a penny. "The key was inside the chest all along. How about that?"

"That's not the key to the chest," Al says.

"Sure it is."

"Too small," Al says, his hand still under the lamp lady's skirt. "Looks more like the key to a cheap jewelry box. Or a diary."

The red diary I found in the basement box flashes in my head. "I'll take that," I say, snatching the key from Tad.

Behind us, the shop bell rings.

"Cool," Tad says, clapping his hands. "Well, the chest's open, anyway. Now we're in business, aren't we, Al?" He's looking at Al like he's an oracle. "Al?"

But Al's looking at the shop door, suddenly pale. "Fuck," he whispers.

"What is it?" Tad says, turning toward the door.

"Her," he says.

I turn to look. But even before I turn, I know whom I will see. Maybe it's the way he said *her* with such contempt and fascination and fear. The woman in red. Dressed in drapey velvet like she belongs to another century, another world. Red parasol crooked in her wrist. Clutching a pair of—is it opera glasses? Yes, actual opera glasses, the long golden handle in her red-gloved fist. "Freak show," Al whispers.

We watch her wandering the aisles like a bride. Touching each item she passes. Stroking it, really. Right beneath the signs that say DO NOT TOUCH! But Al's not clearing his throat. Not reminding her about the signs. He's just staring at her.

"She comes in here all the time," he murmurs, his hand still under the lamp lady's skirt, gripping now.

"Huh," Tad says. "What's with the glasses?"

"I don't ask," Al says.

"She must love antiques."

Al shakes his head. "She loves something."

I watch her zigzag more quickly through the aisles now, as if she's hunting. Stroking a gilt frame here, then a glass animal there. Picking up a pewter goblet and clutching it to her chest, then putting it back hastily. Bringing a glass figurine up to her face and . . . sniffing? No, she couldn't possibly be sniffing. I blink and she's moved to the next aisle, holding up an urn now, a giant one patterned with vines. She's turning it in her gloved hands as though marveling at its design. Holding it up to the light. Bringing it terribly close to her face and . . . yes, sniffing. Her nose is twitching now like a dog's. I watch her take what looks like a hit from the urn. She shudders with ecstasy. Gasps a little. Now she's bringing it to her lips, her long tongue protruding.

Al clears his throat loudly. She whips her head toward him, urn still in hand. Icy stare. Looks through her glasses, then lowers them slowly. She's seen me. Just like that, a light goes on behind her eyes. She's all teeth now. White and shining.

She puts the urn down and glides toward me. Throws her arms wide. Suddenly I'm crushed in her velvet embrace. I smell oceans and roses, and beneath those scents, something else . . . sulfury and mammalian that recalls my placenta serums. But fresher, riper. I'm aware of Tad and Al watching us, exchanging looks.

"Daughter of Noelle," she whispers into my ear. "What a delightful surprise." She looks over at Tad and Al. Is that a growl I hear from her lips? Impossible. She's smiling.

"Tell me, tell me," she says, taking my hands and drawing me away from them, leading me deep into an aisle full of glass animals. "What is Daughter doing here?"

"Taking care of some . . . business."

"Ah," she says, looking over my shoulder at Mother's things by the cash register. "I see." Lowered voice. Sympathy in her eyes now, suddenly glistening like she could weep for me. "Poor, dear Daughter. She is desperate, isn't she? *Désespérée*. Mother left her in some . . . straits."

"What are you doing here?" I ask.

"Oh, I love coming here. *J'adore*. Especially being around . . . *old* . . . things." She seemed to choke briefly on the word *old*. "Don't you?"

She strokes the head of a dusty glass jaguar. "They have so very much to teach us." She crouches down beside the jaguar so they're cheek to cheek. Closes her eyes. A strange, unholy bliss passes over her face.

"Well, I didn't mean to disturb your . . . shopping," I say.

Her eyes fly open. "Nonsense. Daughter of Noelle is so much better than any stupid bit of glass." Suddenly she's very close to me again. I blink and she's standing inches from my face. Looking deeply into my eyes as I'm looking into her eyes. Blue as the outside sky. Red eye shadow around each of them like the strangest, fiery clouds. I'm held by her gaze like a moth to the light.

"A little bird told me you came by La Maison last night," she says.

I picture the little bird. Blond corkscrew curls that made her look like a doll someone forgot to put away. Looking at me with her sapphire eyes full of amused judgment. Her heart-shaped face so like the face I'd conjured long ago in my child's mind.

"A little bird," I repeat, staring into her eyes. "Yes."

"She said you were perfect."

"She did?"

"Oh yes, the Perfect Candidate."

The word *perfect* from that perfect mouth. About me. I smile in spite of myself. And then I think, *Candidate? For what?* I glimpse Tad and Al watching by the register. They suddenly seem miles away.

"Many congratulations, Daughter. You must be terribly excited."

"Yes." *For what, for what?*

"Though she also said you were leaving us? Flying back to the Dark North? Is it true? *C'est vrai?*"

I lower my eyes to the dusty black-and-white floor. I feel her sigh heavily. A cold breeze on my face.

"How that grieves us. When we were just getting to know one another. But of course, we are aware of the dire situation in which Daughter of Noelle finds herself." She looks back at Mother's items strewn by the cash register. Tad and Al watching us, whispering. "She is quite *désespérée*, isn't she?" she says into my ear, her lips grazing.

"Yes."

"It is no wonder Daughter's face is in such a . . . predicament." She looks up at my scar, which tingles hotly under her gaze. "We empathize. Deeply. Which is why we'd love to offer you a free treatment before you fly away from us."

Something in me lifts then. A darkness brightens. *Free treatment?*

She hands me a small red card from inside her red glove. *VOUCHER*, it says in a golden font like runes. "A transformative experience. Highly prized. Of course, *one* treatment—*un seul*—is never enough to achieve the desired results, *tu comprends*. But it's a crucial first step on your Journey. One might even say *the key*." She looks down at my fist like she knows there's a little gold key in there.

"The key?"

"To Rouge, of course." And her face when she says this fills with an impossible warmth like light. The hairy wings of my soul beat excitedly. How the light she emits warms me. I could sleep by it like a fire.

"You would do that?"

"In honor of your dear mother. Whom we so loved like a daughter. So that now we love Daughter, too."

"Belle?" Tad calls from the cash register. "You okay?"

The woman in red glares at Tad. Again, I hear something like a growl from her mouth. Surely not a growl. Surely just clearing her throat. She grips my shoulders, drawing me close. Once more her lips are at my ear. "Tonight at Vespers," she says. And her cold breath makes the skin along the side of my neck sing.

"Vespers?"

"You'll come by the house."

"I'll come by the house."

"And all will be taken care of. Clear your head. When one is offered the key to Rouge, dear Daughter of Noelle, one doesn't say no. One says yes a thousand times." She smiles. "I think you'll find the results quite breathtaking. In fact," she whispers, "I think you'll find they *take your breath away*." She looks at me meaningfully. "Like that old song. *Te souviens-tu?*"

"What do you mean you've *changed* your mind?" Tad calls after me. I'm back outside now in the San Diego sunshine, out of Al's wretched shop. The lady lamp's tucked under my arm. I'm gripping the butler statue by his waist. I don't stop walking until I've reached Mother's car. Tad's behind me, carrying the chest, the painting.

"I'm sorry," I say. "I just can't, okay? I'm not ready to sell her things. Not to that awful fucking lech. Not to anyone." I shake my head. I think I'm going to cry, but I don't. I remember those two tears I shed before the girl-woman in black. One and then the other. How she watched each one drip down my cheek like it was so delicious.

Tad stares at me curiously. Leaning against the Jaguar, gripping the lady lamp to my chest. What does he know about me and Mother? What did she whisper to him after sex, in the dark? Awful truths about me, my childhood, that I can't remember? Though they're still there inside me, aren't they? Rising up in memory fragments. I can feel them folded up in my heart, in my brain, like a dark weight. A black box with many gleaming locks. It only seems heavier as I grow older, weighed down with more and more locks. Mother never spoke to me of the past. But did she speak to him? I picture Mother and Tad in bed in the dark. Neither of them sweaty after fucking. Neither of them sweats, they glisten probably. Tad would be staring adoringly at Mother's profile. Mother loved her profile. She'd turn away in conversation, and I knew she was just offering it up to people like a gift.

My daughter, she might say to the ceiling. Shake her lovely head. Light a cigarette. *Let me tell you.*

Tell me, Tad would whisper, entranced.

I imagine the words that might emerge from Mother's traitorous throat. *Hateful. Jealous. Estranged. What a weird child she was.*

Or maybe she told him nothing at all.

But if she told him nothing on those nights, then why is he looking at me like that? Unsure. Maybe even suspicious. *Of what? Of what?*

"Look," Tad says, "I'm just trying to help you find a solution, Belle. I thought you needed money. My fee is whatever, I can wait for it. But I can't repair the entire apartment myself. There's just too much to do. And some things are far beyond my meager expertise."

He smiles sadly, so handsome, so capable, so clearly Mother's man. The sun beats down on us, making him look divine, making me squint and melt in my black dress, like a witch. I remember I'm not wearing Glowscreen. No moisturizing overcoat to prevent the transepidermal water loss. The loss is likely happening as we speak, to say nothing of the oxidizing damage from unprotected exposure. Marva would be horrified. *Prevention, my darlings, is our mightiest weapon against the onslaught of the elements. Our armor must be thick, thick. The only time you can afford to go without is if you happen to find yourself in a black hole. And we'll all find ourselves in a black hole soon enough, won't we?*

"Belle?" Tad says.

In the distance I see the woman in red walking away hurriedly under her red umbrella. A red umbrella on a sunny day. I don't think it's strange. What I think is: *What a brilliant way to keep out the sun.* I feel the red card in my breast pocket. Right over my heart. It seems to pulsate like it has a heart of its own.

"Just give me a day or two, okay?" I tell Tad.

"But you're leaving tomorrow, aren't you?"

"A day, then."

"Who was that woman in the shop? She seemed to know you."

"A friend," I lie. "A friend of my mother's. I'm surprised you didn't recognize her." I'm turning it on him. I look at Tad's face closely now.

"Well, your mother was popular," he says slowly. "She had a lot of friends, didn't she?"

11

I had to google what time Vespers was. Sunset. The sky is a pink blaze. The dark palm trees swaying, just like they always did in Mother's voice, so lazy and happy with beauty. I'm walking along the cliff by the water's edge in the red shoes. The dirt trail I've walked twice now in the dark. Third time's a charm, isn't it? In the light of day, it's a different beast. Just a winding path through shrubs and low-growing trees, on a downward slope of tall grass and wildflowers. I hear the water to my left, crashing serenely against the rocks, against the cliff walls. Bunnies hop along the path. Lizards dart into the bush as I pass. My phone keeps buzzing but I ignore it. Chaz again. Wanting to know am I selling the place or not, what have I decided? Funeral director reminding me to pick up those ashes, please. Persephone wanting to make sure I'll be back on the shop floor this Sunday. The house should be around this corner somewhere, shouldn't it? Yes, any minute now, I'll see it. Nervous. Nervous but excited, too.

After he drove us home, I told Tad to take the rest of the day off. *But there's so much to do*, he insisted. *It can wait until tomorrow*, I told him. At home, I fished the red diary out of the basement box. Anjelica was sleeping on it, but I lured her away with food. I put the little gold key in the little gold lock and it came right open. I held my breath, just like I'd held my breath when I'd first opened the box itself. And it was funny. When I opened the book, I knew exactly what it would say on the first page, beneath *This Diary Belongs To*. I knew before I saw the words *Belle, Age 10*, in my child's hand. My very careful print. Red and tight and tilting. *1988*, I'd written beneath my name. The year I don't remember. The year that's in a box. Cold rushed through me. In my head, I saw a 45 of "Walk Like an Egyptian" turning slowly on a Fisher-Price record player. A pink room full of spiders, dusk outside the frilly curtained window, a screen full of holes. A princess bed cluttered with staring dolls.

I looked down at the diary. Hesitantly, I turned the page, my whole body suddenly thrumming with the beat of my heart. Blank. I turned the next page. Blank too. I turned the next and the next and the next, more quickly now. Blank and blank and blank—*what the fuck?* I flipped through the whole book. All fucking blank. All but one page, one sentence. Right in the middle of the book, in the middle of the page. Six words on a single line written in that same red ink in which I'd written my name and age.

He came to see me again.

How funny I felt, reading that. *Who?* I whispered. *Who came to see you?*

But the next page had been torn out. Someone had ripped it out hastily. In my mind, I saw a flash of a hand ripping. The pink room in my mind went black then. As I flipped through the book to see if I'd written anything more (there was nothing), a picture fell out. Floated down to my feet like a fallen leaf. I picked it up. Just another clipping. Tom Cruise again. Cut out from a magazine like the other shoebox clippings. It looked like it was from one of those teen magazines. Their ridiculous names came back to me. *Tiger Beat. Big Bopper.* Thin, bright pages full of cheap pinup posters of Johnny Depp and Leonardo DiCaprio. Factoids about them in little heart-shaped sidebars. Tom was wearing a black suit and a red bow tie. His eyes were serious like this was a serious moment. His sober expression was undermined by the hot pink hearts around his face. Strange, the feeling I had looking at it. Light and heavy at the same time. I stared at Tom's eyes, and the room seemed to swim then. The ocean roared outside the windows like a veritable animal. I thought of the glass jaguar in the antique shop. I thought of the woman in red's face pressed against it. Contorted in that strange, hungry bliss. *Clear your head*, she'd said. And then I remembered the red shoes were right there by the door. Shining as if with new purpose. Free treatment, why not? Clear my head, yes. That's what's necessary. *I think you'll find the results take your breath away*, she'd said, her lips hovering by my ear. *Take it*, I nearly told her. *Please.*

As I turn the corner along the cliff, mansions appear like mirages in the jungly green. Old Hollywood monstrosities. Ultramodern temples of concrete and glass. No sign of La Maison de Méduse yet. Huh. On the path, a deep ravine ahead. To cross it, there's a rickety white bridge. Did I cross this bridge last night? I walk right to the shaking middle, look around. The house is still nowhere in sight. Just the mossy green walls of the ravine. Maybe I've gone too far? Below, white waves crash and hiss against sharp rock. In my mind, I see Mother. Standing on a bridge of black iron over a dark, rushing river. The Saint Lawrence in Montreal. She's leaning far over the rail, closing her eyes tight. Younger than I am now. Wearing a white-and-black Yves Saint Laurent coat she bought on credit from the Hudson's Bay Company. Snow falling all around us both like quick, bright fish. Falling onto her red hair and my coarse black hair where I know it doesn't look nearly as pretty. I'm watching her make a wish. *Make a wish with me, Belle*, she's saying. I'm looking up at her. I'm nine years old. The time just before the time that's in a black box. I'm wearing a pink coat the color of sick that I begged her for. She wanted to buy me a navy velvet coat, but I wanted this pink fluffy one. She shook her head at me like I had no idea, no style, like it would take me a very long time to realize things. She's impossibly beautiful with her eyes closed and her face tilted up to the dark gray sky and her lips curved in a secret smile.

Are your eyes closed, Belle?

Yes, I lied, for my eyes were wide open. Looking at Mother, leaning dangerously forward like she could fall into the river at any moment.

All it would take was one push. A sudden wind. I closed my eyes then. I closed my eyes then and I'm closing my eyes now.

Are you making a wish? Mother whispered.

Yes.

"Be careful," says a voice now, its breath on my neck. And I scream. Open my eyes. *Mother?*

No Mother. No Montreal. I'm back on the creaking white bridge in the ravine, above the churning Pacific. The setting sun is blazing red overhead. But I'm not alone anymore. On the bridge with me is a man. I recognize him instantly. The taste of smoke and mint in my mouth. That fake black beard that chafed my face. Now he's clean-shaven. Wearing that same dark blue suit, that hat that shadows the top half of his face. He looks, as always, like he emerged from Mother's nighttime television screen, forever filled with noir or New Wave.

"Don't want to fall," he says. "There are caves down there, you know. Seriously treacherous."

"I wasn't falling."

"If you say so." He smiles. "Following me again, huh?"

"No," I say. "I wasn't following you the other night, either. We just happened to be going the same way."

"Are we going the same way tonight, too, I wonder?" His eyes look pale gray in this light. Knife-sharp face. He comes in closer. There's the scent of green tea again. A warm, woodsy smell too, like forest herbs distilled in a brown bottle. Crack for the vagus nerve. Very spa-like. "Let me guess," he says. "A certain glass house on the cliff's edge. Where the red roses grow."

"So what if I am?"

"Call me interested."

"In what exactly?"

He smiles. I feel him taking in my skin. "Oh, I think you know."

I look at his mouth full of white teeth. He's wearing that lip balm that gives off a scent of roses. An image of kissing him rises up in my mind, but it might just be how close he is to my face. I flush. "I'm sorry," I say. "I don't have any idea what you're talking about."

"Really?" He moves in closer still, his sharp shadows falling over me. "Funny. I thought I'd met a fellow freak." Even closer now, grinning. "Snail mucin?" he says softly, looking at my face.

"Excuse me?"

"A mist, too, definitely," he whispers, eyes grazing like a touch. "Rosewater, maybe birch milk. A double-fermented green tea, algae, and rice essence. The infamous Brightening Caviar for Radiance. And of course the Revitalizing Eye Formula. Diamond-infused for brightness, but it bleeds is the thing." He brushes a tear from my cheek that must have just now fallen.

"How did you—?"

"Call it a wild, wild guess." He smiles. That's when I notice the scar on his cheek like a jagged slash. Flashing redly in the dying light of day.

"Why did you kiss me in the hall like that?"

"Me?" He shakes his head. "Oh, I would never *ever* do something like that. Just like you would never follow me, right?" He pulls out a small tin of what looks like red candies. "Collagen gummy?"

I shake my head.

"You sure? They're really tasty. Cherry, I think. And they're in the shape of a rose, see? Really pretty. Rose shape, cherry taste. Nice little mindfuck." I watch him pop the red gummy in his mouth and hold it between his white teeth. I see his tongue press against it.

"I should—"

"They're interested in you, you know," he says in a low voice. "Very. I'm jealous. *I envy*, to use the parlance."

"Who's interested?"

"They," he whispers. "The beautiful ones." He looks at me meaningfully. The woman in red flashes in my mind. The twins in their veils. The girl-woman in black smiling at my scar as we waltzed backward around the tank. "I saw you talking with them on the staircase the

other night. Never seen the higher-ups do that before. Take so much interest."

I watch him turn the rose gummy around his tongue. Still intact. He's not even chewing, just letting it dissolve slowly in his mouth. Behind him the sky is the color of blood. *Vespers*, I remember. The voucher in my pocket starts to pulse.

"I should go."

"Not lost, are you?" he asks like he's concerned.

"No." Quickly, I scan the cliffs for any sight of the house. No sign. I start to walk away, but my feet are slow moving, my shoes suddenly heavy. I feel them sinking with each step, almost like they're refusing me. Almost like they're whispering, *You are fucking lost*.

"Because if you were lost, I'd be happy to escort you up there," he calls after me. "For your free treatment."

I freeze. Look back at him standing there on the bridge in the darkening light. "How did you—?"

"Another wild guess." He holds out his arm in offering. "You don't want to be late, right? They fucking hate it when you're late. So I hear, anyway." Attractive in the red light, holding his suited arm for me to take. *Sharp*, Mother would say of this man, her highest praise. The cut of his face and the cut of his dark suit and the cut of his shadows. The scar's jagged shape gleaming in the bloody sunset.

"I don't need you," I blurt out, almost reflexively. "To guide me, I mean. Thank you anyway."

He smiles, then looks serious. "Of course not. You're just using me tonight. Letting me be your eyes in the dark. After all, we are going the same way." Still holding out his arm. *Go on*.

I walk over and take it, and he smiles again, like maybe he won something.

"What's your name, by the way?" he asks me as we start walking along the darkening path.

"Belle." When was the last time I told anyone my name was Belle?

Mira, I'll usually say, or *Mirabelle* at best. I can feel Mother smiling at this.

"*Belle*. Of course. You know you look like a Belle? From the fairy tale, right? About a pretty girl who fucks a monster. That's a classic."

"I don't know that they ever fuck exactly."

"Well, maybe not in the story, Belle. But I'm pretty sure they fuck eventually. Watch your step there. Wow, great shoes."

"Thanks." Smiling now in spite of myself. Gripping his suited arm. Breathing in his skincare scent, a heady mix of extracts and botanicals I know so well. Makes me feel . . . strangely happy. Strangely at home with him on this dark road. Dark now, very. Water crashing on one side of me. A smell of roses on the other, close and thick. "What's your name?" I ask him.

He raises his hat from his head, then lowers it again. "Hud Hudson."

"*Hud Hudson?*"

"Don't laugh. My mother wrote romance novels. All out of print now, sadly. Well, here we are." I see we're already at the gates. We must have been very close all along. I look at the man named Hud Hudson, grinning beside me in the dark. I feel tricked. How could I have missed it? Beyond the gates, the house glows red among the eucalyptus trees, glowing red too. The roses sway gently in the breeze, giving off a rich perfume.

"You go on ahead," he says.

"Aren't you coming?"

"In a bit. I'll follow you this time around."

I'm about to walk up when he reaches out a hand and holds me back. "After you get the treatment, I'd love to hear all about it. All the lavish details."

"Why?"

"Don't you want to make me weep with envy, Belle? Doesn't that sound like fun?" He smiles and raises his hat. *That's Monty. That's Alain. That's Paul.* "I'll be in touch. Sorry about your mother, by the way."

"Thank you."

He walks away. Leaving me there alone, wanting to say *wait. Wait.* But the word is stuck in my throat. The sun has sunk. Nothing but a dim red flame over the palms and the rocks and the distant waves I still won't look at. But I can hear them all around me. That gentle, relentless primordial roar. And it reminds me. *I never told you about my mother. I never told you.*

12

The doors open just as I reach the threshold. The woman in silver who greeted me the first night. The one who looked like she'd been eating too many cherries. She seems paler than last time, her eyes ringed in more silvery smoke. She glances at the red voucher in my hand and smiles.

"Well, aren't we the lucky one?"

The grand hall is darker tonight. I can just make out the red chandelier, the looming shape of the giant aquarium, concealed by red curtains.

"This way," she says, smiling, leading me down the hall. Her hand on my arm a firm, caressing grip. I'm about to go on a very exciting journey, she says. I'm about to take the first step. Am I excited?

"Very excited," I whisper, fear swimming in me like a bright fish. We pass clusters of luminous people in exquisite dress—red and black and silver. Their bright faces glow in the dark. Members, they must be. No sign of the woman in red anywhere. On the landing of the stair, I see the twins in silhouette, faces veiled. I feel them watching the woman in silver tug me through the crowd. "An exciting journey," they all echo as she ushers me past. "The first step." They smile knowingly with their eyes. I'm touched by their raised glasses, their eyes on me, so many sky-colored eyes, their hissing whispers of "Bravo." "Bon Voyage." But another part of me thinks, *All this for a free treatment? For what is probably just a fancy facial?* But maybe they take their facials more seriously here. Calling them *treatments.* I nod at them all. "Thank you. *Merci.*" And they just stare at me, these strangers.

"We should hurry," the woman says, tugging on my wrist nervously. I wonder, will we go through the corridor marked SIGNATURE

RITUALS or the one marked VOYAGES MERVEILLEUX? Instead she leads me to an unmarked staircase near the Depths.

I'm having trouble following her down the winding stairs. Suddenly, my feet won't move.

"What is it, Daughter?" she asks, pulling on my arm to no end.

"I don't know."

She frowns. Do I not want the free treatment? Do I not wish to go on an exciting journey? So I say, "Excuse me," and take off my shoes. The insides feel very hot between my fingers. Throbbing like hearts, or a pair of lungs breathing. The stairs are cold on my bare feet, but at least I'm able to descend them now. She smiles, relieved. Daughter's antics on the stair were *très amusant*, she says, but she's very glad they're over now. Because we really don't want to be late for such a momentous occasion, do we? *Such a momentous occasion as a spa treatment?* I think. But I say, "Absolutely." And she tells me to run, "Let's run, all right?" And then the two of us are running hand in hand down the stairs. As I run, I want to laugh. Running for a treatment. Sort of defeats the purpose of the relaxation element, doesn't it? But I run with her, the shoes beating harder and faster in my hands.

I'm in some sort of dark-red waiting room. Heavy with the scent of eucalyptus. Mirrors all around. *Bon Voyage*, the woman in silver said, and then she was gone. She took my clothes and my shoes and my purse with her. Left me standing here barefoot in a white-and-red robe. I hear a waterfall somewhere. The distant sound of chimes. Some red magazines, looks like, on a black marble table. Beside them, a vaseful of what looks like raspberries. Also chilled water jugs filled with . . . what is it, blood vessels? Pomegranate seeds. *Get a grip*, I tell myself. A little nervous, I guess. Why a little nervous? When they've been nothing but kind? Just a spa. Just a free treatment. *I'd love to hear all about it. All the lavish details*, that strange man, Hud Hudson, said. *Me too, Hud Hudson. I want them too.* I always did.

How many times have I sat at the dress shop, looking up pictures of the fanciest spas on my phone? Wishing I could walk through those gilded gates and walk out again, lifted and glowing and reborn? Thinking the secret is just behind those gates. Secret to what? Something essential. And now I'm here. Within the gates. In the waiting room. Better, much better, than my Montreal spa's waiting room with its dated copies of *Elle* and its cheap paper cups of weak tea. I go there twice a year, which is the most I can afford. Twice a year, a woman in a white smock takes me into a darkened cubicle and electrocutes my face. I taste metal in my teeth for weeks after, but it's worth it for that slightly lifted look. After the electrocution (she calls it *microcurrent*), she coats my still-spasming skin with marine algae. I lie there under the cold, black sea goop for as long as she'll let me, dreaming of luminosity. How I'll soon glow in the dark.

What the fuck did you do to your face? Mother would say when we FaceTimed afterward.

Nothing.

Liar. You did something. Tell me.

Don't I have a lifted look?

You have a scared look. Like you've been stunned.

Well, maybe next time I visit you, I can go where you go.

She got silent then. Waved her hand as if to wave my words away. *You don't want to go where I go. I've told you, you don't need any of this stuff. That Egyptian blood saves you. I'm another story.*

Well now I'm here, Mother. I've gone where you go. Maybe I'm not another story after all.

I take a seat in one of the chairs shaped like a wave. I picture Mother sitting in this very chair. Imagine her in a white-and-red robe, listening to the chimes and the waterfall, partaking of pomegranate water. Soaking it all up with a non-wrinkle-inducing smile. *This'll be good.* It makes me smile too. There's another woman with me in the room. She's beautiful. Her dark skin glows in the dim light. Her eyes are pale. Maybe she's mixed too. Ethnically ambiguous, as

Mother might say. *Where are you from?* I would ask this woman if I didn't fucking hate that question myself. The way Mother would answer for me, smile and say *Egypt*, right as I said *Montreal*. The woman's flipping a magazine. Too dark for me to see the cover. Can she really be reading in the dark? She looks up at me and smiles.

"First time," she says. It isn't a question. She knows it's my first time.

"Yes," I say, and my voice echoes in the room like it's a corridor. "They offered me a free treatment."

"A free treatment," the woman repeats, raising an eyebrow. "Me too."

"You too?"

"Lucky us. These cost a pretty penny, so I'm told."

"Is it your first time too?" Not a furrow on her brow. Not a wrinkle. She's flawless.

"I've had one. Still need a few more for the brightening."

"The brightening?" I ask.

"The glow," she whispers. She goes back to reading her red magazine in the dark. I'm glad she's here. Another client. Otherwise I'd feel . . . not afraid exactly, that's ridiculous. Just . . . sort of weird. Getting a treatment at . . . what time is it now? No clock on the wall and the woman in silver took my purse and my phone. Late, anyway, for a facial. Is it a facial that I'm getting though? Never really clarified that. Just took what the woman in red dangled. Said, *Thanks so much.*

"How is it?" I ask her.

She looks up at me like she forgot I was there. "How is it?"

"The treatment."

"Oh. Well, it's different for everyone, isn't it?"

"Right," I say like I understand. I notice black tapered candles on the table now, red rose petals scattered all around. There's a mirror wall beside us, a thousand of me, going on to infinity.

"Deeply perilous," she says, turning to the mirror wall. Smiling at herself there.

"Perilous?"

"Did I say perilous? I meant *personal*, of course."

"Of course. Personal." *Personal? Come on, lady. A facial is a facial is a facial. Even I know that.*

There are white faces on the wall above the mirror, I see. Plaster casts, sticking out of black frames. Making expressions of open-mouthed horror.

"So is it a microcurrent then?" I ask her.

She just stares at her many reflections.

"Or a laser? Ultrasound? Radiofrequency?"

She smiles like all the words I just said are funny. Funny little things.

"A peel maybe?" I press. "Glycolic?"

She laughs, tilting her neck back. Not a ring on that neck. Not a blemish. "You certainly know some . . . *terminology*, don't you?" She takes a sip of the red champagne. Hers looks thick and dark, the color and viscosity of blood. Does it have any bubbles? Not any that I can see. But then again the room is dark, isn't it? Silly to be afraid. Sure the white faces in the wall are a little weird, but it could just be a rich-people thing. Like the jellyfish behind the red curtain. Part of the eccentric spa décor. *Eclectic*, as Sylvia would say.

The woman is still chuckling to herself, still looking in the mirror, her thick red champagne in her hand. "Glycolic," she repeats, shaking her head. "Oh my."

"Daughter of Noelle," someone calls softly. A small woman in a black suit standing in a doorway. A woman like a whisper. "We're ready for you."

The woman with the magazine stops chuckling. She looks at me, suddenly so very serious. "Letting go is *so* worth it," she says.

"Excuse me?"

But she's turned away again, staring at her selves in the dark.

———

Scared. No reason at all to be, really. Just a treatment room like any other. Dark as a womb. Thick with herbal steam. Heated massage table in the middle. The woman like a whisper stands in the corner smiling. She looks like so many aestheticians I've seen before. Serene expression. Eerily ageless. Voice like air. Barely there, really, like a ghost. Her English accented slightly, though from where, I'm not sure. She's telling me to undress, she'll take my robe now. She doesn't leave the room like they normally do. Just stands there and smilingly waits for me to strip. "Great," she whispers. "Just great. Now lie down, please."

What sort of treatment is this? I want to ask, but now the question seems stupid. Ungrateful. It's free, isn't it? I think of those white plaster faces screaming out of their black frames in the waiting room. Anyway, I tell myself, too late now, isn't it? Your clothes and your purse are in a locker a maze of corridors away. You'll have to be led back to them later like a lost girl. You'll have to find the woman in silver somewhere on the winding stair. You'll have to beg her for your shoes. A tightness in my chest. My breath is shallow and quick. The whisper woman is telling me to close my eyes. I feel her lay a blanket over my body. "Breathe," she says. "Three deep breaths, there you go. I'll take them with you. Shall I take them with you?"

"Yes."

And then she rubs her hands with some sort of scented oil. Eucalyptus, maybe? Holds her hands suspended over my nose and mouth. We breathe together. I feel my chest rise and fall. "There," she says. "That's better, isn't it?"

"Yes," I say. And it is. Much better. I close my eyes in earnest now. The eucalyptus-y scent thickens. Fresh steam rolling in from somewhere like a fog. A warmth spreads through me that feels delicious. I let her wash my face about a thousand times. Rag after hot steaming rag descending upon me, smothering my skin. Her soaped hands sliding across the planes of my face, washing me away and away. I start to drift off as she applies a thick, cold paste to my cheeks. The first of several masks, perhaps? Just a facial, then. That much is clear now.

"I could really use this facial," I say. "I haven't had a facial in a while. I go to a place in Montreal, but it's nothing like this, of course."

The woman says nothing. Just continues to massage the cold paste onto my face.

"My mother came here though," I offer to the dark.

Silence. More cold paste.

"She died recently. That's why I'm in town. Taking care of things. That's why I'm here tonight, too. I guess someone here knew her. I guess she was a member."

Still nothing.

"Wouldn't surprise me," I add. "She had terrific skin. Did you ever—?"

A hand on my shoulder, gripping. Then: "I'm afraid not." She begins to knead my cheeks more forcefully.

"They offered me a free treatment. That was nice of them."

I can feel her smiling in the dark. "They're very generous."

I hear that water fountain again in the distance. Soft ambient music. An airy drone like the endless reverberation of some other-worldly bell. I notice something glimmering out of the corner of my eye. I try to look without moving my face, still under her lathering hands. Then I see it: a small white jellyfish. Glowing in the corner of the dark room, in a little glass box full of water. I know it's the tiny one I held in my palm last night. The one light as a wish. *You're going to go on quite a journey together*, the girl-woman in black said.

"What is that?" I ask. "A jellyfish?"

"Shhh," whispers the whisper woman. And then she says, "I'm just going to turn on the light so that I can assess your skin. It's a bright light. So I'll be covering your eyes, is that okay?"

"Of course." And now I'm really smiling. Because, jellyfish aside, all of this is familiar. First some cleansing and massage. Now assessment followed by extractions. I can handle extractions. There was never anything to fear. Which is a little disappointing, frankly. Maybe I wanted to be obliterated. She presses a damp cotton pad over each of my closed eyelids. I can't help but think of pennies on the eyes of the dead. The ferryman taking his change as I float on the river Styx. She shines a lamp over my face. The light's so bright, I can see it even through my closed eyelids and the damp cotton pads. Flaming red. I feel the fact of her eyes. Looking at me.

"Well?" I say at last, because I can't take any more of her silence. "What's the verdict?" And I laugh my nervous laugh that betrays me. "Am I congested?"

"That's a way of putting it," she says quietly.

"Lots of extractions to do, then," I offer. Listen to me offering.

She's silent. No sound in the room but my own breathing and those chimes. The eucalyptus scent is beginning to be oppressive.

"If you have to do extractions, I can take it. I'm very seasoned. I'm—"

"It's all here," she whispers at last, touching my face. I feel her finger pads trace my forehead furrows, the deep creases between my brows. The veins around my nose and the muzzle lines around my mouth. *Nasolabial folds*, I know they're called. Laugh lines that weren't even born from laughing. I feel her fingers glide their way back to my forehead. Trace the scar, its shadowy star shape. She touches it so tenderly that a thin tear leaks from my eye. She takes the cotton pads from my lids. "Open," she says. I do. And there I am in the oval mirror she's holding over my face.

"Memory and skin go hand in hand, you know," she says. "Good memories, good skin. Bad memories . . ." And here she trails off. Because the mirror speaks for itself, doesn't it?

I stare into it. I stare and stare at my own wretched reflection. So close I was once. On certain days, in certain lights. It's the closeness that kills me. The *almost but not quite*. The grasping and the disappointment. The resignation and the desperation. All etched in my face. The hope's still there in my eyes. Dumb, persistent, unquashable. It gives me a slightly crazed, haunted look. Hope is a weed that Marva nurtures in the shade. *Have faith*, she entreats. *Never give up*, she pleads, *on your #skingoals. It might just be a matter of the right combination of acids. Of not looking so closely, so punishingly in the mirror. Under such very bright lights, tsk, tsk.* Herself under very bright lights as she says this. Looking so terribly flawless. Looking like evidence of godly design.

I feel the whisper woman hovering over me, just beyond the glass, smiling encouragingly. She could be thirty-five. She could be sixty-five. Beside her, the jellyfish is glowing more brightly, more whitely in its tank.

"What if we do something about it?" she says in a voice that is like a caress.

"Like what?"

"How attached are you to your memories?"

I look into the mirror again. The shadows and miseries imprinted there on my skin. My pores gaping open at me like silently screaming mouths. The toll of the years casts a grayness that perhaps will never be lifted. I see my paltry almost. My utterly unbearable closeness. *Closeness to what?* Mother's face flashes brightly in my mind.

And I say to my own reflection, "Not attached. Not attached at all." Beside me, I feel the jellyfish quiver in its tank. Like it's sighing.

How long have I been lying here in the dark? In the eucalyptus fog? On the heated table beside the little white jellyfish? Don't know. Time's not here. She said, *Why don't you lie here and we'll get started?* And I thought, *Haven't we already started?* I said, *This is some facial.* And she said, *Treatment. It's a treatment.*

Treatment, I repeated. *Of course.*

There are sleek black discs taped to either side of my face now, at my temples. The discs feel somehow connected to the small jellyfish tank, because the moment she pressed them against my temples, the creature began to glow even brighter. Like a dimmer switch turned all the way up. *For the extractions?* I said. *Exactly*, the woman said. *For the extractions.* She was about to leave when I felt her hand on my shoulder. *You may find you're in a bit of a fog after this. You may find you have some blanks.*

Blanks?

Letting go is so worth it. You'll see tomorrow in the mirror. Now just lie here. Are you comfortable? And the only answer to that was *Yes.* My entire body under the blanket was so terribly comfortable. I was warm to my core. I was floating, floating there on the table. I didn't know where I began or where I ended. I didn't know my own body from the fog, from the bell. There was a smile on my face. A soft one that caused no wrinkles. My eyes were closing and opening on the small, pulsing white jellyfish. Light as a wish. And that's how she left me. *Come back,* I whispered. But my lips weren't moving at all.

Above me now, the ceiling rolls back, look at that. Like a sunroof or a tarp over a swimming pool being rolled back. What's there? A sky full of stars? Not quite. A glass ceiling, awash with blue-green light. The light of water, of aquariums, fills the dark, steam-thick room. Through the steam, I see them floating by. Red, pulsating, trailing tentacles. Giants compared to the small, glowing white creature beside me. I must be right beneath the Depths. The tank goes far beneath the main floor, so I must be deep under. Wow. It's terribly beautiful up there. *Primordial* is a word that floats alone in the lagoon of my mind. I'm in the lagoon of my mind now. Deep in the lagoon, there's a black box. A black box with many locks, like metal teeth. It lies there on the lagoon floor, half covered in silt. I feel the box open its black mouth.

And then?

I can't feel my body at all anymore. The heated table is getting warmer. The room is getting darker, the only light coming from the blue water above. The little jellyfish shines beside me like a star. The steam has grown thick, thick. I'm rising up from the table. Drifting up toward the glass ceiling, to where the giant red jellyfish float. Nothing beneath this body I can't feel but air. The sleek black disks are still attached to my temples, throbbing along with my pulse. I should be afraid. But I'm so comfortable. And the red giant jellyfish are so beautiful up close like this. Look at them drifting redly in the water. They're putting me in the mood to drift myself, to dream. And there, suddenly on the glass, something like a film begins to play. Like the aquarium glass has become a movie screen. *Oh, are we watching movies?* I want to ask. But there's the problem of my mouth again. How it won't move the way I want. How my lips feel dead on my face.

I look at the glass screen. I see a young girl tiptoeing down a dark hall. She's wearing a white frilly dress. She's ugly. The dress is ugly too, but the girl doesn't know this. She's ten years old. *How come you know that she's ten?* asks a voice inside.

"I just do," I try to whisper.

Look. Now she's in the doorway of a blue-and-white bedroom. Her bedroom? No. Not her bedroom. How come I know that? Because she looks guilty.

Also you just know, don't you? says that inside voice. *You know the way you know your own bones. You know the way you know your cells, your breath.*

Yes. I can see the red jellyfish through the glass screen, through the scene of the young girl as she creeps into the bedroom that is not her own. Looking both ways. Looking all around her now. *What are we watching?* I think. And that question is hilarious. As hilarious as the question, *Is this a facial?* I'm laughing though my mouth isn't moving. My mouth is frozen open wide like the black box inside my mind. The black box is where the movie of the little girl is coming from. The film projector is my eyes.

You know what you're watching, says the voice. *You're watching you. You're the little girl, aren't you?*

Yes.

Sneaking into this bedroom that isn't your own.

Not my own, not my own.

Whose? Whose bedroom is it? Tell me.

I look at the little girl there on the glass screen. The answer is a bubble leaving the mouth of the black box. The answer is a single word. Out with it.

"Mother's," I say with my dead lips. The word leaving my mouth fogs the aquarium glass, fogs the film being projected by my eyes. But I still see the girl outside the room that isn't hers. The giant red jellyfish moving through her little body. I feel my mouth stretching open.

"I'm in Mother's bedroom."

13

I'm in the dark hallway with Mother. Mother's gloved hands are on my shoulders. Her face hovering over mine is like a pretty, pretty cloud. She's telling me that she has to go out now. She won't be long. But don't wait up. All right, Belle?

"All right, Mother."

"And don't go snooping around in my room while I'm gone. Especially you know where."

I nod. I know where.

"I *won't*." I'm lying, of course.

"Promise?"

"Promise. Where are you going?" I ask even though I know. I know by her clothes and her hair and her perfume that smells of violets and smoke. She's wearing the white suit by Yves Saint Laurent today. Her hair's done into an old-timey wave like the women in the black-and-white movies Mother likes to watch at night, and sometimes she lets me watch with her. It's Nicholas, her hairdresser, who Mother calls a genius, who did this wave for Mother so that her hair is like a soft cloud of S. He tells her every time she sits in his salon chair that she's his very own Elizabeth Taylor. He told her this today when we went to get Mother's hair done for tonight. And Mother smiled at herself in the mirror. She loves when he says that. I watched the smile creep across her face from where I sat in the waiting area, flipping through a magazine called *Sky*. Tom Cruise was on the cover, and I knew there'd be more pictures of him inside. *Who's Elizabeth Taylor?* I asked her. *Someone beautiful*, Mother said, out of the corner of her red mouth, as if that were all I needed to know. *Someone beautiful*, I repeated to Tom

Cruise, his smile white and blinding. There *were* more pictures of him inside. Quietly, I tore out the one I liked best.

After mother got her hair done, she let Nicholas give me a trim— *just a half an inch, just the bangs,* she said—and I hated when Mother said this. It was like she was sentencing me to myself, which is not a place I want or asked to be. I wanted Nicholas to defy Mother. To give me the S he gave her. In my dreams, he does just this and then we run away together, hand in hand. But today, Nicholas just gave me the trim Mother said to give me, talking to Mother the whole time about something called "the single life," making Mother howl with laughter while she smoked her Matinée 100 in the next chair. He didn't tell Mother to put her cigarette out. He didn't tell me I was his anything. Nicholas smells like shampoo and his eyes sparkle and his hair is very crisp. For a while, I had what Mother called a crush. Though I told her nothing, she knew. She knew by my face alone, which Mother says she can read like a book. Every page. And she said, *Nick doesn't go that way, Sunshine, sorry.* I pretended not to know what Mother was talking about. And Mother read that page too.

"Mother," I ask her again now. "Where are you going?"

"Twenty questions," Mother says, which is a warning. And then she says, "I'm meeting someone."

A man, of course. Always a man. Which one? Mother is seeing two men these days. Will she be meeting Chip or the Troll? I hate them both, but the white suit and the violet perfume probably mean Chip. She wears another dress, another perfume that looks like a poison apple and is actually called Poison, for the Troll. It smells like spiced secrets. The lipstick she has on (that I love) is the one she wears for them all: Russet Moon by Chanel, a deep red that makes Mother's mouth look like it's bleeding. The shiny red shoes on her feet are for all of them too. Not my favorites. My favorites are still in her bedroom closet, second shoe shelf from the bottom, third pair from the left. But these are pretty too. I look at Mother's strappy feet, her made-up face with the Russet Moon mouth, her hair done by Nicholas, for whom she is someone beautiful.

"Can I come?"

"Not today, Sunshine."

"Why not?" There's a whine in my voice. A whine I can't control. A whine Mother hates. I watch her wince at the sound of me. Touch her white hand to her white temple like I'm too much. I've followed her into her bedroom, where she's pulled a hat from the closet and set it on the bed by her purse. The broad-brimmed white hat with the beautiful black ribbon to protect her face from the sun. *Because the sun is our mortal enemy, sweetie*, Mother always says.

Why?

Because it makes us age and it makes us tan. And we don't want that. We certainly don't want to age. As for tanning, it's wonderful when we have it naturally like you, of course, she always says to me, cupping my face in her hands. *You're one of the lucky ones, Sunshine. But when we're ghosts like your poor Mother, we need to be exceedingly careful.* I always thought the sun was nice. In school, whenever I drew the sun in pictures, I made a smiling face inside the yellow circle in the sky. Made it smile over the flowers below, also smiling, and the spiky green grass. But ever since I learned the truth from Mother, I put a frown in the sun. I give him angry eyes. Mean eyebrows, like hairy, upside-down vees. He shoots death rays down onto the beautiful maiden's hat, who is sitting below on the grass.

Why do you make the sun so cruel-looking, dear? Ms. Said asked me, looking over my shoulder at my drawing on the desk. Ms. Said is Egyptian like me. But fully, not half. *Which is lovely*, Mother said.

Because the sun makes us dark, I told Ms. Said. And Ms. Said was concerned. She was already very concerned that most of my drawings featured girls who looked nothing like me. They were either blond and green-eyed like my secret best friend, Stacey, or they were red-haired and blue-eyed like Mother, and they kept looking at themselves in the mirror. There was always a mirror in my pictures, even when they were outside.

It's called imagination, Mother told Ms. Said when Ms. Said brought her into the school to talk about the pictures. She'd laid them all out on the desk, to my great shame. All my angry red suns and my beautiful maidens and my shining mirrors.

Is that what it's called? Ms. Said asked, and Mother didn't answer, just stared at my pictures. Her sunglasses were on, so I couldn't see her eyes. Ms. Said is the one who told me my last name, Nour, means "divine light," did I know that? I thought Nour meant something dark like the French word for *black. Noir, Nour,* a lot of French people get it confused, including Grand-Maman. *Nour,* Ms. Said said. *Looks like "night" but means "light," remember that.* Mother's name means "of the gardens." No one looks at Mother's name with narrowed eyes or says it like a question. *Noelle Des Jardins,* they say, and I know they see a beautiful snowy garden like I do. Her face offers a picture. The red of her lips and blue of her eyes like flowers poking out of the white.

"Belle," Mother says now, "please just stay here and be good for Grand-Maman, okay?"

"But I don't want to be good for Grand-Maman!" Now I'm shouting. *Grand-Maman's evil,* I want to tell Mother. I want to tell her about Grand-Maman's eyes. How they can go from light brown to shining black in an instant. How the blackness seems to fill her whole eye, even the white. This happens whenever she tells me about the end of the world, how it's coming soon. She'll start the minute Mother leaves. *Belle,* she'll hiss from her white island of couch. *Viens ici.* But there is never time to tell Mother because she's always going somewhere.

"Mom, please let me come with—"

"No, Belle." And the words are like a slap. My face stings with it. For a minute, Mother looks cruel. It feels like her beauty was only a disguise. This thin, hard mouth, these flashing eyes, this jaw of stone—this is the truth of her face.

"Stay. Here. Stay here and be good and *don't go in my room.*"

"I don't!" I shriek. I'm a terrible liar. I feel my face go red. I look at the floor, where I see my foot's jittering. I can feel her staring at me, not like she's mad, but like she's sorry for me. She reaches into her purse. Lights one of her long cigarettes. Look what I've done. I've made her smoke. She's been trying to give it up, she really has, but she never will with me around. *Whining.* She exhales a plume of smoke into my face.

"Play with your dolls or something, all right? I guess you're a little old for those now. Read one of your fairy-tale books, how about that?" She makes it sound like such a fun time. Like I haven't read these books a thousand times before.

"All right," I say.

"Chin up, Sunshine. No more long face. Or else what? What do we say?"

"It'll freeze that way," I finish.

"That's *right*. And we don't want that, trust me." And she does an impression of me pouting. Makes her eyes storm cloudy and sticks her lower lip out really far. I don't want to laugh, but I do. And Mother smiles. Pats my head. "Much better." Kisses the air near my face three times. I catch a whiff of her violets and smoke, the waxy animal smell of her lipstick.

"Bring me back something?" I call after her. Pathetic. I don't know the meaning of the word yet, but the minute I heard Mother use it about someone, I knew that's the word I was. She's already going out the door, but she hears me.

"Like what?" she calls over her shoulder.

You, I think, after she's gone.

From the living room window, I watch her go. A man is waiting outside our apartment in a fancy red convertible. Chip. The one who Mother says looks a little like Montgomery Clift. *Monty*, Mother calls him and sort of sighs, like she's actually met Montgomery Clift, like he's not at all a dead stranger. When Mother calls Chip *Monty*, he gets angry. *I'm not a queer*, Chip says, and then he winks at me. I don't wink back. I hate Chip. He looks nothing like the beautiful man I see on Mother's black-and-white screen at night, who Mother calls by his first name only, like they're friends. I think there's something very wrong with Mother's eyes if she sees Monty in Chip. Apparently, Chip is *Connected to the Industry*, Mother says—*whatever that means*, Grand-Maman always adds—and if he could get Mother a role in his next film project, wouldn't that be so wonderful for Mother? Then Mother wouldn't have to slave her days away in Ladies Apparel at the Bay, dealing with those god-awful *ladies. So difficult the ladies are, Belle*, Mother says, closing her eyes as if she can still see them in her mind. But difficult's one thing, she whispers. Mother can handle difficult. Mother can handle anything, she's a survivor, after all. What's trying for Mother about the ladies who shop in Ladies Apparel is that they have No Style. All they want are the saddest slacks. Sweaters to fucking drown in, even when Mother is very happy to show them other options. They always choose Death by Polyester. Mother sometimes wants to ask them why not just go down to Hardware and buy a garbage bag and wade into the Saint Lawrence River and have done with it? It's the lack of style, the lack of dreaming, that gives Mother a migraine every night when she comes home. So that she has to sit in the dark for a very long time watching old movies to do what she calls *cleanse*. And if I'm quieter than quiet, if I let Mother sit and smoke on the couch, watching the TV screen like it's a window to the most magical world, mouthing the words she knows by heart, I can sit with her. And Mother might even pat my hand, point at the screen with her cigarette, at Elizabeth Taylor or Gene Tierney or Catherine Deneuve, and say, *See? Now that's style. I see*, I say, but I'm still looking at Mother's face fixed on the screen, dreaming herself into this other world. Her face looks like it never does. Soft. Open. Like she could cry any second, but she won't. The Bay and its ladies have left her mind. Or it's Mother who left, the screen took her away. Opened a door and Mother walked through it. Movies do that to Mother, open something usually closed. I guess they do that to me, too, sometimes. Certain ones, anyway. If Chip or the Troll or whoever got Mother a good role, *just one*, Mother could leave the Bay and its ladies forever. She'd torch it on her way out the door. Set all the slacks and sweaters on fire, she wouldn't be sorry. They'd burn up quick, she says, made as they mostly are from cheap materials.

Now Chip grins when he sees Mother walking toward him in her white suit, which she bought with her Bay discount—what Mother calls the *one saving grace*. When I look at Chip grinning, I think of wolves dressed as sheep. Fangs hidden in the woolly white. She gets in the car, which opens funny, sort of like the doors of the car in *Back to the Future*. She doesn't see me watching her from the window. Fogging up the glass. Telling her don't go.

"Get away from the window, Belle," Grand-Maman says. Sitting behind me in her nightgown of pink lace, eating religieuse and watching *All My Children* in her dark corner. Even in the bright June afternoon, Grand-Maman somehow makes wherever she sits a dark corner. Her jeweled fingers are sticky with syrup. She's taken her teeth out so she can taste. I become aware of the smell of her. Old bread and throw up and Shalimar. Jewels clinking softly. Stones of all shades shimmering from her neck, her wrists, her fingers. Some given to her by her dead husband, my grand-père, and by my father back when he was courting Mother. Other men too. Apparently, everyone used to give Grand-Maman gold like she was royalty. Now she drips with it. She was a great beauty once, Mother says. When she says that, I think of Grand-Maman's drooping mouth and her tiny eyes in her bloodless face. Her gray-white hair sticking up like an electrocuted puffball. *What happened?* I asked Mother. And for a second I thought she was going to smack me. But she just shrugged. *She threw it away. She gave it up.*

If I had beauty, I decided then, I would never throw it away. I would never give it up.

Now that Mother has driven away with Chip, I brace myself for Grand-Maman to tell me about the end of the world. The horse-filled dark. Her eyes going black. Mother doesn't tell me about it enough, Grand-Maman says. Mother's forgotten herself since she moved down to Montreal from the north. Speaking English to her unbaptized daughter. Not even going to mass most Sundays. If it weren't for Grand-Maman, Grand-Maman says, my soul might be lost entirely to Darkness. But today Grand-Maman says nothing. Just stares at *All My Children* like she's not even seeing it. She tells me to go to my room and play.

"Okay," I say. And on this day, I walk down the hall like I'm going there. But I'm not going there. I keep going down the hall. To the very end of it. To the blue-and-white room I love that smells like dreams. I'm careful to turn the knob of the door a certain way so that Grand-Maman doesn't hear the sound. When I open the door, I sigh. Blue walls the color of the sky. Blue velvet curtains that filter out the light. There's the great white wicker bed with the clean blue-and-white sheets. There's her closet on the left. There's her white wicker vanity on the right with her tray of perfume bottles in so many glass shapes. Tears and stars and strange flowers, gifted by Mother's friends at the beauty counters. I have to be so careful in Mother's bedroom. Because of the wicker, everything hisses when I sit on it, when I touch it, even.

The closet door is white and tall, very closed. I see Mother saying, *Don't open this door. Promise me.* When I open the gliding door, I'm very slow. I've done this before. I know how to glide it very quietly.

Dark in here. Can't seem to find the light switch. But I feel Mother's clothes hanging on either side of me. I smell their violets and smoke. Mother sorts them by color, but mostly there's just the three colors she loves best: white and black and red. She loves red most. Because of her hair and her eyes, she says. Also her skin—what she calls her *coloring*. *Everybody has a season based on their coloring, Belle.* Mother read this in *Vogue* magazine. Mother is a Winter, she says. *What am I?* I asked her. *Probably a Fall*, she said, because of my coloring. *It's all coloring, Sunshine.*

What colors am I if I'm a Fall?

Olive, Mother said. *Earth. Rust. Mustard. Don't those sound nice?*

No. Those all sounded like nightmare colors to me. *What if I don't want to be a Fall?*

Well, Glum Drop, I don't make the rules, do I? And Mother pointed to her magazine. *See?* It was *Vogue* that made the rules, not Mother.

Still can't find the light in the closet, but I can sort of see in the dark now. Anyway, I know what I'm looking for. I sense them there. Second shelf from the bottom, third pair from the left. Glowing like a wish. Red satin with pointed, feathery toes. Spiked high heels. They show off Mother's white feet in a red strappy web. *Like lingerie for the feet*, Mother said when she bought them. And I said, *What's lingerie?* And she said, *Never mind.*

Carefully, I reach out my hand and pick them up. Slip them on while sitting on the floor. *How come you never wear these outside?* I asked Mother once.

Because they're not for outside.

There are shoes for only inside?

There are shoes for everything.

What are these for, then?

Never mind, Belle.

But I knew. These shoes were for sex. Knowing that made me as red as the shoes. Thinking of Mother having sex. Mother and Chip. Mother and the Troll. I heard sounds sometimes through the bedroom wall at night, and I wondered if what I was hearing was sex. I didn't know what sex was, not exactly. Apart from what Mother had shown me in a children's book called *What's the Big Secret?* It starred two ugly old people, a cartoon man and a cartoon woman, who were always naked and smiling and holding hands. I hated that book. My secret best friend, Stacey, who is two years older than me because I skipped a year and she was held back a year, says sex is nothing like that dumb book at all.

What's it like, then?

I can't say, Stacey says like she has secrets. Stacey's like that with me. I'm only her secret best friend, after all. Stacey wears Black Honey on her lips just like Molly Ringwald in *The Breakfast Club*, and she walks in a cloud of Love's Baby Soft because *innocence is sexier than you think.* If anyone knew that we actually hung out, that would be very bad for Stacey, Stacey says. *Socially.* In terms of boys, Stacey's had what she calls *experiences.* The only experience I've ever had was in a dream of Stacey's. She once told me she dreamed that I slow danced with Gabriel Gardner to the song "Don't Dream It's Over" by Crowded House, and then he Frenched me right on the dance floor full of fog. *"Frenched" means he kissed you with tongue*, she said. I almost died from happiness when Stacey told me this. I've since asked her to tell me this dream again and again—what was I wearing, what was Gabriel Gardner wearing, how did he look just before he Frenched me, in what part of the song did we French?—but Stacey always says she doesn't feel like it right now. The last time I asked her was when she slept over, and Stacey said she was too tired, then closed her eyes. I looked at her closed eyes through her feathery blond bangs. All I could think was that dream of me was in there somewhere. Floating around inside her skull like one of those jellyfish I once saw at the aquarium. Slippery. Fragile. Mine.

Mother's heels are very high, so when I try to stand up, I nearly fall down. But I grip the closet doorknob just in time. It makes a groaning noise.

"Ça va?" Grand-Maman calls.

"Oui." Quickly I teeter to Mother's vanity. Spritz the violets-and-smoke perfume from the bottle shaped like a jagged star. Does Mother have another red lipstick? She took the best red with her, but there's a lesser red right here in her drawer. In a blue-and-gold scratched-up case shaped like a hexagon. *Rouge*, it's called. By someone named *Dior.* I coat my lips without looking, I don't want to look until I'm done.

In Mother's vanity mirror, I can see only the top half of myself, and I can't see the shoes. She used to have a full-length mirror on the back of the bedroom door, but she took it down. The door still has the shape of the mirror though. I can see the holes where Mother nailed it there. I always thought that mirror must be magic because Mother couldn't stop staring into it. I'd call her name again and again, *Mother, Mother,*

Mom!, and she'd keep looking in the glass like she was in a fairy-tale trance, like it was telling her something.

Where is that mirror now? I look all around her bedroom. Nowhere.

"Belle? Are you sure you're okay?" Grand-Maman asks from the living room.

"Fine."

I teeter back into the closet, ready to take off the shoes. And then I see the mirror. Leaning against the closet's back wall. Turned to the wall like it's mad at Mother. Or maybe Mother turned it away because she was mad at the mirror, like when she makes me stand in a corner. I turn it around, quiet as I can. Heavy. There's a crack right down the middle. Mother must have broken it once. It's dusty and smeared, too. But at least I'll be able see all of myself in it. As I wipe the mirror with my hand, I suddenly fill with hope. Maybe with her red shoes, and her lipstick, maybe in Mother's mirror, I'll see something else. Someone else. Not this face or this body. Not this skin I wish I could slip out of like a suit. Someone who makes me not want to look away. *Who?* I wonder.

But when I look in the mirror, what I see is what I always see. My bulbous body. My monster face. *Beautiful*, Mother says, but I know by now she's lying. I can read Mother, too. Every page. My gold Egyptian bracelet—*a gift from your father*—glows on my hairy wrist. There's an eye in it that's always staring. The Eye of Horus, Mother explained when she gave it to me. *An Egyptian god from mythology. You love mythology*, Mother insisted.

What's mythology?

Old stories. Like your fairy tales.

I looked at the strange, painted eye. It looked nothing at all like fairy tales to me.

Think of it as Father's eye, Mother said. *Watching over you.* She never lets me take it off. I slide it off my wrist now. Let it clatter to the ground. Right away, I feel lighter. I close my eyes. A land far away. A castle by the sea. That's the story Mother tells me each night. About the beautiful maiden. I smile because I can see her. When I close my eyes like this, I am her. Wandering the castle with my glowing skin and my hair like an S.

I open my eyes. What I see in Mother's mirror isn't me anymore. The crack down the middle is gone. The glass is shining. And there's a shape. A dark shape shimmering in the mirror. Waving like smoke. Suddenly, I'm excited. Frozen as I watch the smoke gather into something.

Not something.

Someone.

A man.

An actual man in the mirror. He's blurred around the edges, like a pond rippling after you throw a pebble in. But I see him there. He's beautiful. Dark, waving hair. Eyes of bright blue-green. He looks like he's from the movies. He looks like a fairy-tale prince.

"Are you a prince?" I whisper.

He smiles with his red lips. "Am I a prince?" he whispers back. Looking at me from the other side of the rippling glass. Intensely. So intensely, I shiver. His voice is playful, though. *You know me*, his voice says. *Don't you?*

I nod. *Yes.* His voice, his face. I know them.

"The movies," I whisper. "You're from the movies."

And just like that, he's not blurry anymore. He comes into vivid focus. His smile shows teeth. Long and white, slightly crooked. *Yes. That's exactly right.*

My heart hammers. The movie. Seeing it in the theater with Mother, then again secretly with Stacey. He's not wearing aviator glasses or a pilot's uniform, but otherwise it looks just like him. It *is* him. I know it like I know my own hammering heart; it hammered just like this in the dark theater. My breath catches.

"Oh my god," I whisper into the glass, "is it really you?"

"It's really me," Tom Cruise whispers. Tom Cruise. Standing in Mother's mirror. Tom Cruise, in the flesh. Right there on the other side of the glass, his smile white and blinding. Looking just like the movie except for his clothes, which are all black. Like the picture I tore from *Sky* magazine while Mother was getting her hair done into an S. I don't know why I did that, just looked into his sky-colored eyes and ripped. Quietly, carefully, so Mother wouldn't hear or see. Folded it three times, then tucked it deep into my dress pocket where it is still. Tom's smiling at me. His lips are a little redder than I remember. But he sounds just like Tom Cruise sounds. Smiles just like Tom Cruise smiles. Suddenly, I feel very hot in the face.

"What are you doing here? What are you doing in Mother's mirror?"

Tom keeps smiling with his long white teeth. One is longer than all the others, like a fang on one side. His eyes say some things are secrets, right? Best kept that way. Something inside of me catches fire. My skin goose bumps right down to my feet. I know why he's here. I know before he even says the words: "I'm here to see you, Belle."

Me. Tom Cruise is here to see me. Of course he is, though part of me thinks, *It can't be*. I notice he's holding a red rose pointy with thorns.

"Aren't you supposed to be in Hollywood?"

When I say *Hollywood*, I think of Mother, even though she's the last person I want in my head right now. Hollywood's where she wants to go eventually. Because how is she ever going to be the star she's meant to be in Montreal, *for fuck's sake*? Doing theater? A commercial here, a film there? She's tired of being a big fish in a small pond, making peanuts in Ladies Apparel. *Someday we'll get there, Sunshine*, she whispers to me at night, gripping my hand in the dark like it's my dream, not hers.

Tom Cruise shakes his head. He's still smiling at me. "I had to see you," he says.

"You did?"

"Definitely."

The rose glows in his hands. The rose, I know, is for me. My heart flutters, brightens. We're swaying to this music that's suddenly playing.

That song I love from the movie, the one about breaths being taken away. Tom takes a step closer to the glass that separates us. He looks serious now. His jaw tightens, just like it does in the movie when he feels the need for speed.

"Can I come in?" he whispers. Tom is asking like the mirror is a door I can open. Will I open the door for him?

"Yes," I hear myself say. "Please."

And then? Tom Cruise walks through Mother's mirror. The mirror is like jelly. As Tom walks through, it makes a sucking sound that reminds me of squids. And then he's here. In Mother's closet with me. Standing on the same floor I'm standing on in Mother's very high-heeled red shoes. So high that Tom's eyes are only a little above my eyes. His face is inches from my face. And everything seems to happen in slow motion then. Like a movie. A movie I'm inside of. He smells like the ocean, like the sky over the ocean, the breeze the water brings. My body is swimmy. I can't breathe because Tom's taking my breath away. He's smiling at me just like he smiles at that blond woman in the movie, like Chip smiled at Mother just now. I'm fire. I know no words but his name. There are no eyes but Tom Cruise's eyes, which aren't blue-green anymore. They're red. Red and shining like the shoes on my feet, like the rose in his hands.

What's wrong with your eyes? I want to ask Tom. But I don't want to be rude. And maybe very close-up like this, Tom's eyes were always red and I just didn't notice before. But wouldn't I have noticed before?

"Here," Tom says, handing me the rose. "For you."

"Thank you." No one's ever given me anything like this. I can't wait to tell Stacey—

"Don't tell anyone," Tom says, knowing my thoughts. Knowing my heart. He looks very intense.

"I won't," I whisper. And though I'm sad about Stacey, I love that Tom doesn't want me to tell. That it's a secret.

"Our secret," Tom says. "From Mother, too."

"Mother, too?"

He nods. Takes a step closer to me. He cups his hands around my face. Tom Cruise does. His hands feel slightly sticking and cold. I shiver at his touch. "You know about secrets, don't you, Belle?"

"Yes," I tell Tom.

He smiles. "Good." Even with his red eyes, he's the most beautiful thing I've ever seen. More beautiful than any of my dumb dolls. More beautiful than any prince or Snow White. Way more beautiful than Gabriel Gardner or even Val Kilmer, the actor from the movie where I first saw Tom Cruise. *Iceman*, Stacey sighed in the theater, and now her bedroom wall's plastered with his cold, smirking face. I thought, *How is it possible to see Iceman when there's Maverick?* I didn't say anything though. *Iceman*, I agreed, but I thought no, never in a million years. Tom's skin gleams like glass. He has red lips like he's wearing Mother's Russet Moon lipstick or like he's been eating cherries. He wants to dance with me. *With you, Belle.* Like Mother, he calls me Belle too. He bows a little, like he's from a fairy-tale world. He holds out his glossy hand and I take it. It feels just like a hand would feel except lighter, colder. More jellylike.

"Take My Breath Away" is playing all around us in Mother's dark closet. Tom and I are dancing. I've never slow danced with a boy before, apart from once in Stacey's dream. I watched Stacey do it with Gabriel Gardner at our grade six dance, while I waltzed with Ms. Said. They put their hands on each other's shoulders and rocked like they were on a boat. Their arms were so straight, like zombies. Later, Stacey said it was so hot.

Slow dancing with Tom Cruise is nothing like that. It is incredible. His cold, sticking hands on my shoulders, only a little lower than his thanks to Mother's shoes. His red eyes locked with my eyes. His smile making my skin shiver and burn like it's freezing and on fire at the same time. He's lighting me up on the inside. Like I'm a candle in Grand-Maman's dark church. He tells me he has a castle by the sea.

In a land far away. He doesn't tell me this in words so much. We speak in another language. A language of eyes. Tom's eyes. And his smile full of white teeth, sharp and long.

"I like your shoes," Tom says, just like Tom would. He's very serious about it. "Wow," he whispers, shaking his head at my feet. "They're so pretty."

"Thank you," I whisper. I don't tell him that they're Mother's.

"So pretty," Tom repeats. Not looking at my feet anymore. Looking into my eyes, the color of mud. "Like you."

And when he says this, tears fall. I lower my head so Tom can't see.

"I'm not," I say, shaking my head. I shouldn't be telling him the truth about how I feel. "Mother's the one who's beautiful," I say to the red shoes. "Not me." The words just fall from my mouth like leaves from a tree. There's a game the girls at school play called Honestly. We sit in a circle and take turns closing our eyes. When you close them, you ask the circle, *Am I beautiful?* and people raise their hands if they think *Yes* and don't raise them if they think, *No, sorry.* And someone counts the hands for you, and that's how you know honestly. The last time we played, every girl, when she closed her eyes, sang, *No one is raising their hand, no one is raising their hand*, and we all laughed, though mostly we raised our hands. When it was my turn, I closed my eyes and sang, *No one is raising their hand, no one is raising their hand*, and no one laughed. *How many hands?* I asked when I opened my eyes. *One*, said Valerie, who was our Counter, who Mother said looked like a gopher. She'd had three hands. *Well at least now you know honestly*, Ashley said. She'd had five. I nodded. Now I knew honestly. Ashley looked at me like *sorry*, like maybe she was the one who'd raised her hand. But I knew who it was because I'd peeked. Stacey. She'd even glared at everyone like *seriously?* Later, I told Mother about this game and she looked at me for a long time. *I don't want you playing that fucking game ever again*, she said.

Why?

Because it's stupid, that's why. She lit a cigarette. On the TV screen, Grace Kelly was about to change from a beautiful evening dress into an even more beautiful nightgown while Jimmy Stewart sat in his pajamas and watched from his wheelchair. *Go,* Mother said to me, eyes on the screen.

I thought we were watching right now.

I don't want you watching right now.

Where do I go?

She shook her head at the screen. *I don't know. Run. Climb a tree or something, okay? Climb a rock. Be a kid.*

So I went outside and sat on a rock until it was dark. Until I heard Mother's voice calling me. Sounding soft now. She looked beautiful in the doorway watching me walk toward her. If she closed her eyes in any circle, I know everyone in the circle would raise their hands.

Now Tom lifts my chin so my eyes look right into his eyes, blue-green again. Tom's face is inches from mine. Still serious, a little angry, maybe. Glowing like he's lit by his own personal sun. So beautiful, I can't breathe. "Forget about Mother," he hisses.

"Forget about Mother?"

"Her Beauty's a lie, a trick. Not like yours." And he smiles like I'm sweet. When Tom says the word *Beauty*, it sounds like he's uttering its name.

"Mother is the moon to your sun," he says.

And then in Tom's eyes, I see the sky and the sea all at once. Creatures gliding in deep, dark water. Above the waves, the bluest sky going up and up into black space. Eclipsed suns and a Milky Way of stars. I'm shivering and shivering from his touch.

"The moon is pretty," I whisper, lost in the universe of Tom's eyes.

"The moon is nothing," Tom snaps. For a moment he looks angry. The universe goes red. Then he smiles again. "Without the sun, what's the moon? Just a rock in the outer dark. Its illumination just a trick. Just a trick from the sun's light, which it steals. And that's what Beauty is too."

"It is?"

"Definitely," Tom says. He seems so sure. A smoke surrounds us like fog, like it does sometimes in movie scenes when people dance.

"Beauty," Tom says through the smoke, "is a mystery, Belle. A spell. Some have it for real like the sun." He smiles at me. "Or like this rose right here." He takes the rose and tucks it behind my ear. "And you can have it for a while. You can bloom and bloom. But Beauty also disappears. Just like that. Here one day, then poof. Gone. Smoke and mirrors."

"Where does it go when it goes?"

"Where we all go in the end."

"Where's that?" I ask, afraid. Thinking of my father. I remember almost nothing about him. Just a lullaby he sang to me once about a goose and a duck. Mother says he's in heaven now, he's all the stars I see, and if I look up, I'll see him there in the twinkling lights, looking down on me. Waving. Now I feel bad about taking off the bracelet with Father's eye.

Tom just smiles at me like I'm sweet again. Where we go isn't up there with the stars, his face says. *Trust me.* I don't want to know where we go.

"When Beauty goes, it fucks with people, Belle."

"Fucks with them," I say, mesmerized by Tom saying the word *fuck*. My own mouth saying a word Mother once smacked out of it.

Tom nods slowly. He leans into me close. "They'll do anything to get it back. Even stealing Beauty that doesn't belong to them."

"Really?" I whisper. "They do that?" I think of Mother's mean face.

"Oh yes. It happens all the time," he says softly. He fingers the rose in my hair.

I flush. Lower my eyes to Mother's shoes. "That's so bad."

"It's the worst," Tom says, sighing like he knows. His breath like a breeze on my neck. I'm sure he knows all about this. People must try to steal Tom Cruise's Beauty all the time.

"But you know what you have to do, of course," he says. "When they steal it."

"Take it back," we say at the same time. And then I smile.

"How?"

And now Tom smiles too. Tom's smile. My body is jelly. Cold hands on my face making me shiver even as I burn. The smell of him like oceans and sky and something else, something that makes me think of creatures gliding in deep water. "Magic."

Suddenly, his expression darkens. Like the sun on his face went behind a cloud. His smile disappears. "I have to go."

"No! Wait. Take me back with you, Tom Cruise," I whisper. "Please."

There's a flash of anger in his eyes. Then he sighs. Strokes the side of my face with his cold, sticking hand. Not like Mother does. Not like I'm some pet. Like I'm his lover. I don't know what a lover is exactly, but somehow I know that's what I am to Tom Cruise.

"My name's not Tom," he says. "It's Seth."

"Seth?" *But you're Tom Cruise, I know you are.* He looks exactly like the Tom I saw in the movie except for the red in his eyes sometimes. But Tom's face says he's just told me his name. And that it's a secret. Like the rose. Like this dance. Like the fact that I'm his lover. And I can keep secrets, right?

Don't fucking tell anyone, Stacey said when we first started hanging out. Just after the Honestly game. I went up to her in the schoolyard the next day while she was with the grade seven girls. *You raised your hand for me*, I said, and all the girls smiled sideways and Stacey told me to fuck off. Later, though, she came up to me. *Hey*, she whispered. *They're just being little cunts, the girls in your grade.* That's what she called them, *the girls in your grade*, though technically it was her grade too. *Come over sometime*, she said. *Maybe we can rate each other or something. Okay*, I whispered. I had no idea what she was talking about. And that's how it started. After school we'd go to her house, which it turned out was only a block from my apartment. It felt like a different world with its huge rose garden and its many floors. She'd lead me through the bright red flower beds spiky with thorns, and then through the back door, down to her basement. There she'd change into a black bodysuit and lower the lights. Tell me to sit on the plaid couch covered in the hairs of her many golden dogs. Then she'd turn on *Flashdance* and dance it for me until she collapsed. My job was to rate her ability to be Jennifer Beals on a scale from 1 to 10. At first I gave her all 10s, but then I learned to give her an 8.7 or a 9.2 sometimes so she'd trust me. So she'd know I was really honestly watching each time. *Don't fucking tell anyone we do this*, Stacey said. *It's secret.*

Like being best friends, I said. I said it like a question. Stacey didn't answer. Closed her eyes like she was tired and it was time for me to go home.

I look at Tom smiling at me with his red lips. Tom who just told me his name is Seth.

"Yes," I whisper. "Yes, yes, just take me with you, Seth, please. Away from here," I say. I'm shaking my head. I'm in tears.

He brushes them away tenderly with his cold, cold hand. "I'll take you, Belle," he whispers. "I will. *Definitely.*"

When he says this, I shiver. Fresh goose bumps on my skin. He feels them under his fingers and laughs. Cups my cheeks in his hands. I look at his face shining like glass. I can see a shimmer of myself in his red eyes. Not at all like the girl I am. Beautiful. My true face in his eyes like universes, like mirrors.

"When?" I whisper back. "When will you?"

"When the time is right. You'll know. I'll give you a sign, how's that?"

"What's the sign?"

But he's already slipping away from me. Smoke all around us now.

"Belle?" calls a voice. I hear footsteps in the distance.

"What's the sign?" I shout to Tom/Seth, slipping away into the smoke.

The door bursts open. I lose my balance in the shoes and fall to Mother's floor. I smell violets and smoke. And there's Mother in the closet doorway.

"Belle!" she hisses. Lips a tight line. Eyes flashing with anger. She's looking at me sitting in a heap on the floor. Her red sex shoes slipping off my feet.

"What the hell are you doing in here?"

"Nothing."

She raises an eyebrow. "What did I say about coming in here?"

I'm silent.

"*What*. Did I *just* fucking say about coming in here?"

I stare at the floor. My whole body ringing with the anger in Mother's voice.

"Tell me what I *SAID*!"

"Not to," I whisper to the floor. I see the gold bracelet lying there. Father's lidless eye staring up.

"And did you listen?"

I shake my head. Tears fall. Drip, drip onto her blue carpet. The bracelet is a glowing, blurry circle by my feet.

"Who were you talking to in here?"

"No one."

"I heard you talking to someone."

"I was playing."

"Why is this mirror turned around?"

"I just wanted to see myself."

She looks at the mirror, then at me. She reaches down and picks up the gold bracelet. *Your father's bracelet. On the floor.*

"It fell off," I whisper.

Mother's shaking her head. "You're not to come in here again, do you understand me? Ever." I hear a rustle and look up. Chip now behind her in the doorway, grinning at me over her pale shoulder. He loves this. That I'm finally getting what's coming to me. Feeling Chip behind her, Mother's face softens, remembers itself. Puddles back into its usual Beauty. She pats her S hair, disarrayed by her shouting, into place. *"Well?"*

Her Beauty is a lie. A trick. I nod.

"Good. I'm glad we understand each other."

She turns away from me and grabs her white hat from the bed. That's why she's back. Can't forget the hat that keeps out the sun. That will keep her from ever being tan like me. That will keep her Beauty a lie. From the doorway she looks at me, her hat in her hand.

"Go wash your face and then go to your room and stay there. Until I come back."

She looks at Chip, shaking her head—what is she going to do with me?—and slams the door. I hear the sound of laughter in the hall. The click of their footsteps fading. And I'm alone in Mother's blue bedroom. Staring at the floor-length mirror in the closet. No more crack. No more dust. The crack's sealed up and the glass gleams. Empty now. Tom's not in it anymore, though the ocean animal smell is still all around. Just my reflection. Same old face slashed with Mother's lesser red. Except I look a little flushed, like I've been running or something. My heart's pounding in my chest. My heart is full. With what?

A new secret. *Our secret*, Tom said.

Seth.

I close my eyes, the better to savor it.

Part III

14

Bright afternoon seeping in through a crack in the red velvet curtains. Slept long. Slept deep. Now the sound of birds and waves outside. *What a sky that is,* I think as I lie here. I'm in a bedroom. Whose bedroom? Oh yes, that's right: Mother's. Mother's dead and I'm here in California, wrapping things up. That's why there are palm trees outside the window. Look at them waving in the blue breeze, almost like hands waving. I wave back a little. *Hi.* That's why there are wave sounds too. Mother lives by the ocean, remember?

Lived. Right.

There's another sound I hear along with the waves. Vibratory and celestial, like chimes or the endless gong of some great sacred bell. Sort of like there's spa music playing somewhere, funny. Nearly brings a tear to my eye, though it's quite pretty. I could lie here listening to it all day, actually, just that there are things to do. What things? Funny, can't remember just now. When I try to think, there's a kind of mist over my thoughts. I can smell it, if that makes sense. Like eucalyptus almost or sage surrounding me, burning. It's pleasant like a perfumed fog. All I see in my mind is a tall black vase of pretty red roses. White, red-nailed hands arranging the stems. Huh. Maybe if I shower or something it'll all clear and the things I have to do will come back to me. That sounds really nice.

But I hear voices out there now, beyond my bedroom, over the chimes and the waves. A man's voice and another man's voice. Both familiar. Both distressed-sounding. Rising in pitch like the gulls outside. Who's out there? Better go see. I grab a robe from the back of the door, white silk with black roses, very pretty. It gives off a violets-and-smoke scent, also pretty.

Just as I'm putting on the robe, I remember last night. Went somewhere, where did I go? Oh yes. The house on the cliff for my free treatment, that was nice. Very nice of Rouge to offer me that. I remember the red waiting room and the white faces in the walls and the glowing woman staring at her many mirror selves in the dark. I remember the lovely sound of chimes, like the chimes I'm hearing still. I remember a cold white paste being lathered onto my face, a marine algae mask, maybe. Pretty conventional stuff in the end, for all the baroque trappings. Probably drank too much of that red champagne, because I'm drawing a bit of a blank after that. *You might find you have a few blanks after this*, didn't someone say that? I recall a hand leading me down a dark, endless hall. I held the hand like I was blind. *You might find you're in a bit of a fog. But you'll see the results in the mirror quite clearly. Letting go is so worth it.*

What did I let go of? I wondered. But all I said was *Oh good. I hope so.*

Can't expect miracles, of course. Know better by now. But maybe I'll have a bit more of a glow today. That would be a very nice surprise. I take a quick look up in Mother's ceiling mirror before I go out the door to meet those voices, getting louder now.

Oh, look at that. Yes. I do seem to be glowing a little today. How nice.

Two men are in the living room, so my ears were right. One is wearing a linen suit and holding a briefcase; the other is shirtless and holding some sort of squeegee. Briefcase man looks a little like a goblin. The shirtless squeegee one looks like a merman, except instead of a fish tail, jeans. He's very pretty. It's a little funny to see the two of them talking. Such an odd couple. Who are they? I know them, I know I know them, but it's taking my brain a second to give me their names. While I wait, I watch a pretty white cat do figure eights around their legs as they talk to each other in low voices. Now they both turn to look at me. The looks on their faces are very strange.

I smile. "Hello, good morning," I say, because my brain still hasn't given me their names. "I was about to shower but then I heard your voices over the chimes and the waves."

They both just keep staring at me like they've seen . . . someone dead. *Boo*, I want to say. The pretty man with the squeegee looks stunned, why stunned? Just a bit of a glow. He grips the squeegee like a gun pointed right at me. I laugh to put him at ease. "Don't shoot," I say, but he doesn't laugh with me. Maybe he's an idiot or something. I turn to the goblin man. He might be more reasonable since he has a briefcase. But he looks just as shocked as the pretty squeegee man. His shock isn't so pretty because of his goblin face.

And then I remember. Of course. Mother's lawyer. This goblin man is Mother's lawyer.

"You're Mother's lawyer. Tell me, is there something wrong?"

That seems to snap him out of it, though he's still looking at me funny. "Belle," the goblin man says, like he's confused, like my name is a question. "Sorry to barge in like this . . . I came by because I've just received a notification from your mother's bank."

"Mother's bank." Huh. The roses in my mind flash redly in their vase. "What about Mother's bank?"

"Well, I was hoping you'd tell me," the goblin man says, trying to smile. Sweating a bit.

"Tell you?" *Tell you what?* I hear a faint swelling of those chimes. The mist over my thoughts grows thick. "I think you better tell me first."

"Well." And the goblin man clears his throat. He looks very pale. "It looks like all her debts—"

Beside me on the wall, one of Mother's many mirrors shines and I can't help but look into it. I'm a little nervous to look, I have to say. The way both these men are gaping at me, you'd think I have tentacles growing out of my face or something, haha. But when I turn to the mirror, I'm pleasantly surprised. Very pleasantly. My, my. Look at that.

"Belle, did you hear me?"

"What was that?" I'm still looking at my reflection, my face, which looks really very—

"I said, it looks like all of your mother's debts have been paid off."

"Paid off?"

"Yes. She's totally cleared."

"Cleared," I say to my glowing face in the glass. Looking into my own shining eyes. "Unbelievable. Well, that's wonderful, isn't it? A very pleasant surprise."

"It is. But—"

"What? Cleared is a good thing, isn't it?"

A very good thing, my mirror eyes say. Now I look at the goblin man in the glass, though it's hard. Very hard to look away from my own reflection just now, which is smiling at me like of course cleared is a good thing. The best thing. The happiest turn of events. He's still staring at my face with that strange, scared expression. Why scared? Shouldn't I be the scared one? Doesn't he look even more goblin-like in the mirror?

"Of course," he says. "I was just very surprised. I was under the impression . . . I was under another impression . . . about your finances."

"Another impression." I stare at his face in the mirror. Definitely he looks more like a goblin there. And his mouth movements don't quite sync up with his words. Sort of like there's a lag, if that makes sense, how funny. Maybe I'm still a bit out of it from last night. Or maybe there's a glitch in the glass. My eyes or the glass? Can't be my eyes, because I can see myself so incredibly clearly. And what I see. What I see is so—

"So *you* cleared her debts, then?" goblin man asks.

And the answer that comes to me right away is *Yes. Definitely. I cleared them.* In the glass, I feel my reflection nodding. *Definitely, we cleared them.* I'm nodding with her, of course. Nodding at both men because they're looking at me like they can't believe my face, let alone my words. "Definitely I cleared them. If not me, then who, right?"

"You really did?" the pretty squeegee man asks me softly. He looks incredulous. "When did you do that, Belle?" He knows my name, so I really must know his.

"Who is this man?" the goblin says, pointing at squeegee man, who's still staring at me like he's enchanted, a little afraid. Mouth open. Eyes wide. Really very like a merman if he weren't wearing jean shorts. What is he doing out of the sea? Nothing to be scared of, Tad. *Tad,* that's right.

"That's Tad, of course," I say, like I knew all along. "He's Mother's boyfriend. He cleans the windows."

The goblin frowns. "Boyfriend?"

"He does a wonderful job, don't you think? Each day he washes the dust and the spray and the grime that collects over the course of the day before. Washes it all away—right, Tad?"

"Yes," he says quietly.

"So that everything is always wonderfully clear. So that it doesn't even look like there's glass there. Nothing at all between you and the sea." I smile at Tad in the mirror. "Which creates such a pretty effect. But also a little scary. Maybe that's why you look a little scared."

He's still staring at me like he's in a trance.

The goblin's still frowning. "Belle, about the debt. Can I ask where you got the money?"

"The money?" In the glass, I can still feel my reflection smiling, though she's getting a bit annoyed with these questions now. So am I. "I found a chest of black pearls," I tell them. *Yes,* I can feel her thinking. Funny that I can feel her thinking.

The goblin and Tad exchange looks. "A chest of black pearls. Where?"

"In the lagoon," I say, staring at my face in the glass. Shining and nodding. *Definitely.* It's a little joke, of course. A pretty way to say, *Stop asking me ugly money questions on this lovely morning, please. Because I don't know the answers, sirs. I only know* cleared *is a good thing. I only know this Glow I'm seeing in the glass is really quite something, can you go away so I can look more closely, more freely at this Brightness?* Like someone turned a light on inside me. Right beneath my skin. No wonder I'm smiling like that. Haven't smiled like that in a long time, I think.

"The lagoon," the goblin says, so suspiciously. "I see. So you're saying you forgot that you had hundreds of thousands of dollars. You forgot that."

"But then I remembered. Which reminds me." And it really does remind me. "I'm late for work."

"*Work?*" they both say.

But I'm really too late to explain. "If you'll excuse me."

"So wait," the goblin says. "Then your plan is to keep the apartment?"

And it's when he says it that I know. Suddenly the floor beneath my feet solidifies. I feel something soft slinking around my ankles. The pretty white cat walking circles around my legs now. Beside me in the glass, I feel my reflection nodding and nodding.

"You are?" Tad says.

Of course you are, she mouths.

"Of course I am. I'll have to fix it up. Tad's going to help me with that, aren't you, Tad? Sell some of these things. Get a very nice price."

"I thought you said you didn't want to sell her things, Belle," Tad says. "I thought you said you had an emotional attachment, remember?" He's pointing to some sort of black chest on the floor. I look at it and feel nothing. Just an old box of wood. Taking up space.

"Not attached at all," I say, a smile in my voice. "We can't form silly attachments like that." And my reflection's shaking her head as if to say, *No, no. Can't do that.* "Have to cut things out. Cut things off. When they do us no good. Letting go is so worth it, n'est-ce pas?"

He's just looking at me.

"Are you all right, Tad? You look like you've seen . . . someone dead."

"Just surprised," he murmurs. "By the change in your . . ." He trails off, staring at my face. "Feelings," he says at last.

"Belle, can I talk to you for a second?" This from the goblin, trying to look fatherly. It's hard with his evil sprite face. He pulls me away into a corner of the living room, a pretty room now that I really look at it. "Are you all right?" the goblin whispers. Perhaps he doesn't want to be overheard by the merman. "You seem a little . . . off."

"Off?" Over his shoulder, in another one of Mother's mirrors, my reflection smiles at me. A smile that warms my heart. "Not off at all. Roses."

"*Roses?*" he repeats, staring at me. Like he's not so sure about that. About my smile in the morning light. He's looking for cracks. "Maybe you should talk to someone," he says.

In the mirror, I see my reflection is laughing at him now. I laugh with her. It *is* funny. *Talk to someone.* "I am talking to someone. I'm talking to you right now, aren't I?"

"Yes," the goblin says softly. This is true. He can't deny it. He's staring so deeply into my face, like he's lost in some kind of dream.

"And I wish I could talk more," I lie. "But I really am late for work, I'm afraid."

"Where do you work, Belle?"

But the answer to that isn't one I have just now. Not in my head or on my tongue. Just roses beaming in the thickening mist. Just the lovely sound of those chimes from the Treatment Room, I can still hear them vibrating all around. Just my bright reflection smiling at me in the glass.

It's then that I notice it. Just beyond the goblin's hunched shoulder. The many mirrors in the living room. All of them sealed back up. All of them uncracked and shining now. All of them reflecting me back to myself. All of these selves smiling. All of them glowing. Well, more than a glow, really.

Way more than just a little glow, isn't it?

15

Outside, the chime sounds are still playing somewhere, seeming to follow me. The light from the sun stings my eyes. Had to put on Mother's black hat with the widest brim, her sunglasses with the frames big as a bug's eyes. I'm walking on the shadow side of the street. The *shady* side, I mean. Sometimes the words I think aren't quite the words I mean. Maybe just part of the fog I'm in this morning. When it comes to the words I mean, there might be a lag or a blank. Sometimes the blank stays blank no matter how long I wait for it to fill up with something. Like when I said goodbye to the goblin man just now. He had another name besides Goblin, I knew that, and I waited for it to come back to me so I could say goodbye in a nicer way. But when I looked at his face, the only word in my head and on my tongue was *goblin*. My reflection was even mouthing it beside me in one of Mother's many mirrors. I could feel myself in the glass going, *Goblin, goblin, goblin*. So in the end, I just said, *Farewell*. I said it in French, which was funny. *Adieu*, meaning "to god." Curtsied as I closed the door, to make it look like I meant to say it that way, to make it pretty. *Pretty* is a word that's always there for me in the fog. And the French for it, which is my own name, Belle. That's lucky.

Very *belle*, this town. I never really saw that before, or maybe I'm seeing it today in a new way. Palm trees. Curving streets. Shop fronts of glass like an endless maze of mirrors. Better hurry to work, don't dawdle. But I can't seem to stop smiling at her in all the reflected surfaces along the way. Myself, I mean. When I say *her*, I mean myself. In the shop glass, I'm not wearing the hat and sunglasses, funny. Don't seem to need them on the other side, I guess. I guess that makes a sort of sense. I look good, don't I? More than good. Glowing, lifted, eradicated. *Eradicated* is the word that comes most strongly to my mind, but it can't be the word I mean. Doesn't *eradicate* mean "destroy"? My face looks the opposite of destroyed. Well, but somehow it fits. Fits like the dress I'm wearing today, Mother's dress, which I'd never seen before. It was tucked deep in her closet, buried among the black and white silks like a hot little secret, like it was just waiting for my hand to find it on the rack. When I saw it, I hesitated, but then I thought, *Why not put it on?* She won't be wearing it anymore. And a funny thing happened then: in the closet mirror, I saw I was already putting on the dress. I was putting it on in the glass while my actual hand was still on the hanger, hesitating. I watched for a while and I thought how funny to see me getting a little ahead of myself like that. In the glass. Can that be right? Can we sometimes see ourselves just slightly ahead of ourselves? I thought of how I saw the goblin's mouth in the mirror earlier, not quite syncing up with his words. How I saw my reflection smiling and nodding before I was actually smiling and nodding, laughing before I thought to laugh. Even mouthing my thoughts. So maybe it happens sometimes, a lapse or a kind of jump ahead, a glitch in the glass. Maybe I just forgot how mirrors worked because of this morning's fog. It looked very pretty on me in the mirror, anyway. Mother's dress. In fact, when I saw my reflection slipping her arms into the armholes, I quickly slipped into them too, catching up with myself so that we smiled and zipped up at the exact same time. A red dress, which is nice. Goes with the red shoes, which we're wearing too. I do love red.

But I'm dawdling again. Got to get to work. My reflection in the shopwindows is actually jogging slightly ahead of me, I see, her heels clicking a beat faster than my heels, like she knows I'm late. *Wait*, I nearly say to myself. *I'm coming.* Which is a very funny thing to want to say to oneself. Surely I'm just not seeing things right. My phone buzzes. Heart jumps. A name and number I recognize, but not off the bat. Persephone. Goddess of the underworld. Why is she calling me?

"Hello?" I answer, a little nervous.

"Mirabelle, how *are* you?" Her voice sounds falsely mournful. And familiar. We seem to know each other, Persephone and I, but in what capacity?

"Been trying to get ahold of you for a while," she says. Her voice insinuates power. Like it has some sort of dominion over my soul. In the shopwindows, I see I'm still clicking just a little ahead in my red shoes. I haven't even answered the phone.

"Yes, well I've been busy. You know how it is."

"Of course," Persephone says. "I can only imagine. Well hopefully you're at least getting some sun while you're there?"

In the glass, I seem to be smiling right up into the sunlight, like it's telling me a very pretty secret. Funny because I'm actually in the shade, shivering. "Some," I say.

"Well listen, Mira, I just wanted to check in. First to see how you are, of course, and then also to confirm when you were coming back?"

"Coming back?"

"To *work*," she says. Her voice is starting to sound tense, frustrated. The glove of power tightening on the hand. My boss. That's why she sounds like she has a claim on me. "We're expecting you at the shop tomorrow. For the afternoon shift."

"Oh, well there must be some mistake. I'm actually coming in now."

"You are?" I can feel Persephone raising her eyebrows on the other end of the line. I've shocked her.

"I should be there in the next few minutes. So it's funny you called."

"Few *minutes*? Well. That's wonderful. We weren't expecting *that*, but that's wonderful. I didn't realize you were already back home?"

"Home." I look around me. Blue sky. Palm trees. Street that curves like a seashell, all the shop glass windows reflecting back my glowing self to infinity. I see I'm walking quite far ahead now. Quite far ahead of myself. But I can feel the smile on my mirror face. "Yes," I say. "I'm home."

As I approach the shop, I have to smile. I was worried about being late, but we're right on time, look at that. *I'm* right on time, I mean. Even with all the dawdling and that phone call from the under-world. I'm here at Belle of the Ball, where I work. Where I've always worked, right? Worked with Mother until she died recently. A pretty dress shop right in the heart of . . . the area. Can't miss it. Some-thing's different about the shop front though. Things that used to be here, pretty things, aren't here anymore. Drawing a blank on what exactly, but I know they're gone. Where did they go? Does Mother know about this? There I am in the window. Glowing, lifted, *eradi-cated*, which may or may not be the word I mean. I'm smiling in the glass though the window display itself upsets me a little, not going to lie. Who cut off the heads of these mannequins? Why are they wear-ing these sad gray sacks?

In the shop, no one's on the floor. Well, maybe because my shift's starting. I walk behind the counter. Place my hands on the glass jew-elry case. When did the jewelry in here become so . . . not pretty? The first chance I get, I'll have to do something about that. For now, though, I'd better stay here on the floor. Can't leave the register, Mother would hate that. Yet she used to leave all the time. Loves to leave while I'm forced to stay and watch her float around and disappear into the back for god knows how long. *Loved* to leave, I mean. *Be my eyes and ears, Belle,* she'd call over her shoulder. And I was. I am. Her best sales-woman, she always said. My reflection has wandered off, I see. Wan-dering the shop floor just like Mother does. Like Mother *did*, what is it with me and tenses today? I'd call myself back but that seems like too strange a thing to do. Call oneself back. And anyway, maybe it's just this glitch in the glass today. Following me from mirror to mirror like the chimes seem to be following me. They're playing here now. Right here in the shop, right around my ears. It would make me maybe a little nervous if they didn't sound so pretty. My reflection seems to be swaying a little to their music as she wanders away. Smiling, though we're not loving what we see hanging on the racks. With my eyes, I try to follow her from mirror to mirror, Mother installed so many along the shop walls. Where is she going? Where am *I* going, I should say. Do reflections really wander off like this?

"Hello? Are we here?" Someone's snapping their fingers in my face.

My eyes focus. A customer right in front of me. Tight, wet-looking curls that remind me of seaweed in a tide pool. A face that screams she's chosen what Marva calls *the Procedural Approach*. I can't tell if she's angry or frightened or extremely surprised.

"Hello." I smile at her. "How can I be of hell to you? *Help* to you." Funny, these word slips I'm having today.

She looks at me, a little scared maybe. Again, very hard to tell with her face. "You work here?"

I smile like *what a question*. I'm behind the counter, aren't I? But sometimes, in retail, one must state the obvious. "I work here, yes."

She looks at my hands gripping the counter. "I've never seen you here before." In my pocket, my phone buzzes.

"Well, maybe we missed each other. Ships in the night." I look around for my reflection. Nowhere in sight. Where did she—?

"Well maybe you can help me now." She already looks like she doubts it. Doubts me, Mother's best salesperson. I smile like *sure I can, of course*. My mission. My absolute pleasure to try. After all, how many doubtful shoppers just like her have I asphyxiated over the years? *Assisted*. She raises her hand, weighed down with the very strange, sad clothes we seem to sell here.

"I want to try these on."

"Wonderful."

My phone's still buzzing. Persephone. Why Persephone? *I'm right here*, I want to tell her. Would tell her but I'm busy just now. The customer's still standing there as if waiting for something. "*Well?* Would you mind showing me to the fitting rooms, *please*?"

I smile. "I would never mind at all. Follow me."

The fitting rooms. Surely I know where those are. Surely if I walk toward the back, I'll find them there. I'm keeping an eye out for my reflection, too, of course, but it's nowhere to be seen. Where have I wandered off to now? *I, she, it* . . . what do I even call that shape I see in the glass? Never really thought about it until now. Maybe my reflection needs a name, my mirror me. Where is mirror me? Nowhere in the nearby glass. Maybe over—

"Excuse me, do we know where we're *going*?"

"Definitely."

Finally I see mirror me in the far corner. Glowing in a grand oval mirror. Standing there in the glass, beaming brightly, patiently, like she's waiting for me.

"*Finally*," mumbles an annoyed voice beside me. I turn and see that the fitting rooms are actually right beside this mirror. Three chambers, each with its own little locking door. So mirror me led me here. Not always a bad thing to let oneself go, to get ahead of oneself, I guess. *Letting go is so worth it*, didn't someone say that recently?

I'm about to go back to the cash register when the customer says, "You stay here. I could use another pair of eyes."

"Another pair of eyes. Of course. We can be that for you." Why not? Me and my reflection, two other pairs of eyes. She frowns at me though we're smiling at her, waving as she disappears through the door. I turn to look back at my reflection, just to admire the Glow again, when I see someone standing between me and the glass.

"Mirabelle?" she's saying. A little woman. Staring at me. Cropped blond hair. Pearls. A disregard for sunscreen that shows in her rampant lines and moles. Persephone? No, but she does look like a boss. Maybe I have two. Something about her reminds me of a small, yipping dog.

It's snapped at my heels before. I know her. I'd know her crisp white shirt and pearl-wattled throat anywhere, but when I try to recall her name, all I can think is *Yip Yip*.

The little woman looks surprised to see me. More than surprised. Shocked, really. Like she's just seen someone dead. Like Tad did. "Mira, is that really you?"

I look in the mirror. The glass is empty, shining. I'm nowhere to be seen. I look back at the woman and smile. "Who else?"

"What happened to your . . . ?" She brings her hands up to her own face, as if to check that it's still there. "What are you doing here?"

"I'm on my shift, of course," I say, gripping the fitting room door handle.

"Your *shift*? Here?"

Where else? "Yes. I work here."

"You *work* here?" She looks at me confused. "I'm sorry, but I don't understand."

I feel my phone buzzing again. I smile at the woman. "It's very simple."

"But . . . aren't you supposed to be heading back to Montreal?"

"Montreal? I'm not sure where you're getting your . . . information."

"I see. Well maybe you'd like to come with me in the back? And have a little chat?" She's looking at me like I'm a wild animal and behind her back is some sort of tranquilizer gun.

"That's going to be a problem," I say.

"Problem? Why a problem?"

"Well if I go back there with you, I can't be another pair of eyes. For her." And I gesture to the fitting room door. "I promised to be her eyes."

"Esther can take care of that. Can't you, Esther? She's just back from her lunch break now." I see another woman beginning to creep into my peripheral vision. She's holding a container full of some sort of soggy salad. Glasses on a chain around her neck. Bloodless face looking at me blankly. "A little *late* coming back today," the woman says to Esther, her voice slightly scolding.

My phone buzzes and buzzes. I shake my head. "No," I say loudly.

"*No?*" the little woman repeats.

"I'm staying here for now."

She looks at me for a long time. Not just confused, frustrated. And what else is in her face? Some sort of pity, why pity? Why can't I remember her name?

"I know you're in a great deal of pain right now, Mirabelle. About your mother. Is that what this is all about? Coming in here? I know grieving can be such a journey. Perhaps you're working through something."

I stare at her and she stares at me. Sylvia. That's her name. Right there in the tight lips, the parched skin, the cropped blond spikes. My phone continues to buzz loudly. Persephone again. I silence it. Smile at Sylvia.

"I'm definitely working through something, Sylvia. My shift. Now if you'll excuse me, I actually think I hear my customer calling."

"I don't hear anyone calling. Do you, Esther?"

Esther just stares at me.

"Mirabelle, listen—"

"Hello?" from behind the door. "Can you get in here, please?"

"Yes. Of course," I say, looking at Sylvia. Frowning at me now. "I'll be right in."

In the fitting room, I find her standing in the ill-fitting dress without her shoes on, staring at me. Her arms are out slightly as if the dress has arrested her.

"Well mirror, mirror," she says, locking eyes with me in the reflection. "Tell me. Is this worth the absurd amount of money you people are charging for this?"

I look into the full-length mirror. There I am, standing behind the seaweed woman just as I'm really standing behind the seaweed woman. Wearing Mother's red dress. Still glowing, lifted, eradicated. So good to be synced up with myself again finally. I feel such relief seeing myself there in the glass. Smiling as I'm smiling. Ready to be of service, another pair of eyes. Everything nicely aligned in time and space, no more weird glitch. The chimes are still playing, maybe a little more loudly, but they're pretty. I'm Mother's best saleswoman.

"So are you going to tell me or what?"

"Definitely." I smile at her in the glass. And it's the funniest thing: the seaweed woman's suddenly a bit blurry in there. Right when I go to really look in the mirror. I turn to my own glowing reflection. I'm perfectly clear. Sharp even, against the customer's blur. Huh.

"Well?"

"It's not entirely clear."

"Not entirely *clear*?" She lets out a guffaw. "That's a new one."

And then I see in the glass, I'm staring at her coldly. Very coldly. Am I shaking my head? How can that be when here in the actual dressing room, I'm nodding and smiling?

"What does that mean *exactly*?" she presses. Annoyed, but also curious. Deeply wanting the words I'm supposed to give. I always have the perfidious words to give. *Perfect*, I mean of course. I meet my eyes in the mirror. Eyes that are supposed to be the other pair of eyes for this suddenly blurry customer. So bright and entrancing my mirror eyes are. But are they mocking? Surely not. Not when I'm smiling and nodding like this, being so nice and polite. Nodding so hard, my neck hurts, really. And yet mirror me is doing more of a grin. A wicked grin.

"Just tell me, do I look good or not?"

I watch my reflection lean over the woman's blurry shoulder, my mirror eyes still on my eyes. A chill down my back from our cold, mocking stare. My red mirror lips hover by this woman's out-of-focus ear. Lips so very red in the glass, did I even put on lipstick today? I'm mouthing a word right into the black hole of her ear. *No.*

"What was that?" she whispers.

Awful, chants my mouth in the mirror. *Awful, awful, awful*, right into the woman's ear with my very red mirror lips. But on this side of the glass, my own lips are sealed. Literally pressed together as tight as can be. I'm shaking my head. "No," I whisper. *Yes.*

"*No?*"

"I can't say that. I won't say that," I whisper to mirror me in the glass.

"Won't say *what*?" the blurry woman snaps. She grabs me by the shoulders and turns me away from the glass so I'm looking right at her. "*Just tell me what you see!*"

I stare into the woman's face. Not blurry anymore. All too clear. The awful dress. Her awful soul. I hear an ocean roar suddenly all around us. Like crashing waves right here in the dressing room. Does the woman hear it too? No. Her mouth still seems to be saying, *Tell me, tell me.* So I do my best to tell through the roar. Words I can't hear in the wave sounds, though I feel my mouth making their smiling shapes. I only hope they're the perfid—perfect words. The ones I can always give. The ones she's so desperately looking for. The woman just stares at me, her dark eyes going wide. Finally the roar around us quiets. I fall silent. The mirror is empty now. Shining like nothing. Once again, my reflection seems to have slipped away.

The seaweed woman shakes her head at me like I'm monstrous.

"I can't believe," she whispers, "what you just fucking said to me."

Oh god, what words did I give?

"All right in there?" Sylvia says on the other side of the door, knocking. Her voice is smiling, but I hear the panic and rage beneath.

"*Fine,*" the seaweed woman snaps. She slowly turns to me, her dark, wet ringlets trembling before her eyes. I think she's about to hit me. I wait for it, bracing myself. Then she sinks to her knees as if felled. I drop to my knees too, like a good reflection. She looks at me. "Is it really true?"

What did I say? "I should really let Sylvia or Esther help you now," I tell her quietly.

I'm about to rise when she reaches out and grabs my wrist. "Wait."

Desperation in the press of her fingers. I look at her. Still shaking her head at me. Not with anger anymore. With a kind of wonder. A tear drips from her eye. "How did you see all that?"

Maybe I gave her the words she wanted after all.

"It's all here," I say, stroking her cheek softly. And then I recall the Treatment Room last night, the spa woman's hands on my face in the eucalyptus fog. *It's all here*, she said. Stroking my face just like this. Offering me the terrible mirror of her eyes. What I saw there.

"What?" the woman prompts now, bringing me back to the dressing room floor. "What should I do?" I'm on my knees with this stranger who's also on her knees. I'm crushing her cheeks between my hands, giving her a fish mouth. She's gazing hungrily, fearfully, into the mirror of me with bloodshot eyes. I see her soul, shattered like so much glass. Yet the shards are sharp and hungry, whispering *feed, feed*. Looking into her eyes, I feel a flicker of awful recognition. And then it's gone.

"Mirabelle!" Sylvia shrieks, pounding on the door, rattling the handle.

"Boleros," I whisper. "Or a blazer maybe."

The customer stares at me. Her pink gloss is a slash across her face. Her ringlets have gone limp. *"What?"*

"They really finish a look. Especially in spring."

I turn to look in the mirror. My reflection's back, locked in. Blinking when I blink. That's nice to see. But I don't appear to be in the dressing room anymore. Not even at Belle of the Ball. When I look in the glass, I see myself standing at the gates to a house on the cliff. *The* house on the cliff where the red roses grow. The roses are swaying gently around me in an ocean breeze. I can smell them from here. I can hear the waves and I can hear the chimes making a lovely music. I'm smiling at myself with my very red lips. I'm telling myself it's time to go.

16

The darkness is thick as the mist over my thoughts, but in a way that's very pretty. The red shoes lead me right to the house along the winding path, along the cliff's edge. The chimes play all around me, like a music of the spheres I'm hearing, like I'm privy to the vibration in all things. The damp, twitching grass, the shivering palms, the movement of clouds over water—a kind of hum of the world and my own clicking feet part of its pulse. Not sure what happened back there exactly. The woman on her knees in the fitting room. Sylvia rushing in, telling me to go, *just go*. And I did go, even though the woman kept calling after me to come back, *please come back. Tell me more.* Like I was some sort of awful oracle. Like we were an oracle, me and my reflection. Never had word slips like that before. Never had such a glitch. Almost like what's inside and outside are just a little bit scrambled now. I'd be troubled by it, very troubled, if it weren't for the pretty mist over my thoughts, making it already feel so faraway, farther with each step. And the promise of my reflection, being reconnected with her, hurrying me along. Funny to think of reconnecting with your own reflection. What is she doing at the house, I wonder?

When I arrive at the gates, all is dark. I can't see anything beyond the glass walls of the house. Not the great chandelier or the glittering people or the Depths. Only my glowing reflection in the glass walls looking so happy to see me, so very happy we came. I can see her smile from here. I'm smiling too, so happy to see her, so lovely she is. Of course I have questions. Why does she keep wandering away from me? Why are we having these glitches? Why did she lead me back here? I push at the gates, but they're locked. The red roses in the front garden sway behind the black bars, looking alive as ever. Apart from the flowers and my reflection beaming at me, all is still. Empty-looking. Like no one lives here. Odd, I think. Lots of people live here. The woman in red, for example. The young girl in black with the shape-shifting face. I danced with her backward around the tank, her pale eyes burning like twin flames. Those twins in the black veils, stroking my face with their gloved hands. Telling me they knew Mother and they knew me, too, Daughter of Noelle, oh yes. Mother's friends, they all are. My friends too now, right? I'm gripping the black iron bars. Trying to shake the gates, but they can't be shaken. I should be on the other side with my smiling reflection. I should be inside, not outside, shouldn't I? I watch her wave at me and then disappear into the wall of the house.

"Wait!" I call out. "Where are you going? Don't go, please." Later, when all the mirrors right themselves, when this glitch goes away, I'm going to laugh about that. How I called out to myself glowing like a moon in the dark. Told myself not to go, please. *Please stay. Don't leave me here on the other side, gripping the gates.* I'm going to laugh and laugh. Because it really is funny, isn't it? Right now I'm not really laughing at all, though. Right now I feel something else watching her, watching myself walk away like that. Leaving me alone here, the sound of chimes still humming all around.

"Hello?" I call in the dark. A light flashing behind me. I turn around, but there's no one there on the footpath. Just the cormorants perched along the cliff walls like bats. Just the water crashing against the rocks where Mother fell. A red glow on the waves tonight. A phosphorescence on the white foam. And then a voice. I hear it through the roar of water calling my name. *Belle, Belle.*

My heart thuds in my chest. *Mother?*

Belle, says the voice in the water.

And I'm running. Sliding down a steep dirt trail toward the roaring water in my red shoes. They wink at me from the mud while the voice calls, *Belle, Belle.*

I'm coming, Mother, I think. *I can't believe you survived.* I quicken my pace, though I'm afraid.

When I reach the shore, just sharp black rock slick with seaweed. A swelling ocean, hissing spray. The red light on the water is flashing, flashing. *Mother, where are you?*

In here, says the voice in the water. *Closer.*

Now I'm on the tip of the black rock where the shimmering red waves crash. Mother's in there somewhere. I'll have to go into the water and look. Mother will carry me in the red wave, and in the wave, we'll talk. I'll ask her, *Why did you leave me?* I'll tell her a lot of things seem to be leaving me, even myself. *But I'm glowing, just like you did.* Or at least I seem to be when I catch myself in the mirror. Now I close my eyes. Let the wave rise, taking me with it. The cold water shocks my body, freezing the air in my lungs. Her voice is all around me now. *Belle, Belle, Belle.* But there's nothing down here. Just dark water. Do I know how to swim? Surely Mother taught me once. A picture in my mind's eye as I thrash in the waves. A little girl and her mother on a beach long ago. The girl is on the shore and the mother is in the water, waving at her to come in, join, *don't be afraid.* But the little girl is afraid. Doesn't wade into her mother's arms. Doesn't trust, even though Mother's hands say, *It's okay, trust.* The little girl shakes her head from the shore. *Don't feel like it now*, she lies. And Mother drops her extended arms. Giving up. Disappointed. Oh, a coldness then. A shame, too. Drowning in it. I'm drowning now.

I see Mother on the rocky shore. "Mother!" I cry, my mouth filling with water.

She doesn't move. She's watching me drown because I never went out into the waves to meet her long ago.

And then she's gone.

I'm alone and sinking in the black. Is this where Mother went, the black? Is this where the roses are? Is this the way? My lungs fill with cold darkness.

A hand grips my arm.

Pulls me up out of the water.

I'm gasping, lying on the rocks, looking up.

A man framed by a night sky full of stars. He's got a hat on. The brim is dripping water onto my face like cold rain.

"Caught you," he says.

When I open my eyes, I'm no longer by the ocean, on the dark shore. No longer wet, though still cold. I'm dry and in a bed. A hotel room with pink walls. Is it morning or afternoon? Can't tell by the light from the half-drawn curtains. THANK YOU FOR NOT SMOKING says a little sign on the cherrywood nightstand. Someone's watching me lie here. I feel it in the prickling of my skin. The hairs on my neck are standing on end. I see a silhouette in the dark. *Who are you? What am I doing here?*

The silhouette turns on a soft light. The man in the hat from the beach. Sitting and watching me from the desk with his feet up, wearing a white shirt that opens to a white undershirt. Red suspenders. A silk tie around his neck in a loose noose. His hat's not on his head, it's on the desk. His hair is wet, slicked back into a dark wave.

"Good afternoon," he says. So it's afternoon, then.

"You caught me."

He smiles. "And you wet my hat," he says. "It may never dry."

"I'm sorry."

"I have other hats."

I see he's got a glass of Scotch in his hand. Looks luminous, like liquid gold. If I drank that, maybe I'd be warm again. Maybe I'd fill with light. As if he can read my mind, he walks to the edge of the bed and hands me the glass. As I sip, a fire sparks. All the way down to my toes. He stays on the bed's edge, watching me. Face half in shadow. Quite pretty, really. If pretty had a shadow side, it would be this man's sharply cut face. Telling me he can order room service if I'm hungry. I should probably eat something, he says. Fine for now, I tell him. Thank you, sir. *Sir*, I call him, which seems to amuse and disturb him. It amuses me, too, sort of. Because I know him, of course. I saw him at a bar once. I saw him once too through a red fish. And of course, I met him on a bridge only yesterday, though his name's slipped my mind just now. *What's your name, sir? What am I doing in your bed, wearing a man's silk robe the color of midnight?*

"That's mine, by the way," he says of the robe. "You were drenched."

Now I see Mother's red dress hanging over the mirror on the bureau by the open window. *Oh god, did we—?*

"We didn't," he says. "If that's what you're thinking."

"Didn't what?"

"I would never take advantage like that. I'm not a monster. Well, not that kind of monster, anyway. We're all some kind of monster, aren't we, Belle?"

I look at the mirror covered by Mother's red dress, the only mirror in the room. The skirt obscures my reflection, the entire glass covered in a bell of red silk. There's a vase full of red roses on the bureau. Some red jars and vials.

When I look back at the man, he's smiling at me. "That was quite the swim you took."

"I can't swim."

"If you can't swim, why go in the water, Belle?"

"I forgot that I couldn't." It's actually true, I did forget. Though how could I forget? Suddenly I want a cigarette. He gives me the one still burning in his mouth. Bringing it to my lips, I taste his rose lip balm. A whisper of a green tea essence or a cloud jelly he must wear on his face.

"Funny thing to forget," he says, watching me puff on the cigarette, a little longingly. "Seems pretty important to keep that in mind, don't you think?"

But there are roses in my mind, I want to tell him. Freshly cut in a tall black vase. A white, red-nailed hand arranging the stems to best advantage as we speak.

"Been a bit scrambled lately? Forgetting names, faces, places? Mixing past and present?"

How does he know that? "How did you know that?"

"Oh, a wild guess. But it's worth it, right? For the *Glow*," he whispers.

I feel myself flush now under his gaze. "Excuse me?"

"Quite the Glow," he says. He raises his glass as if to toast my face.

"Who are you?"

He feigns looking hurt. "Oh Belle, am I really so forgettable?"

"I remember you walked me to the house last night. For my free treatment."

"Wasn't that nice of me?"

"You were also at the hotel bar the other night. Then I saw you at the house. You had a black beard then." *And you kissed me, didn't you kiss me?*

"I did." He smiles. "And I still have the beard, by the way." He points to his desk, where I see there are a number of mannequin heads lined up, each of them sporting different configurations of wig and eyewear. I see the black beard hanging on a white face. Those strange spectacles. I look back at him and he puts a finger to his lips. "Shhh," he whispers. "It's resting."

I should be afraid, maybe. Ask him why he has all these heads. *Also, why do you seem to be following me, Hud Hudson?* Hud Hudson, that's his improbable name. But by catching me he did save me, remember? Can't forget that. Although maybe he saved me so he can kill me, that's possible. Still, I'm not afraid. He's very pretty, for one. Like an ad for some beguiling perfume, something with leather in it. Something with dark woods. He has a Glow himself, maybe marula oil is responsible or some sort of snail. It's nice to watch, anyway. Also, I don't seem able to speak accusing words just now. Something to do with Mother's dress over the mirror. Feels like it's muffling me in red silk. Without the mirror, I'm not quite oriented, not quite . . . *myself*, if that makes sense. The only mirror in the room is really Hud Hudson's face. How it's staring at me with such . . . what?

"I have to say that Glow is really something, Belle."

"Is it?"

Sitting on the bed in his suit, he really looks like he belongs in Mother's old movies, her fascist magazines. *Fashion*, I mean. The nefarious gentleman gloating after his nefarious night out. God knows what happened among the stylish shadows. Only Hud Hudson.

"Oh yes," he says. "There's a dewiness."

"There is?"

"A luminosity. Some might even say a *Lift*. An eradication of free radicals. We should talk."

"So talk," I whisper.

"You first. How long are you going to keep me waiting?"

"Waiting?"

"The treatment, Belle. I'm slavering for details here." He reaches out and I think he's going to touch my face, but he just takes the cigarette from my lips. Slips it between his. Stares at me, transfixed, waiting. Some dark shame rises up in me like a wave, why shame? I look away from him at the red dress hanging over the mirror, at the roses gleaming redly on the bureau. *Shhhh*, they seem to whisper. *Secret*.

"Nothing to tell."

He raises an eyebrow.

"Really," I say. "It's really just like . . . a facial basically. From a . . . beauty house. Like any other beauty house. The usual severings."

"Severings?"

"Did I say *severings*? *Services*, I meant of course."

Hud Hudson grins at me from his stylish shadows. "Just like a facial, huh?"

I nod. I'm getting sort of hot in the face, the way he's looking at me.

"A facial that makes you forget you can't swim?" he presses.

"I just . . . forgot that I can't swim. Separately."

He's still looking at my face. I feel him taking in the skin. What is he taking in? If the mirror weren't covered, I could see. He takes a deep drag of his cigarette. "Why am I getting . . . the very distinct impression . . . that you're holding out on me here, Belle?"

"Why is that mirror covered with my dress?"

"It's drying under the heating vent. Also, that mirror is hostile. Some mirrors are, as I'm sure you know."

Hostile? He hands me his cigarette again and I take a drag, tasting his roses. Feeling Hud Hudson's eyes watching me through the smoke. He's sitting very close. I'm surrounded by his leather and dark woods. Deep in the stylish shadows.

"Come on, Belle," he whispers. "Don't you want to make me weep with envy?"

I watch the dress rise and fall against the mirror glass in the window breeze. Is my reflection beneath the dress? Is she there in the glass? I can feel her looking at me through Mother's red silk. Shaking her head. Putting a finger to her very red lips. *Don't. No. Secret.*

"Just some steam and apocalypse in the end," I say.

He looks at me. *Apocalypse?*

"Eucalyptus," I correct. Funny how those words slip and slip.

"Interesting. Because I have to tell you, it really doesn't look like *just* a facial to me."

"It doesn't?" *What does it look like?*

He shakes his head. "A little more than marine algae masks going on down there in the Treatment Room, I think. Call me crazy."

"What are you, some sort of detective of beauty?"

He smiles. "Of beauty. You could say that." He's leaning in even closer now. Almost like we're fucking but we're not, obviously. I'm here and he's there, isn't he? If I had the mirror, I could know for sure.

"Why do you want to know so badly?" I ask him.

Something flashes in his eyes then. Some dark emotion. A wound exposed. It's there and then it's gone. He smiles over it. "Because I'm just like you."

"Like me?" There's a word for what I saw there in his eyes, but it's slipped my mind, filled and shining as it is with roses, slipped my tongue muffled by the red silk. "How are you like me?"

He takes my hand and places it on his cheek. Terribly smooth. Tiger grass maybe? An Orpheus flower peptide. A fermented tea elixir or some sort of moon drink. Makes me shiver. Haven't shivered in a long time at the touch of someone else's sin. *Skin*. Even my hand is shivering at the smoothness of Hud Hudson. Or is it shivering at something else?

"I told you," he whispers, his eyes on my eyes. "I'm a fellow freak."

He should move away from me now, he's so close. Too close. But he just stays there. I feel his whiskey breath in my face. I smell all of his skin products—he definitely uses a cloud jelly. Or is it a snow mist? With the late-afternoon light coming through the windows, I notice there's a long, jagged scar across his face.

"Why not just get a treatment yourself, then?" I ask him. "If you're a freak."

He smiles darkly now. "Because I'm not one of the anointed ones, am I, Belle?"

"Anointed ones?"

"They only seem to give them to very special people. Like you. You're very special, did you know that?"

"Me?" In the corner of the room, the red dress waves and the roses gleam. I shake my head no, but Hud Hudson is nodding yes.

"What they call perfect. A Perfect Candidate. The rest of us bottom-feeders have to pay. Too rich for my blood, sadly. I'm a poor peasant, didn't you know?"

I look at him, his clothes and his face literally glowing with money just like this hotel room. Not just money. *Style*, Mother would have said. *Now that's style, Belle*. "You don't look like a peasant to me."

"Well, looks can be deceiving, can't they?"

"They can be," I agree. "When I first saw you through the jellyfish, you had no beard, even though you did."

"Those aren't jellyfish, Belle."

Fear suddenly at the memory of those red pulsing creatures in the dark water. "What are they, then? Some sort of . . . squid?"

He laughs. *Squid.* That's good. "Let's just say you wouldn't encounter them in the ocean. Not part of the usual fauna."

"How do you know?"

"I'm a detective of beauty, remember?" He takes a long sip of the whiskey. Gestures at the red vials of cream on the dresser by the roses. "All backwash. Swill. Useless potions. They save the aqua vitae for the anointed."

"Why am I anointed?"

He glances at my forehead. "You tell me, *Daughter of Noelle.*"

Why is he calling me that? Only my friends at Rouge call me that. "Are you saying it's because of my mother?"

"I don't know. Am I saying that?"

"I know she was a member. She died recently. An accident," I add quickly.

On the mirror, the red dress waves and waves in the breeze.

"Noelle," he says softly, like the name is a tender thing. "That's a beautiful name."

"It is. She was. Very beautiful."

"Grief's funny, isn't it?" He's not laughing at all.

"Yes." I feel an ocean of something welling up inside me, but only a single drop falls from my eye. He's brushing it away, and I'm letting this stranger do that. This stranger who looks like he walked right out of Mother's movies. Right out of her fascist magazines.

"It makes us do funny things, I know." He pauses. "I lost someone myself not too long ago."

"You did?"

"My brother. My twin, actually. Believe it or not, there were two of me once." He tries to smile, but it cracks.

"I'm sorry. What happened?"

"That's a story for another day and a lot more Scotch than we've got in this room." He takes another long sip. Looks at me. "You know, when I saw you on the bridge, you had a birthmark right there." He touches my forehead, gently grazing. "Star-shaped. Very pretty, I thought. Still there, but faded. As if the color's been leached out or something." He looks fascinated. I sense Mother's dress waving at me in the breeze, like it's calling me.

"I should go."

"But your clothes aren't even dry yet."

"So I'll wear them wet."

He reaches out for my wrist. "I'm sorry. I'm pushing too hard, aren't I? You've just nearly drowned and here I am asking you about a treatment. Us detectives—beauty detectives, I mean. We're relentless. I promise I'll shut the hell up for a while if you stay and rest. Then we can talk about this a little more, okay? You waded into some deep, dark water, Belle."

On the bureau, the mirror shimmers and the roses gleam. *Come over here.* I look at Hud Hudson, who's getting far too close. The stylish shadows swallowing me.

"I wonder if you can run down and get me some tea," I say.

"Tea?" He looks at me awhile. "I'll call down for some."

"I'd like it now, please. I'm still quite cold. Nothing warms you like tea."

Still looking at me. So closely. "You promise me you'll stay here?"

"Green, please. If they have it. I'd really appreciate it."

"They'll have it."

He leaves at last with a soft click and a *Be right back. Don't go anywhere.* Once he's gone, I run to the mirror, to my dress hanging over it. Lifting and falling so gently in the breeze. I take Mother's dress down, still damp and cold in my hands. In the glass, I watch the silk fall away, part like curtains. The mirror is like a window now. In it, I see the house on the cliff. I see the tall black gates are open. The glass walls of the house are glowing red. And there I am inside its walls, inside the house itself. My reflection standing on the stair, beside the woman in red. Glowing, lifted, eradicated. Smiling at me with the reddest lips. Waving at me to *come in, come in.*

17

The Treatment Room has a different smell tonight. But it's the same fog, the same bell and chimes, the same soft-voiced woman with me in the tea-lit dark. Rubbing her hands in a heady oil while I lie on the heated table, smiling in wait. She holds those hands over my nose and mouth, telling me to breathe in, that's it. Deeply, please. "Three deep breaths. We'll take them together again. Shall we take them together again?"

"Yes, please. And what is this scent, may I ask? Apocalypse? Sage?"

"Oh, why it's our special blend."

"It's different than the last one you gave me."

"It is a little different," she says. "Are you ready for that?"

And I nod yes. I'm ready. My head starts to feel very warm. And fragrant. Like pine trees on fire. On fire? That doesn't sound so good. The little white jellyfish is beside me in its small tank. Not so little and pale anymore. It's grown since the last time. Turned a pinkish-red like it's blushing everywhere. "We were able to do quite a significant extraction last time," she says to me through the fog.

"Really?" I say, looking at my pulsing fish. "That's great, right?"

"It's wonderful. We were very successful. Well, didn't you enjoy the result?"

"Yes," I say. I'm radiant with fiery pines. "I have a Glow now, don't I?"

And the woman just smiles. Because surely I already know the answer to that. My Glow has been causing a stir all night. The woman in red couldn't believe it when I walked through the doors of the house this evening, led by the woman in silver, who also couldn't believe it. *If you'll allow me to say so, Daughter of Noelle*, the woman in silver said, *you're looking quite luminous ce soir*. There was a party in the hall. Larger than last time. People in silks of red and white and black. Music, heavy with harpsichord, played somewhere. The chandelier was ablaze. *We're doing a number of treatments tonight,* the woman in silver said, tugging me down the hall. *Including yours, Daughter.*

Mine?

You've been Selected. Bravo, Daughter.

Bravo, people echoed as I passed. Everyone appalling. Applauding, I mean.

Bon Voyage, Daughter, they said. Some smiling. Some not so smiling. Some maybe even glaring a little.

Dear Daughter, one woman hissed, *how excited and happy and fortunate you must feel.*

Yes, I said uneasily. *I feel all these things.*

The woman in red applauded the hardest of all. She stood on the landing of the stair as she'd done that first night and, as I approached, she put her hand to her mouth with such shock. *Could this be?* She raised her opera glasses to her eyes. *Surely this couldn't be . . . our very own dear Daughter?*

Our very own, said the twins behind their black veils, standing on either side of her.

In honor of your Beauty Journey, she said, handing me a flute full of red stars. *And to celebrate Mother's debts being cleared, of course,* she whispered into my ear. I looked at her and she winked at me.

You cleared Mother's debts for me?

We can't have our dear Daughter furrowing her brow over such mundane concerns as Coin, can we? Not when she is on her Beauty Journey.

I don't know what to say. How can I ever repay you?

Oh, I wouldn't worry about that, Daughter. We're just so terribly thrilled to see you pursuing your Most Magnificent Self. Aren't we, Lord and Lady Vichy? she said, turning to the twins. So they were royalty.

They smiled at me through their veils. *Oh, very much.*

At its heart, you'll find Rouge is a deeply human-loving enterprise, Daughter.

Very deeply. Lord and Lady Vichy smiled.

I nodded. That made sense. Much more sense than what Hud Hudson was telling me in the hotel room, his face very close to my face. What was he saying again? Something about wading into some deep, dark water. I was having trouble recalling anything but his eyes, full of deep, dark water themselves. Didn't know what he was talking about. Look at all these lovely people, drinking and dancing under the brilliant chandelier, I thought. Not laughing, but only because they didn't want laugh lines. They were laughing on the inside, though, I heard them. I was laughing there too. I was having such a good time on the landing of the stair with the twins and the woman in red, all of them stroking my shoulders with their silk-gloved hands. Deep water, what deep water? Just a beauty house. Just a beauty house full of caring fiends—*friends.*

I am wondering, I said to them. *I mean, I am a little concerned about my memory lately.*

Their faces fell then. *Concerned?*

Well, I've been forgetting things like names and places.

Names? Places?

And faces, I added. *I can't seem to put the faces to names. Or the names to places. Words, too, seem slippery suddenly.*

The twins looked at the woman in red. They shook their heads behind their veils. The woman in red appeared to frown, though her face stayed very still. *Interesting. Well, Daughter, I think you'll find that there are some faces and places that simply aren't worth recalling. Perhaps you're discovering that on your Beauty Journey.*

But it really does feel like I'm a little scrambled, I said. *For instance, I forgot that I couldn't swim, if you can believe it. I ended up nearly drowning.*

And they smiled with their eyes. *Oh well, being a little scrambled,* the woman in red said, *is to be expected. Absolutely a normal side ef-fect of the treatments. Memories are all connected, aren't they?*

They are, they are, Lord and Lady Vichy said.

If you extract one memory, the bad one, the absolutely unneces-sary Free Radical of the Mind, the Comedo of the Soul, the one that's dulling and creasing and darkening your visage so hideously, it's bound to affect the others, isn't it?

The others need a little time to adjust, so to speak, said the Lord.

They get a little turned around, that's all, said the Lady.

But I'd happily be a little scrambled for this . . . Brightness. She pushed me closer to the giant mirror on the wall so that I could see for myself. There was mirror me. Synced and smiling with very red lips. Beaming at me with shining eyes. And my skin . . .

There is a whiteness, isn't there? I whispered. *Brightness,* I meant to say. Not a whiteness, I told myself, call it a Brightness.

Oh yes. Like the moon if it had its own Light, is it not so, Lady Vichy?

The Lady smiled. *Like if the moon were plugged in,* she agreed, over my shoulder.

For a Glow like that, the woman in red said, *I'd be willing to forget quite a few things, let me tell you. The day of the week, who needs to know it? Which breakfast tisane I favored, a chance to try a new one, n'est-ce pas?*

You'll find life is full of lovely little surprises this way, said the Lord.

The opportunity to live moment to moment, in the present tense, like never before, said the Lady.

They pushed me closer still to the mirror, so that I was inches from my reflection in the glass. And though I was afraid, I was smiling at myself the whole time. *Of course, we're not quite there yet, are we?* the woman in red said, over my shoulder.

Not quite, not quite, the twins whispered, staring at my face in the mirror.

But that's why you're back here, isn't it, Daughter? Because Rome wasn't built in a day.

Or a treatment, offered the Lord.

It was built in three treatments, the Lady said.

But didn't Rome fall? I heard myself ask. *I recall it crumbling.*

Look at our Daughter, recalling things! And they smiled at me with their eyes. *Please don't worry about a little mental reshuffling here and there. A little rearranging in your head.*

I thought of that white hand arranging the roses in my head.

A small price to pay for this level of collagen regeneration, n'est-ce pas? Speaking of which . . .

And then the woman in silver came and ferried me down to the basement. In the waiting room, I drank the blood vessel water. The pomegranate seed water, I mean. It was very cold, vaguely sweet, with a bitter finish that surprised and delighted me. I stared up at the horrified white face masks on the red walls. Twisted in varying degrees of terror. As if each face had been frozen confronting its worst nightmare, really. It was lovely. The glowing woman I met last time was sitting there beneath them, reading her red magazine. The one who I thought might be mixed, like me. Ethnically ambivalent. *Ambivalent,* is that the word I mean? *Hello again,* I said. *We must be on the same treatment schedule.*

She looked up at me like she'd never seen me before. *I'm sorry,* she said, *have we met?* I didn't want to confuse her, so I said, *Sorry, maybe I have it wrong. I've been confusing names and faces lately.*

And she said, *Funny. I'm confusing them too. I'm told it's a harmless psychotrope. Side effect.*

I was also told that.

But worth it for the Glow. Don't you think?

She looked in the infinity mirror and I looked there too. I stared at thousands of her. Between us, she really was the one to look at. Paler than last time. As if the color had been leached out of her skin a little. She had a whiteness. *A Brightness, call it a Brightness.* There was a Glow greater than before. I envied it.

I envy, I said.

And she smiled. *Thank you.*

Now in the Treatment Room, the black discs are on my temples, the cold white paste's on my face. "Is this a marine algae mask?" I ask the whisper woman.

"You could call it that," she whispers.

I'm strapped to the bed, why strapped this time?

"So you can relax. These extractions can be quite visceral," she says. "Memory lives everywhere in the body. Down the back. In the neck and in the hands. Even the feet."

The feet, I think, and then remember that it took a while to get down here to the Treatment Room. Because of my red shoes. Again, I had to take them off. I had to follow the woman in silver barefoot, with the red shoes gasping in my fingers. It was so silly. I really shouldn't wear them to the house anymore. And yet if I didn't wear them, I don't know that I would know how to get here.

Dark in here now. I'm alone. Such a warm feeling spreading through me. So there are straps, it's fine. Don't fuss. Don't struggle. The straps are meant to protect me just like the whisper woman said. From what?

Yourself, of course, says a voice inside. The roses in my mind seem to have vanished now. Nothing in my head but a dark, scented fog, the sound of chimes. Who is speaking in the fog?

I look up and see the ceiling is being retracted to reveal another ceiling of glass. A sky of water, the red jellyfish floating by, pulsing. Someone recently told me they weren't jellyfish. Who? What someone? Some silly person. They're obviously jellyfish. Look at those red tentacles. Look at those pulsating heads. Like translucent hearts beating in the water, aren't they? So pretty. And again I feel my body floating up, up to the ceiling, which is weird, what about the restraints?

But your mind has no restraints, says the voice inside.

Now I'm so close-up to the ceiling glass. I'm right near the jellyfish. I see a pattern like flowers on their bodies, beautiful. The aquarium glass becomes a screen where a movie plays. Oh god. *Good*, I mean. It's very good. I love movies. Which one is this?

On the glass screen, I see a little girl. She's standing in the closet of a blue-and-white bedroom, in front of a large oval mirror. She's dressed in her mother's clothes, waiting at the mirror like it's a door. She's ugly, I think. Jellyfish swim through her little ugly duckling body. Look at her intense face. Pained. Familiar.

Huh. What film is this again? Don't think I know this one.

Oh, but you do, says the voice. *Definitely. You know this one well. Trust me.*

18

I'm sitting slumped by the mirror in Mother's closet. I've been waiting here awhile for Tom to show up in the glass, any minute now. I'm in the red shoes and the white dress he loves best. I'm wearing Mother's violets-and-smoke perfume and Mother's lipstick, the lesser red she leaves in the drawer. *Although there's nothing lesser about you,* Tom always says.

Really, Tom?

Seth, remember. Remember, I'm Seth.

Okay, I say, but he really does look a lot like Tom Cruise. I know that for sure now because I've been watching his movies. I watched them in spite of Mother, behind her back. I asked Mother to rent them for me, I begged her. This was after Mother screamed at me about being in her room. Later, she called me into the living room and said she was sorry for screaming, she was just tired of me not listening, okay? *Okay.* Also mirrors were not playthings, did I understand that?

Mother was curled on the couch in one of her silk robes Father brought her from Egypt. Egypt was like a pretty robe she could put on or take off. She had a copy of *Vogue* magazine on her lap and a Matinée smoking in the pointy glass ashtray on the pointy glass coffee table. Everything in our apartment is shiny and pointy and cold, Stacey says. Or it's white and hissing like the wicker. It's what Mother calls *style*, I tell Stacey, who says *whatever*. She doesn't like coming to our place because *we can't rate each other there*. Rating is something we do only in Stacey's basement, where I watch Stacey twirling in her bodysuit in the dark until my eyes water. Sometimes I'll look away from her, through the cloudy basement window near the ceiling, into the endless rose garden. I can't always see the tops of the flowers, just the spiked stems in their beds of dirt, which her Russian mother Alla's always turning. Alla doesn't know how much I come over because we always go through the back door, but she met me a few times when we were cutting through the garden. She was smiling, but her eyes were hard and glittery as Grand-Maman's diamonds, and her hand, when I shook it, was a limp fish. *What have we talked about traipsing through the garden, Anastasia?* Alla tells Stacey, her eyes still on me. *No more back door, okay?* Alla's blond like Stacey. *Very Stepford,* Mother says when she comes to pick me up, making a face, though I know she admires their house, the garden with its gazebo. Still, Mother prefers her own style in all things. I prefer it too. Even the cigarette in Mother's ashtray, idly smoldering, had a pretty mouth of Mother's best red around the filter. She smelled of violets and smoke from her jagged star.

Belle, Mother said from the couch, *are you even listening to me?*

Yes.

What did I say?

Mirrors aren't playthings.

That mirror especially, understood? Look at me. She was holding my chin, tilting my head up so there was nowhere else to look except Mother's face, shining and pointy and cold. But her eyes were soft. Wanting me to really understand about this, okay? For my own good. *Comprends-tu?* Mother said, speaking in French the way she did only when she was very upset. And she shook me a little.

Oui. Mom, I said, *do you know Tom Cruise?*

Tom Cruise? Mother said, letting go. *Of course I know Tom Cruise. Who doesn't? He's a big movie star.*

Can we watch some of his movies maybe? Can we rent them from the video store?

Why do you want to do that all of a sudden?

And I went red in the face. I couldn't tell Mother that Tom Cruise was my boyfriend. That I felt like he knew me better than anyone. Better than Mother even. *Just to see, that's all*, I said to the floor. *He's a good actor, isn't he?* Mother's always talking about who's a good actor. *Don't you like him?* And then Mother's eyes went a little soft again suddenly. *He looks a bit like Monty. I'll say that for him.* Like she could see Tom in her mind. I would've been jealous, but Tom had already told me what he thought of Mother. That she was awful. Ugly. Old. Her Beauty a disguise. Just a painted mask. It would slide off her face in time. It was already sliding.

Mother smiled at me. *A good actor, huh?* She looked amused. *Well, all right. Next time we go to the video store—*

She's a little young for those movies, don't you think? This from Chip, stretched out on her love seat. Watching some sort of car race on TV. Not even looking at us.

Is she?

No, I'm not!

Think about it, Chip said, ignoring me. Risky Business? He raised his eyebrows at Mother in the way I hate.

Oh right. It's true, Belle. You are a little too young for his movies, I think.

What?! I screamed. *But I'm ten already! Ten isn't too young.*

And Chip smiled.

Maybe in a couple of years, Mother said.

Mom! You can't listen to—

Darling, there are scenes that are too . . . adult for you. I'm just remembering.

But you were going to say yes!

Well, I'd forgotten about some scenes.

But what about Top Gun? *We saw* Top Gun *together, remember? Can't I at least rent—*

No, Belle. There was a scene there, too. And I blushed. I knew the scene Mother was talking about. Tom and Kelly McGillis in blue silhouette. Tom lying on top of her. Sticking his tongue into her mouth and how I hated her. All to "Take My Breath Away," which was our song. It made me hot in the face, thinking about that.

Mom, that's not—

Belle, that's enough. Room!

So I waited. So I waited and rented them with Grand-Maman. *Mother doesn't want me to watch Tom Cruise movies*, was all I had to say and Grand-Maman immediately rented all of them for me. *Risky Business. All the Right Moves. Top Gun. The Outsiders. Legend.*

Ooh, a Tom Cruise marathon, the girl behind the video store counter said, and Grand-Maman said nothing, just wrote her a check from her book of checks. We watched them together in Grand-Maman's bedroom dark on her big black box television, even the kissing parts. Even the sex parts. She didn't fast-forward anything. Just sat there in her creaking rose-gold chaise saying nothing at all. Part of me wanted her to fast-forward sometimes. Because I hated watching Tom kiss or touch or even smile at any girl. Kelly McGillis. Rebecca De Mornay. They all looked pretty much the same to me. Their hair, their eyes, their skin. Even the dark-haired, dark-eyed ones like Mia Sara in *Legend* or Mary Elizabeth Mastrantonio in *The Color of Money* were still somehow more of the same. More like Mother or Stacey than me. It burned my face up seeing that. It hurt my heart. I felt a pain to breathe, like someone stuck a knife there, right in the middle of me. Watching Tom kiss Rebecca in *Risky Business*, I had a feeling that was so many feelings at once. The angriest angry. The saddest sad. A want so big and deep and aching, it made my stomach a sinking pit. The want was like drowning. There was a word for this feeling, I knew. *Envy*. Mother taught it to me when she first read me *Snow White*, what the evil queen feels. *When someone has something you want so much and you hate them so much for it.* Envy is what I felt. I envied every girl who came near Tom in the movie, so I could barely stand to watch. But I watched, through tears sometimes, wanting to run through the screen and push the girl out of the movie, out of the world.

Tom doesn't love you, I would scream at them as I hurled them out into space. I would scream and scream until I lost my voice.

Qu'est-ce qui se passe avec toi? Grand-Maman said at one point, while we watched Tom wrap his arms around Rebecca De Mornay's naked body. Her hair was the same strawberry-blond shade as Stacey's, I realized. Her eyes blue as Mother's eyes.

Are you crying?

No, I said. *I'm watching. This is how I watch. Grand-Maman?*

Quoi?

Do you think he really likes her?

Ben non. It's a movie, cher. He's acting.

Okay, I whispered. I loved Grand-Maman then. I was so close to telling her that Tom Cruise was my boyfriend. That I was the only one who knew his true name, Seth. I was the only one who knew about Tom's eyes. How they could go red in an instant, then back to blue-green again when he was calm and happy. But then I remembered that it was a secret. *Our secret*, Tom said. There were times when we were watching that I felt Tom looking right at me from Grand-Maman's dusty TV screen, and I thought the screen was a mirror and that Tom would step through it in his varsity jacket or in his pilot jacket or in his white shirt and underwear and sunglasses.

Ça va? Grand-Maman asked me. *You're breathing very funny.*

Because Tom's taking my breath away, I thought. But of course I didn't tell Grand-Maman that. All I said was, *Ça va, oui.*

Once, in the middle of *Top Gun*, I saw my face reflected in the screen's glare, right next to his. Tom was flirting with Kelly McGillis in an elevator, so sometimes it was Kelly on the screen, sometimes Tom, both of them beautiful and smiling beside what I saw was my very un-smiling face, which looked hideous, warped with want. *What's wrong?* Grand-Maman said. She turned off the TV suddenly and then I just saw myself. Close-up and cross-legged on her scuffed floor, Grand-Maman rocking beside me in the dark. My face was dreamy and open like Mother's when she watched her movies. But my dreaminess wasn't at all pretty like hers. It was terrible. It was nothing Tom could ever love. *I'm going home now*, I said.

After seeing the movies, it really seems like Seth is Tom Cruise. But if Tom Cruise wants me to call him Seth, then I can do that. I'll do anything for Tom Cruise. Seth, I mean. We're getting so close. Every time Mother is out these days, I go to her bedroom closet and he's there, waiting in the mirror. She told Grand-Maman to absolutely not let me go into her room ever again after the last time. *It is of the utmost importance, do you hear me?* she said to Grand-Maman, and Grand-Maman told Mother, *I heard you.* But the minute Mother leaves, Grand-Maman always turns a blind eye. I walk right in and surely Grand-Maman hears my creaking footsteps going down the hall, surely she hears the turn of that wobbly doorknob. Maybe she turns a blind ear, too.

The next time I went back to Mother's closet, I didn't see the mirror at first, and for a minute I couldn't breathe. Then I saw it glinting behind her row of dresses red as blood. The glass was turned to the corner like it'd been bad. So I picked it up, I turned it around, it wasn't so heavy really. I always take off Father's golden bracelet first. That Eye of Horus. Father's eye, Mother said. Watching me, it feels like, and I don't like it. The minute it falls to Mother's floor, the mirror begins to shimmer, and he appears on the other side of the glass like a dream. Blurred around the edges at first. Rippling like water.

Tom, I whisper.

And then he comes into blinding focus, his smile a flashing white that burns me. *Hello, Belle*, he says. *Can I come in?* He is so beautiful, I have no words, though my mouth's wide open. My breath is taken just like the song. But Tom hears the *yes* in my pounding heart. And he walks through the glass with a sucking squid-like sound. And the song, our song, is all around us. He asks me if he can have this dance. Even though of course he knows he can have it. He can have anything.

And then we dance and talk, for hours sometimes. I'm surprised Tom Cruise has so much time on his hands. Shouldn't he be so busy making movies and doing interviews and things? What is he doing here in the dark of Mother's closet dancing with me? But I don't dare ask. I talk about other things, mostly because I'm so nervous to be slow dancing with Tom Cruise. I think of my face reflected in Grand-Maman's TV screen, ugly and distorted with dreaming. I look nothing like the girls in his movies, and yet he's looking at me like I'm Kelly McGillis in the elevator. I'm Rebecca De Mornay wandering into his living room like a literal dream. Honestly. Tom's hands on my shoulders. Tom's eyes on my face. It's so much. Too much. When I find my voice to talk, I barely know what I say. I tell him dumb things. How much I hate school, I don't want to go back this fall. How Stacey has a boyfriend now, Gabriel Gardner, and he told her she looks just like Christie Brinkley. That my turtle died last spring and I'm afraid I killed him somehow. Tom seems amused but annoyed by my chatter.

Stacey sounds like your run-of-the-mill slut, he whispers.

School is a waste of time, Belle. You'll learn nothing there except lies.

Death is inevitable and the world is full of murder, Tom says, tenderly brushing a lock of hair from my eyes.

If Tom talks, he really only wants to talk about two things: my Beauty and how Mother is evil. *A terrible person, Belle.* A vile bitch queen. It surprises me that Tom Cruise feels this way about Mother when she looks so much like all the girls he kisses in his movies. But he's so serious-sounding that I believe him. When Tom talks about Mother, his eyes go red. His fang shines in the light more. There's a heavenly glow on his face. He's so beautiful. The most beautiful being I have ever seen.

Mother's Beauty is a trick, Tom whispered last night. *Not like yours, Belle.* Right now, he says, I'm just a little bud in the grass. Not even a bud yet, a seedling. Deep in the dark earth, among the worms and spiders. That's where Mother's keeping me. But Tom says he sees me down there in the dirt. Sees the green shoots that will soon rise up. The red petals that will unfurl. A rose I will be someday, little seedling. Just like the ones in Stacey's mother's garden. Just wait. Wait and see. And what will Mother be? Rotted. Fallen petals. Dead earth.

Now Mother's still out but she'll be home soon. Grand-Maman is asleep in her chair in the living room. Tom's really late. Maybe he's busy filming a new movie or something. But didn't he say just yesterday to meet him here tonight?

But Mother might come back early, I warned him.

Fuck Mother, Tom said. Did Tom Cruise really say that? He put his cold, sticking hands on my shoulders, and he said, *Belle, your mother is a real problem.*

I nodded like I knew. *Yes.* But I really didn't know. *It's just that this is her room*, I said. *And she told me not to go in. So she gets mad when I'm here. In her shoes.* And I wanted to tell him if he came into my mirror in my bedroom, we wouldn't have to deal with these issues. We wouldn't—

I don't mean that, Belle.

What do you mean, then? What's the problem with Mother?

And Tom looked at me and smiled in the dark. His fang shone, sharp and white. Surely I knew what the problem was. But I didn't really.

She's taking your Beauty away, he said.

She is?

Oh yes, definitely. And I, for one, won't stand for it. I told you. I hate stealing.

I nodded. I hated stealing too. I thought of Mother's many robes from Egypt. How sometimes she'd line her eyes like Elizabeth Taylor in *Cleopatra*. Wear a blue beetle on her wrist, a scarab. She didn't steal any of it. Father bought it all for her. *From Egypt*, Mother would say of the jewels and robes. So why was it that when I watched the beetle wink against her light skin, I sometimes thought *liar*, I sometimes thought *thief*? Because she was Noelle Nour with creditors only. I'm Mirabelle Nour, no matter what I wear, no matter where I go. Can't take it off like Mother's wrist beetle. Can't even take it off like Father's eye. But was Mother really stealing? Wasn't she born like that and wasn't I born like this? And wasn't I the actual thief, coming into her room where she told me again and again not to go? *Little thief. Little bitch*, isn't that what Mother calls me under her breath each time she catches me? She says it after I've left, but I hear her through the wall.

Tom—

Seth.

I don't know for sure if she's stealing. Maybe she's just beautiful. I pictured Mother when she took me apple picking last fall. Her face beaming up at me through the branches of a tree fuzzy with caterpillars. I handed Mother the very first apple I picked. The red of the apple was almost the same red as Mother's Chanel lipstick, so it matched. I told her so and she laughed and said, *Oh god, I've created a monster, haven't I?*

It's a lie, he said, stroking my hair. *I see through her. I see the truth. And I hate lies.* He closed his eyes. *So much.* It's true that Tom Cruise hates lies. He has a lot of honor. I saw that firsthand in *Legend*. In *Top Gun*, too.

Please take me away with you, Tom Cruise, I begged.

He opened his eyes, which were red now. A flash of anger. I thought surely he would correct me again: *Seth, remember?* But he just smiled to himself, amused. He sighed. Shook his head of waving dark hair.

I'd love to take you away, Belle. Definitely, I would. You know I'd do anything to keep you close. It's just your mother would be very, very angry at me . . . He put a hand to his chest just like Tom Cruise would. So suddenly sincere.

I don't care, I whispered. *I'll do anything.*

Tom's smile flashed white. *Anything?* He took my face in his hands. His hands were so cold, it was like being plunged in icy water. I gasped. *Well. There is one thing.*

I looked into Tom's eyes, now blue-green again. Full of the laughter and light I loved. So much like Tom Cruise's actual eyes, I could barely breathe.

Tell me. I was shivering in Tom's hands, but he didn't seem to mind.

It involves Mother, of course.

Of course. I shouldn't be surprised about that. I was afraid, but I tried not to show that to Tom Cruise. *What about Mother?* I said.

The lies need to be stopped, Belle. She has to pay for stealing your Beauty. And you have to take it back to be able to come with me to California. You'll need it there. Will you do that, Belle?

Do what exactly? I thought. I don't know. But Tom Cruise was so close to me then, I couldn't speak words anymore. His smile a flashing white that made jelly of me. I was lost in the laughing waters of his eyes. He leaned in closer still. Like he was going to kiss me, this was it. *Don't be nervous,* I thought. Stacey wouldn't be nervous. She wouldn't get stiff. She was leagues ahead of me with her Black Honey lips and her hair a blond swishing curtain like Rebecca De Mornay's. Gabriel Gardner had just Frenched her the other day, apparently. Tom's smile flashed and flashed at me, blinding like an eclipse. His hands on either side of my face, making me shiver. Tom's eyes on my face like he could truly see me. Could see my great Beauty deep down in the dirt. Could he really see it? I felt his breath on my skin like a cold, cold wind. I closed my eyes, not believing this could be. Tilted my head up just like those terrible girls do in Tom's movies, those girls I wanted to push off the screen, out of the world. Except I wasn't one of them, was I? Nothing could change that. Not my slash of lesser red or Mother's sex shoes or the Dior I was drowning in or my stolen cloud of violets and smoke. How could Tom Cruise ever want me? I started to tremble, knowing he was so close now. Then at the last second, I suddenly lowered my head, afraid. Tom ended up kissing my forehead. And where he kissed me, it burned. I felt the fire through my whole body. I felt shame, why had I been afraid suddenly? I lifted my head back up and waited for him to kiss my lips. I parted them even. I was ready this time, though I was scared. Tom Cruise was my boyfriend, after all. This was what a boyfriend did. *Tom, you can kiss me now*, I thought with my eyes closed.

Nothing.

When I opened my eyes, Tom was gone. Just Mother in the doorway. Looking at me.

My forehead was throbbing, burning where Tom had just kissed me.

Mother didn't say anything. Not about going into her room. Not about wearing her lesser red or her shoes or her Christian Dior dress she'd bought discounted from Ladies Evening Wear. Not about Father's eye bracelet being on the floor. She just stared at me. *What the hell is that on your forehead?*

Nothing.

Not nothing, there's a mark.

No there's not.

Yes there is, like a bruise. Did you hit your head?

No. It's nothing.

She raised an eyebrow. I was really going to lie like this? Right to her face? *That's it, I'm putting a lock on this door.*

Mom—NO!

One minute, Mother said through her teeth. *One minute to get dressed and come out here.* And then she slammed the door. And in the empty mirror, I saw it on my forehead. Glowing like a star. A mark where Tom Cruise had kissed me with his cold red lips. The skin was still burning.

She hasn't put the lock on the door yet, but she says she will. *Watch me.* Tonight, I have to tell Tom Cruise about the lock. Seth, I mean. I have to find out what he wants me to do before Mother separates us forever. I have to tell him to come to my bedroom from now on, not Mother's. I won't have her shoes or her dresses or her Dior Rouge, but at least I'll have privacy. We can talk about the things Tom wants to talk about. This thing he wants me to do that involves Mother. *One thing*, Tom said. But the mirror's still empty. Just me in the glass. I hear Grand-Maman leaving. If Mother finds me here, I'm cooked. The sun's going down now. I wonder if I did something wrong. Did I upset Tom? There's still a mark on my forehead. He meant to kiss my lips and I gave him my forehead and maybe he's angry now. *I'll let you kiss me next time, Tom Cruise*, I promise him in my mind. I mean *Seth*.

Key in the front door. Mother's home, fuck. *Fuck Mother*, Tom said. And the mirror is still dark, still empty of all but me waiting.

Tom, you've abandoned me. Because I didn't kiss you? Because I hesitated about Mother?

"Belle," Mother calls out sharply.

Quickly, I get out of her shoes and dress and I stuff them all back in the closet. I wipe my mouth of her Rouge. I look once more in the mirror before I walk out the door. Just me looking hideous as ever. No wonder Tom didn't show. Maybe now he sees what everyone else sees.

In the living room, there is Mother with a man. Not Chip. Not the Troll. A new man.

"Hello, Belle," he says.

That voice. I'd know it anywhere.

I look up. Dark hair like a wave. White crooked smile. Blue-green eyes that could flash red any second.

"Tom," I whisper.

Tom Cruise standing in our living room beside Mother. Smiling at me. "What are you doing here?"

Tom just blinks. He looks at me like he's never seen me before.

"No, darling, this is *Bryce*," Mother says. "He's a film producer from LA."

"Hello there, Belle. Your mother's told me so much about you." He puts out his hand for me to shake. Like we've never slow danced. Like he never left a bruise on my forehead with his lips. Like he's never seen me before, he's a stranger. I stare at his hand. The hand that touched my cheek, my hair, my shoulders. Acting like it never did.

"Belle," Mother snaps, prompting me.

"Seth," I whisper.

He just stares at me. He looks at Mother. *Seth?* "Belle, I told you, this is BRYCE. Sorry about this," she tells him. He nods like he understands. "He thinks Mommy could be in his new movie, isn't that exciting? And maybe we'll move to LA for a bit."

"Your mother's very talented, Belle," he says. "I think she's a star."

He smiles at Mother. And Mother smiles at him.

"Why are you doing this?" I whisper. *Why are you lying like this? I thought you hated lies. Is it because I didn't let you kiss my lips? I was just nervous!*

"*Why?*" Mother repeats. "Because it's an opportunity, Sunshine. Wouldn't you like to move to LA?"

Tom Cruise puts his arm around Mother's white shoulder and smiles at me.

"No!" I shout.

And just like that he turns into someone else. Just a dark-haired man looking at me intently, with a question in his watery eyes. Not blue-green or red. Not Tom's eyes at all.

I run out of the room. I run to my pink bedroom, where I shut the door.

"Sorry about that," I hear Mother say. And she laughs her clucking laugh I hate, that sounds like her anger putting on a face, trying to sweep itself away.

"Don't worry about it," I hear not-Tom say. "She okay?"

"God knows. She might be playing pretend or something. She's been going through a phase of some kind. Maybe because of her father. I don't know. Who knows, you might be an evil wizard in her mind right now. Or a handsome prince."

Not-Tom laughs. "Well, she's uncovered my secret, then. I'm both an evil wizard *and* a handsome prince."

And Mother laughs again too. "God, I wonder who I am." I hear the sound of her lighter going *click, click*. The cigarette catching fire. A drag and then a breath. "Probably the evil bitch queen."

And then not-Tom and Mother laugh together.

Dinner with Mother and not-Tom. *Bryce*. Is he really Bryce? Is he really not Tom? Hard to tell by the light of Mother's candles. I said I wasn't hungry, but Mother said, *Do not do this to me, please*. She forced me into an ugly green dress she'd bought me from the discount rack of Little Miss. Mother calls the ugly green *olive*, says it shows off my *golden skin*. I'm sitting beneath the painting she bought in a Metro station, all red slashes in a white sky. Grand-Maman says she doesn't understand it. The painting or why Mother keeps buying this *fancy trash* instead of paying off her many debts. I'm watching not-Tom eat a snail Mother has cooked in garlic butter and served on a plate specially for eating snails. He and Mother are drinking wine that looks like blood. Smiling at me.

"Your mother tells me you're Egyptian."

I stare at Mother, who's nodding at me from across the table. It's going to be one of those nights. Where Mother wants to do what she calls *show off. Can't I show you off a little?*

"Not me," I say. "My father."

"Well that's you, too," Mother says, and her voice is a smiling warning. "That's why she's so exotic-looking," Mother says, her eyes still on my face, telling me, *Please. For me?* "Aren't you?"

I stare at my plate of snails.

"That's why," not-Tom agrees, smiling.

"And beautiful. If it weren't for the long face."

"Even with the long face," not-Tom offers politely.

"So jealous," Mother says. *Liar*, I think. She's wearing the scarab necklace and her red Dior. The same Dior Tom Cruise kissed me in. I watch the blue beetle shimmer on her white neck. Egypt is an accessory tonight. There will be honey-and-pistachio pastries later, which

Mother will say she made, which she did not. She gets them from the Arab store, taking me with her because *this is your heritage.* I hate going there with her. Every dark eye on Mother, then on me. And Mother loving every minute.

"You know I visited Morocco recently?" not-Tom tells Mother, who looks at me with such delight. All the lights in her face are shining violently on me.

"Really?"

"Magical place."

"Magical, magical," Mother agrees, even though we've never been there. She beams at me like I'm Morocco, sitting right there in front of her. "Belle and I visited once, didn't we?"

"No."

"Not Morocco, Egypt. Similar. With your father." She lowers her voice on the word *father.*

"And how was it?" not-Tom asks.

"Oh, interesting. Exotic. Unforgettable, really. Wasn't it, Belle?"

I shake my head. "I don't remember." I remember. Riding a bus with Mother and everybody staring like they do at the Arab store. Holding her hand in what she said was a pyramid but felt like a cave. Walking in a white dress with Father through the Valley of Kings. Sun in my eyes. Dust on my dress. His hand warm and dry. His gold watch ticking by my ear.

Now Mother's eyes flash darkly at me across the table. Then she smiles. "Belle thought the Sphinx was talking to her."

"No I didn't."

"Oh yes you did. It was just a recording, of course. But we let her think it. We said, *Oh yes, of course it's talking to you, Sunshine.*" More laughter. More blood.

"Well, maybe it was," not-Tom offers, accepting even more blood from Mother, who pours and pours.

"You know, when she was little, she would go into my closet looking for Narnia. Or Wonderland, wouldn't you? Or Oz."

"No." Yes. I remember knocking and knocking on the closet walls. *Hello, hello, hello? Do you hear me? Are you there?* The mirror wasn't in the closet then. It was still hanging on the back of Mother's bedroom door. She wasn't mad at it yet.

"I told her, *It's not there, honey. I wish it was. Believe me.*" Sweeping laughter that sweeps it all away. "She still goes in there. Still looking for something, aren't you?" Now her eyes are sad. Looking at my forehead, still burning where Tom Cruise kissed me.

I look back down at the snails. I'm hot in the face.

"Well who knows, Belle. Maybe it is there. Anything's possible, right? Definitely." This from not-Tom. Something in his voice. I turn and look at him.

Tom. He suddenly looks like Tom again. So much like Tom Cruise that I can't take it.

"I love the movie *Top Gun*," I whisper into Tom's face.

Tom nods. "Oh, it's a great one. All those fighter planes. Was it the planes that you liked? All that flying around in the sky?"

"No." I'm looking right at him.

"Oh?" He smiles at Mother. "What did you like, then? Tell me." Reaching out for Mother's hand across the table.

"I don't know why you're being like this," I whisper.

"Belle."

And then he's not-Tom again. Just a strange man blinking at me like he doesn't understand. I walk away from the table with Mother calling and calling my name to *come back here*. And then: "Fine. Go. Go ahead."

I lie in my bed, watching the sun set through the white frilly window. Fiery red. All the rose-gold shades I've seen in Tom's face are in the sky tonight, the same blue as the universe of his eyes. *Tick, tick* goes my Snow White clock. I let the seconds and minutes and hours go. *Go ahead.* Through the wall, I hear the laughter of not-Tom and Mother together in the living room, eating pastries, clinking fishbowls of blood, and I think of squids. Not-Tom or Tom? He looked so much like Tom Cruise, and then he didn't. Not even close. He just looked like a boring old man. *Bryce*. Before I came in here, I went into Mother's bedroom. I was fearless, because Mother's Sting was playing so loudly in the living room, the walls were vibrating with "Englishman in New York." I crept into her closet, took the mirror, and carried it back here. Now it's shining in the corner of my room where it belongs. Empty of all but my silhouette. I stared at it until I couldn't see myself anymore. Until I was just a black shape in the blue dark. *Fine*, I told myself. *Go ahead*. Now the sky's black. It happens in the blink of an eye, the movement from blue to black. I stare at my ceiling full of glow-in-the-dark stars. In each corner, a spider's spinning a web. I was so afraid of those spiders in the corners for so long. *Mother, please kill them*, I'd beg her each night. But Mother said no. She said this is what happens when you live in an apartment on the ground floor, on an island by the river. Things creep in through the cracks, through the screens. *We can't keep them out, Belle. Get used to it. I can't kill every creepy-crawly for you, honey. There are far too many for that*. I hear them both walk down the hallway now. Mother's clicking heels, then the deeper clack of not-Tom's shoes. At my bedroom, the clicks and clacks stop. Mother pausing at the door. Should she open it and deal with me? No. They walk past to her blue bedroom, *click, clack*. Door closes with a thud. Through the wall I hear new music, a song I know. "In the Air Tonight." I know it because it's a Tom song. From *Risky Business*. When Tom and Rebecca are on the train. The sound of it makes me sick, my stomach sinking, sinking. But it's not just the song that makes me sick. It's the sounds I hear underneath the song, like sighing, like breathing. The breathing of Mother and Tom or not-Tom. Soft. Heavy. Together. Like a knife, I feel it. Right in the middle of me, twisting. I close my eyes but I can't cover my ears enough, not with my hands or my pillow or one of my dumb dolls with Mother's hair and skin and eyes that watch me. My forehead burns. Dumb to cry. To feel this . . . what? *Just sick*, I tell myself. But no, not just sick. I know the word I feel. The one Mother taught me from *Snow White* that is so many bad feelings at once. That I feel when I watch Tom Cruise with any girl, when I watch Mother put on her hat with the wide brim to protect her pale face. The dark, twisting poison one that aches and eats and empties. And wants. All by itself.

Silence now. No creaks, no gasps, no music anymore. I hear not-Tom leave her bedroom, then the apartment. Get in his car and drive away.

I fall asleep staring up at the stars Mother pasted on my ceiling. Because I was afraid of the dark, she put them there. *There*, she said, *better? Like a night-light but less childish.*

She didn't even get the constellations right, Stacey told me when she slept over. *So each night when you look up at those stars, you're looking up at the wrong sky. You're looking at the wrong heaven.*

So?

That's fucked, Stacey said quietly. *But it explains a lot.*

Still dark when I open my eyes. Woke to a sound like a song. "In the Air Tonight" playing again. Again? But it's midnight on my Snow White clock. Mother is surely asleep. So why do I hear the song still? And a sound under the song again. Not breathing or sighing this time. Footsteps. Maybe it's part of the song? No. Footsteps aren't part of the song. Different footsteps than earlier. Not a click or a clack. Fear in my stomach. Opening up like a black pit.

Then I see the mirror in the corner is shining. I see someone walk through the glass like it's a door. I smile in the dark.

"Tom," I whisper.

"Seth," he says.

His silhouette makes its way to my bed. Putting a shadow finger to his shadow lips. *Our secret. Like Beauty, remember?* He sits on my bed's edge. Right where Mother sits when she tucks me in. It feels like he sits closer to me than Mother ever sits. My skin is goose bumps, my breath is caught. "You're here," I whisper.

"Of course I'm here."

"I thought you left me. I thought you were gone forever." Tears fill my eyes. I hope he doesn't see.

He leans in and strokes my hair. So softly. His hands are cold and sticky. That's how I know it's him, though I can't see him so well in the dark.

"Why didn't you meet me in the mirror today? I waited and waited for you, but you didn't come."

"It wasn't safe," he whispers under the music. "I knew your mother was plotting something. So I found another way."

"Through her new boyfriend."

Tom nods. "He's a fool. Very easy to infiltrate."

"Was it you drinking and laughing with Mother all night? Did you have . . . ?" Saying the word *sex* to Tom is impossible.

Tom smiles, shaking his head. His hair waves in the dark. "I just did it to get to you."

"You did?"

"Definitely."

I thought of what Grand-Maman told me when we were watching Tom's movies, Tom and the girls. Just acting.

"Are you really going away with Mother to California? Are you leaving me?"

"Belle, don't you trust me by now?"

"She's going to put a lock on the door, Tom," I whisper.

"Seth," he says quietly.

"Seth. Then I'll never see you again."

He walks over to Mother's mirror in the corner. I watch him stroke his own jaw in the shining glass. There's a dark shape in the glass, I see, doing the same. Tom's reflection.

"Who's that old actor your mother likes again?" he whispers.

"Montgomery Clift."

"Right. *Monty*." He smiles to himself in Mother's mirror. "How could I forget?"

"She says you look a little bit like him."

"Does she? Interesting. I guess I do, don't I?" He looks lost in his own reflection, shimmering darkly in the glass.

"Only because Tom Cruise looks like him," I whisper. "Only because you're Tom Cruise."

For a second, he looks like he's going to laugh. But then he smiles in the mirror, almost sadly.

"I won't let her separate us," he says to the glass. "Ever."

"How?"

"You know how. But I need your help. We have to get rid of your mother, Belle. There's really no other choice if you want me to take you away to California."

I knew Tom Cruise was going to say this. I knew he was going to say it just as he said it. I might have even said the words with him, like when you sing along to a song.

"But I can't get rid of her," I whisper. "She's my mother. I love her." I'm devastated that this is true. I think of Mother and me in the apple orchard that day. The warmth of her hand in mine, her laughing voice. "I love her," I repeat, but there's a crack in my words.

Tom hears it. He looks at me in the shining glass. "You know I'd really hate to leave you here, Belle. All by yourself on this island you hate, beside your muddy little river. With the spiders that Mother won't kill. With these dumb dolls that look just like Mother's stolen Beauty. Reading your fairy tales rather than living them. Do you want that?" Standing by the mirror, he looks like he's about to leave me right now. Disappear through the glass.

"No." I shake my head. "Please. Please don't leave, Tom. Please come back and lie here with me for a while." I can't even look him in the eye when I whisper these words. A whisper of a whisper. When I look back up, he's smiling at me in the glass. His smile like a sunrise in the dark.

He walks back to my bed. Moves my dolls away carefully, one by one by one. Not making a single sound. He lies right by my side so we're face-to-face, Tom Cruise and I. I've never had anyone lie in my bed before besides Mother. And only when I was sick with pneumonia and couldn't breathe so well in the nights. I opened my eyes and there were her pale eyes staring at me with a crumpled look. That was the last time. Even Stacey, when she sleeps over, sleeps on a blow-up mattress on the floor. *Tell me a secret*, she always says. And I never had any to tell besides the secret of me and Stacey, that she twirls for me in her basement to "Maniac." Until now. Tom's eyes glow from blue-green to red to blue-green to red in the dark. His face just like the movies I watched on Grand-Maman's box TV. No screen of glass between us now. His smile shines like the stars on the ceiling. So beautiful. The way he looks at me, I can't believe it. Like no one looks at me. Like I'm so beautiful too. Maybe I'm dreaming like Tom dreams at the beginning of *Risky Business*. *The dream is always the same*, he says in the movie. *If this is a dream*, I think, *let it always be the same*.

"You have to promise me," he says, serious now. "Do you promise me, Belle? In a way, you know, you've already promised."

"I have?"

He nods slowly. His jaw gets so tight, his cheek begins to tick like a clock. The most beautiful clock. "It's the only way." He reaches out and strokes my face softly with his squid hands. It sends such a chill through me. Again, I think of being plunged into cold, dark water. I shiver in the hot June night.

"Is it going to hurt her?"

And Tom just smiles at me in the dark, under the wrong heaven. "Those are pretty stars up there," he says. "Pretty as you are. So pretty you are. God. To be here with you. I definitely feel like the luckiest guy in the world right now." I die inside when Tom says these words to me. Like we're in a movie. The girl's been pushed out of the world, and it's just me and Tom now. I picture her falling off the edge, her honey-colored hair floating behind her, her pale skin glowing like Mother's.

Can it really be you saying these words to me, Tom Cruise? Of course it is. This is your face like the sun. These are your eyes like the sea. I watch him turn his smile to the stars. He doesn't say anything about them being in the wrong place. He looks up at the ceiling like everything is exactly where it should be. The stars up there, and down here, me and Tom Cruise. Leaning in so I smell the ocean of him. Cold and blue and deep.

"Do you promise me?" he says.

I watch a red jellyfish float across his face. "If it's the only way," I say.

He kisses me on the lips. Just once. So light, like a touch of a touch. This time it doesn't burn. It burns, yes, but not in a bad way. It's like that wrong heaven of stars up there are all in my body now. Little dots of fiery light. But it doesn't feel wrong anymore. It feels exactly right. Just like the right heaven.

"It is," Tom says, stroking my hair. "Trust me, okay?" He takes my hand, and then sees the gold bracelet on my wrist. A funny look passes over his face as he looks into Father's eye. Like he knows it, though how could he? "What's this?"

"Nothing. Just a gift."

"It's ugly," he hisses.

"I know," I whisper. "Mother makes me wear it."

Of course she would, Tom's face says. "It doesn't belong on your pretty wrist." His voice is nearly a growl. So I slip off the bracelet and push it between the pile of dolls. A twinge of some bad feeling as I slide it away. Like I've abandoned Father. His eye is sad and alone now. I'll put it back on after Tom goes. For now, I push it away.

Tom smiles. Red jellyfish are floating through his body. Not just his body, but the whole room. My whole bedroom is lit up like we're underwater, how strange. There's mist all around us now, like we're in a strange fog. Maybe I'm really dreaming. Or drowning. Doesn't matter.

I'm in heaven with Tom. Seth, I mean.

It's heaven either way.

Part IV

19

It's the light that wakes me. Morning light from a window, searing the backs of my eyelids red. What a strange, strange dream I had. Can't remember any of it now, funny. Must be those blanks again. But the feeling of it lingers in my body—like I went deep down into the depths of myself and to wake up was to swim a long way back up to the surface, to come up gasping for air. And now? Now, my heavy lids are still closed, and I hear the sound of chimes like a strange church is nearby. A very pretty mist over my thoughts. As I wander through the mist, I see the reddest roses in vases being arranged by white hands. Their downward-pointing thorns like shining spikes.

When I open my eyes, what greets me is the nicest surprise. Other. *Mother*, I mean. There's Mother right above me, smiling down at me from heaven. She's lying in a red bed on the ceiling, what are you doing up there, Mother? She looks like she, too, awoke from a very strange dream, like she may have been wandering in some mist of the mind herself. What did you dream about, Mother? Will you tell me?

But Mother just smiles like some things are secrets.

Well, that makes sense. Everything was always a secret with you, wasn't it? Like Beauty. You haven't changed a bit. Must have been a good dream, whatever it was, because you look so unbelievably refreshed. Not like someone dead at all. You're glowing, Mother, truly. It's amazing to see you. Making me a bit emotional in the morning, I have to say. I feel a tear slipping down.

Oh look, Mother, you're crying too. Don't cry, we can't both cry. Look, I'm happy again, okay? See? I'll be happy for you.

Mother smiles again. She's being happy just for me, too.

Oh, I see. Not Mother up there after all. Me. The ceiling is a mirror and that's me looking up at the glass, me smiling down. Must be my bedroom. This is my bed and these are my red silk sheets. For a minute I'm very sad that it's just me alone here. An emptiness opens up that feels bottomless. A blackness sits on my chest, pressing its knee into my throat. But I have to smile, too. Because that means that the face up there is mine, isn't it? My face, not Mother's, yet it looks so like Mother's. My face defying how many natural laws. That Glow, a most heavenly Glow. I'm mesmerized. If only Mother could see.

As I rise from the bed, I notice red jars shining prettily on the insanity. The *vanity*. My vanity. So very shiny and red, they do catch the eye. Gleaming like sentient apples. Each one full of skin stuff that's mine to plunder. So I'll plunder. Make a real morning of it. In the Journey of Beauty, after all, the ridicule is key. *Ritual*. Though it's going to be hard to improve upon what I'm seeing up there. If that's me.

Of course that's you, the jars seem to whisper. *Who else would it be?*

I derange—*arrange* the jars into exfoliants and mists, into toners and essences, into serums and emulsions, and finally moisturizers and oils, which are the somethings of the skin. Capes? Cardigans? Some sort of outerwear, anyway. The jars have no labels or instructions, which is funny, so I do it by texture or by guess. As I derange, I smile to myself. I keep thinking it's Mother I see there in the insanity mirror, what a strange trick. Wait, not a trick. It *is* Mother! She's back, oh joke! I mean, *joy*. Joy. Are you back to do the morning ridicule with me, Mother?

And Mother smiles with her very red lips. *Definitely*.

Now, we don't need to wash our face, right? At night, one must wash off the day, and in the morning, one must wash off the night—you taught me that. But what if we wake to find the night has already been thoroughly washed away? It appears we were thoroughly washed by the very nice people at Rouge, our friends. Your friends and now my friends, Mother. Our face is so terribly clear this morning. If we washed any more, that would just be going too far. And then what would we even have left of our faces, right?

Mother's nodding with me, *yes. What would we even have left?*

Let's skip cleansing and go right to acid, my favorite. Mother's favorite too. Acid is like cleansing but better, right, Mother? It goes deep into the ick you can't see with your human eye, and it just melts that away like a witch. Shall we do the one that smells like it'll numb your face or the one that smells like burning? You pick, Mother.

Mother's smile says, *Surprise me.*

Now normally, if your face was on fire, you'd scream like a witch, wouldn't you? Not me and Mother. We smile while our faces burn, we love it so. Because we know magic is happening, just like in a fairy tale. Transformational. We light a cigarette so as to add to the smoke. First one of the morning is always heaven, isn't it, Mother? Mother actually appears to be in a kind of heaven in the glass. A garden, it looks like. Surrounded by such tall red flowers. Red and spiky with thorns. What garden is that you're in, Mother?

But Mother doesn't want to tell me. Mother just smiles while our faces burn and we smoke our cigarettes in tandem. Another secret she wants to keep. She loves sitting here at the insanity with me—*our* insanity, I should say—even though I'm on one side of the glass and she's very much on the other side in what looks like another, more beautiful world. Will you tell me about it, Mother? Mother shakes her head no. She can't. She's with me here in the glass, though. She loves this morning's ridicule that we're doing together. It's hers, after all. She taught it to me, didn't you? Well not willingly, never willingly. I learned it by watching you in the mirror. How many nights and how many mornings. How many mirrors and how many years. How many ridicules. Watching just over your shoulder, you were such magic to my eyes then. And I'd say, *What's that you're putting on your face, Mother?* And you'd look at me in the glass like you're doing right now. Smiling sadly just like that. And remember what you said to me every time? Something about never minding. Something about blood. How mine saves me, I remember that. Can't remember what about my blood saves me. I'm having just a bit of trouble this morning with my memory. Those blanks I seem to get after I see our friends at Rouge. It'll come back to me, I'm sure. Everything will. It'll all come dancing back like a pair of red shoes, right?

Now that we're done burning our faces, what's next? Oh a mist, that's right. How could I forget? A hydrating mist to put out the fire, to set the stage for the rest. A pretty mist like the one swirling in my mind, over my thoughts, where the flowers bloom. Like the mist swirling around in the garden Mother seems to be sitting in right now, there on the other side of the glass. Looking down at our insanity, I see we have many mists to choose from. Here's a spray and here's a spray and here's a spray. Which should we pick? Can't read what's in any of these red bottles. What language is this? Looks pagan. Can you read runes, Mother? I can't, and Mother can't either, because she's shaking her head like I'm shaking mine. Better spray them all to be safe, right? We spray and we spray and we spray and it's lonely. *Lovely*, I mean. I smell an orchard of chokeberry blossoms, a field of Orpheus flowers, a dead sea of rose milk. That's the lonely thing about a mist, isn't it, Mother? The *lovely thing*. It's not just a hydrating possibility. It's another world to wander, a bit of dreaming, right? And if you mist just enough, you can even maybe go to that other world. Maybe that's how you got to where you are now. To the other side of the mirror, to that pretty garden. Maybe the lonely mist took you there. Maybe if I spray enough of one or all of these, I can follow.

I spray and I spray and I spray and it's very lonely. All these worlds of hydrating possibility waft around us now, and in your garden the mist grows thick, but I'm still here and you're still there, sadly. It's hard to see you somewhere so pretty where I'm not also. Of course that was always the way with us, wasn't it? You in your world of hydrating possibilities and me in mine is sort of like old times. Yet so close that I can almost touch your hand. But not quite, right? When I reach out my hand now, there's just glass there. Cold under my finger pads. You're reaching out too now, looks like. Just glass for you, too?

Mother smiles with her very red lips. Red as the flowers in the garden growing tall all around her. Are they growing even taller now, Mother? Am I losing you in the mist? Well I'll just keep spraying until I get myself there. I'll spray and I'll spray and I'll—

"Belle?"

Just then our bedroom door opens. And we both scream, Mother and I.

But it's only a beautiful blond man, naked from the waist up. He looks like a merman. What is he doing out of the sea? Interrupting our ridicule, which we don't love. Do we know who he is, Mother? Mother's red lips smile in the glass like she's been eating too many cherries. Of course we do. Our boyfriend, Tad. Your boyfriend or my boyfriend, Mother? Can't remember. But he washes the windows so preternaturally, it's amazing. You'd never know there was a glass there.

"Hi, Tad," we say.

He's dumbstruck, of course. No surprise there. After the transformational magic of acid, after the lonely mist, our Glow is really out of this world. Our Lift upends the natural law. To say nothing of the Brightening.

"Good morning," we say.

Tad says nothing still. Look at him just looking at us like he's afraid. Afraid? That can't be right, can it, Mother? But he really does look afraid. Well, Beauty can be scary sometimes, it can take your breath away. Maybe that's what's happening to Tad. Maybe we need to give him a minute to collect himself. Regain the power of speech. We smile at him. Not too sluttily or anything. We try hard not to be *too* dazzling. Oh, but we're failing. The Beauty just drips from us like our many hydrating possibilities.

"Jesus Christ," he whispers at last. "What happened to you?"

"Happened?" Like we were in an accident. Well, we *were* in a kind of accident, weren't we, Mother? In a manner of speaking, sure. Beauty, when you come face-to-face with it like Tad is right now, can be very like a collision. A kind of violence. This must be what Tad is

experiencing. *Beauty happened, Tad.* A Glow. An unfurling of the red
flowers of our faces.

"Belle. Please tell me."

Don't tell him, right, Mother? Because Beauty is our little secret,
isn't it? So we seal our lips into a smile that says *over my dead body.*
The mystique must be putrefied. Petrified? *Preserved.* The mystique
must be preserved. Far more magical that way.

"Belle, say something, you're scaring me."

Why does he keep only talking to me, Mother, when you're here in
the room too? Well, maybe not in the room so much, but in the glass,
definitely. Smiling there with your very red lips in your misty garden
of tall red flowers. And now look, he's marching over to us, he's sinking
to the floor, his head is right between our knees. Jesus, this is quite the
scene he's making. But then, that's what Beauty does, right, Mother?
It makes people make scenes. It makes crazed fools of those who bear
witness.

"What?" we say, so casual-surprised. Like we don't know that we're
blowing Tad's mind right now. His mind, his dick, his eyes, his soul,
really.

"Belle," he says. "Are you . . . sick? Did you give blood or something? Do you feel faint?"

Blood? Sick? Faint? Is he insane, Mother? Is he blind? Look at
you, smiling in your lonely garden where the mist grows thick. Look at
me positively dripping with hydrating possibilities. We're the furthest
thing in the world from sick, right? Mother? But Tad turns me away
from the mirror so I'm forced to look away from you. Forced to look
right into this merman's eyes, so worried yet still serene. He reaches
up and feels my forehead with his cold palm, what the hell? Like I'm
a child with a fever. I want to shake him off, but his palm, the way it's
pressed into my skin, reminds me of something. Another time someone put their hand on my forehead. A long time ago. I think it was you,
Mother. Can't remember. I don't know about you, but my memory

hasn't been the best lately. Making me emotional again, I admit. Look at me, ruining my misting like this.

"Belle, I'm sorry," Tad says, wiping away my tears tenderly. "I know this is hard. Maybe it's finally hitting you all at once or something. Maybe that's why you look so . . ." And as he's looking into my eyes, his expression shifts. Moves from concern to something else. He's so taken with us, Mother.

"My god," he whispers, his eyes fixed on us now, deep. Surely he wants to kill us. *Kiss* us. He's our boyfriend, after all, and that's what a boyfriend does. Who wouldn't want to kill a lonely dream?

"You look just like . . ." But he's drawing a blank. Looking at my face, words escape him. Which makes sense. I understand all about blanks, about words being slippery.

"I look just like . . . ?" I say, leaning in, waiting.

"Like her," he says at last, looking afraid.

Her?

"Just before," he says. "I can't believe it." He pulls away—why would he pull away, Mother? But Mother's gone. Just me and Tad in the glass now. No misty garden of tall red flowers. No Mother smiling there amid the blooms and thorns. Just Tad standing up. Leaving me sitting here alone at my insanity with my open hands empty.

"I don't know if you should sleep in this room anymore," Tad is saying. "The energies are off. Or maybe it's mold."

Mold?

"I told her a long time ago that it might be. Maybe it's in the walls. Maybe I should call a doctor," he offers. "Get you something to drink."

A doctor. Something to drink. Is he serious? He seems to be. Though maybe playing like I'm sick is his thing, what excites him. Maybe he'd like to save me. "Well, before you do that, you'd better come back and feel my forehead again," I tell him. "I'm feeling a bit faint."

He reaches out tentatively and I pull him down and kill him hard on the lips. Surely this is what he wants. But instead of melting beautifully into my kill like a witch in acid, Tad stiffens. His lips stay very pressed together. "I'm sorry," he says, pulling away, getting up. "It's just . . . It's too weird, right?"

"Weird?" *Why weird? You're my boyfriend.* "No. How is it weird?"

"Belle," he says, and something in his voice makes me look away.

I stare down at my hands gripping his. Many mists drip from my face. I hear the sound of chimes in my head, and underneath, a roar like water. Through the roar, Tad's voice comes to me very faintly. Something about rest. How it's all I need right now. Something about juice and how we're out of fruit. He'll just go out now and get some, okay? His hands in mine are lax, patient, waiting for me to let go. *Please let me go.*

So I open my hands. Watch Tad run out of the room. *It's fine,* I think. *Go ahead.* Leave me here, I'm not alone. I'm lovely. I have my mists. Each one a world to wander in. All of them running down my face in rivulets, so very luminous I am. Dripping from my eyes onto my empty hands gripping air. I guess in the end we misted too much, Mother. But Mother's not in the mirror anymore, must remember. Through the mists, I see a gold bracelet winking on the table. Nested between the red jars. Mother, did you leave me a gift? The bracelet itself is so small, so delicate, the gold thin as thread. It could have belonged to a child. Perhaps it did. What a slim little wrist it must have fit once. It has an eye in its center, I see. Strange, slanted. Staring at me like it can see my heart. Have I looked into this eye before? Why do I feel I have?

I slip it on—and look at that, it fits. Makes me smile a little, clears the mists. The chimes quiet, the roar of the ocean in my head goes still. I remember I've got work today. At my shop, of course. That's right. I've got a shop, don't I? How could I forget?

20

By the time I get to Belle of the Ball, I can see and think very clearly. Clear as a bell. Just like my name, Belle. Just like my shop, Belle of the Ball. There's Mother in the shop glass. Mother, I'm so glad you're here. To be honest, I thought you left me there back in my bedroom, left me for your garden world. I wouldn't have blamed you. But it's good to see you here in the window display, and look, you took your pretty garden with you. Wearing a dress red as its flowers, just like I am, the same red shoes to match. I chose it after Tad left me to get some fruit for a juice I don't even need to drink. And he never came back, can you believe that? Mother can't. Once more, she's shaking her head just as I'm shaking mine. Or is it something else you can't believe, Mother? Mother, why do you look so horrified?

Then I see, of course. Why she looks horrified.

There's something else in the window display, something else with Mother in her garden. A horrible obstruction that hurts my eyes like the light. Hurts Mother's eyes too, it looks like. A row of gray headless . . . are they scarecrows? Garden statues? They look like corpses. Standing all around you, Mother, oh god. Almost as if on ghoulish display. Each one backlit and wearing some sort of sack dress and . . . is it chunky silver jewelry? I know it sounds crazy. Because who would do something like that, right? Mother, no wonder you look so upset. What are these wretched creatures? They must be statues. And yet they look so much like corpses, I can't help but whisper to them: *When was the beheading? And why wasn't I here, protecting you from the guillotine? Who dressed you in these fashion sacks? Who put chunky silver jewelry around your necks like chains?*

Thank god I'm here now. Have to fix this immediately, right, Mother? Put the Belle back in Belle of the Ball where she should be.

"Can I help you?" says a voice. A woman poking her head out of the shop door. Grim face. Fish eyes. Red glasses hanging from a red chain around her neck. She looks a little afraid of me, like Tad did.

"Can I *help* you?" she repeats. Which is funny. Because *we're* the ones who work here, aren't we, Mother?

"We should really be the ones asking you that, Esther," I say to her, and smile. She has a name tag, that's helpful.

Esther looks around, confused. *We?* She must not see that I'm with you, Mother. She must not see you in the shop glass or she must think we're one and the same. We look so much like each other today, it's true. Esther doesn't seem to see very well. Completely immune to the abomination in the window display.

"How can *we* help *you*, Esther?" we say in our best salesperson voice. I say it; Mother mouths it along with me in the shop glass with her very red lips. We make the delight drip.

"I work here," Esther says.

She does? Oh god, then things are even more not pretty than I thought. Mother, did we really hire this woman? With the dead-fish eyes and the resting bitch face, who's scared of Beauty? But we can't let on that we forgot her.

"Of course you do." We smile. "Sorry we're late, Esther."

"Late?" Esther says. "How can you be late? You don't even work—"

"We were pursuing our Most Magnificent Selves," I say. "But we went a little too far with the mists. You know how it is." Probably Esther doesn't, but it's always good to banter with your staff like this. "First chokeberry blossoms, then Orpheus flowers . . . the ocean of your mind roaring along with the chimes." I laugh and Mother smiles. "Always trauma—I mean *tricky* to get out the door, isn't it? But we're here now. We're here to sever. *Serve* of course." And we bow like we don't own the place. "Have we been bury? *Busy?*"

Esther just stares at me. She's standing in the doorway sort of blocking our way to the shop. "I'm not really supposed to let you in, Mirabelle. I'm sorry."

I look at Mother in the shop glass. She's horrified. Just as horrified as I feel, she looks.

"Not supposed to let us in? To *our* shop? Esther, that's crazy. You need us now more than ever." I squeeze by her, making my way inside. But Esther's dogging my heels. She scurries past me and runs behind the counter as if to block me from it, can you believe this, Mother? I look up at Mother in the mirror behind the register. She can't believe it either.

I turn to Esther and smile. "Why don't you go on your lunch break?" It would really be best to get her out of the way for the plans we have. Not necessary, but best.

"Sylvia says I'm supposed to be on the floor," Esther says, hands on the counter.

Sylvia? Who the hell is Sylvia? "Well it can be our little secret. I won't tell if you won't, Esther."

"I can't. Sylvia said."

"Esther, do we really need to do everything 'Sylvia' says in this life?"

Esther says nothing. She reaches for something under the counter. A gun? A phone. She's texting something quickly, what is she texting, Mother? Making me nervous, but in the mirror, Mother looks just fine in her garden. She's picking red flowers now. Gathering them into a basket crooked in her arm. A pretty black bird alights on her shoulder and they appear to be singing to each other softly. You're right, Mother. It's not for us to be nervous. If anything, Esther should be nervous. Texting on the floor in front of her bosses like this.

"If you want to stay here and text, you go right ahead," I tell Esther. "We'll just wander around the floor." In the glass, I see Mother's already starting to drift away along the mirrored walls of the shop. Mother, wait!

"I think you better stay here at the register with me," Esther shouts limply.

"Oh, we can't have three of us crowded behind that register. That would be *such* a waste." I walk away from her, my red shoes leading me along. And in the glass along the shop wall, Mother's red shoes are doing the same.

"Where are you going?"

"Here and there." But we know exactly where we're going, right, Mother? Mother knows. Mother's already far ahead.

"Sylvia says we're not supposed to change anything!" Esther blurts after me, almost like she anticipates our plans.

"Does she?" I sing over my shoulder. "How interesting." And then I run to the display window. Why do I feel like I need to do this in a hurry? I don't really. Not doing anything illegal. This is our shop, isn't it? We've let it fall into the wrong hands, obviously. Hired Esther for some reason, what were we thinking? And now this woman *Sylvia* to contend with, apparently. Where have we even been? Don't know, isn't that funny? Anyway, we're here now. To put things back, to make things right.

Mother's already there in the window glass, waiting. Smiling at me among her tall red flowers, though she's surrounded by such violence again. Her smile says, *Surely you know what you have to do here.*

Of course I do, Mother.

First things first: get rid of these gray headless monstrosities. I say *monstrosities* because when I look at them straight on, I see they're just ugly dress forms. And yet when I look in the window glass where Mother is, they're most definitely corpses. So which are they, Mother? Dress forms or corpses? Mother's face says *potato potahto*, and I have to agree in this case. The point is really to get them out of her garden. So I topple them—one, two, three. Because they're already dead, they don't feel a thing. I gather one of them into my arms. Surprisingly light and silvery she is. I'll have to bury her, all of them, somewhere, I guess, right? Or should I call the undertaker? *Who is your next of kin, ladies?* But that's such an absurd question. How can they possibly answer it? They don't have lips because they don't have heads. And dead on top of that, remember? Can't forget.

"Mirabelle!"

I turn to find a little blond woman standing behind me. Clutching her pearls. Looking aghast. Of course we would have a customer pestering us just now. Always when you're in the middle of something.

"Just a moment, please. We'll be right with you, okay?"

The woman just gapes at me. She's looking at me like she knew me once (I must have severed her before) and she can hardly recognize me now. "My god, Mira." She shakes her head. "Is that really you? You look . . . ," but she doesn't finish that thought. Her mouth just stays open. Taken aback by the Glow, I suppose. Our Brightening—or is it our Lift?—has cut out her tongue. Not very nice or polite, but that's retail. Sometimes you have to finish people's sentences. Sometimes their thoughts.

"Thank you. I'd tell you my secret, but here's the thing: everyone's Journey is different. Very perilous. *Personal*," I whisper. "So what works for me may not work for you and so forth." Right, Mother?

But when I look in the window glass, I just see the garden. A black bird sitting on the basket of red flowers. Mother, where did you go?

"Mirabelle," the woman says, and closes her eyes. "What the hell is going on here?"

A nosy one, I guess. Some customers are. "Just doing some deranging in my shop."

"Your shop? *Your* shop!"

"It didn't always look like this, promise. We've had some real issues with staff lately, but we're sorting them out, definitely."

"I need you to get out of that window display *now*."

"Well, as you can see, you've caught me at a bit of an awkward time." And I hold up my headless corpse. "But I'll be with you in just a minute, all right? Unless maybe you'd like to purchase one of these dress sacks? Take them off our hands? We're having a sale, just announced. And I see you're already a fan." She's wearing one, the little woman. Swallowed by an asymmetrical sea of slate.

"Mirabelle, this has gone too far. Far too far, do you understand?"

"Oh have you soured on the sack, then? Can't say I blame you. They're not very pretty, are they? Not my idea," I whisper. "I think some person named *Sylvia* is responsible. Probably she was the one who severed you. I'm very sorry. I wouldn't trust her in the future, not a drop. I think she also may be responsible for this," I say, pointing to the corpses. "Call it a hunch. Now I have to go bury them in the basement I didn't know we had, can you believe this job? Retail. Not for the faint of heart." And I laugh. Mother isn't here to laugh with me just now. So I laugh for both of us because it's really very funny. *Retail.* I know she'd laugh if she were here.

But the little woman doesn't laugh with me. "Listen, I know you're grieving. And I know grieving can be difficult but—"

"Grieving? Oh no, I hardly know them." I smile sadly.

"Mira, I really think you need to see someone, do you hear me? Talk to someone. If not me, then someone else. Who can help you."

"Help us?" That's very funny too. Makes me laugh again all by myself. Because it's this woman, clearly, who needs all the help she can get. If only Mother would come back from her wandering in the other world, she could explain for both of us. That we don't need any help. "That's silly. When *we're* supposed to be helping *you*. Speaking of which, I'll just go into the back room and see if I can find something for you there." And when I step forward with the corpse in my arms, the little blond woman backs away immediately. She looks very afraid. Understandable. Retail, like Beauty, can be scary sometimes.

When I get to the stockroom, what I see makes me drop the corpse: my sisters. Alone in a dark corner. Stripped of their lovely clothes, their finery. They used to be out front in the display window, I remember. Now imprisoned back here. Standing still as you please, the picture of elegance even in their fallen state. I know they're my sisters because they look exactly like Mother. And Mother looks exactly like me. Of course, Mother's not here just now. But when she comes back and sees us all together, she'll smile at how we all have the same Brightness.

"Sisters," I say, and I curtsy before them, "I'm so sorry you were left here in the dark. I'm so sorry I didn't rescue you sooner. I don't know what witch put you back here, but I have an idea who it might be. Don't worry, I'm here now. I've taken the corpses out of the window. I'm putting you back out on display where you belong."

But what will they wear? I think. Oh look, here are some dresses, hanging on a rack. Dresses we used to sell that we apparently don't sell anymore. Dresses of silver and of gold. Dresses of starry midnight and dresses white as snow shimmering under the sun. I dress one sister in gold, one in starry black, one in silver. And me wearing a dress red as blood completes the picture. My sisters smile at me with their eyes. *Thank you so much, Sister*, they seem to say. Their golden irises come alive. Their red lips, too. Oh Mother, I wish you could see.

"Mirabelle," screams someone behind me. That pesky blond woman again. Looking even more outraged and afraid than before. That's right, I was supposed to help her find a dress. But this is far more important, sorry. These are my sisters, after all. "I'm sorry but your dress is just going to have to wait. This is a family emergency, I'm afraid."

She looks at me gripping my sister's shoulder. "Mirabelle, please. If you just leave now, I promise I won't press charges, okay? I won't file a complaint. I'd hate to do that given my friendship with your . . . given everything. But if you don't leave right now, if you continue to harass my staff and terrorize my customers and destroy my merchandise, you'll be tying my hands. Do you understand that?"

Her staff? *Her* merchandise? And it hits me. This woman isn't a customer. She's the infamous Sylvia herself. The one who beheaded the corpses, who locked my sisters in this back room. And now she seems to think this is her shop, can you believe this, Mother? Mother's gone, must remember. When I look in the nearest mirror, there's no one in the glass, just the garden that looks nearly underwater now. The flowers seeming to sway like sea flowers on a seafloor. The sky is a blue of light-filled water. And Mother nowhere in this ocean world. But she'll come back, surely? I look at my sisters. *Won't she?*

They stare at me with their eyes so golden and sorrowful.

"Mirabelle, did you—?"

"Sylvia, if anyone should be pressing charges, it's me. You've destroyed my shop, my family." I wrap my arm around one of my sisters tight. I look right at Sylvia, her mouth gaping at me. "I'm afraid you've given me no choice but to let you go."

"That's it," she roars. "I'm calling the police!"

She's about to storm out, but there's a man standing in the doorway, blocking her path. He's wearing a hat and a dark blue suit. He flashes something like a badge very quickly. "That won't be necessary."

"Speak of the devil," Sylvia says, wiping her eyes. I can feel her wondering if she summoned him with her thoughts. "Officer?"

The man nods imperceptibly. You could say he nodded or you could say he just stood there. He looks like he walked out of one of your old movies, Mother. His dewy face all shadows and sharp angles. A scar on his cheek curved like a hook. Familiar. Where have I seen him before?

"Officer, thank god, I was just going to call."

"What seems to be the trouble here?"

"Oh, this is so difficult. So very difficult." She sighs and shakes her head like it's all too much. "This," she says, gesturing at me, "is the daughter of a friend who passed away recently, you see. A dear friend. I don't want to press charges, but she's been harassing my staff, destroying merchandise. She gave one of our customers a nervous breakdown just the other day. And she seems to think she still works here."

He nods. "I'll take care of it. Belle?" Acting gruff, but there's a softness to how he looks at me, speaks my name. I see a rickety white bridge over the Pacific. A hotel room in the half-dark. The smell of whiskey and flowers and smoke. His face very close to my face, like he wanted to kill me. Kiss me? Wanted something, anyway.

"You're not going to arrest her, are you?" Sylvia says. "I don't want anything to happen to her, I just don't want her in the shop. I'm afraid she's not in her right mind. Maybe you could call a psychiatric hospital?" So concerned, when just a moment ago she was ready to throw me out of my own shop.

"That won't be necessary, Miss Holmes."

Sylvia raises her eyebrows. How does he know her name? "Have we . . . ?"

"No, but I'm familiar. Belle, would you please come with me?" Gray eyes full of dark water. I know that his lips taste like roses—why do I know that? I don't necessarily want to go with him, but I also don't want to stay here with Sylvia. In the mirror, no Mother. No ocean garden anymore. Nothing now in the glass but my three sisters. Looking at me with their golden eyes. Myself standing between them, gripping one by the shoulder. There's a gray dress form on the floor at my feet. "I'm not leaving without my sisters," I say.

Sylvia looks at him like *you see, you see?*

The man ignores her. Stares at me. "So bring them along."

21

On my couch with a detective named Hud Hudson, who keeps staring at me. He gave me his business card and that's what it said in silvery-blue font above the words *Private Investigations*. "Have we met?" I ask him.

"A few times now."

"I had a feeling."

"Belle," he says, "I hope you know this is getting very serious."

"Serious?"

Hud kindly drove me and my sisters home, carried them into the apartment since they didn't seem to be able to carry themselves. Two under one arm, one under the other. Now they're sitting all around us, smiling. At least this is how it seems when I look in any one of the mirrors in Mother's living room. The mirrors are where my sisters come alive, so that's where I mostly keep my eyes. It's lucky Mother has so many, a wall of glass right across from where we sit. Whenever I look at this wall, I see them offering various kinds of support. One sister is sitting on the carpet playing with the coffee table flowers, deranging them like she's a florist. Another is slouched by the open window, watching the water. Leaning pretty far out, she loves to breathe the ocean air.

"I hope she won't fall."

"I'll keep an eye on her," Hud says, not looking at her. Looking at me. I see that in every mirror and even when I look at him straight on.

My third sister sits beside us on the couch. Keeping the closest eye. She looks the most worried, the most suspicious of Hud Hudson.

She can't deny that he's beautiful, of course. We all think that. He's a detective of Beauty, after all, isn't he? Or a beautiful detective. Either way. And how he's looking at us right now, with such intensity, such *I want to get to the bottom of you*. Even my most suspicious sister concedes it's entrancing. But we've always liked a bit of distance, haven't we, Sisters? Arm's length is best. Not that we don't have desire. We are human, after all, aren't we? Just that in our bodies, something is sealed up, closed like the CLOSED sign I used to put in the shop door at night. Something is holding itself away as if behind glass, isn't that right, Sisters? In the mirrors, my sisters smile. *Exactly*.

Meanwhile, Hud's staring at us like he doesn't know where to begin.

"May we offer you a drink?" I ask him.

"God yes," he whispers. "Please."

I pour some of Mother's cognac for him, myself, and my sister on the couch. He and I raise glasses, but my sister leaves hers where it is. Doesn't trust Hud at all. *I don't like this*, she whispered again and again on the ride home. And I told her *shhh*, even though Hud didn't seem to hear, and her mouth stayed pursed in that secret smile. It was in the rearview mirror only that I saw her mouth moving, that her eyes were wild with just how much she didn't like this.

"If you don't mind, Belle, I'd like to ask you a few questions," he says now. And then he pulls out a pen and a small notepad from his pocket. Clicks the pen.

My heart begins to thud in my chest. "Questions?"

"For our records is all."

In the mirrors, I see my sisters stiffen. They don't like this for me.

"What's your name?"

"Belle."

"What is your *full* name?"

Nothing comes. Only one of those blanks. Is there a word that should come after Belle? Feels like there should be one, one that never felt like mine. Alien. Heavy on my tongue, a strange-shaped stone. *Looks like "night" but means "light"* is a phrase that suddenly appears in my mind. But it means nothing. So maybe this is a trick question?

"Belle," I say. I watch him scribble on his pad.

"What about your father?"

A slanted eye of gold winking on my wrist, watching me. "I'm afraid I don't know."

"What's your mother's full name?"

My sisters and I smile at one another in the mirror. That's an easy one. "Mother."

Furious scribbling with his pen. "And where do you live?"

I gesture out the window at the blue sky, whose brightness hurts my eyes. "Eden. Obviously."

"Where were you born?"

In my mind, I see a wretched island wreathed by a slushy river the color of Hud Hudson's eyes. That can't be right. "Here."

"Where do you work?"

"At Belle of the Ball. A dress shop. You know that."

"Your name isn't Mirabelle Nour and you don't live and work in the Plateau area of Montreal, Canada? At a shop called Damsels in This Dress?"

"In *Distress*? That sounds awful."

"What about Montreal?"

"I've heard it's pretty there but very cold. Too cold for me."

"So you grew up here? And you've never lived or worked anywhere else?"

"That's right." Along the wall of glass, my sisters nod encouragingly. They love my answers so far.

"Where is your mother now, Belle?"

"Not sure, to be honest."

"Do you know what happened to her?"

"Happened to her?"

"That she died?"

And I have to laugh. Isn't he the one who's supposed to be the detective of Beauty? He should really have his facts straight. "She was just here."

"Where? Show me."

"No." For one, Mother isn't in the mirrors at the moment. Just me and Hud in the glass—and my sisters of course, smiling a little more sadly now.

"Belle, listen. You're in grave danger, do you understand? You've fallen into the hands of some very evil people."

"Evil people? I don't know any evil people. I only know my friends at Rouge. And you. You're a friend too, aren't you?"

Hud Hudson's turn to look at me sadly with his clear gray eyes. "No, Belle. At least, I haven't been. But I want to try and be one now."

"What do you mean?"

"I should've been straight with you from the beginning. I just never thought they'd move so quickly. So fuck me for that."

"What do you mean?"

"Your second treatment."

How does he know about the second treatment? I look in the mirror at my sister on the couch. She's seething. *Oh, he's clever, this one, isn't he? He thinks he's very clever indeed.*

"Second treatment?" I say. "I haven't had a second treatment."

He looks at me like *come on*. Am I seriously going to lie about this?

Why am I lying about this? I ask my sisters with my mind. And in the mirror, my sister on the couch smiles like it's really very simple. *Because Beauty is our little secret. Because we never tell. Not even over our dead body. We deny everything. We deny all.*

I think you should be honest, says my sister deranging the flowers. *Honesty is the best policy.*

Don't listen to her, she knows nothing! shouts my sister on the couch. *Denial is really the only way forward.*

The water looks so pretty from here, sighs my sister by the window.

"Your face gives you away, Belle. That *Glow*."

"Plenty of people glow, Detective."

"There's the Lift, too. The Smoothness. The Whitening," he adds, lowering his voice.

Whitening? And we all have to laugh, me and my sisters. *Call it a Brightening.* "I'd call it a Brightening."

"Is that what you'd call it?" He looks at me until I find I have to look away, in the mirrors, at my sister on the couch. She appears outraged by his terminology. Regards him coldly. Her looks could cut.

"Also that mark that was on your forehead. Barely there anymore," he marvels. Still looking at me, entranced. Not just entranced, another shade of feeling in his expression. Darker, sharper, I used to know its name.

Envy, snaps my sister on the couch. *Envy is its name!*

Not envy! Desire, says my sister by the flowers. *He desires you, because you're so very entrancing, Sister.*

Well, envy and desire are often one and the same trance, murmurs my sister by the water.

I look at the scar across Hud Hudson's sharp cheek. Like someone took a hook to the skin and ripped. Seeing me notice, he turns away and pours himself another drink. "Taken all together, I'd say the evidence is pretty damning, Belle."

Evidence? Don't let him get to you like this, he knows nothing! What is he going to do: arrest you for a Glow? Ha! Since when was Beauty a crime? Envy, now there's a crime for you!

I think he just likes you, says my sister by the flowers. *Really likes you and this is his way of saying it.*

I think you should sit by me, Belle, says my sister by the window, who won't meet my eye in the mirrors. *We should walk to the cliff's edge. I know a game we can play. We can play it together, you and me.*

"Belle, are you listening to me?"

"Of course we—I am."

"You did it, didn't you?"

"No."

Very good, denial! cheers my sister on the couch.

"You followed the path to the house on the cliff. There was a party, and everyone applauded. Said how you glow and glow. *Like a moon, Daughter.*"

"No." I shake my head. "No, no."

"And once you were good and drunk on the bubbly drug, a woman, maybe in silver, maybe in red, she took your hand and led you downstairs, below what they call the Depths. They made you lie down on a table, sort of like a massage table, in a dark room full of fog. And you took some deep, deep breaths. What were you breathing in, Belle? Maybe eucalyptus. Maybe ether. Maybe a special blend of both."

Wow, says my sister by the flowers. *He seems to know the whole story. He's very smart.*

He THINKS he's smart, shouts my sister on the couch. *He knows nothing!*

"And then they took something from you, didn't they? What did they take from you, Belle?"

A little of your cloudy skies, says my sister by the flowers.

Nothing you couldn't do without, says my sister on the couch.

Please walk out to the water with me, says my sister by the window.

"Nothing, nothing," I whisper.

"Something they said you didn't need, maybe? Something dark and sad from your past. A humiliation. A childhood trauma. A painful labyrinth of memory you unknowingly walk in the night that shapes your dreams. Maybe even a crime. What did they call it? *A Free Radical of the Mind. A Comedo of the Soul.*"

Don't listen to him, Belle! screams my sister on the couch.

Oh, listen to him, he's so intense, says my sister by the flowers. *So filled with conviction, this detective of Beauty. It's quite entrancing.*

Let's please run to the cliffs now, beckons my sister by the window. *The waves are high and crashing against the rocks. And I have a game for you and me.*

"And now here you sit, memory scrambled and full of holes. But who wouldn't want to exorcise a few demons, kick a few skeletons out of the closet for that Glow? Letting go is so worth it, isn't it?"

"I don't know what you're talking about." I'm shaking and shaking my head.

"Maybe we should ask your mother if it's worth it? Oh wait, that's right, we *can't* ask her, can we? She's dead."

He's lying!

"You're lying," I shout, along with all three of my sisters.

"I wish I were," he says quietly. His gaze holds mine. Sorrowful, knowing. Hurts to look at. He reaches for my hand, and my sister on the couch hisses and my sister by the flowers shudders and my sister by the window sighs. "Listen, Belle. Please. There are those who go through those black gates, walk up that rosy path, and they never come back. They disappear. Or they wind up dead on the rocks like your mother."

What is he saying to me, Sisters? Can this really be true? But when I look at the wall of mirrors, all three are dead silent now, and still. My sister on the couch stares straight ahead coldly. My sister by the flowers has given up on the flowers. She's facedown on the coffee table. My sister by the window looks out at the water with a tear in her eye. Her face is filled with some secret grief.

I turn back to Hud Hudson. Eyes still sorrowful. Gaze holding mine like a glass. "How do you know all this?"

He lets go of my hand. Lights a cigarette. "Didn't I tell you there were two of me once?" In the mirrors, he's in shadow now. The smoke hangs over his face like a veil.

"Your brother."

"Edward. He was a member, like your mother. An actor like her too. Who knows, maybe they even saw each other at the house. Shared a glass of the bubbly drug by the Depths." He smiles darkly, takes a long sip of his drink.

"What happened to him?"

"He disappeared about six months ago." Another drag from his cigarette. I watch his scar gleam as he smokes.

"I'm sorry."

"Me too." His voice is cracked with pain. So familiar to us. "We weren't very close, not since we were kids. Sort of estranged, actually. Especially after our mother died."

A sigh from my sister by the flowers.

"About a year ago, I'd started to notice that on the phone, he'd have these word slips. Blanks. Little things, then bigger things. Mix past and present. I worried it was drugs at first—Edward was never all that . . . stable. Or early-onset dementia. Our mother had it. The last time I saw him, he was playing Iago at the Playhouse. He kept messing up his lines. It was painful to watch, he was always so flawless. I stayed after the show to see how he was holding up, though I worried he'd see that as some sort of insult—Edward took any dent in his armor so terribly. But when he opened the door to his dressing room, I couldn't believe . . ."

And now Hud's just staring at himself in the mirror as if struck.

"What?"

"His face," he says. His eyes look afraid. And there's that other shade of feeling creeping in again, what is its name again, Sisters?

"He'd looked different onstage," Hud continues, still lost in his reflection. "I'd thought it was just lighting, makeup maybe. Maybe another one of his procedures—Edward had always been into those, always a little vain. But this was something else. This transformation was unreal. Not any of his newfangled treatments, not even surgery could account for . . ." He turns to me. Reaches out as if to touch my face. Instead he runs his hand through his own dark hair, takes another drag of his cigarette.

"I didn't say anything to him, of course. Edward didn't like to talk about his looks, but he was obsessed. Sort of like it was a . . . secret for him. Or something. You know?"

We do, mumbles my sister by the flowers in her sleep.

"So I just congratulated him on his performance. And the way he looked at me . . ."

"How?"

"Like I wasn't his brother. Like he didn't know me at all. Sound familiar?"

Not at all, murmurs my sister on the couch from behind her hands. But her voice is full of pain like Hud Hudson's. I see Mother's face in my mind. Looking at me like I was a stranger. Like she was empty. Emptied. And me looking at the emptiness, feeling sick, afraid. Responsible—why responsible?

"*People disappear*, the police told me, if you can believe it. I started looking into it and that's when I stumbled upon our house on the cliff. On Rouge."

My sisters sigh at the sound of this word. The way Hud Hudson says it. How it lights up his eyes, darkens his voice.

"*Try looking into Rouge*, I told the cop. He said, *That fancy French spa by the water? My wife's a member. Loves it. Barking up the wrong tree there, Hudson.*" Another angry drag of his cigarette. He shakes his head at Mother's mirrors. I know he sees nothing there in the glass. Just himself on the other side, broken and looking in.

"That cop didn't know it, but he confirmed something for me. Some people, like his wife, seem to be enjoying the services of Rouge, paying for them, without losing their minds or dying. Others, like your mother, like Edward, aren't so lucky."

I look at my sister by the window, frozen but still gazing out at the water, a tear midway down her cheek.

"That's the thing I don't fully understand yet," he says. "Why do some members pay, why do others get free treatments? Why do some lose their minds from the treatments and disappear? Why do some disappear quickly and others not so quickly? There seems to be no standard timeline, no—"

"Well, everyone's Journey is different, isn't it, Detective?" I say. Didn't someone tell me that in a waiting room once? "Very peril— *personal.*"

"Like our demons. Maybe some are more appealing to Rouge than others." He's still staring at my face, his eyes tracing its particular configuration of contour and shadow. Why is he looking at me like this, Sisters? But they all still seem to be dreaming.

"You know Edward tried to kill me once?" he says, eyes on my eyes. A sharp shiver runs through me. "He did?"

"When we were nine. For some reason, he had it in his head that I was the prettier one, if you can believe it. Even though we looked so alike, most people couldn't tell us apart. But Edward was convinced. So one day he broke one of our mother's perfume bottles and he did this." He points to his scar, shining in the light. A burning on my forehead suddenly. Cold rushing through me like wind.

"After that, Edward went to live in Santa Cruz with our father for a while. It was the strangest thing . . ." He breaks off, shaking his head as if to shake it all away. I reach out my hand to his face. My fingers trace the raised, pale slash on his cheek.

"What?" I whisper.

He looks at me. Presses my hand against his face. "I used to be able to look at Edward and know his thoughts. I could feel his joy, his fear, his pain. Whether I wanted to or not, I felt it. But when I saw him again, that was all gone. He was like a different person. He'd forgotten what had happened, what he'd done. He was smiling, but distant. So distant with me." Crack running through his voice like a crack in a glass. Eyes still on my eyes. A sorrow there, fathoms deep. His sorrow or mine? I'm drowning in it like dark water.

"Why are you telling me this story, Detective?"

"Because he was a Perfect Candidate. Like you."

I drop my hand from his face. "Me?"

"Your mother paid for her treatments, like the cop's wife, like many people seem to. She paid, but she still lost her mind, still disappeared. That's less common from what I've seen, though it happens. Typically it's the ones who don't pay, who get free treatments like you and Edward—the *Perfect Candidates*, they call them . . ."

A skipping of my heart now at that phrase. A flicker of some recollection. Hud Hudson sees it. "Those," he says, "are the ones who—"

"Go on a very exciting Journey," I cut in.

Exactly, Sister, whispers my sister on the couch. In the mirror, she's suddenly wide awake. Glaring at Hud Hudson, who's looking at me with such *let me in*.

Because he's a little in love with you, says my sister by the flowers. Awake now too in the glass. Elbows on the coffee table, chin in her palms, watching us like we're a film, an old favorite.

He's not in love, spits my sister on the couch. *He just desires what he doesn't understand. Men love a mystery, don't they?*

The true mystery is the ocean itself, isn't it? says my sister by the window. *The first mirror of the world. Reflecting back the heavens.* When I look in the glass, I see she's smiling at the waves, still with that tear in her eye.

"I still don't know what makes a Perfect Candidate," Hud says. "I just know some people are marked. And Rouge knows how to spot the mark." He glances up at my forehead. "Knows what they want when they see it. And what they want, they take."

He's very close to me again, this beautiful detective. Looking deeply into my eyes like he could look there forever. It's the true mystery. Reflecting everything he's lost and now found again. Can't lose it now. Can't lose it again ever.

Well, this is very entrancing, says my sister by the flowers.

All he wants to do is pull back the curtain, says my sister on the couch with great bitterness. *Once he's wrenched it down and stared into what he thinks is the cold light of the truth of you, he'll walk away.*

Walk away with me to the water, Sister.

Suddenly, beside us, I feel the wall of mirrors start to shimmer. Does Hud Hudson see it? No, he's still looking into my eyes. I'm the only mirror he wants right now. But like a magnet, I'm drawn back to the wall of glass, shining like it's beckoning me. It doesn't look like a mirror anymore, but a window. Through it, I see the house on the cliff. The grand hall with its great chandelier. And is that Mother I see on the stair? Yes! In a red dress just like mine. Walking down toward the Depths. Oh Mother, is that really you? There's a man in shadow behind her, who is that man, Mother? Who's walking behind you? But Mother still doesn't answer, doesn't turn to me.

Beside me, Hud Hudson's calling my name. "Belle, what are you seeing?" He turns and looks in the mirror, but I know he sees nothing. Doesn't see the house on the cliff. Our friends at Rouge on the stair. Everyone waving for me to come join them. And Mother walking down toward the Depths. Disappearing behind them. The mirror going black.

"Detective, I'm afraid I have to leave now."

"You're not going back there, Belle. Not on my watch. Not without me."

My watch? repeats my sister on the couch. *Who is this man? Does he think he's in the movies or something?*

He could be in the movies, says my sister by the flowers. *He's very beautiful, but in that broken way we like. A detective of Beauty, remember?*

I really think we should just dive into the sea, says my sister by the window.

"I should go," I say.

"Let me come with you." Gently, he reaches for my hand.

Presumptuous, mutters my sister on the couch. *Thinking he can save you from yourself.*

I think it's sweet, says my sister by the flowers. *Look at him, so intense and well-meaning. It's quite sexy.*

You should probably just seduce him, Sister, says my sister by the water.

Seduce him?

It's the only way to go to the house alone. To get to Mother. Also, you really want to, don't you?

The wall of mirrors is just glass again now. No window to the house. No Mother. I look back at Hud Hudson, beautiful detective. Eyes clear and deep as the first mirror of the world. Warm hand gripping mine. "All right," I tell him. "I'll let you come with me."

He raises an eyebrow. "Really?"

"Absolution—solutely."

"Okay, then." He sighs with such relief. Oh god, how do I do this, Sisters?

Remember, says my sister by the water, *envy and desire are often one and the same trance.*

"First, though, I think you should take a closer look at this Glow," I say. And then the look in his eye shifts. Slowly, I take his hands and bring them up to my face. Press his palms into my cheeks. I feel his hands trembling against my skin or am I trembling at his touch, Sisters? But my sisters are sighing. Sighing as Hud Hudson is shuddering, shaking his head like he shouldn't, he shouldn't, even though he's only moving in closer as I'm moving in closer. Not pulling back, not like our boyfriend did earlier. Sighing now as he strokes my face. At first very softly, tenderly, like he might break me. Then more intensely, with hunger and wonder. "Holy fuck," he whispers into my ear.

All around me, my sisters are sighing at the touch of the beautiful detective. Our souls open like a flower opens to the light.

Entrancing, whispers my sister by the flowers.

So long as we're just using him, mumbles my sister on the couch.

Finally, the sea, sighs my sister by the water.

I lean in and kill him on the lips and he kills me right back. *Kisses.* Deeply. I taste roses. I feel the want in his hands and lips, deep as my own want, its mirror. Deep as the mystery of the first mirror.

And something else is there too, in his touch that can't get enough. Something under its want, in its depths, I feel it creeping in. A dark, aching thing, I used to know its name. The one that empties. That consumes and is consumed. It tastes bittersweet, thorny like the roses in his kill. My sisters turn away their golden eyes.

22

I arrive in the grand hall, my red shoes panting on my feet. "Right on time," the woman in silver says when she opens the door. When I'm announced, the applause is deafening. A full-on roar. For me? But this is so unexpected. Thanks so much, *merci*.

"I'm actually just here because I'm looking for someone. Have you seen—?" But my voice is drowned out in the roar. A raising of red fizzing flutes in their opera-gloved fists. The grand hall is all lit up tonight. The red curtain is drawn and the Depths are exposed. The blue-green water glows gloriously as if lit from beneath. Even the red jellyfish seem to be clapping for me. Their bells pulsate in time to the human applause, tentacles undulating wildly. Except one. A large one, very red. Its strange jelly eyes are fixed on me. Sadly? Can't be. Oh well, never mind. I'm looking for someone, aren't I? Mother, that's right. Is she here? Don't see her. The hall is crowded like never before with shimmering people trailing silks of red and black and white. Their sin looks made of actual diamonds. *Skin*. Not sin, why sin? All of them are smiling at me. Never too widely, of course. They have their own sins to think of. *Skins*. They congratulate me as I pass. They've mastered the art of speaking without moving their lips, quite like my sisters.

"Many *félicitations* on reaching the Precipice," they say through their teeth.

"Thank you," I say. And I think, *Precipice? I've reached a Precipice?* "I'm actually here because I'm looking for my—"

"What a big fucking night this must be for you," a woman says as I pass. "Reaching the Precipice so quickly." Gripping my shoulder so hard, her red nails nearly sink into my shoulder flesh. "Who did you have to fuck?"

"Excuse me?"

"That's right, they don't fuck. Was it extra money, then? What did you do to move through the treatments so fast? Tell me!"

Another woman won't stop stroking my neck. "*Incroyable*, astounding really," she whispers, nearly throttling me. "I envy."

But I'm saved at last by the woman in red, who pulls me away.

"Now, friends! *Mes amis!* Let's not congratulate Daughter of Noelle *too* much, all right? There'll be plenty of time for more *félicitations* later. We don't want to exhaust our dear Daughter. Let's just have some bubbly for now, yes?"

I see the twins on the stair, the Lord and Lady, staring at me from behind their black veils. Raising their red fizzing flutes as if to toast me.

"Yes," I say, and feel them smile through their veils. Can nearly feel the cold silk of their hands grazing my skin from here. So happy they are to see me. Music plays, a harpsichord-heavy opera, and a powdered man in a red ruff sings soprano on the stair. I dance with many partners, and my partner keeps changing. My shoes seem to want to dance me very close to the Depths, very close to the glass behind which the medusae drift and pulse.

"I hope you don't mind," I tell my partner, who stares at me, trembling. "I'm actually looking for someone." She's an extremely pale woman with very blond hair. Her features suggest she wasn't always so pale, she was something else once, hard to say what or from where, but don't I always hate when people try to guess a place from my face? Anyway, she's Brightened. Washed away like how at night we wash off the day. She wears a long white dress, spilling diamonds from her throat. She's looking at me with a pained expression. "My plight—*pleasure* to dance with Daughter on the eve of her third treatment," she says.

"Third treatment? It's tonight?"

"Of course it's tonight," she says, like it's obvious.

"What a happy surmise that I'm here, then."

"Such a happy surmise," she hisses. "Very woeful. *Wonderful*."

"I actually came here because I'm looking for someone. Funny, I can't remember who just now. Drawing a bit of a blank."

"That is funny," she says, not smiling. "Daughter is very amusing and delightful. And why shouldn't she be when she is on the Cusp of achieving her Most Magnificent Self," she says through gritted teeth. Obviously lying. And yet I'm charmed by her troubled energy, the way she's looking at me like I physically hurt her to look at, but she can't look away. She looks so lonely. *Lovely*.

"You have so much Glow," I tell her.

I think this compliment will soften her, but it makes her smile sharp. "My Glow is Shadows," she says, "compared with yours, Daughter. A cold rock in the outer orbit of your Impossible Brightness. The literal embodiment of Dull." She's spoken the truth, she knows it. Tears fill her eyes because it stings. "I envy," she whispers. "So much." She looks at me through stinging tears. And I see the dark love there in her eyes. Veritable soul poison. How it loves and looks in spite of itself.

"Thank you," I hear myself say. "I envy too." But mine's a lie. I don't envy. I know I'm the Impossible Brightness. I know she is the cold rock. She sees the lie in my eyes and she runs away, crying. Everyone around us keeps dancing like nothing. Envy, it happens all the time. The harpsichord music keeps playing and the white man in the red ruff keeps singing operatically. I should follow after her. Tell her, *I'm very sorry my Glow hurts your eyes. I wish we could all Glow like I do.* These would be more lies, of course. I'm not sorry. I don't wish that. But I would be very happy to tell them if only to dance with her again. I enjoyed her wanting eyes on me so much. But wait, wasn't I looking for someone? Just then, out of the corner of my eye, I notice something funny. One of the jellyfish has moved very close to the glass, right beside me. The large red one that didn't applaud when I entered the hall. I see it has a pattern like petals on its bell, how pretty. Its eyes, slanted and strange and translucent, are fixed on me. It wants to say something.

"What is it?" I hear myself ask.

"Talking to the fish, Daughter?" says an amused voice. I turn away from the tank to see the woman in red beside me now. We seem to be dancing—when did we start dancing?—and she's smiling at me with her sharp white teeth. I look into her very blue eyes, flecked with gold like bits of sun, and I think *lie*.

"Not talking. Just one of them seemed to be staring at me for a while."

I'm about to point to the jellyfish, but it's drifted away to the opposite side of the tank now.

"Ah, the anthropomorphizing impulse," she sighs. "We are all guilty of such projections. We impose our humanity on creatures of the Deep. Understandable, but rather . . . childish. Like believing in fairy tales!" She laughs. "Have another drink," she says, taking one from a servant bearing a silver tray full of flutes. "Now tell me, Daughter, did you have any trouble getting here this evening?"

"Trouble?" I say. "No trouble."

But I recall that there was trouble, wasn't there? A dark, handsome face floating over mine, transfixed. The hunger of strong hands all over my body, of lips that tasted of roses. Brushing against my sin like they could never get enough. A breath hot in my ear, whispering *god*, *god*, *god* as my fingers gripped his dark waving hair. But I can't tell the woman in red how I seduced the beautiful detective. So much so that afterward he fell right into sleep like my sister dreams of falling right into the sea. I watched him lie beside me, drifting against his will. *You know I understand it*, he murmured as he drifted.

What? I said.

You. Rouge. Why you keep going back. We all have our demons, don't we?

I looked at his scar catching the fiery light from the window. Sunset, it must have been then. *And what are your demons, Detective?*

He smiled. *Let's just say I'm not invulnerable to our friends. To* the Depths. *That I've had my moments of temptation. I still do*, he said, stroking my face. And as he looked at me then, I felt a pang. Deep in my chest. Of *I know, I know. I, too, have been in those shadow places, those basement places.* I watched his eyes close, felt his hand fall from my cheek like a cold, dead thing. And then I left him there in my blood-colored bed, his scar shining red in the darkening light of Vespers. Beautiful it was, that slash of pale, raised sin in the crimson evening shade. I leaned down and killed it. Felt a burning on my lips.

I'm sorry, I whispered to it. *I have to go. I know you understand.*

The only worry I had was whether he might feel the empty space I left behind. *I'll happily fill the space for you, Sister*, one of my sisters offered from the living room. The one at the coffee table, deranging the flowers. She always liked him. So I put her in the bed with him and left them together. He wouldn't notice the difference, surely. My sin was as smooth and bright as hers was now.

"No trouble at all," I tell the woman in red now. But then I see I'm no longer dancing with her. I'm dancing with a man. Tall. Blond hair, blond beard, and muttonchops that don't quite match his tawny face. Monocle over one gray eye.

"No trouble?" repeats this man. "Belle, I'm hurt."

"I'm sorry, sir, do we know each other?" I ask Monocle Man. He looks very worried that I asked this question. But over the worry, he smiles.

"Your sister was a poor substitute. She couldn't really compare to you." And then he grips me tight and I see the man I just fucked through his disguise. The roses of his lips I killed. The scar I traced in the red light. "Belle, listen. I'm getting you out of here tonight, okay? Now just dance with me, follow me. Trust me, okay?"

Out of here? Why out of here? Why would I trust anyone who would lead me away from the exact place I need to be just now? When I'm looking for someone? Where I'm on a Precipice, no less? A Cusp?

"Now look," Hud says. "The party goes on forever, see? So we'll just make our way down that dark hall. Dancing like we're doing right now. We've gone down that hall before. Where I didn't kiss you because you weren't following me, remember?"

I stare at the dark hall that gapes like a black hole. So unlike the dazzling party all around. "I don't want to go down the dark hall. I want to be here. I'm on the Precipice, you see."

"You're on a precipice, all right." And he sort of sneers. Envy. There's envy in it, I see, which delights me but it also sobers me. I hold it close like saving knowledge. To hold it, I must stand very still. The dancing people around us are dancing more slowly now. The music around us seems to slow too, to quiet as if it has ears and wants to listen.

"See behind me on the stair?" Hud whispers. And then I notice the ones in black veils on the landing. The twins have been joined by a number of others, it seems, all dressed just like them. A small, murmuring cluster staring down. "Do you realize who those people are, Belle?"

I look up at their luminous faces, shining through their veils. How their silks fall like such dark water. How their pale eyes, cold and smiling, seem to know the name and shape of my every dream.

"Important people," I whisper. "Very important to Mother and me."

"Listen to me," he says. "Please. You can't have that third treatment. If you do, you'll be lost, do you understand? Lost to me, lost to yourself. Completely. I won't be able to save you." He looks at me. Envy's gone. His eyes are full of some other tender feeling. It could melt me away if I let it. If I let it, it could destroy me. The veiled ones are descending the stair. The music has quieted even more, pricked up its ears. Even the medusae in the tank seem to hover and wait. The dancing people are watching openly now.

"Who says I want you to save me, sir?" I whisper. I look right at him when I say it, right into his clear gray eyes, where his soul sits open. I feel something in him break. See it breaking on his beautiful, sadly scarred face.

"Excuse me," says a voice right beside me. A woman all in black.

Not a woman, a girl, she's a girl-woman, really. Tall like a grown woman, tall as I am in my heels, but with a girl's face. So beautiful, like a doll's. One I might have clutched and loved, even as I envied and hated. Her blond corkscrew curls erupt from her perfect skull like a golden fountain. Her preternaturally pale eyes are full of smiling. Her alabaster face is the True Brightness. She puts my Glow to great shame. It is a Shadow Glow compared with hers. It takes our breath away, mine and Hud Hudson's, though he's still gripping my arms. She knows of her effects. They please her greatly. Yet she's beaming at us both like the most innocent of innocents. "May I cut in," she asks, and it is not a question. We couldn't possibly say no to an innocent child, could we? say her eyes. We're not monsters, after all.

But Hud Hudson is going to say no. "I'm sorry," he says. "We're still in the middle of—"

And just then, another hand takes mine and pulls me away.

"Belle," says a voice.

And it's funny what happens then. I hear no music anymore. I hear only this voice. I hear it at the very bottom of my brain stem. Like a leash, tugging me. And then I'm in the arms of this voice, saying my name, *Belle, Belle, Belle.* I can't see his face because he's holding me tight to his black-suited body, so that I'm locked in, stuck looking over his shoulder. We're dancing away. I could say, *Do I know you, sir?* But I say nothing. It's like his arms are a drug, making jelly of me. So familiar these arms are, like the voice. Taking me to a basement place, a shadow place I know so well. I might have known these arms since I was a child—did they hold me then? I think they did. I know their feel, like being plunged into cold water. I know their ocean scent. Did I long for them to hold me in the dark, though I was afraid? Impossible. This man is a stranger, isn't he? *No,* says my brain stem. *Not a stranger, this one.* I let him spin me around and around the floor though it makes me dizzy, the drug of him.

A little farther away, I see the girl-woman in black dancing with Hud Hudson. He's looking wildly around the room for me. Where did

I go? He can't lose me. He must still try and save me. *But I'm already lost*, I'd tell him if I had words, if the spinning weren't making me dizzy. So I just watch him look for me. The girl-woman in black takes his hands and presses them to either side of her small, heart-shaped face. He looks down at her. And then his face suddenly changes. Entranced. So taken he is by her skull shape, its exquisite symmetry of bones. By her Smoothness. By her Glow, most of all. He's shuddering. A hairy moth moving toward her light.

She's whispering something to him now, what is she whispering?

Whatever it is, he's taken with it. A man in a dream. Lost himself.

She reaches out and touches his face too. And that's how they're dancing now. Cupping each other's faces like you might cup a flame to keep it lit. Turning the slowest of circles in the middle of the floor. Until they aren't really dancing at all anymore. They're standing still. And she's removing his disguise. His beard, then those blond muttonchops. First one chop, then the other. Then finally, the monocle. She drops it to the ground and crushes it with her little patent leather heel. He lets her. Doesn't move at all. Lets himself be revealed, this tawny-faced man with glossy black hair, shuddering before her now. I watch her fingers float up to his naked face, tracing the deep scar there. She's whispering something to him again. I watch her red bow of a mouth making words I can't hear. There are tears in his eyes. And now he's allowing himself to be led by the hand like a lost child. Down the very dark hall where only a minute ago he wanted to go with me, to save me.

"Belle," says a voice now in my ear. The drug voice that is like the movies, like music. The only music I hear. And then the man I'm dancing with, the one who's been holding me so that I can't see his face, holding me in a way that brings me right back, like a scent that brings you right back, now holds me apart so that we're facing each other at last. Black suit. Black-horned mask over half his face. Familiar. I know the dark hair like a wave. I know the blue-green eyes shining out of the black mask. I remember the cold ocean of them. I remember drowning.

"You haven't changed a bit, Belle. Except that you've grown. So much." Long white teeth. That smile that used to light me up, like wrong stars in my child's body.

"I know you," I whisper, shivering. Very cold suddenly. But happy. So happy. I know him, though my mind's a blank.

"We know each other well, Belle. Definitely. Allow me to escort you to your final treatment. Seems fitting, don't you think, that I should be the one?"

I nod. Of course he should be. We're dancing so slowly. Like time itself has slowed. There are no bodies in the hall anymore. Just us. No harpsichord or opera singer. This man brings his own music, just like he always did, and I hear it inside and outside of me. A synthy, dreamy pop song. It sounds like bodies in blue silhouette. It sounds like all my dreams. I'm jelly like the fish.

"I always knew," he whispers, swaying me, "that you would take your Beauty back, Belle. I knew you would find me here. A long road. A long, lonely road for you, hasn't it been?"

"Yes," I hear my soul say. It's my soul speaking to him through my mouth now. He has a direct line to it.

"But you've followed the footpath to the castle by the sea. To me."

"To you."

"Didn't I always tell you this place was a magic place?"

I look around the dark, empty hall. The arched ceiling, I can finally see it, like a cage of white bone above us. The tank of red jellies has gone black now. All around me feels like a void. Like nothing at all. "You did."

"Well now you see for yourself, don't you?"

And then we're walking down a winding stair to under the Depths. He holds my hand, his own gloved hand cold and slightly sticking. I remember the cold and the sticking of his touch, but I still can't place him. If he would only take off his mask and I could see his face. But my body remembers. My soul remembers. *From where, from where?*

We stumble at first down the stair. My red shoes won't walk me down. But he just smiles. Kneels at my feet like a prince. He's going to take them off. "I always hated these fucking things," he says. "I never told you, of course. Because you loved them so much."

"I think I wore them for you," I say. Somehow I know this is true.

But the shoes don't come off, won't come off, they're fused to my feet flesh. I think he's going to flip out about this. Instead he just picks me up like a literal feather. Carries me down. I'm in his arms that are like a drug, and we're going down and down. I'm smiling into his neck though I'm afraid. Shouldn't be. Just my final treatment. This man's accompanying me. *Who are you?* is still a bubble of a question, iridescent and floating around in the dark of my mind. I know the answer to it somewhere. Somewhere deep under everything—all my words and thoughts.

We pass through the red waiting room of mirrors with the white screaming faces on the wall, empty but for a pale, glowing woman reading a red magazine in the dark. I've seen her here before. She doesn't smile at us as we pass. Just watches us, a little afraid-seeming. To her, we're a strange ship in the night.

He carries me into a half-lit room full of fog. Lowers me onto a table in the center. The Treatment Room, of course. My final treatment tonight, that's right. Very exciting. The ceiling of glass is exposed, and I see we're under the Depths, blue-green as the eyes of the man in the black-horned mask. A sky of water shimmers above us like the northern lights. Red jellyfish swim over us like so many strange moons. The man stands over me as I sit on the table. Normally a woman comes in at this point, doesn't she? Tells me to strip and I do. Lie down and I do. Breathe, and she breathes with me. Then a cold white paste on my face while I drift. But no woman comes. Just me and the man in the fog.

He walks over to a small aquarium tank on the other end of the table. Inside floats a single red jellyfish. Mine. My red jellyfish that started off so small and white. That I first pulled out of the black pool, held in my palm, where it glowed like a whisper of a wish. It's grown so much bigger and redder since last time. The man in the mask is staring at it. "Beautiful," he says, "isn't it, Belle?"

"Beautiful," I agree, looking from the man to the creature. Though I don't know that it is anymore. It looks scary to me. Hideous. But the man in the mask doesn't seem to think so. He's lost in looking at it, like it's a dream.

"Is it really so beautiful?" I ask him, jealous maybe. "Just a jelly-fish."

"Oh, it's more," he says, still smiling softly like it's telling him a secret. "It's something else now, thanks to the treatments. Can you guess?"

I stare at the creature. Its red bell pulsing like a strange heart. The hairy tentacles undulating. I shake my head. The man smiles his smile of long white teeth. His smile is a constellation. His smile is a movie and I'm in the dark, dreaming. Gently now, he takes my hand. "It's the story of you and me."

Inside the tank, the red thing begins to pulse more quickly.

"You and me," I repeat. There's a shiver in my voice now. The touch of his hand is making me cold. Something black and closed and buried deep in me opens. "What story?"

I look at the jellyfish, a pattern like roses on her back. Her eyes, I see she has eyes, translucent and red like her body, are wide and afraid. *What story?* But somewhere inside me knows. Knows exactly. I feel the knowledge pulsing just like the red thing in the water.

"*What story?* Oh Belle, *Belle*, now you're hurting my feelings. Now you're *wounding* me." He presses his gloved hand to his chest like I stabbed him there. But he's still smiling like the movies. His eyes in the mask flash from blue-green to red to blue-green. He brushes my hair away from my face, and I shiver.

"It started the day you found me in Mother's closet, remember? Beastly little thing in Mother's lipstick and cheap sex heels. Dreaming of another self, a princess self, in a castle by the sea. Dreaming of me. And I heard you. Dreaming on the other side of the glass."

He squeezes my hand, that cold, slightly sticking touch that dives me in dark water. He's standing over me now as I sit hunched on the table, cold coursing through my body.

"You heard me," I say, and I'm shivering, shivering.

"But the story's not over."

"It isn't?" I say. I'm so very cold. He lifts up my chin with a hand of ice, so I'm looking right into his flashing eyes. Still smiling that smile that burns me.

"Let's finish it together, shall we?"

We're lying together now on the table, he and I, and in the glass, the jellyfish is beating wildly like my own heart, like the black buried thing inside me. He's taken his mask off so I see his face. His face lights up the architecture of me, my cage of bones brightening. Not just his smile, but his whole face is the movies. As beautiful and unreal as a dream, but somehow right here with me. I must have watched those movies a thousand times in the dark, on dusty TV screens. I've seen him on another kind of screen too, a screen of glass. Smiling like he is right now.

"We lay together like this once, remember?" he says. "In your silly pink room with the dolls and spiders. Under those dumb stars. And you made some promises to me. Do you remember?"

"No," I say. My lips find it hard to make the word.

"Let's remember together."

"There's supposed to be a cold white paste on my face," I say with my half-numb lips. "The whisper woman puts it on. And black discs on my temples. There's supposed to be an oil I breathe in and she breathes with me."

He shakes his head. "We don't need her tonight. We don't need the fucking accessories, you and I. The oil, the discs, the paste—those are just flourishes to impress the idiots. The essence is just this. Just you and me."

And he takes my hand again, my first love. Somehow I know that he was my first love. How nice to know that I am holding the hand of my first love and I'm not cold anymore or I'm so cold, I'm burning. It was a troubled love. There was something between us, always between us, what was it? A kind of wall. Shiny but smeared. Made of cracked glass. Hiding in the dark. Turned toward the wall, until I turned it to me.

"I would come through it to be with you, remember?" he says.

His name is nearly on my tongue. And my heart is frantic inside me.

"Yes." It's all so familiar, there are tears in my eyes. He tells me to look up at the glass ceiling exposing the Depths. At the red jellyfish floating by like comets with fiery tails.

"What do you see? Tell me."

The table we're lying on floats up now toward the sky of water. The small tank with my red jellyfish floats up with us. Beating fast and wild as my own heart is now. I am burning with cold and very still. There's a movie playing up there on the ceiling glass like a screen. I see a young girl. Lying in her pink bedroom. Night outside. A low moon lights up the room. She's not alone. There's a man with her in the room. Lying beside her. She's holding him tight. There are tears in her eyes. She's saying, *Don't leave me. Please don't leave me.*

"Who's that?" he asks me.

"Her first love. She's holding her first love," I say with my mouth that's so very hard to move now.

"What's his name?"

I look up at the little girl on the glass screen. Her eyes shut tight. Tears streaming down her face as there are tears streaming down my face. I feel them tingling on my skin. Her mouth saying his name again and again. And I remember. I start to say the name along with her with my now dead mouth. Together, we're mouthing his name like a refrain in a song. And the man beside me is smiling at the sound.

Part V

23

"Tom," I'm whispering. "Oh god, Tom. Don't go."

But Tom leaves me. He holds me once more and then he becomes smoke in my arms. And I'm holding nothing. Air. But he promised that if I do what he says, we'll see each other again. He'll see me on the other side if I do it exactly. Exactly like he said.

I'll do it, Tom, I promise.

Not Tom, Seth.

Alone in my bed, I look up at the wrong stars that were just the right heaven when Tom Cruise was here. What did I just promise him? What did Tom ask me to do?

There's a garden, he said. Whispered in my ear only minutes ago. *You know the one. Behind your so-called friend's house across the way.*

And in my mind, I saw the bright red petals. Stacey's hand leading me quickly through the thorny beds, toward her back door. Alla smiling hard at me, a spade in her gloved hand. I nodded.

Her Russian mother doesn't like you coming over, does she? Doesn't want her daughter playing with the Egyptian girl. Not even a Christian. Never baptized.

I nodded again. I hated that Tom knew this. I was so ashamed.

It's not you that should be ashamed, Tom said, knowing my every feeling as I felt it. Can't hide anything away. *They should be fucking ashamed*, he said. *But they do grow the most beautiful roses, don't they, Belle?* he said, smiling at me under the stars.

Yes. And I pictured them through the cloudy glass of Stacey's basement window. Red flashing in my eyes while I watched her dance.

So you'll go to the ripest bed. So you'll pick the blooms off the stems, he said.

I looked at Tom in the dark. *But that's stealing.*

Not stealing, Tom said. *Stealing back.*

Now I'm standing in Stacey's garden alone. Still in my white night-gown, which lifts in the breeze. The moon is red and full and low in the black clouds. No stars I can see like the ones in my bedroom. I guess the right stars are too far away to see tonight. Or the clouds are too black and thick. I've never been outside at night alone before. The wind is soft on my face like a hand. I'd like it if I weren't stealing.

Stealing back.

Tom was right about the gate latch, very easy to lift. The house is dark. A pretty brick house in a line of pretty brick houses, the nicest on the island. I think of Alla meeting me in her garden. How I knew by her eyes that she hated me. *She just doesn't know any better*, Mother said when I told her. *Small-minded people, Sunshine. You'll find them everywhere.* Yet when Alla invited Mother for tea once, Mother said *why not?* They sat in the solarium off the garden, sipping tea from gold-rimmed cups patterned with roses and smoking long, thin cigarettes. They laughed and laughed; I heard them from where Stacey and I sat in the den watching *Degrassi*. No way could we rate each other with our mothers there, Stacey said. Listening to Mother's laughter, I felt angry. I thought she said Alla was small-minded, but apparently not to her face. Maybe because Alla was a fellow Christian. *Mother, why can't I be Christian too?* I asked her when we left. *Because I promised your father, darling*, Mother said. *He had a different religion, so we made a deal.* And I said, *But Grand-Maman thinks you're leaving me open to dark forces.* And Mother laughed. *Dark forces. Do you believe that woman?*

In the garden, my bare feet make no sound. The grass is spongy and soft, and the earth smells green and sweet beneath my feet. *Some people have gardens*, Mother said when we came home from Stacey's. *We will too someday, Belle. In a much better place than this.* She sounded drunk. Maybe Alla's tea wasn't just tea. *We'll have a garden with fruit trees. And we'll have fucking flowers. Not roses, though. You know Mother's allergic.*

I know.

I'm supposed to pluck thirteen petals, Tom said. From the bed of roses in the farthest corner, whose throats are the most open. So very pretty this place is where I'm not supposed to be. Where Mother sat drinking alcoholic tea with the woman who thinks I'm godless. Who looks at me with eyes of ice. I'm creeping toward the roses and my hands are closing and opening at my sides. Don't even need the light of the low red moon to lead me there. The smell would lead me, like the most alive perfume. What Mother calls *heavenly*, though never about roses. It opens something inside me, the scent. The same thing Tom opens whenever he looks at me. *Don't wake anyone, Belle*, he said. *Be quieter than quiet. As quiet as a mouse, my mouse. Remember, it's a secret. Our secret.* And the universe of his eyes was shining in the black. In my head now, I can feel Tom smiling at how quiet I'm being. My footsteps are nothing. I'm barely breathing. My heart's hammering inside me, but hearts don't make noise, do they? I remember Stacey has a white cat, Luba, that's always slinking around out here, hissing. God I wish Tom were with me. But Tom's gone. He's smoke. The only way back to him is through these roses. Why roses, Tom?

Oh, you'll see, Tom said.

I see a bed of them growing by the basement window, glowing under the moon just like he said they would be. Sharp and red and shining in the dark. Long snaking stems. Petals that curl open prettily like bells. And inside, a tight swirl like a secret, the secret of Beauty itself. I hear them breathing quietly in the soil. The same cold, damp soil I'm standing in with my bare feet. They look like the word *no*. *Don't touch. Don't pluck.* They look like the word *forbidden*. These are the words I said to Tom in the dark about these flowers. And he smiled his white smile and said, *All the more reason.* His eyes like the sky the roses were trying to reach, his face glowing like the sun that made them bloom.

I look back up at the dark house of brick. The windows are still black. No light but the moon's. Stacey's in there somewhere, dreaming.

Tom, which rose, which rose? I asked him.

You'll know the one when you see it, mouse.

And I do know the one. Growing in the very center of the bed, shining with thorns. The tallest, the most beautiful. The queen. Its throat of swirling petals seems the most open, an open secret. Its scent the most alive perfume. It puts Mother's violets and smoke to shame. Fills me with something so happy and sad all at once. Like how Tom's eyes are the sky and the sea all at once. *Beauty is a spell*, isn't that what Tom Cruise said? I'm reaching my hand out to the rose like I'm in a spell, I'm in a dream. My heart's beating so hard, surely it makes a noise now. I have to really lean forward, dance my hand through the thorns. As I reach, I feel something drop from me. *Oh god, what dropped?* Before I can look, a light goes on in the dark house. I feel it before I see it, a square of yellow light falling on me, freezing me in the mud. I remember the eyes of ice, imagine a white arm gripping me—*What are you doing here?!*—and I lose my balance. Fall into the thorny bed. My skin sings with pain, the thorns cutting me all over—*oh god*—but I don't cry out. Quickly I gather as many petals as I can. Stuff them into the black silk bag Tom gave me.

Luba the cat slinks out of the dark, hissing.

"Please," I whisper to her shape. "I'm just here to get some roses."

But she knows I'm lying. She knows I'm Tom's dark mouse. She looks at me with Alla's eyes of ice. She presses her paws into the soil, arching her back.

"Please," I whisper.

She lunges into the air and she's on me, scratching my arms and face, and I scream. Another yellow square in the dark house. "Who's there?" says a soft voice.

The little cat runs away, shrieking. I run too. I'm running through the garden on the damp, sinking grass. Running back to the gate I left open, still open. Bare feet running so fast through the flowers while I hear the voice calling louder, sounding afraid and excited: "Who's there? *Who's there?*"

I don't stop running until I'm back home, until I've climbed back through my window, back to my bedroom. Still night. The longest night of my life. I'm alone now, standing in the middle of the room with the bag of rose petals in my hand. No Tom anywhere. Mother still asleep in the bedroom. My heart. Beating so hard, it's going to break through my skin. But I'm still not breathing, still quiet as a mouse, Tom's mouse. The police are going to call, any minute, any minute. They're going to bang on the door, break it open. Point their guns at me. *Deny everything*, Tom said. First thing, hide the bag of flowers. Not in the closet, too noisy to open a closet now. Under the bed, then. Shove it way down into the dark under. As under as it can go. Then get back into bed like nothing. Nothing ever happened. *Close your eyes like you're sleeping*, that's what Tom said.

I tell myself I can still feel the shape of him there. I can still smell him like oceans, the cold breeze over oceans. But what I really smell is my crime. What I smell is the word *forbidden*, red and sharp and bittersweet, rising up like crushed roses under the bed. And even as I lie there all night with my eyes closed like I'm sleeping, it's not until morning that I feel it missing on my wrist. My gold bracelet. I slipped it back on after Tom left, feeling bad about Father's eye sad and alone in the sea of dolls. Stupid. Where it is now is so much worse. More alone than ever before. Gleaming in the dark soil of Alla's rose beds.

12:01 on the Snow White clock. Bright light of day floods my bedroom. Mother thinks she's letting me sleep in, but I'm not sleeping. I'm standing in front of Mother's mirror that I stole last night, staring. Because in the light of day, it's so much worse than I thought. My face, my arms and legs, my whole body's covered. So many scratches and cuts, I can't even count them. The bruise on my forehead from Tom's kiss is darker, bigger than it was before, how is that possible? I hear Mother singing to herself in the living room, some Sting song about beating hearts being still. I wish my heart could be still, but how can it ever be now? Mother will know. She'll take one look at me and she'll know everything. *All I have to do is look at your face to know you're lying*, Mother always says. And she'll drag me in front of a mirror to show me. My face, whatever it's telling Mother. I never had any idea what I was supposed to see there, apart from what I always saw. Until now.

A knock on my bedroom door. "Sunshine?" A happy singing still in Mother's voice. So Stacey's mother hasn't called yet.

"Yes?" Tears in my eyes right away at Mother's voice that is so sweet and gentle this morning.

"Someone slept in today." I feel her smiling on the other side of the door.

"Yes."

"We're going out for the day. But Grand-Maman's coming to stay with you. She'll be here later this afternoon, okay?"

"Okay. See you."

"Come out and say hello before we go. Bryce's here."

In the mirror, I'm still looking at my scratched-up face. My bruised and cut body still smelling of the word *forbidden*. Bittersweet. *Tom, what do I do?* And I hear his voice inside like a whisper of a whisper. *You're tired today.*

"I'm tired today," I tell Mother, staring at myself in the glass. I can almost feel Tom nodding on the other side.

"Belle," Mother says, and this time, there's no more singing. "You slept all morning, how could you be *tired*? Come out and say hello. You were very rude to Bryce yesterday. Today, I want you to be *nice*. Shake his hand, okay? Apologize. Oh, and wear the little white sundress I bought you from work."

That one has spaghetti straps that tie at each shoulder. A bow tie at the back. Wearing that will show all the cuts. "Do I have to?"

"Yes." And now her voice is cold. "Two minutes to get out here."

So I put on the white dress. There's a folded piece of paper in the pocket. That picture of Tom I tore from *Sky* so long ago. I stare at his glossy face. Smile though I feel strange. He looks different than when he's in person. But that's how pictures are sometimes, right? It's Tom, of course. I fold it up, tuck it back in my pocket. Put a sweater over the dress, though it's hot and it itches and it doesn't cover everything. Not my neck or my hands or my face. *All I have to do is look at your face*, Mother says, *and I know everything. I can read you like a book, remember? Every page.*

When I come out in the dress and sweater, I expect Mother to scream, but Mother is smiling. She looks like *Vogue* magazine. Like she stepped out of the movies she watches to cleanse from Ladies Apparel. She's wearing the black Saint Laurent suit today. Lips shining with her best red and her hair a soft wave. White sunglasses on her head, the lenses big as a bug's eyes. There's a gold chain on her neck with a gold Nefertiti head.

"How sweet you look," she says, not looking at me. Looking through me, it feels like. There's Bryce beside her. He doesn't look anything like Tom Cruise today, not even close. He's a completely different man. Very tall. Glasses. Beard. Small, bloody, watery eyes. Something spidery about his long legs and arms. He's wearing a look on his face like he expects something from me. My apology. That's when I know I hate him. *Creep*, I think.

My hands are behind my back so Mother won't see the scratches on them. Though she has to see the bruise on my forehead is worse. But she doesn't at all. She keeps glancing at herself in the mirror behind me, nervous. Checking her hair, her jacket, her best red. Checking that Nefertiti's head hangs from her neck exactly like it should.

So I reach out my hand to Bryce the Creep.

"Sorry," I say. "For yesterday."

He doesn't smile at first. He just looks down at my hand like it's a bug. And Mother doesn't tell him to stop being a baby like she would to me if I did that. She just stands there, looking at Bryce like she's nervous. She doesn't scream at the sight of my scratched-up hand either. Finally, he takes my hand, shakes it, but he doesn't hold it back. It's like I'm holding something dead.

"It's fine," he says. But he's lying. Now I know what Mother means when I'm lying and she says, *Do you see your face?* Because I see the lying in his. I want to ask Bryce if he sees his face. I want Mother to ask him that. But Mother is looking at herself in a gold compact now. Sometimes her best red smears beyond her mouth corners and she needs to check. On the back of the compact, there's a picture of a lady also looking at herself in a compact. She's checking her best red just like Mother is.

Any minute now she's going to snap the compact shut. Really look at me and scream. She's going to notice my forehead bruise, so much darker now. The cuts and scratches on my neck that my sweater doesn't cover. She's going say, *What the fuck happened?* She'll be so mad, she'll say *fuck*. And I'll have to deny everything, like Tom Cruise said. But she'll read my eyes and she'll know the whole story. Tom's kiss. The bracelet with Father's eye lying in the dark soil of Alla's garden. The crushed stolen roses under my bed in the black sack. Probably I stink of their alive perfume. But Mother doesn't notice, even though she's snapped her compact shut. She's looking at Bryce the Creep mostly now, his lying smile.

"Mother has her audition today," she says to me. So that's why she doesn't see. On audition days, Mother sees only herself, her dream of herself in what she calls *that other world*. Far from Ladies Apparel. Among the lights and palm trees. "Wish me luck."

"Good luck." And suddenly I'm angry about Mother not seeing. When usually she sees a button missing on a dress, a loose thread on a sweater. *What the hell is this?* Mother will say, poking at the hole where the button was, holding up the loose thread like evidence. *What happened? What did you do? Do you know how hard I work to buy you these things?*

But Mother's just smiling now. "All right, Sunshine, we're off. We can't stay and wait for Grand-Maman today, okay? But you'll be fine."

She's not asking me. She's telling me.

"Yes," I say. "I'll be fine." My face is full of lying, but she sees nothing. Not even when she leans in close to kiss the air by my cheek and I smell her dead perfume. *Thank god,* I tell myself. Which god, I don't know. Between Mother's and Father's gods, I picture a wide black space full of stars. That's the space I whisper up to. Maybe there's a god there, too. My own.

Find a pestle and mortar, Tom said to me last night. His eyes were shining in the dark. Blue-green then red then blue-green again. *Your mother has one in the kitchen. She likes to think she's a cook.*

What's a pestle and mortar? I asked.

And Tom smiled his white smile. *It's a tool, my dear mouse. You'll use it to crush the roses.*

It takes me forever to find it in the kitchen. I have to open all the cupboards and drawers. Turns out Mother hid it under the sink, behind a carrot juicer that she bought a long time ago. For a week after she bought the juicer, we drank nothing but carrots because Mother said it was good for us and also it might make us beautiful. Then it turned our skin orange and Mother was frightened. *So much for that.* The mortar and pestle is a black heavy bowl of stone that comes with a rock for crushing. I can't remember Mother ever using it. The sky is still bright though it's evening now. I bring it to my bedroom and put it under the bed with the roses, which are really starting to smell. I have just enough time to hide it before Grand-Maman arrives.

When she comes in the door, she looks at me and I know she sees everything. Her eyes take in every cut, every scratch. She sees the dark bruise on my forehead, and that's where her eyes stay.

"Que s'est-il passé?" she whispers.

"Nothing."

But Grand-Maman knows it's not nothing. "Is it that man? The new one? The producer?"

I hesitate. Look at Grand-Maman's face. "Yes."

And then Grand-Maman's eyes go like I've never seen them go before. Soft and hard at the same time. Like she's going to cry, but then her eyes say *never*. "Je le savais. I knew something."

And her hands holding mine are shaking.

"I'm going to go to my room and play records now," I tell her. *You'll need to play them loud,* Tom said, to cover the sound of the crushing.

Grand-Maman looks down at our held hands. My tan hands and hers white with tan spots. All the jewels on her wrists and fingers. All the shimmering gold and pretty colored stones. I picture her young, beautiful, holding out her white, spotless hand for each shiny thing the men give her.

"Go play records," she says.

Loud, Belle, remember, Tom said. I play Madonna, who Mother hates. *Why don't you play that record by the Bangles instead?* Mother always says. *With "Walk Like an Egyptian"? Mother bought it for you, remember?* And she hums the song, does the dance from the video, arms and hands bent at strange angles. At a parent-teacher meeting, Mother told Ms. Said she bought the record for me. *And do you like that song, Belle?* Ms. Said asked me. *Yes,* I lied, to protect Mother. I hate that song. Whenever Stacey sings that song to me, which she loves to do, breathing it hot and close into my ear, I go red in the face and want to not exist. But Mother loved me for saying I loved it to Ms. Said. She even bought me the Madonna record *True Blue* on the way home as a surprise. Rolling her eyes a little but smiling when she handed it over. *Trashy with that blond hair now*, Mother said on the bus home. She was watching me stare at Madonna on the cover, I could feel her eyes. *Always trying to transform herself. Into what this time? Marilyn Monroe?*

Now I play *True Blue* the loudest it can go. My very favorite song, "Live to Tell," which is like a secret at the end of side one. When I first heard it, I thought I dreamed it there. It sounds like smoke. I take the black bag of roses out from under the bed, and the mortar and pestle. But it's funny, when I open the bag, I see the petals have changed. Not soft and red anymore, they're dark and crisp like they've been burned. *I'll start the process*, I remember Tom said. *The bag will start the process. You'll finish it, mouse.*

Petal by crisp petal, I put them in the bowl and crush. *Very important to go petal by petal*, Tom said. *It needs to be a fine powder in the end. A very fine dark red powder is what you'll have*, Tom said. *If you really crush.* I crush all night in my white dress, never once looking in Mother's mirror in the corner. Can't seem to bring myself to, though I can feel Tom there somewhere. I can almost smell the ocean of him through the roses. Nice to feel him there. It takes a very long time to crush, longer than I would ever think for thirteen petals. Grand-Maman doesn't knock on the door. She won't now that I've told her that lie about Bryce. She'll leave me alone. Maybe she'll pray to her and Mother's god for me. But she's not praying now. Even over the sound of "Live to Tell," I can hear Grand-Maman watching *Wheel of Fortune* in English out there. I can hear the rickety turning of the wheel and the applause. Then *Jeopardy!* and Grand-Maman never knowing the answers. Never shouting them out like Mother, even when I know she knows them. *Not the answers, darling, the questions*, Mother always corrects. *In* Jeopardy!, *the questions are everything.*

Midnight on the Snow White clock when every petal is crushed. My ceiling stars are glowing. Grand-Maman is dead silent. She could be

sleeping in the rocking chair. She could just be staring at the dark. She
does that sometimes. I have no idea what she's seeing there. The perfume of the roses is so thick in the bedroom. It smells just like I'm back
in Alla's garden and the yellow squares of light are coming on behind
me, freezing me in the soil. The phone rang twice earlier. Once and then
once again right after. Maybe Alla. Maybe Stacey. *What the fuck were
you doing in our garden?* Grand-Maman never picked up, though.
She let it ring and ring. It rang so loud, it rattled my pink phone. The
spiders in the corners are awake now, spinning bigger webs, dangling
down from threads, but I'm not afraid of them anymore. Funny, I'm
not afraid of anything anymore. Mother's still not back. *She won't be
back till dawn*, Tom says. He says it at the very back of my mind. That's
where I still hear his voice when I need to. That's where he reminds me
of everything I need to know.

The next step, Tom says, *is the trickiest of all.*

To go into Mother's bedroom. To her vanity with the three mirror
faces. To find the jar of night cream on the table. The one she uses
every night. Rubs tenderly into her face in counterclockwise circles. I
sometimes watch from her bed, making wishes in my head until she
tells me to leave. *Why do I have to leave?* I always ask her. *Because
this is Mother's secret*, Mother says, and her face is suddenly a closed
door. The night cream smells like perfume and is named after the sea
in French. Because the cream has red algae in it, Mother told me once.
Plus a magic sea broth.

Like a potion, I said.

Yes. Mother laughed. *Exactly like that. Mother needs all the help
she can get these days.*

I look at the jar shining on the vanity in the blue light of the moon
through the window. I'm supposed to open it, Tom said. Take the dark
red powder from Tom's black bag and mix it in. *Easy*, Tom said. I
picture Mother's throat closing. I think of the open throat of the rose
whose petals I plucked.

This will hurt her, I tell Tom in my mind.

And in my mind, Tom smiles, amused. Didn't I already know that? Didn't I fucking know that when I plucked the red petals? When I crushed them one by one by one with the heavy black stone? I'll have to mix them into Mother's cream. *Your mother's cream comes with a little gold spoon, remember?*

Yes. Of course I remember. Mother using the gold spoon to scoop. How she dabs it on her face dot by dot like she's anointing herself, she says. I always ask if she can anoint me, too. And Mother always says my skin is young and plump and perfect just as it is, so I don't need anointing. I won't ever need it anyway because of my father. That Egyptian blood. It will always save me in the end. How she wishes she had it, Mother lies, so it could save her, too. And she cups my face between her hands like a light she wants to keep lit.

Can you believe that cream actually comes with its own little gold spoon to mix? Tom said in the bedroom last night, delighted. Shaking his head at the ceiling stars like how perfect was that?

Yeah. And I just stared sideways at his so perfect face. Glowing like a sunrise right beside me. If I touched it, would it burn me?

Too perfect, right? Tom whispered, turning to me.

Too perfect, I whispered. I smelled the cold ocean of him. And I thought, how could someone be a sky and a sea and a sun all at once? How could someone be heaven and also the endless deep? Tom, I thought, this is what you are to me. This is what you will always be. Everything all at once.

It's fate in a way, Tom said, oblivious to my staring. Or maybe not. Maybe that's why he was smiling. *Do you know what fate is, Belle?*

I thought of the picture of him I'd torn from *Sky*. Folded three times then hid like a secret. And now here he was in the flesh, here with me in the flesh.

It's what's meant to be? I whispered.

And Tom nodded in the dark. *Definitely.*

Like you and me, then, I said. Shy suddenly. My turn to look away up at the stars. But I could feel him still watching me. I could feel his fang shining in the dark. The fang was my favorite part of Tom.

Yes. Exactly like you and me, seedling.

But Mother will see, I told the stars. *She'll notice the red powder. She'll smell the roses.*

Which is why you'll have to mix it well, Tom said. *So well that Mother won't be able to tell. She won't be able to see or to smell that anything is amiss. It's a good thing her cream is red, too. Red like roses. Red like blood. Red like the algae she steals from the Deep to make her look young and beautiful forever. But it won't save her in the end.*

It won't? Why not?

Nothing saves us in the end, Tom said, stroking my hair. *Not gods or shadow gods. Not heaven or the endless Deep. Not blood or cream red as blood. Rouge, as they say.*

And he smiled his smile that lit me up.

In Mother's blue bedroom, I'm quick and light as a mouse. But not like I was in the garden. Not stiff and afraid and waiting for a yellow square of light to fall across the garden, exposing me. I'm not afraid of being caught, even though Grand-Maman's not sleeping. I can hear her breathing in the living room. I can hear her still staring in the dark. She doesn't say, *What are you doing in your mother's room?* She gives me all the time I need. To open the jar. To tip the red powder in from the black bag. To mix it with the little golden spoon that's too perfect. To mix it well by the light of the June moon. To not look in any of the three mirror faces. Tom won't be there anyway. Just me alone in the glass, though I don't dare look. Three of me mixing in my white dress stained red from the flowers. And my memory of Tom's voice in the back of my head like a song.

Now you'll also want to dust some red powder onto her hairbrush.

Which hairbrush, Tom?

Oh, you know the one, Belle.

And I do know the one. I'm reaching for it just as Tom tells me: *The gold one she bought for you that doesn't even work on your coarse dark hair. So she had to take it back. It works such magic on hers. So let's see what sort of magic it works now*, Tom says as I sprinkle the powder on the brush and my hand not at all shaking.

And then her perfume. A few roses for her dead violets and smoke. Just a sprinkle in her jagged star. Very good, Belle. Now shake it up. Perfect. Oh wait. Don't go just yet.

Not yet? I say.

No, no, Tom says in my head. *There's one more thing.*

What? But I know what Tom is going to say.

The drawer, Belle. Where Mother keeps her lacy hideous things she wears for her Creeps. The red ones with the little garters hanging down. I open up the drawer. The scent of Mother's skin hits me. I smell it through the roses. Powdery. Sweet. So familiar. How she held me in the night when once I woke up screaming from a bad dream. *Oh Belle*, she whispered. *Dreams aren't real, remember? Dreams are just dreams.* The powdery sweetness enveloping me then like now. Making the tears in my eyes sting.

I don't know, I tell Tom, shaking my head. *Will it kill her?*

Belle, what am I, a monster?

I think of Tom's burning kiss, his cold, sticking touch. His insistence that I call him Seth—why Seth when he looks just like Tom Cruise except for the red in his eyes sometimes? Suddenly I'm not so sure. But I shake my head no. *You're Tom Cruise*, I say.

I feel him smile that amused smile. *We're just giving her a little rash is all.*

Will it hurt? I ask him.

Nothing like you hurt. Not even close. It'll just give her a taste of the hurt you feel. So she'll definitely know. So she won't lie to you anymore about wishing she had your face.

Now go on, he says. *A little red powder there, too, for good measure. And Mother won't even notice the red. Because her lacy hideous things are red too. Good. Very good, Belle.* His voice is so clear in my head now, so near, like it's at my ear the whole time. I can almost feel his breath on my neck.

And then it's gone. And then it's done. I've sprinkled it all. I've closed the drawer. Nothing in my hands but red dust. And a pounding in my chest like a petal crushed.

I've done it. Which means . . .

I run back to my room, to Mother's mirror shining in the corner. *I'll see you on the other side*, Tom said. Now that I've done what he's asked, he'll be there, won't he? Waiting. Maybe holding roses for me. I'll step through the mirror and we'll go to California, where the water will be as blue-green as his eyes. An ocean of Tom's eyes to swim in. And I'll be beautiful.

But when I get to the mirror, all I see is me. My stained white dress. My scratches and cuts that look like black bugs in the dark. The bruise of Tom's kiss is glowing like a strange star on my forehead. Underneath, I'm the same. A seedling in the dirt. My same ugly face full of every ugly thing I have done. Telling it in my eyes of mud and in my pale worm mouth even though no words come out. *Tom, where are you? You're supposed to take me away now, remember?*

But Tom's voice is gone from my head. I'm alone.

I call his name. *Tom, Tom.*

I knock on the mirror like it's a door.

Tom Cruise, I whisper. *Where are you? Where are you?*

But he doesn't come.

Just me in the glass and my hands full of red dust. My pounding heart, I can see it pounding through my skin, darker against my dirty white dress. My breathing ragged like I've been running miles.

Like I'm running still.

———————

In the morning, the sound of sirens. A red flashing light outside my window. A phone ringing and ringing and a man shouting in the next room. The scream has the word *fuck* in it.

"Fuck! What the FUCK happened?"

I remember it was Mother who first taught me what a siren meant. *An ambulance, darling*, she said. *It means an emergency. That someone's very sick. Or hurt.*

Will they be okay? I asked.

Maybe, maybe not, Mother said. *That's why the ambulance comes.*

I see there's a trail of red powder on my bedroom floor. I didn't see it last night in the dark. The red trail goes from my bed to the door. It goes past this door, I know. All the way down the hall. To Mother's bedroom, where there's screaming now. I look down at my red hands trembling.

And then? It's like a nightmare except I'm awake. Still in my white dress. Lying in my pink room, where I barely slept. Hearing shouts and loud voices now in the hall. That man who was screaming *fuck* is saying, "In here, in here!" I hear the word *unconscious. Poison. Reaction.* My heart is pounding and pounding. Oh god. *Oh god oh god oh god.* I follow the red trail to the hallway, where men in uniforms are running to the bedroom blue as dreams. No one sees me or hears me asking, "What's wrong? What's happening?" I run after them to the bedroom, my heart pounding so hard in my body, surely they hear it pounding. Then I see her. Lying on the floor between their crouched bodies. Lying like she fell there. I'm crying. One word over and over. I try to run to her but someone's holding me back. Bryce. Creep. Shouting words in my face I don't hear because I'm crying, "Mother, Mother." Tears in my eyes make the blue room swim, make her body on the blue floor seem to float like a swan on a lake. *Please, god, don't die, Mother.*

"What is she talking about?" Creep whispers.

Over Creep's shoulder, I see her face. The white skin is red and raised like it's been burned all over. The skin on her neck and chest is red and raised too, all over. I'm screaming, *No, no, no*, but then I see her breathing. Quick and shallow. I hear it too, rattling, like when I had pneumonia. "Please," I cry through my tears. "Please be okay, Mother." She looks over at me then, through the bodies of the emergency men all around her. Tears in her eyes that make more tears in my eyes right away. "I'm sorry," I whisper. And then the look in her eyes changes. I see she reads everything. Every page all at once. Shakes her head like she can't look at me anymore, can never look again. Close the book forever. The hurt in her face is a stab in my heart. Her eyes close.

"Mother, no!"

I try to run to her again, but Creep's still holding me fast. I watch the emergency men lift Mother from the floor onto some kind of bed. They lift up the bed and carry her like the seven dwarfs carry Snow White's body. I see Snow White in her glass coffin when they carry her away, *please don't take her away.* But Creep is carrying me into my room now. There, he sits me on the bed and holds me down by the shoulders. Looks at me with new eyes. "You better stay in this room for now."

"Where are they taking her?"

"She had an accident. We're going to the emergency room."

"Please let me come!" I try to get free, but he's still holding me down. He looks down at the floor and I follow his eyes. But there's no trail of red powder on the floor anymore. All is gone like nothing. Nothing at all happened. *Magic*, Tom said. Only my hands are red now.

"I didn't mean to," I whisper. I can hardly speak because I'm sobbing, shaking. I can hardly breathe. I hear them carrying Mother out the front door, toward the red flashing lights outside. Away from me. I feel the hurt in her heart. It makes my own heart hurt like never before. I look back up at Creep. His face has no expression at all.

"Please," I tell Creep. "Please let me go with her to the hospital."

And he just shakes his head. Leaves, slamming the door. I hear the slam of the front door soon after. I feel the slam in the back of my head, in my chest.

I run out to the front door but the siren's sounding and the ambulance is already pulling away, speeding down the island road toward the river, the bridge to the city. I'm alone now. More alone than ever before. Standing in the living room in my dirty white dress with my red hands open and empty. The phone is ringing and ringing, it will never stop ringing. I pick it up before I remember about Stacey, the garden.

"Let me speak to your mother." A woman's cold voice. Russian accent thick. "Now."

I hang up. The phone rings again.

Covering my ears, I run to Mother's bedroom. The door is wide open. The jar of night cream named after the sea is open, oozing its red onto Mother's white wicker vanity. The drawer full of her red lacy things is open too, the lacy things spilling out like red tentacles. The jagged star of dead violets and smoke has been shattered against a wall. Someone broke the gold brush that never brushed my hair in two. But the red dust is gone. No evidence of it anywhere.

The phone is still ringing. Alla wanting to tell more, wanting me arrested. I have to get away from here. Mother won't look at me ever again. Mother will never love me again. She'll never forgive me even though *I am so sorry, Mother.* I can't breathe. Creep is going with her to the emergency room and he'll never leave her side now. He'll be her knight in shining armor forever. Protecting her from me.

Tom.

I need Tom.

But Tom hurt Mother. Tom, you said it wouldn't kill her. You said we were just taking my Beauty back, that it would hurt only a little. *Belle, what am I, a monster?* Isn't that what you said?

But I don't hear Tom's voice in my head anymore. He's gone like Mother is. Somewhere on the other side. Didn't he promise he would take me with him? *Definitely*, Tom said.

I remember the folded picture in my pocket. I pull it out and stare into his kind, light-filled eyes. I think of Tom's eyes. Red as my trembling hands.

Do you trust me? he said.

Yes, Tom, I trust.

Seth, Tom said.

I shake my head. *No.* Run to the mirror in the corner of my bedroom. Once it was Mother's and now it's mine. Once it was cracked and hidden away, and now it's sealed and here with me. Heart pounding, slow steps, eyes closing and opening, wanting and not wanting to see what's there. Will he be there? Tom, will you be there on the other side, waiting? To take my hand? To take me with you to the other world? To save me from all this. *Please save me from all this.* I look into the dark, shining glass. But all I see is my red face, my red hands. White dress dirty and torn. The scratches on my arms still black and raised. My bruise isn't glowing anymore, just an ugly blotch on my forehead. My hair's one big dark tangle. I've never looked more ugly, more alone. I've never looked more like Father's child. Tom is nowhere. Not in the mirror, or a breath on my neck, or even a voice in my head. I don't feel him on the other side of the glass like I did before. It feels like a light there went dark. I look down at the crumpled picture in my fist. Something in me is sinking, drowning. The not-breathing feeling. I knock on the glass.

"Tom," I call, and my voice sounds broken.

Nothing.

I knock again and again. "Tom, where are you? Will Mother be okay? What did you do to her? Please. Please take me away like you promised. I can't stay here. I can't stay." And my voice sounds more and more broken. Like my heart is right there in my words, breaking like my words, and still I call for him.

Now I hear a knock at our patio door. From a pounding white fist. The fist wants to come in. It won't take no for an answer. I know the fist. I know the eyes of ice peeking through the door. Alla. I pound on the mirror so hard the glass cracks, but I don't feel the pain.

"Tom, please! Please take me away from here. Please save me. I can't stay." But even as I say this, as I knock and knock on the cracking glass, even as I scream his name, my heart is breaking. I remember his face like a sunrise in my bed. Smiling in the dark when he said, *Nothing saves us. Nothing saves us in the end.*

Seth, I whisper.

The mirror shatters. It makes a sound so much louder than my scream. I've fallen to the floor. Lying here just like Mother was. Not screaming anymore. All is suddenly silent. Broken glass falling all around me, so many shards, shiny and sharp. They fall and fall over me in slow motion like the prettiest snow. The snow hurts terribly. I feel it cutting me everywhere, deeper than the thorns cut. I watch my blood flow onto the floor, onto my bed of snowy glass like a small red puddle. The puddle becomes a pool. I stare at the man in the crumpled picture in my hand, his smiling face eclipsed by red.

And still it snows more.

24

"All that broken glass," says a voice. I open my eyes. Tom's there, smiling beside me. Shaking his head. We're back in the dark Treatment Room, in the room full of fog. Lying side by side on the floating table under the sky of water. The red jellyfish pulses beside us in the glass tank. Pulsing fast like the heart in my throat.

"It's amazing you didn't go blind," he says. "Healed beautifully, didn't you, just like Mother."

"What did you do to her?" I whisper, but my mouth is frozen. It sounds like nothing. A whisper of a whisper through my dead lips. I'm still under. Still in the treatment. Still half dreaming. "What was in that red powder? Not just roses." Though it's a whisper, Tom hears.

"Belle. I think it's time to take some responsibility, don't you?"

I'm shaking my head, but it won't shake; it won't move. Tom's nodding and smiling. *Oh yes.* "Didn't you envy? Didn't you want? A mirror is only a mirror, Belle. It only ever reflects back what we desire and long for."

"You made me."

And Tom's smile fades then.

"Who crept into Mother's closet where she said not to go? Who turned the mirror around? I didn't make you do anything. I just saw what was inside you, seedling. Saw you tell it in the eyes of mud. You want to know what was in that red powder? You. Your dark feelings about Mother. Want. Hate. Envy. That's what poisoned the roses. Poisoned Mother, sad to say. That's what made the red dust."

"No."

He strokes my numb face. So tenderly, like I'm a child. "I was only ever a mirror for your darkness, seedling. I only gave words and a shape to what you wanted to do all along. Gave permission. Showed you what you fucking wanted. So much. Took your breath away." And he smiles his sunrise smile that burns me. His red eyes go the blue-green of Tom Cruise's eyes, filled with laughing light. Shame rises in me like a dark wave.

"You tricked me," I whisper through my dead lips.

"You saw what you wanted to see, Belle. You still do. Something shiny and torn from a magazine. Folded three times, then tucked in your little dress pocket like a secret. No matter how many times I told you my name."

I look at his face, the face that lights up my blood. For a second, he seems to ripple and blur around the edges like an image going out of focus.

I shake my head. *No.* "No, you lied to me. Tricked me into hurting her and then she never forgave me. My whole life. She abandoned me."

"Well who knew Mother would hold such a grudge?"

"You abandoned me too."

The white smile reaches its zenith. "That's what this is really about, isn't it?"

No. But Tom's nodding yes.

"I believed you," I whisper, but my mouth is still frozen. It's so hard to say any words at all. Like a nightmare when you try to speak and your mouth can't move right. My words come out garbled, at different volumes, in fits and starts. "I . . . loved you."

Tom sighs, amused. He knows. Of course I loved him. Look at him, for fuck's sake. A dream in the flesh. A movie in the dark. Rippling around the edges now, blurring slightly if I look too close.

"And I loved you," he lies. "Definitely." He's saying it like it's a line in a movie.

"You broke my . . . heart. You hurt my . . . mother and you broke my . . . heart. I felt it . . . shattering inside me . . . like glass."

"Tell me about your heart, Belle. Tell me what happened next."

I'm afraid. I try to shake my head, but it still won't shake. "Don't remember. I don't remember."

He looks back up at the sky of dark water and sighs. "Oh, you do. This part, I know you definitely do. You don't have to tell me. We can watch it together." And on the sky, the screen is back. A dark beige bedroom. A young girl lying on the bed, her face covered in bandages. Staring straight ahead.

25

In summer, the river around the island turns red. Like the color of mud plus blood. Flies swarm the air in dark, buzzing clouds. A kind of fly I've never found anywhere since. You walk outside and you're covered. The flies have a smell that's almost sweet. I'm watching them darken Grand-Maman's window. Blocking out all the light that comes through the green leaves. Grand-Maman's guest bedroom is just like her own bedroom. The same beige everywhere, but darker, shinier. I lie on a beige satiny pillow edged with crackling beige lace. On the beige wall there's a painting of a man with a beard of feathers in a heavy gold frame. There's a painting of a dark house in a dark wood, also in a gold frame. A dirt path leads up to the front door. That's the one I look at. The one I can't stop looking at. What's hidden inside the dark house, I wonder.

Between the pictures, there's supposed to be a mirror on the wall. Grand-Maman took it away when I was in the hospital. Nothing there now but its ghost. I open my eyes to beige. Close my eyes to beige. My body burning from cuts that are healing just fine, the doctor said, but I still feel them burning. And my heart broken. Shattered like glass. Over Mother leaving me, why did she leave? Something happened. Grand-Maman won't say what. When I try to remember, all I see are flashes now. Broken glass. Red powder. A man smiling at me in the dark. Mother on the floor.

When I opened my eyes in the children's hospital, that was my first word: *Mother.*

Cher, said an answering voice. Not Mother. Grand-Maman. Sitting beside me and dressed up in her black lace like she was going to bridge.

You're up, she said in French. *Thank god.*

Where's Mother? I asked. And Grand-Maman looked at me.

Gone.

Where?

You should rest.

Grand-Maman, what happened? As I asked, flashes came. Mother being carried away in a hospital bed. Red powder on my hands. A man in my bedroom turning to smoke. *Tom, Tom*—I started to cry. And Grand-Maman gripped my hand. *Shhh*, she said. All her gold rings were on her fingers and I stared at the different-colored stones. I stared at the stones because I couldn't look into her eyes. Could never look at what I saw there for long. *Listen*, she said. *Now is the time to bury. Now is the time to forget. We take what hurts us and we put it here.* And she made a fist. She put it over her heart. The bright stones on her fingers flashed. And in my head, I saw a box. Like Grand-Maman's jewelry box for her rings. It looked just like a tiny closet, a *garderobe*. It even had a little gold key like my red diary. *We put it here and we lock it up.* She pressed her fist to her heart. *We keep it for ourselves. We keep it closed. We never open.*

We never open, I whispered.

And Grand-Maman smiled at me for the first time. She opened her fist of stones. Put her hand on my hair, greasy and unbrushed. *And then it can't hurt us*, she said. *Ever again.*

Now Grand-Maman leaves food for me outside the door. Leaves it with a little knock and then tiptoes away in her fuzzy socks. *Cher*, she always calls me. I don't answer and she doesn't make me answer. Mostly, I'll leave the food at the door. Usually things out of cans and jars. Smoked oysters. White asparagus that looks like skeleton fingers. Beef consommé, which is a soup that's clear, so I can see right through it to the bottom of the bowl, where an old-timey man and woman dance. I like that best, though to look at the dancing makes me feel strange. Mother sends me postcards from California. She lives there now with Creep, somewhere called Malibu. There, Mother will be making a movie starring Mother, produced by Creep, they're just waiting on something called funding. *Hope you are well*, Mother writes in a looping black hand. She doesn't sign it with love. She doesn't even sign it *Mother*, just *N* for her name. She doesn't call and I don't ask Grand-Maman if I can call. Even though I want to know does she still love me? I want to say, *I'm sorry, Mother. Whatever I did that made you leave, I'm sorry*. Mother doesn't want to hear it just now, Grand-Maman says. Mother feels some distance might be good for us, and Grand-Maman agrees. More than agrees. Let her try this movie thing, get it out of her system. She'll leave that producer soon enough. Once they've made that movie, anyway. *If* they make it. But yes, of course Mother loves me, Grand-Maman says. Even if Mother doesn't say.

At night, I come out of the beige guest room and go into Grand-Maman's beige bedroom, where I watch *Wheel of Fortune* then *Jeopardy!*, while she sits in her chaise and eats pastries from a box with the prettiest ribbon. Sometimes we watch *Murder, She Wrote* after. Grand-Maman and I always know who did it before Angela Lansbury does. Or maybe Angela Lansbury knows all along and she just doesn't say until it's time. I lie on her sagging beige bed watching television upside down, my head hanging over the bed's edge and filling with blood.

Grand-Maman looks over at me a lot. Worried, I guess. Sometimes I'll still burst into tears for no reason. Like tonight. She's just flipping channels like she does during commercials and there's Tom Cruise talking to David Letterman. And she looks at me and smiles, thinking I'll be happy. But I'm crying suddenly, I don't know why. My scars and cuts are burning again like they haven't in a while.

"What's wrong, cher?"

"I don't know," I say. Though somewhere inside me I feel I do know. Looking at Tom Cruise's face, I'm seeing roses, why am I seeing—?

Then Grand-Maman flips the channel again to a rerun of *Wheel of Fortune*. She lets me cry and I do very quietly. Tears drip from my upside-down eyes to the floor full of cracked, dusty tiles.

"You'll be starting school here next week," she says. On the upside-down television, Vanna is turning letter after letter around. "At Sacré Coeur."

Sacred Heart. The French Catholic school on the island where Mother never let me go. She sent me to an English public school in the city. *Where there are different people from different places, with different religions,* Mother said. *Like Ms. Said. Like you. Do you really want to be taught by a bunch of nuns, Belle?*

"But you have to be Catholic to go there," I say to Grand-Maman.

"I'm having you baptized. I've made arrangements with Mon Père."

Last Sunday, Grand-Maman took me to church and introduced me to the priest, whose watery eyes kept going to my forehead. They talked in a fast whisper behind me while I sat in the pew, staring at Jesus on the cross. I heard the word *troubled*. I heard the word *Mother*. I heard the word *devil* and I heard the word *touched*. Mother never wanted me baptized *out of respect for your father*.

"But Mother—" I say.

"*French*," Grand-Maman says, "is your mother tongue even if your own mother is too proud to speak it to you. Your mother forgot herself and where she came from when she moved to this city. But I never forget. It's time you spoke French and it's time you were baptized. You are not an English girl and you are not a godless girl, and if your mother hadn't raised you the way she did, we wouldn't be here."

"But my father—"

"Your father was a gentle soul," Grand-Maman snaps. "Very agreeable. He agrees with me, under the circumstances."

How could Father agree? And then I remember Grand-Maman talks to the dead. Every Sunday after church, she lights a candle at the dining room table and talks for hours while she plays solitaire. She does it in quick, quiet French, while she lays out the cards. She talks to my grand-père and my grand-tante Shirley, her sister, and her own mother and father. And now my father, too, I guess.

"He agrees?"

"You know your father knew French before he knew English. He would be disgusted that she sent you to an English school. As for religion, your mother likes to paint him as such a Muslim, but he's really far more agreeable than that."

I have a flash of a man in her doorway nodding and smiling. Agreeing very politely with whatever Grand-Maman said.

I stare at the television. My scars suddenly hurt again though the bandages are long gone. The doctor says I healed beautifully. Very beautifully, in fact, and he stared at me awhile. All that's left of the Day We Don't Speak Of is my forehead bruise. But it doesn't glow like a star anymore. It's just a bruise. *Now is the time to bury*, Grand-Maman said. To put it away like jewelry in one of her many boxes. So many boxes she has of very dark wood on her dresser, each one with its own lock. The Wheel of Fortune is turning now. Vanna is clapping lightly. She's always clapping lightly. I wonder if she'd clap lightly if the wheel caught fire. Isn't Mother ever coming to get me? Has she forgiven me? Can I go home?

But I don't ask if I'm ever going to California with Mother. I don't say anything to Grand-Maman but *Okay*.

The priest whispers French words, dribbling water onto my forehead from a golden cup. School is a sea of staring faces I drown in. They all seem afraid of me for some reason, I don't know why. There is whispering in French, but the whispering is too quick and slippery for me to catch. I keep my eyes on the blackboard or on the ground. I do homework in the beige guest room. Stacey calls to ask why the hell aren't I back in school? I'm going to the Catholic school on the island now, I tell her. Stacey says that's terrible. Now there's no one for her to talk to because everyone around her is a fucking child. She asks me if I can come over. I remember the dark basement. Stacey in her black bodysuit spinning for me to "Maniac," her blond hair flying around her like a golden cloud. How I watched her leap and turn until she collapsed on the plaid couch beside me breathless and flushed. Looked at me, her dark mirror, waiting for whatever rating I'd give her. It was the only time I ever felt power. That I had something she truly wanted.

"Well, Belle?" Stacey says. "Can you come over or not?"

Grand-Maman, playing solitaire nearby, hears Stacey's question through the phone. She shakes her head at the cards. "I don't know," I say.

"Don't you at least want your bracelet back?" she whispers.

"What?" My heart. Suddenly pounding inside me.

I feel her smiling on the phone. "I saw you," she says. "That night in the garden."

"What are you talking about?" A flash of red petals. My feet in the cold black soil. My heart beating hard in the dark, like it's beating now.

"My mother's really fucking pissed at you, by the way." She sounds happy about this. "What were you doing out there, anyway?"

I see myself running under a low red moon, the slick grass sinking beneath my feet, while a voice called after me. I shake my head. "I don't know what you're—"

"Never mind, I know."

"You do?"

"Sure. You were trying to see me." She lowers her voice again. "Weren't you?"

I close my eyes. "Yes."

"I knew it. Look, just come over, okay? We'll just have to plan it for when she's not home. Because if she sees you, she'll fucking freak. She doesn't want me dancing for you anymore."

"I have to go," I tell Stacey, and the phone makes such a click when I hang it up.

And Grand-Maman nods her head. *Thwack* go her cards on the table. Whisper, whisper to the dead.

I never see Stacey again.

The air grows colder. I watch the flies disappear from the window. Then the leaves are the color of fire and they're falling. One by one by one. At night, the wind makes a howling sound and the air smells like smoke. I close my eyes. Sometimes I see Mother. Sometimes a man made of smoke. When I open my eyes, the trees are bare and snow is falling slow and fat. It falls forever. And the ground glitters cold and white like Mother's skin. Christmas comes and Mother sends me a card with a palm tree covered in Christmas lights. *Happy Holidays*, it says. *XO, N.* Mother's first *XO*. A good sign, Grand-Maman says. For Christmas, Grand-Maman gives me a Good News Bible, a necklace with a little gold cross, and a brush that works on my hair. She brushes it for me while we watch the ball drop in Times Square on New Year's Eve. The gold cross glitters on my neck. It makes me remember my bare wrist, where Father's eye bracelet used to go. And in my mind, there's a rose garden. A bed of black soil. A flash of gold glinting there. *Now is the time to bury*, I think, watching the snow fall thick and slow. *Now is the time to forget*. And for a long time, the world stays white and shimmering and cold.

Four times the flies darken the window. Four times the river turns the color of mud-blood. Four times the world turns the color of Mother and melts away again. And then the buds are on the branches, and they give way to green leaves. I'm fourteen years old going on fifteen in three weeks. I'm sitting with Grand-Maman in her bedroom watching *Wheel of Fortune*, watching the rickety wheel turn and turn. I've made us dinner. I know exactly what jars to use now. Spring is in the window.

Looking out at the blue sky over the drab apartment buildings, I feel alive and awake in a way I never have before. Grand-Maman is telling me that Mother wants me to be with her in California. She's all settled in a place called La Jolla now. There's a high school I will go to in the fall.

"What about Hollywood?" I ask.

"Well, that didn't work out quite like Mother planned," Grand-Maman says. Now she has some sort of shop. Dresses.

"Like Ladies Apparel?"

"Like your mother's idea of it. You know."

I nod at Vanna White. Yes. I know. Sometimes I play a game where I flip through *Vogue* magazine and I imagine Mother somewhere among her palm trees, the sun in a different place in the sky, flipping at the very same time as me. What would she call *style*? What would she call *a fucking eyesore*? What would she point to and say, *Now that's sharp*. I never knew before. I'd look at the glossy page of a girl Mother was pointing to and have no idea what she was talking about. Now I see. It's in the cut and how it falls. It's in the clothes and the girl and the spirit they make between. I wish I could tell Mother how I can see it from a mile away now. What's sharp.

I stare at upside-down Vanna White on the television screen. Still clapping her hands. Still smiling white and wide. I had a feeling this was coming. Mother has been signing *Love* next to the *N*. She's been addressing the postcards *Dear Belle*. She even called once. *How are you?* she said.

I'm okay, I answered in French. *I'm going to school on the island.* Mother was silent at first.

I heard, she answered in French at last. *And how is that?*

Good.

But Mother wasn't listening. She hadn't called to ask me how it was. *I do love you, Belle*, she said in English.

I love you too. It's the truth. Just not the whole.

"I don't want to go," I tell Grand-Maman in the beige room now.

"I know," Grand-Maman says. "But she's your mother. And you're still a child."

"But you weren't a child anymore, were you, Belle?" Tom says, calling me out of the beige room, back with him in the Treatment Room, under the sky of water. Where we still lie side by side on the floating table. My lips are deader than ever. I can't move my body. He's touching my face and I can't feel his hands. Tracing it like he made it himself, made every shape and shadow that lives there. The forgotten touch I somehow still longed for each night in the beige dark, watching the flies in the window, watching the leaves of fire, watching the glittering white snow and then the green buds. Closing my eyes to the beige and the paintings in their gold frames and the mirror ghost. Finding him only in the very corners of my dreams. Turning to smoke the minute I reached out my hand.

I shake my head at Tom but it still won't shake. He's blurrier around the edges, his face flickering on and off like the most beautiful light.

"Not a child anymore," I say. Beside us, in the glass tank, our red jellyfish has grown bigger now. Nearly the size of the glass tank itself. Not quite the size of the red jellyfish floating up there in the sky of water, but close.

"You blossomed in that beige room, didn't you? Grew up faster than the seasons change. Raised up out of the dirt just like I said you would. Bloomed like a hothouse flower, the red throat of you opening. It was stunning. Even with the mirror gone from the wall, you knew. You could see it in all their eyes whenever they looked at you. Teachers. That sleazy priest. Even the dumb, cruel children at that stupid island school. The dark, aching want in their eyes. That wants in spite of itself. That looks in spite of itself, transfixed. That consumes and is consumed."

I nod with my eyes.

"Envy," Tom and I both say, basking. A smile ripples across his face. He loves how I can say the word even with my dead mouth, clear as a bell.

"You knew that feeling, didn't you? Because you'd looked at someone else like that once. Who did you used to look at like that?"

But he knows the answer.

The answer is up there in the sky of water.

Her face. Its pale eyes looking surprised. Then troubled. Very troubled at what they see . . .

. . . Me. Arriving in San Diego to meet her after so many years away. She's standing at the foot of the escalator, a long airport escalator at arrivals. I'm at the top and she's at the bottom and I'm making my slow way down.

I've just flown over the clouds for six hours. Staring at the sky going bluer and brighter the farther west we went. On the plane, a movie called *A Few Good Men* played, starring Jack Nicholson and Tom Cruise, both very good actors. I mostly watched the screen while I listened to Nirvana on my Walkman that Grand-Maman bought me as a going-away present. To watch Tom Cruise made me feel strange. Made me grip the armrests whenever he came on the screen. Wanting the truth that Jack Nicholson told him he couldn't handle. Still wanting it.

All okay? said the man sitting beside me.

He smiled in a way I would come to know very well. Like even though I wasn't saying anything, my face was telling him something. Some secret thing. Something that pleased him. But when I turned to look at this man, my heart stopped. Dark hair a wave. White movie-star smile. Eyes blue-green as my dream of the sea. He looked just like the actor up there on the screen.

Tom? I said, stopping the music.

Excuse me? the man said. Still smiling at me though he didn't understand.

And then I said, *Seth?* Which was funny. Where did I get that name from?

He looked at me like he wished that Tom or Seth were his name. *I'm Jeff.*

Sorry. I thought . . . you were someone else.

Oh, don't apologize, please. I'm sorry not to be who you thought I was.

Why would someone be sorry for something like that? I thought. But I didn't ask. I turned to the window, turned my Walkman back on. I didn't want to talk to Jeff. But Jeff wanted to talk to me. I could feel his want oozing out of him. He tapped me on the shoulder until I turned back.

Flying home? Jeff mouthed, and smiled. Like there were more questions in this question. And my answer would answer them all.

I looked at Jeff. Businessman. Boring face. Earthly smile.

I don't know yet. And I turned up "Lithium" and looked out the window. Jeff was still looking at me. I turned it up as high as it would go, but I still heard the want of Jeff the whole way across the ever bluer and brighter sky.

When we landed, Jeff asked me if I needed a ride. *My mother is picking me up,* I told him as we walked down the long, wide arrivals corridor, my headphones still on. They'd stay on, in one form or another, for the rest of my life.

Your mother, Jeff said, like that was something he wanted to see. *Where is she?*

We're riding the escalator down together toward baggage claim. A long, slow ride down. Jeff is asking me if I'm sure I don't want a ride. If my mother doesn't show up, he can take me. More than happy to, definitely. Anywhere I want to go. He has a limo, have I ever ridden in one of those? Oh, they're fun. He's surprised that a pretty girl like me has never been in one before. Striking, has anyone ever said that? *Definitely.*

And then I see her. At the bottom of the escalator. She's alone. Doesn't see me yet. She's looking all around for me, her eyes wide open. Worried. Maybe a little afraid, which hurts me. I almost don't recognize her because she's cut her hair to her chin like Isabella Rossellini. Dyed it ice-blond. She looks beautiful still. But older, smaller. The blue of her eyes is less bright, more watery. Her mouth is still red, but small and puckered like now the world has a sour taste. There's a new softness around the edges of her face, like she eroded. When she sees me, she smiles. I smile back. And just like that, she stops smiling. It's only for a second that she stops. Something dark comes over her face like a shadow. And then it's gone. When I get to the bottom of the escalator, she's smiling again.

"Belle," she says, and her eyes flood, and mine flood too. She hugs me and Jeff scuttles away. I smell her violets and smoke, and something else—a ripe sourness, a faint rot of the flesh. She holds me at a distance. "Let me look at you."

And in Mother's watery eyes, I see it. The dark ache. Consuming and consumed. She looks like my face is telling her something and she's deciding if she wants to tell me. Whatever it is makes her happy and sad and scared all at once. And then she smiles over it, a window with a drawn shade. Shakes her head.

"I'm just . . . So happy to see you, Sunshine."

"I'm happy to see you, too." It's a lie and the truth. The tears in my eyes sting with it—the lie and the truth. She hugs me again, a hug full of air. Her body so far away, I can barely feel her arms there. "I love you," she says into the space by my ear. There's a space between us now. A space that feels as big as the years. It's been there ever since.

"Why did she stop smiling at you?" Tom asks me, pulling me out of the dream, back into the fog with the red jellyfish.

"I don't know."

"You do," Tom says. "Because of what she saw. What did she see, Belle?"

"I don't know, I don't know." Though of course I do.

"You. Her Beauty in your face. Her Beauty that you took back. You thought I didn't keep my promises. But I did, Belle. Didn't I get you to California in the end?"

Tom's smiling his constellation smile, his gaze an ocean wave. If I try to focus on his face, he nearly seems to dissolve before my eyes. I remember longing for him, loving him even as I hated him because of Mother, because he left me. I remember standing in the mirror, knocking and calling his name until the glass shattered and the shards cut and my blood pooled red as roses onto the floor.

"But you weren't there," I say with my dead lips, with my broken voice. "You said we would be together, but you weren't there."

"I was everywhere," he says. "All around you. I was the air you breathed and I was the ocean you swam in. I was the breeze that came through the window and lifted the sheets where you slept."

And as he says this, my body grows cold. I'm deep in the cold, rippling ocean of Tom's eyes. "I grew up swimming in your eyes," I whisper. "I became more beautiful in my way and I grew taller and Mother grew shorter and older and her smile turned into a smirk. And the world never got cold, never turned the color of Mother again. It stayed green and blue like the great Pacific. I floated on its white waves while Mother sank to the silty bottom. Quit her acting career and opened up a dress shop. She gave it my name. I got a job as a princess and even dated a prince. And a fellow princess. But they were nothing like you. There was a space there, too, like the one between me and Mother. Like the one between me and everyone forever after. There has been a space between me and everything ever since you turned to smoke. There has been a wall of glass."

A smile on Tom's shining face, rippling like water.

Though I'm still speaking through dead lips, my words garbled like I'm underwater, he hears every word, he knows it's the heart's blood. My heart's blood. The exact true music of our story. To the very last note.

He kisses me on my dead lips.

Behind us, the red jellyfish bursts out of its tank, shattering the glass.

We watch it from our floating table, the story of Tom and me in one red pulsing fish. It drops to the floor. Flails against the wall like a still-beating heart among the glass shards. Right beneath a giant glass tube along the wall that runs from the floor to the ceiling. The tube is like a vacuum, it makes a sucking noise now. My pulsing red jellyfish is rising up toward the sucking mouth of this tube in spite of itself. It's afraid, I know it. I feel it in my heart beating in time with the pulsing bell. I watch the tube suck it up by its tentacles. I watch the jellyfish float up the clear tube toward the ceiling.

"Where is it going, Tom?" I ask with my broken voice.

But Tom isn't with me on the table anymore.

I'm alone watching the red jellyfish move up through the glass tube. There's a hole in the ceiling that connects the tube to the sky. I watch our story join the sky of water. All its red tentacles. Its red bell still beating like a frantic heart. Its pattern of roses. And then it's floating above me, looking down at me through the glass ceiling with eyes both familiar and strange.

And all goes black.

Part VI

26

A dark, warm room full of fog. White faces frozen on the red wall above me, so many faces. Not faces, masks of faces. Their eyes and mouths wide open like black holes. Are they in the midst of horror or in the midst of bliss? Hard to say. I'm lying on a white chair shaped like an S. Slippery, no armrests. I'm in a robe of white silk that shines in the dark, how pretty. There's a red flowerlike thing on the breast pocket. It could be a flower, it could be a fish. The petals look like tentacles, very pretty. Where am I? What is this place? Whatever it is, I'm not the only one here, it seems. Others with me, sitting in S chairs of their own. Everyone smiling. Everyone looking so peaceful, like we're in a spa place. Perhaps we are. And this is the waiting place before. There's a sound of chimes, a perfume in the fog that's lulling. All very peaceful, but I'm a little nervous, funny. Maybe I should get up, take a look around in the fog. Orient myself.

"Oh, don't get up," says the woman next to me. "Not yet, they said."

She's smiling at me in the dark. She's also in a chair like an S, wearing a white robe with a red flower-fish on the breast.

"Who's *they* that said it?" I ask. That can't be the right way to ask, but it's how I ask.

She smiles sleepily at me. She's so extraordinarily beautiful. Her face is like a lake. Lakesmooth. Pale, but something tells me she wasn't always so. Like she's been drained a little of her color. Brightened.

"Who's *they*?" I ask.

"Can't remember," she says. So dreamily. Everything is a dream. The fog is a dream. I'm a dream. She's smiling in it. "They're a color."

"What color?"

"Can't remember the color," she says. "Funny, that. It's so close in my head, you know?"

"Yes," I say.

"It's roses. Blood. Fish that float with many legs. You put it on your face with a brush to make yourself pretty. Anyway," she says, "soon. Soon is when they're coming for us."

She knows so much, I think. She's so wise. And familiar, too. I feel as though I may have sat with her before in this very waiting place. So I ask, "Where are we?"

"The Relaxation Chamber. Where you come post treatment. The After Place."

I look up at the white faces on the wall frozen in screaming. I breathe in the perfumed fog. The After Place. Yes. It makes sense. So I've just had a treatment. "And who are you?"

And she smiles, but then stops. "I'm not sure," she says. "Funny."

"Yes, that is. Really funny."

She looks at me. "Who are you? Maybe if you know, then I'll know too."

I try to think, but my mind is a blue pool empty of fish. Light from a sun streaming down. But no words there. No name that's mine.

"I'm not sure too."

"Funny," we both say.

And we smile. You have to smile or you'll something else. The thing that happens to your eyes when they begin to leak salt water. It's a little funny how we don't know. It's also not funny. It's the opposite of funny. What's the opposite of funny? Forgot. Whatever it is, I'm feeling it spread through me and it's making me cold. It's spreading through her, too, I see. See it on her . . . face. She looks the opposite of funny.

"Can you favor me something?" she says.

I look at her. "Course, yes."

"Do you mind telling me if I look . . . how I look? If it's beautiful at all? Because I can't see a glassthing anywhere."

"I can't either," I say. "Just these white faces on the walls. Do you see them?"

She nods, looking all around. "I see them. I see them and I don't love them at all."

She begins to do the opposite of smile again.

"Don't," I say. "Please. Look at me. I'll be your glassthing."

She looks at me and I look back at her for a while like I'm really looking. Like I'm finding the words in her face though I already know what to say. "You're beautiful," I say. "Like a lake of ice. Smooth and Bright."

This makes her smile again. "It's true?"

"Very. Can you tell me what I am now? What about me?"

She looks at me.

"There's a Glow," she says. "A Glow like a light. Moonbright."

We smile at each other in the fog. Who needs glassthings when we can give each other our eyes? But oh god. Feet sounds now. We hear them coming our way. A gong thing ringing through the chimes. Rings through me. Making me vibrate like a bell. I watch the fog clear like clouds parting.

"Sounds like soon is coming," the woman whispers.

"Sounds like soon is now."

27

We're in a long line of us. All of us in white silk robes with red flower-fish things on the breast. Lined up, two by two, in a grand, dark hall where I've never been. Where are we now? Why are we lined up like this? Where does the line lead? Only They know. There's a perfumed fog still, all through the hall. There's the sound of chimes coming from somewhere. "Have you ever been here?" I ask my new friend, beside me. She's my partner in the line.

"I haven't," she says. "It's a no." She shakes her head. "Definite."

I see a woman in red at the very front of the line, at the very end of the long, dark hall. Two people in silver stand on either side of her holding out what looks like bags for each of us to take.

"Must be gift bags," my new friend says. Since we can't remember our names, she will call me Moonbright. And I will call her Lake. Just until the mist lifts. Until the blue pools of our minds fill back up with the words of us, and our names come swimming back like fish.

"This must be the way out, Moonbright," says Lake. "The exit. And look, they're giving us a gift bag full of samples. For keeping up the Bright and Smooth at home. The Lift. Oh, they are so kind."

"They are so kind," I agree.

"And our shoes and clothes to walk home in too," she says. "Must be."

"Yes," I say. "Oh, that makes such sense."

"Because how can we walk home in these?" She touches her white robe. "It would be silly."

"It would be very silly," I agree. We're moving along in the dark hall, two by two, toward the woman in red at the front of the line. The chimes sing and the mist grows thick.

Lake does the opposite of smile again. "Do you know where home is, though, Moonbright?"

"Home?" I try to think but all I see is the blue pool of water. I'm afraid again. "I think so. It's on a street, I believe. That I know for sure," I tell her.

"Yes. Mine too," Lake says. "On a hill, I believe. In a house with thirteen windows."

"Well that should be easy to find. We'll just count windows."

She smiles. "Yes, that's true. And roaring water. I live beside roaring water. Like a lion, it roars all night."

"Well we'll definitely find it, then. Once we're outside, we'll know where to go. We need outside to orient us, that's all."

"Right, of course. Hard to orient when there's a fog still. And all these chimes. And the dark filling my eyes."

A blond woman just ahead in line turns to look back at us. She is lakesmooth and moonbright just like us. She glows in the dark like we must. So beautiful, our breath is taken. She has old eyes in a very young face. "They keep it dark in the hall because of sun," she whispers. "It's our enemy now. We hate it and it hates us. Forever."

"Who says so?" Lake says. And her voice sounds like a fight.

"They," the woman says, pointing to the woman in red and the two people in silver at the front of the line. We're moving toward them steadily. Getting closer. I can see the flashing white of their smiles as they hand out the gift bags.

"But I like sun," Lake says. There's a frown in her voice now.

"Suns melt lakes of ice, remember?" the woman ahead of us says.

"Not all suns," Lake says.

As we move through the line, the wall on my side becomes a glass tank running from floor to ceiling. The tank is filled with blue-green water sparkly with light. Filled too with many red, strange-shaped fish. They look like pulsating mushrooms or flowers, each one trailing a tangle of tentacles.

"Like jelly- or brainflowers," Lake says. "Trailing spinal ropes."

"Yes." We watch them pulse prettily.

"Like hotels have in the lobby sometimes," I say to Lake, pointing to the tank. "The fancy ones. This must be a fancy spa place." I'm surprised at how easily the words come to me. "This must for sure be where we're checking out." When I say this, I feel so much better. This is the line to leave here. The long, dark hall leads to an exit. And then I realize I don't have my purse with the cards in it. Or my phone cell. Fuckshit. But maybe that's what they're giving us up front, our purses plus our shoes plus our clothes plus the gift bags.

"They must be giving us our purses up there. So we can leave and pay."

"Yes," Lake says, but she doesn't sound convinced. She's still looking at the jellyflowers in the tank. Pulsing with thoughts and dreams. "There's just so many of them."

"They're pretty," I offer, but I don't know. Are they? They scare me.

"I don't love them at all. Too jelly and hairy. Look, one of them is looking at you."

"It is? Who?"

And Lake points at the one jellyflower. Red and staring and floating very close to the glass. Pulsating softly. It's looking at me, Lake is right. I see its red eyes staring into my eyes. And then it moves when Lake and I move forward in the line. Moves with us.

"See how it's following you?"

"It is not," I say. But it is.

"It is. Maybe it loves you," she says, a little longingly. The longing creates a ripple of sadness on her lakesmooth face.

"No," I say. "How can it love? It's a creature made of jelly." And with my mind I tell the jellyflower to go, *please go, swim away*. But it won't. It keeps moving forward as we move forward. Head pulsing to the beat of my own heart. Tentacles fluttering like my nerves.

"How ugly it is," Lake says. She shudders. Draws her white robe tighter around her Brightened body. "And look at it looking at you."

"Yes," I say.

"Your fairy godfish." She laughs. "Maybe it wants to go home in your bag of samples. Will you take it home?"

I look at the jelly. Something fluttering in me as it flutters behind the tank.

"It would be very silly," I say to Lake.

"Yes. And how ugly it is too." She says it like she didn't just say it a second ago. "Though maybe you could kiss it. And it will turn into something less ugly. Like one of those silly stories—"

"And which story might that be?"

We look away from my fish and find we are at the front of the line now. Standing before us is a woman in red. She looks like a Queen of Snow, so white and beautiful, she freezes the breath in our lungs. Makes winter in my heart. She wears a long dress of red silk. I've met her before, haven't I? Looked into her blue eyes flecked with gold like twin suns each in their very pale sky. On either side of her are two Statues of Cold. They are not smiling. Their eyes are ice. The Queen of Snow does not appear to have my purse for me. Neither do the Statues of Cold. Then one of the Statues hands me a clear bag of clothes. *My clothes, at last*, I think. But these are white-and-red silk. Very pretty. Very pretty, but not my clothes.

"These aren't mine. There must be a mistake, sorry. I need my clothes to go home in, please."

The Statues of Cold smile. Then so does the Queen of Snow. "Of course these are your clothes." Her voice is terribly, eerily beautiful like the chimes. They nearly lull me into saying, *Yes, of course these are my clothes, you're right*. But I catch myself.

"No. I mean, they're very pretty. Thank you," I say, curtsying to the Statue of Cold who gave them to me. "Just not mine."

The Queen of Snow is still smiling with her eyes. "These are your clothes. And you are home," she says in her chime voice.

"Home? I am?"

In the tank beside me, I sense my following jellyflower hovering close by. Pulsing just behind the glass. *No, no. No, no.*

"Definitely," says the Queen of Snow, smiling.

"Oh," and I fill a little with relief. Though I feel my jellyflower flailing its tentacles as if to catch my attention. As if to say, *Not home, not home.* "I thought home was outside. I thought I'd have to orient myself."

And now they all smile coldly. "No need for that."

I look at Lake and she's smiling too. What a relief.

"So I can pay, then," I say. "For what you've done to me. Making me moonbright." *Making my mind a blue empty pool,* I think, more complaining. *Will it ever fill back up with fish?* I want to ask, but now is not the time for accusing words, I sense this. Even though I am the customer. The customer is always something. Not wrong. The other thing.

The Queen of Snow smiles again with her eyes. "You'll be paying soon enough. Now off you trot," she says, looking at me and Lake. "Run along and get dressed and ready for the Feast."

"There's a feast?"

"Oh yes, a very big Feast tonight. And you all are the guests of honor."

"Are we?"

Beside me, the jellyflower pulses more quickly. Like it's shaking its head.

"Oh yes. Isn't that wonderful?"

"That is," I say. "I love a feast. But excuse me, my purse is where?"

"You won't be needing your purse. In fact, you won't be needing those, either," she says, pointing to my feet. I see I'm wearing red shoes. "Or this, what is this?" She holds up my wrist, where I see there is a gold bracelet with an eye in it. How did that get there? The eye looks at me and I look at it. I smile and the eye seems to smile too. I had this eye, I think, in some olden time. I look back up at the Queen of Snow, who's now very frowning.

"Take them off," she growls. "Shoes and bracelet."

But they won't come off. I try and Lake tries and the Statues of

Cold try. Even the Queen of Snow tries, grabbing my wrist and pull-ing, nearly breaking my shoulder bones. And still, there it twinkles on my wrist, all golden and untroubled. The painted eye unblinking and watchful. And now the Queen of Snow's frown is times a thousand. Yet she smiles over it.

"The power of accessories can never be overestimated, it seems."

"It seems." I laugh. I'm trying to lighten things. But no one laughs too. Lake stands beside me, afraid. "Shhh, Moonbright."

"Shhhh," I agree.

An exchange of looks between the Queen of Snow and the Statues of Cold.

"Move along," the Statues of Cold whisper to me. "It is already late." And then the Queen of Snow smiles again.

"Remember," she says, and now the Statues of Cold chuckle, "this is your last stop on your Beauty Journey. The final step on the Way of Roses. You are almost to the Roses. Run along to the Lounge now and get dressed in your new garments. Chop-chop. Can't be late."

And she laughs and laughs.

28

The Lounge is a grand white hall with red beds. It reminds me of a cage of ribs with many hearts. A perfumed fog here, too. Chimes play, very loud. They make my bones vibrate. They thrum in my skull. I am here with Lake and many others like us. Different ages, we seem to be, with skins of varying shades, all of them Brightened. Some of us, like the blond woman we met in line, have paid very good money to be here. Others, like Lake and me, are still waiting to pay.

"Everyone's Beauty Journey is so individual," Lake says happily as we enter the Lounge. "Like we are so individual." This word *individual* seems to make her very happy to say.

"Individual," I agree. *So why, then, do we all look and dress the same?* All of us so beautiful. All of us glowing in the dark. We are lake-smooth and moonbright. Some smoother and brighter than others, of course, and Lake and I among the smoothest, the brightest, it seems to my eye. There are no glassthings here, the Statue of Cold who escorted us said. The reason being simple. Because we are so terribly beautiful now that if we were to look in a glassthing, we'd never ever stop. And we can't have that. Then we would never make it to the Final Destination on our Beauty Journey, which is just around the corner, apparently. Unlike me, Lake is happy that home is here. That she doesn't have to find her house, the one on the hill with thirteen windows by the roaring water. It would have been hard to do that. Very hard with her mind and my mind in their current states, so sky bright and empty of fish. We might find ourselves lost on a street, looking for a hill, counting windows, turning around and around in our white-and-red silks forever. Scary. Especially since the sun is our enemy now. That's what the Statue of Cold said who led us here. That it might melt us. And we don't want to melt. *There's a witch that melts in a movie*, Lake said. *Remember her dissolving into a black pool screaming. Terrible*, Lake said. We don't want that. Lake wants to stay lakesmooth, a lake of ice. No, she's happy this is home. She finds a narrow red bed in a corner and she stretches out on it. "This is my bed," she says. "Home," she says, like she's insisting.

She smiles at me, but there is something behind the smile. I see it. The opposite of all her words.

"Home," I say. And there is something behind my smile too.

But the gong goes. And we vibrate like bells.

"Chop-chop," cries a Statue of Cold moving through the hall, watching us. Because the Feast is imminent. Time to get dressed.

Our new garments, the ones they gave us in the bags, the ones we put on, are beautiful. "Just beautiful," Lake says, standing up and twirling in hers. "Do you not think so, Moonbright?"

I look down at my new white-and-red dress, the only dress I have now in the world.

"Look, it has red roses on it," Lake says. "Such pretty roses."

But to me the roses look like other things. Tentacles or tangles of blood and guts. A web of veins. I tell Lake and she laughs.

"Tangled blood? Guts? How are you seeing that, Moonbright?"

"Or like the jellyflowers in the glass tank," I say.

"Speaking of which," Lake says. "Your jelly is obsessed with you."

"Not obsessed," I say.

"Didn't you see it panicking when it couldn't follow you in here?"

"I didn't see." I did. I don't know why I'm lying to Lake about this. I saw its distress plainly through the glass when I was led away, and it made me feel strange. *Why are you so distressed for me, jellyflower?* I wanted to ask. But I couldn't ask before the Queen of Snow, before the Statues of Cold, who were leading us away.

"How funny it was," Lake says, though she doesn't look like it was funny. She must mean something else, but *funny* is the only word that comes to mind.

"Yes, very funny."

"It loves you. Love is funny, I guess." She sighs. There is that long-ing again. That ripple on the lakesmooth surface of her face. But then it's gone.

I wish I could stretch on the bed and smile at the ceiling like Lake. I wish I could wear my white dress of red roses and not see tangled veins.

"I wish I knew how I looked," Lake sighs. "Before we go to the Feast. Because perhaps there will be princes there. I'd love to meet a prince. Or a princess. Royalty, at any rate. So long as I look good. Can you tell me what word I am?" she asks me.

I look at Lake. She is still lakesmooth, but paler. There are dark rings around her eyes like eye shadow. Like she went to a makeup counter and got a smoky eye from someone. Or they punched her. One punch for each eye. Her lips are blue now, blue as her eyes. Her white dress with the red silk flowers looks like guts spilling out of her.

She is looking at me, waiting for what word she is.

And then it comes to me. Swims up like a small gray fish. *Dead.* I look at Lake and I know that is the exact word for her face. But I say, "Beautiful, Lake. Beautiful."

And Lake smiles.

"And me?" I ask.

And Lake looks for a long while. And then she says "Beautiful" too.

29

We are walking two by two in a dark corridor, up a twisting path to where the Feast will be. In celebration of our Beauty Journey. Held in our very own honor. Are we very excited? We should be, the Statues of Cold tell us. It's a very long walk up a winding stair. Along the wall on one side, my side, is the glass tank again full of blue-green water where the red jellies pulse and swim. Some are very big. Some are the smallest things, like whispers. Lake walks beside me in the line again. We are partners in this Beauty Journey, it seems.

I would like to hold Lake's hand, but she's holding a silver tray.

I'm holding one too.

We all are. All the moonbright ones I walk with. All the lakesmooth faces on which there is not a ripple of sad or happy or mad. All wearing white-and-red dresses patterned with what the Statues of Cold keep telling us are roses but which look like something else to me. All gripping their silver trays close, like Lake and me. Each tray's surface is covered with a black circle of paper, but nothing else. *Because we don't want you to look until it's time* is what the Statues of Cold told us. Strange to carry a tray. "Almost like we're the severed ones, isn't that right, Lake?" *Serving ones*, I meant to say. But Lake understands.

"It seems so," Lake says. Ever since we left the Lounge, she's been sounding faraway. The dark rings around her eyes are getting darker.

"But why would we be severed? *Serving?* Aren't we the honored guests? Aren't we the people who paid for here?"

"I haven't paid for here yet. Have you?"

"No. Because they have my purse. So it's a misunderstanding." And then something in me lifts. "Maybe this is why they're making us sever now," I say to Lake. "Because we got our treatments free. And now we must pay in some way. We should explain to them."

Lake looks down at her tray. "I don't know. That sounds like a lot to do. Anyway, I think this is right. I'm a Perfect Candidate, they said. You're perfect too. That's why we walk together. Maybe *perfect* means we don't ever pay." Then she looks up and smiles so suddenly.

"What?"

"Your jelly. Following you. Look." And with her chin, she gestures to the glass.

And there it is. Swimming beside us. Floating along. One among many, but I know it's the one from before by its eyes. Red like its jelly body, and watchful. It makes me smile a little inside. But on the outside, I do not smile. "Oh?" I say.

"Your prince," Lake presses. "Or your fairy godfish maybe?"

"Hardly either of those," I say.

"Yes," Lake says. "How ugly it is," she says, like she hasn't already said this. "Maybe you'll kiss it and it will turn into something beautiful. Like a silly story someone told me once. Every nighttime for so many nighttimes. The same story I asked for, over and over. Over and over they told it. Never tiring. In a voice of love. Love is funny."

"Yes, it is."

"Over and over," Lake repeats in a trance. "The moon in the window. A hand on my hair. How ugly it was."

"The story or the moon in the window?"

"Me," Lake says. Not smiling now. Salt water spilling from her eyes of smoke. The silver tray in her hands begins to shake.

"Lake," I say. "You're beautiful." Though I'm no longer so sure about that when I look at Lake. I think of the word that swam up like a gray fish when she asked how she looked. *Dead.* As I look at her Brightened face, more words come swimming.

Eradicated.

Destroyed.

Used.

A whole school of gray ones. How well they all seem to fit Lake's new face.

"Look, we're here," she says. And she nods at a black hole up ahead of us, like a giant mouth. It reminds me of the mouths of the white faces in the After Place.

The red jelly that swims alongside me seems eager, like it wants to tell me something. Its head is pulsing so very fast behind the glass. Fast as my pounding heart. Its legs are like hands waving.

What? I say out of the corner of my lips.

Nothing. Silence. Or maybe not silence. Maybe it's speaking but I don't understand fish. "I'm sorry," I whisper.

And then Lake and I walk through the black hole.

30

A dark dining room on the top floor. The grandest dining room I have ever seen. A high ceiling of glass so I can see the night sky full of stars. A long black table decked out so beautifully. Rose petals scattered everywhere. Black candles, the flames tall and still. There isn't a wind in this room. There is no air at all. That must be why it feels difficult to breathe. Is the grand table for us to sit at? No, there are already people sitting there. People all in black. Black suits and black dresses, wearing black veils over their faces like curtains. Beside the table is a large glass tank of water, like an open aquarium or an aboveground swimming pool. Seems like the same water we walked beside when we were going up the winding stair two by two. Same blue-green shade. Same red jellies floating and pulsing within. So this must be the very top of that glass tank, where it ends, like our Beauty Journey, where it opens up, like a flower-shaped pool. The way the table is facing the aquarium, it seems like the aquarium is the main event, the show, and the table is the audience, with all the seats taken.

"But where will we sit, if these seats are taken?" I ask Lake. "Aren't we the honored guests?"

But Lake doesn't answer. She's mesmerized by all around her. Especially by the ones in black veils, staring and staring at us. "Who are they, Lake? Do you know them?"

"They?" Lake whispers. "The ones who architect our dreams, of course."

"Who give them their shapes and names," says a woman beside Lake, her skin so very dewy. "Their silky textures and wondrous colors and timeless scents. Bottle them in the prettiest of red jars."

"Make creams and sprays of them," Lake adds, "which they then sell, and which we are so lucky to buy."

"There is no price too high," agrees the dewy woman.

I look at the table of veiled ones. Their faces so shining, their pale eyes staring behind their black veils. "Well how exciting to dine with them, then," I say, though in my voice I hear fear. "Right, Lake? With the architects of our dreams? Who know their shapes and names?"

I look back at Lake. The empty tray is shaking in her hands. If she wouldn't grip it so tight, it wouldn't shake. All of the moonbright ones like us are standing along the walls, holding their empty silver trays like we are. Some moonbright hands are shaking like Lake's, their faces very still and smiling. Many are looking down into their trays. As we came through the black mouth, a Statue of Cold took the black circles off the trays, revealing their shiny surfaces. *Mirrors* they are, our trays, the Statues of Cold told us. The moonbright ones are staring down at their reflections now, smiling, many eyes leaking salt water, overcome by what must be joy. So happy with the results. "Beautiful, Brightened, Poreless," they whisper like a chant. But I don't dare look down into my mirror tray. It's something in how they're all looking down. Like they can never stop. Never look back up again. I feel my gold bracelet tingle on my wrist. I am watchful like its painted eye.

At each of the four corners of the long table stands a Statue of Cold. They are watching over the veiled guests, watching the roses and candles as if it is their job to monitor. They each hold a very big net like for catching butterflies. Or fish. Interesting. Perhaps what we are eating at this Feast will be fresh caught? Live?

"Will they kill it in front of us at the table?" I ask Lake. "Like they do in the finest restaurants and markets? That must be what this is."

"I hope not," Lake says. "I hate that."

"It's a very fancy way," I say.

"I don't want a fancy way. I want to go home now," Lake says. "My home on the hill. A house with thirteen windows. You'll help me find it."

"Yes, of course. It's just . . . I'm not sure where we are." I think of the long winding stair we just walked up. All those twisting corridors. We're on the top floor, that's clear by the night sky above, but I don't know how far down and away the exit is. It's comforting to look up at the night sky through the ceiling. To see the sky is to know something, however small, of where we are.

"There is sky up there at least," I say. "Look"—but Lake won't look. "Lake," I say. "There's sky up in the—"

A clearing of a throat. Then the Queen of Snow steps forward from the shadows. Smiles. I stand up straighter in my white-and-red dress. All of us moonbright ones do. It's like the Queen of Snow's smile has invisible threads connected to all of our spines. And when her lips curve, we straighten.

"We have a very special guest to welcome for tonight's Feast," she says. "One of our very best. Who has given us so much. Contributed so deeply to the Source, the wellspring of our Mission. One who has, over the ages, planted many a seed in many a Vessel and watched the Roses grow." And she gestures to us moonbright ones along the wall. We are the Roses, apparently. Or are we the Vessels?

"In fact, this guest planted one of the Roses here with us in this very room right now. Which is why we invited him to join us tonight."

One of us? Which one of us? I look at my fellow moonbright ones. But they are all too busy looking at themselves in their mirror trays. Even Lake is looking down now. Smiling at herself. "Beautiful," she is whispering. "Brightened." Salt water dripping from her eyes.

The veiled ones clap. Murmuring among them. *Wonderful* is a word I hear. "Oh, oh! A delightful surprise."

I see there's an empty seat at the head of the table. The Queen of Snow's gloved hands are resting on the back of this chair. The sort where a king or a queen might sit. The word *throne* appears in the pool of my mind. Probably this throne is for this honored guest.

"I wonder who this guest is," I whisper to Lake. "He sounds very impressive."

"I don't know, I don't know," Lake says, shaking her head, still staring at herself in the mirror tray. She says it like I'm bothering her. She's getting paler. The darkness around her eyes is blacker. I'm worried. Maybe she needs to eat something. Good thing we are at a feast. Hopefully once this honored guest arrives, they'll start severing us.

Applause as someone enters the room from the dark mouth. Another person in black. A man. He wears a black-horned mask. Though I don't see his face, the veiled ones sitting at the table seem to know who he is very well. The clapping gets much louder, is thunderous. All those black silk hands. Little gasps and squeals of delight behind the veils. The man bows slightly. I feel his smile in the back of my neck. He appreciates the claps. His stance says, *Yes. I am all of this.* There's something in his footsteps that's so familiar. I've heard those footsteps before in my life. Walking through the dark rooms of my life. Entering a door of glass. A door of glass?

A crashing sound. Someone has dropped their mirror tray. Me, I have dropped my mirror tray. What a sound it makes. A rattling and a rattling. And then what a sudden silence. All the ones in black are staring at me now. The Queen of Snow, too, she has murder on her face.

I am frozen, but the sound has snapped Lake out of her trance. She tries to bend down to pick up my tray for me, but the honored guest raises his gloved hand like *stop.* Allow him, please. He reaches down and picks it up like it's the most delicate thing. Smiles and hands it to me.

"Here you are, seedling," he whispers. A soft ripple of laughter among the veiled ones. He turns away from me, continues to make his way to the throne at the table's end where the Queen of Snow waits. As I watch him walk away, there is a pain in my heart, familiar and deep. This man is its shape. The hand beneath the black glove has stroked my hair in the dark. The mouth once spoke words like a cold breeze in my ear, making my heart drum and drum. The eyes behind the mask have looked into my eyes. Suddenly there is a name on my lips. It swims up like a quick, bright fish. "Tom," I say before I can think.

All is dead silent again. All the veiled ones look at me. Hands stop clapping. The Queen of Snow's face changes from murder to surprise. The man whom I called Tom stops walking to his throne, pauses in mid-step. I stare at the back of his white neck, a pale, smooth slash between the collar of his black suit and his waving dark hair. I stare so hard, salt water drips from my eyes.

"Tom Cruise," I whisper.

Laughter. From the veiled ones, from the Queen of Snow. They laugh and laugh, even the Statues of Cold chuckle. How funny are the words *Tom Cruise* that I have whispered. They repeat it to themselves. "Tom Cruise, *Tom Cruise, the actor*? Oh, Seth, Seth, how brilliant. Stroke of genius, really. And the resemblance *is* striking. *Take my breath away.*"

I can't laugh with them. I can only stare at the back of Tom's neck. My fellow moonbright ones aren't laughing either. They also stare at the one I called Tom Cruise, whose name apparently is Seth, their faces full of the opposite of laughing.

Meanwhile Seth takes his throne, smiles indulgently at the laughing table. *Yes, yes,* says his white smile through the mask. "It serves its purpose, I suppose." He pretends not to look at me, but I feel him looking still. "Definitely it does."

The table's laughter at me makes him smile awhile, but then suddenly he doesn't like it anymore. He frowns, and the laughter stops immediately.

He raises his goblet.

"Thank you all so much for having us," he says. *Us?* I think. *But aren't you only one?* And then he turns to us moonbright ones along the wall. "But we are not the only honored guest, of course. The true guests of honor are all around us here. We are so happy to have you."

Some of the moonbright ones smile shyly. Most are still looking at themselves in their mirror trays, saying "Beautiful, Brightened, Pore-less" over and over. Beside me, Lake is shaking. "I want to go home," she pleads. "Take me there, Moonbright."

Laughter again from the veiled ones, this time milder. Seth joins the laughter.

"Well"—he claps his hands—"shall we eat?"

Roaring applause.

"Oh thank god," I whisper. "Lake, we're going to eat now. They're *finally* severing."

Lake is shaking and shaking her head. "I don't want to eat in this room. There are too many red jellies in that tank. How ugly they are."

Two Statues of Cold step forward—the ones standing on either side of the tank, holding their nets. Now a great light shines down onto the tank water. It is the light of the full moon shining directly over the floating red jellies. Oh, it's beautiful.

"Isn't it beautiful, Lake?" I ask her.

"I want to go," Lake is whispering in my ear.

"But we're about to eat, Lake." And inside, I'm thinking, *Eat what? Eat what, I wonder?*

"I'm not hungry, I'm not hungry!" Lake cries.

The Queen of Snow is frowning. She hears us. "Why doesn't *Tom* select this evening's catch?" she shouts, looking right at me and Lake with a scolding face.

Laughter again from the veiled ones. "Yes, *Tom*. Why don't you?"

Seth isn't smiling. He's looking at me and Lake. Lake releasing a hand from her tray to clutch my arm. Telling me again that she isn't hungry right now. Her house has thirteen windows. It's on a hill, she believes. If I can only take her there.

"She," Seth says, pointing a gloved finger at Lake.

The Queen of Snow smiles. "Oh, a young one. Only just opened, just joined us. Perfect, I can assure you. Full of our favorite delicacies.

But perhaps still requiring some . . . marination. Are you sure you wouldn't prefer—?"

"She," Seth says again. And he's looking at me as much as he's looking at Lake. With eyes cold and bright. With a smile that is movie-star white, blinding.

The Queen of Snow nods. She looks at the Statues of Cold and they smile. They begin to walk toward me and Lake, still gripping my arm. Her nails are sinking into my flesh but I do not scream for Lake's sake. But when they approach, she smiles suddenly. Lets go of me. Looks at the Statues of Cold. The ripple of longing is in her face again. It is a dangerous rippling. It says, *I will go anywhere with you.* The Statues are so extraordinarily beautiful up close.

"You have been Selected, Beautiful," they say. Their voices sound like an echoing music.

At the word *Selected*, all the moonbright ones look up from their mirror trays.

"Selected?" Lake repeats. Salt water in her eyes again. "Did you hear that, Moonbright? I've been Selected." She looks so terribly happy. Her happiness hurts to look at.

"Yes. I heard." And it's funny the feeling that comes over me then. A feeling full of shadows. A dark, aching want that consumes. A hate for Lake.

Lake sees it in my eyes and smiles. "I am sorry, Moonbright," Lake says to me, "that you weren't also Selected." But she isn't sorry, I can tell this. She's too happy to have been Selected herself.

"I am sorry too," I say. "But it seems like only one of us can be." I look at the Statues of Cold. They're smiling at each other. They reach out their hands to Lake. Not for her to take, her hands are full, holding her mirror tray. But for her to come away from me, away from the wall of moonbright ones. To follow them, please.

Lake follows them toward the open tank full of red jellies. This is her Final Destination, apparently. When she arrives there, one of the Statues of Cold takes her tray and hands her a net.

It seems like Lake will catch her own dinner. A fresh-caught dinner. Of jelly?

"This is a very intense buffet," I whisper to the woman beside me, a very white woman. She has the eyes of someone old, yet her sin is like a child's. It is strange to behold the old eyes in the child's face. "Perhaps the most intense seafood buffet I have ever witnessed, wouldn't you say?" But the woman is just staring at herself in her mirror tray like all the moonbright ones along the wall seem to be. All but me. The bracelet tingles on my wrist. I stare down at the painted eye glowing there in the dark. *Watch*, it seems to say.

I look back at Lake with her net. Another Statue of Cold gives Lake a handful of red petals. They whisper instructions to her. Lake listens, smiling. *I have been Selected*, her face says. *I, among all the moonbright ones*. Didn't she want to go home just a moment ago? But Lake seems to have forgotten all about home. I watch her drop the red petals into the water where the red jellies swim. Immediately one floats up to the surface, like a moth to a light. And the Statues of Cold smile, the veiled ones in black clap lightly. Lake squeals in delight like she did something so extraordinary. She coos at the creature. Is it my prince she's cooing at? My fairy godfish? If it's mine, I'll scream. Lake wouldn't catch what's mine, would she? A moment ago, I would have thought not, but her *I have been Selected* face is a different face, makes her a different Lake. Maybe this new Lake *would* steal what's mine. But no, it's another jelly that swims up to nibble Lake's flowers with a mouth I didn't know it had. It makes Lake smile and clap her hands. Water drips from her eyes. The look in them is strange. Don't know what it's made of, joy or sad or afraid. Maybe it's knowing. *I know you, little one. I know this shape. It is the shape of something inside of me. Something essential.*

Now the Statues of Cold point to the net Lake is already holding in her hands. She lowers it into the water and her jelly swims into it easily. Her jelly wants to be caught, to be with Lake. How can she eat it now? She lifts up the net, heavy with her creature, and all the veiled ones in black clap. All but Seth, who just watches as Lake lowers her wriggling catch onto her waiting silver tray. So this is what the tray was for. And then the tray is hers to carry, quite heavy, full of her very own red jelly. Thumping on the tray like a wildly beating heart, and Lake so happy as she brings it to the middle of the table where the veiled ones sit waiting. Their hunger is palpable. A panting breath. A shudder. Lake sets it down between the black candles and the rose petals. Sets it right down where the Queen of Snow waits with a carving knife and fork and such a smile on her face. But the Queen of Snow never gets to carve the jumping, wriggling thing. Because one of the veiled ones reaches a hand out and there is a ripping sound and then a scream. And all the black silk arms are reaching, descending upon Lake's creature, still wriggling as it is ripped apart by their tearing hands. I see it torn and thrashing between their bodies. I see mouths full of red between the black veils. Chewing and slurping up the many red tentacles of Lake's jelly. Dangling from their mouths like a bloody, alive spaghetti. Every mouth at the table and every gloved hand covered in blood and fish bits. And the Queen of Snow is smiling. Even as her white-as-snow face gets splattered with the reddest blood of Lake's jelly that they eat so violently. But the Queen of Snow doesn't seem to mind. She licks whatever blood splatter comes to her face with the tip of her long, pink, hunting tongue. Whatever bits she licks make her shudder with pleasure. Her eyes roll back into her head with the pleasure. Meanwhile someone is screaming and screaming. The wildest, loudest screams I have ever heard. Like they are being physically torn apart. Ripped wide open, and they are alive and seeing it at the same time. The screams deafen my ears, where are they coming from? Every mouth is too full of jelly to scream. Lake. Lake at the end of the table, standing between the two smiling Statues of Cold. Lake barely standing, the Statues of Cold are holding her up by her arms. Lake screaming as her jelly is eaten before her eyes. Screaming as if she is the one being eaten, even though she is not, it is only her jelly. But Lake's eyes are wide open and her screams bloom from the wide-open throat of her soul. The bloody thing on her dress looks like a stomach slashed open now more than ever before. The Statues of Cold keep holding her in place, each with a gloved hand. And the veiled ones keep eating and eating, making gasping, shuddering sounds of such pleasure, and will no one stop this? But the moonbright ones along the wall are all still looking into their mirror trays and smiling. "Beautiful, Brightened, Poreless," they chant over and over at their own reflected faces. I try to move to stop this. Lake is so upset, I must calm her down, but I find I cannot move. Something is holding me in place. I look down and see two thorny roses have come out of the wall behind me, oh my. They have slithered around my middle. They have made a tight knot at my waist with their blooms. When I try to move away from the wall again, I am stabbed by their thorns. "Lake," I say, "please. It's only your jelly they're eating." A jelly that won't seem to stop wriggling even as only pieces of it are still left on the table. Pieces that the veiled ones are fighting for, black silk hands wrenching it from other black silk hands. Everyone eats but the man who I thought was a man called Tom Cruise, but whom they call Seth. Seth sits at the head of his table on his throne. Watching it all. Watching the Feasting. And then he turns to me. He puts his gloved fingers to his lips. He looks at me, his eyes red now. And he kisses his fingers so tenderly. Blows this kiss to me. I feel it as the coolest breeze on my forehead. An ocean. Welling up behind my eyes, falling drop by drop. For what is being done to Lake that I can't stop. For the tenderness of Seth's kiss that cools me like a breeze in spite of myself. That soothes me in spite of myself. In spite. In spite.

He smiles. How he loves my ocean of drops. There is no food in the world that tastes as sweet as this ocean looks to his eyes.

The screaming has stopped. Lake has fallen between the two Statues of Cold, who carry her away now. Back through the black mouth of the door. I want to call after her, but the breeze of Seth's kiss has silenced me, has emptied me of all words. And the thorns hold me fast against the wall.

At the table where the veiled ones sit, Lake's creature is no more. Only sputtering black candles, scattered red petals. An empty silver tray smeared with blood. The ones in black murmur behind their veils. Dab at their mouths. Through their veils I see their sins shimmering like pearls. So radiant they are now. It's Lake's jelly, I realize, that's made their faces shimmer so wondrously as they do now. So lake-smooth and moonbright. They pick at their teeth.

"That was . . . fine," they murmur. "That was just fine. But. We are still quite . . . peckish. Yes, this peckishness. It is a most unfortunate thing. *Malheureusement.*"

I feel dissatisfaction rising from them like a cloud of ink. Lake's creature has only whetted an appetite that is fathoms deep.

The Queen of Snow looks panicked. Looks at Seth, who says nothing. He's still looking at the ocean dripping from my eyes, getting his own sustenance.

"An *amuse-bouche,*" the Queen of Snow declares. "Only an amuse-bouche to get things started. The true Feast is just beginning. And for this next course, the next *two* courses, rather—the *pièce de résistance,* so to speak—we owe so much to our most honored and esteemed guest." And here she touches Seth's shoulder. But he takes one look at her hand there on his shoulder and she lifts it immediately.

"*He* is responsible for tonight's main menu. Both the *hors d'oeuvres* and the *entrée, n'est-ce pas?*" And she laughs, but Seth does not laugh. The veiled ones make sounds of interest.

"Allow me to recount the story," the Queen of Snow begins, standing at the helm of the table. "We had a most surprising Catch of late, one of our most intriguing Roses to join the Depths. Not even a Perfect Candidate, if you can believe. A paying Vessel who walked willingly through our front doors in the light of day." Lake's blood spatter gleams on her white face.

"And yet, when we did the extractions, what we found was quite unexpected." She looks at me in the dark. "Quite an extraordinary story, quite a Rose we found hidden inside *that* Vessel." She smiles, licks some of Lake's blood spray from the corner of her mouth. "Of the *intergenerational* variety, no less. *Repressed* as we like it best. And chock-full of our very favorites." And here she winks at me—does she *wink* at me? "*Délicieux.*"

The veiled ones make sounds of delight. "Chock-full. Repressed. Of the intergenerational variety. How *succulent.*"

"Why we have always insisted on casting the widest of nets," the Queen of Snow jokes, winking at the Statues of Cold, who laugh a little, gripping their nets tight. Laughter too from the veiled ones.

"C'est ça."

"Tout à fait."

"But unfortunately this Vessel," she sighs, "expired prior to the last Harvest. Wandered away from us as they sometimes are wont to do. Fell upon some rocks. Rendering its delectable Rose quite un-catchable, quite lost to the Depths, ever elusive to our nets and hands. *Malheureusement.*" She makes a fake sad face at me. "As you well know, a Rose can only be caught by its own Vessel."

The veiled ones make sad sounds. "Ah *oui*. Too true. This travesty, this wastefulness occurs at times. And it really shouldn't."

"Stricter security has since been put in place, *bien sûr*," offers the Queen of Snow.

"Good, good."

"What we like to hear."

"But how lucky"—and now the Queen of Snow smiles—"how *for-midable* for us that this prize Vessel had a daughter Vessel. And this daughter Vessel came to visit our little Maison most recently. Found its own way here. And it had a most delectable Rose too, did it not? A Rose that our most esteemed guest planted with his own hands."

She turns to Seth, who's staring at me.

"When we first glimpsed his signature, his mark upon its brow, you can imagine our great excitement. Hence our invitation to have him join us tonight. And he came most willingly, didn't you?"

Seth says nothing. Still staring at me.

"It grew into quite a flower." The Queen of Snow smiles. "Which we did manage to pluck. A Perfect Candidate, obviously, given its lineage. Repressed and full of our favorites, too. Positively brimming with them, just like its mother. Perhaps more than its mother. It has now joined the Depths. And it is our belief that this daughter Vessel should be able to catch both the mother and daughter Roses for us this evening. Ce soir! Two birds, one stone. Or rather two Roses, one Vessel. Or rather two fish, one net. Should make for a most *unforgettable* Feast. Inoubliable."

"Inoubliable," murmur the veiled ones delightedly. "A most happy turn of events." They applaud lightly.

A mother and daughter Rose, I think. "Well that is an interesting story. Very *intéressante*, isn't it, Lake? But what is this about the Roses being repressed? Full of *our favorites*, they said. What are the favorites, I wonder. What makes them so délicieux?"

But Lake isn't here anymore. She must have left or something? Which is a shame since we seem finally just about to eat. Feeling a little nervous now, can't say why exactly. Maybe it's the thorns around my waist. Also when I think the question *What? What* are we about to eat?

"A very interesting story," I say to the very white woman beside me, to cover the nerves. "About two Roses and one Vessel, the mother and daughter. Did you happen to hear?" But she, like all the moonbright ones, is still looking deep into her mirror tray with her old eyes. Smiling at her sin.

Two Statues of Cold are now walking toward me.

The flowers around my waist unfasten like a belt and go wriggling back into the wall when the Statues approach. Their faces are so extraordinarily beautiful up close that I can do nothing but stare. My breath is gone from my throat. My heart has stopped. I can only look upon these faces, smoother and more moonbright than mine or Lake's could ever dream of being. Than any face could ever dream of being. Everything I look at for the rest of my life will pale in comparison to these faces. Their eyes have universes in them, complete with forests and mountains and seas and starry skies and beyond, to the outer black. On either side of me, they lean in close. I smell what I know is heaven, stardust. The cold burning of the outer black.

"You have been Selected, Daughter," they say with their perfect shining lips. They have the voices of angels. I hear their words like a chorus not only in my ears but deep in my heart, making it Brighten.

"I have been Selected?"

"You," says one with their angel voice. Making me shiver.

"You," says the other.

"Oh my god," I whisper. "*I*."

They take my arms, one takes one and one the other, and it is the most perfect touch, the softest caress. The touch of these hands knows everything I have ever wanted. It's promising it to me as they lead me now, gently, slowly, to the water garden they call the Depths, full of red jellies or Roses floating. The most beautiful garden I've ever seen in my life, I realize, now that I'm really here. Now that I'm seeing it up close, standing right by the glass pool, my arms in their hands on either side of me. Under the moon still full and beaming its silver light down on us from the sky above.

"How beautiful," I whisper.

"Isn't it?" says one.

"Here," says the other. She releases one of my hands from the tray I'm gripping, and tips into my palm a handful of rose petals.

"Drop those into the water. Go ahead, Daughter."

I drop the red petals into the open throat of the tank, where they fall upon the blue-green water. For a moment we watch them float prettily on its very still surface.

"It's pretty," I say, turning to the Statues of Cold. But they won't turn their faces to me. They're still watching the water, waiting. For what?

I feel the waiting behind me too. A table of veiled ones waiting. The

Queen of Snow waiting. Seth waiting. The waiting like a held breath. And then it happens. A red jelly swims up to the surface. Begins to nibble on the petals. It is a giant jelly. My jelly. The one Lake mocked, calling it my prince, my fairy godfish. The one that followed me along the corridor of water. *How ugly it is,* Lake said. But Lake was wrong. I would tell her, wherever she is. It is not ugly. It's not beautiful like the Statues of Cold either. What is it?

Mine is the word that comes.

"Mine," I say to the Statues, who just stare at the water. They still look like they are waiting.

And then a second, slightly smaller jelly swims up and begins to nibble the petals too. It swims right up beside the bigger jelly, the two now side by side. The big and the little. Like they know each other well. Maybe the big one is the parent of the little one. The mother and the daughter? That is sweet.

Behind me, I hear applause from the veiled ones at the table. "Excellent. Very good. Ah, a triumph."

And then a Statue is touching my hand. Handing me her big net. "To catch both your Roses with, Daughter," she says.

"My Roses?"

"Or if you like, your soul." They smile at each other. "However you like."

I look at the jellies both nibbling the petals. The mother and the daughter.

"Yours alone to catch. You'll find it very easy," the Statue says. But there is a note of uncertainty in her chime voice. "You'll find they *want* to be with you."

"You'll find they swim right in," the other says. And then they both smile at me. I am devastated by the effect. Undone in my blood. Whatever they ask of me, I will do. To the ends of the earth. I lean closer to the open throat of the tank. A hush behind me at the table. Seth's waiting silence like a roar. I lower my net into the Depths. I wait for them to swim into it like magic. But my Roses, my jellies, do not swim in. They stay exactly where they are, nibbling the petals. A cough behind me. A tapping of gloved fingernails upon the massacred table of petals and blood. I move the net closer to my jellies. And as I do, they drift farther away to the opposite side of the tank. The daughter one is very close to the mother one now. The Statues clear their throats. I hear one of them sigh. It is a distinctly human impatience. Not at all celestial.

"Come on, now, this is silly," I say. I move the net closer again. This time, something happens. The little jelly moves even closer to the big jelly, as if seeking protection. And the big jelly embraces the little one with its tentacles, seems to hold it so close. Then in one swoop, it takes it into itself. Absorbs it so there is no more little one, no more daughter. Only the mother now.

A gasp behind me at the table. Seth's silence is thunder. And then a growling voice: "Get. The. Other. Now."

"Catch your Rose, Daughter," sings a Statue beside me. "And become your Most Magnificent Self."

"Fulfill your Destiny," sings the other.

The mother jelly looks at me with its strange fish eyes. It's trying to say something. *What?*

"Catch your jelly, Daughter," the Statues sing at the same time now. Tugging my wrist where the bracelet tingles and the eye watches, as if to say, *Careful, careful. I am here. I am with you.*

The Statue's touch no longer feels like the perfect touch. It feels terribly cold. I hear a knife in each chime voice, pointed at my throat. I look at the mother jelly pulsing in the blue-green pool, looking up at me; her daughter's inside her jelly body somewhere. I remember Lake screaming. Red tentacles hanging from mouths at the table. Black silk hands ripping at the still-wriggling flesh.

"No," I say before I can think.

"What?"

"Help me," I whisper to the moonbright ones along the wall, all still looking at their silver trays like mirrors. Only one looks up. Old, pale eyes. Beautiful dark sin that looks far too Lifted, very Bright. She looks at me with the net in my hand. Shakes her head. "Selected," she hisses. When I'm so not worthy, her face says. *She* should have been Selected. As for helping me, well, I shouldn't need help now.

The veiled ones watch all of this, impatient. The Queen of Snow smiles nervously. "Theater," she says to them. "Just a bit of dinner theater for you to enjoy between courses." She looks at me. "What is this about, Daughter? You have been Selected. Do you not wish to reach your Apotheosis? To take the last crucial step on your Beauty Journey? To become your Most Magnificent Self?" There are still blood flecks on her very white face from Lake's jelly. I think of Lake. Screaming in her white-and-red silk. Her stomach looking slashed open. *Used.*

"No," I say. And then all the moonbright ones look up from their mirror trays. All the veiled ones at the table gasp. "What did she say?"

I look at the veiled ones, staring at me very silently. "No, *merci.* I'd prefer to . . . not."

The Queen of Snow's smile grows cold. "You'd prefer . . . to *not*?" She takes a step toward me and I feel myself take a step back. My red shoes feel awake now on my feet.

"I see," she says. She takes another step toward me. Again, my shoes take me a step back. *I'll go with you,* I tell them in my mind.

"Yes," I say to the Queen of Snow, backing away. "So sorry. Desolate. *Désolée,* I mean."

"Well. We are also désolée. *Très désolée* to hear that you are dissatisfied with your Beauty Journey. Particularly when you are so close to the End."

I nod like this is indeed a sham. *Shame.* "So if you'll just give me my purse, I'll pay you for your very wonderful severings thus far. And then I'll be on my way."

The veiled ones laugh now, uneasily. Ha. Theater, is this? Well, all right. We were not expecting to be entertained as well as fed. How *charmant*. Though the entertainment is a bit . . . willful? Obstinate for our taste. Pas à notre goût. Speaking of taste, can we . . . *eat*?

The moonbright ones no longer look at their mirror trays. All shining eyes are on me. They cannot believe that I won't take this last crucial step in my Beauty Journey. When I have been Selected. When I am on the Cusp. They shake their heads. Whisper to one another. "She has been Selected and yet she will not take this last step, why? She is a fool. She is stupid. We would never be so stupid."

The Queen of Snow looks at me, and now her smile is ice. "You have been *Selected*." Another step forward.

"I don't want to be Selected." Another step back. Me and my red shoes take it together. "I did not ask to be Selected."

"You are on the *Cusp*." Another step forward.

"I don't want to be." Another step back, and I'm back up against the tank now. I feel the glass wall behind me, the railing digging into my low back. Behind me, I feel my red jelly float. The mother Rose who absorbed the daughter Rose into her body in an embrace of tentacles. She has not gone back down to the Depths. She's staying here with me even though I tried to catch her. Even though I tried to kill her, to feed her live to the veiled ones. She's not leaving me. She's still here. Trying to say something. What is she saying? *Come with me.*

"Well that is perfectly fine," the Queen of Snow says.

"It is?"

"*Bien sûr*. You are a free agent, after all. And the customer is always right, n'est-ce pas?"

Now the veiled ones really laugh.

And then the Queen of Snow nods at the Statues of Cold. They come toward me from both sides. How could I have ever thought they were beautiful? How could I have ever thought they were angels? They're smiling like they are going to kill me.

The black mouth of the door is behind them. The black mouth

into which they dragged Lake, who was once beautiful, who is now no more. Along the wall, the moonbright ones regard me darkly. Not so moonbright-looking now. They're holding their mirror trays up like shields. At the table, Seth sits looking at me. No expression. His eyes are black holes.

Come with me, I hear from behind me in the pool.

I try to take one more step back, away from the Queen of Snow, away from the table of veiled ones. And there isn't a step to take, turns out. There is only falling. Backward falling.

And I'm in the tank.

I'm deep in the blue-green water.

Cold, very cold water.

Can't breathe, sinking.

Through the water and the glass I see the veiled ones silently screaming.

I see the moonbright ones drop their shields and wring their hands.

I see the Queen of Snow tear out her red hair.

I scream and water fills my mouth.

And then the mother is on me, its beating heart-head pressed against my chest, its tentacles wrapping around my neck like it's holding me fast. And we're sinking, down through a grand tunnel of water. Sinking or swimming? Don't know, but down we go. And I'm dying, I feel myself dying, my heart and lungs frozen in mid-spasm. And as we sink down through water, more and more red jellies wrap themselves around my body, legs, arms, chest, all of me covered in red jelly, all but my eyes wrapped entirely in jelly bodies as I sink or swim down. Then suddenly my lungs open, underwater they open, and I'm breathing underwater, covered in jellyfish; these are jellyfish. The jellyfish are breathing for me, or I am breathing through jellyfish? And we're not sinking, we're swimming, they're swimming me down the endless tunnel of water, through the many floors of this house. I can breathe and open my eyes and watch us swimming down. Through the water and warped glass, I see the grand hall where I danced and drank of the red stars, where people are dancing still. In horror, they watch us turning and swimming down. They bang their fists on the glass. I feel things being thrown at us. Champagne flutes. The sound of shattered glass like rain against the tank walls. We swim down faster, down to the very bottom of the tank. They know where they're going, these jellyfish. I hear what I think are voices all around me. Saying, *Hurry.* Saying, *This way.* We've reached the bottom of the Depths, which is a floor of glass. Through the floor, I see a dark room with a white massage table. The Treatment Room. Where I lay with Seth, I remember now. Where I grew my little jellyfish from a ghostly white wisp into a red creature like the ones wrapped all over me. The water down here feels so much colder, why? Where is the cold coming from?

The jellyfish swim my body toward a dark grate in the tank glass. The cold rushes in from the grate like a cool breeze from an open window. Except instead of a breeze, it's water. Darker, colder like the water of night. I feel the jellyfish sighing.

Ocean, all the voices say as one voice.

They swim me up to the grate. The cold water is a wind in my face. In all our faces. They sigh around me. *Yes. Here.* Gently, they guide my hands, covered in pulsating heads and tentacles, to the lock. They slide farther up my arms, leaving my hands suddenly empty, free of jelly. My fingers that can open the lock. That will open the lock for them, *please.* They who have no hands and fingers. Who can only swim me here. Up above, I hear shattering glass, *oh god.* Someone has broken the tank and the water is spilling out onto the floors above. I can see Seth at the very top. Standing in the open throat of the tank high above us, his body shimmering darkly. Watching the water flood, the glass break, I feel his eyes on me like voids. I see the Queen of Snow running down the stairs with her Statues of Cold. "After them. After them."

Hurry, hurry. Unlock, unlock, the creatures say.

But my fingers are slippery on the lock. Numb with cold on the cold metal lock, *oh god, oh god.*

Please hurry, Belle.

The water empties above us. The glass is raining down. The lock gives in my fingers. Opens.

And together we swim into a dark night of water.

I do know how to swim after all.

31

How long does it take us to surface from the night of water? It was a long way down. It is a long way back.

In the ocean, I see faces in the red creatures that surround me. Human faces. Mostly children's faces.

Once upon a time there was a little girl.

Once upon a time there was a little boy.

I hear the whisper of *thank you, thank you* in my ears. *You saved us.*

They swim away into the dark one by one. Unwrapping themselves from my arms and hands and legs. Until there is only one creature left with me. The one wrapped around my chest. The one with its bell-shaped head pressed against my neck, beating like a heart against my heart. The mother. I am still breathing as she swims me. She will not let me go. She alone is helping me to breathe through this dark night of water. Maybe she alone always was.

A light above us now, creating a brighter pool of blue. And I know this is the night lifting, I know this is the bright dawn we're swimming to, she and I. *Are you swimming me or am I swimming you, Mother?* Does it matter? There is the sun above us. The sun she was always afraid of and then I was always afraid of. Though not anymore. They told us it was our enemy, can you believe it?

She swims us toward the light.

I'm lying on the shore. Sand on my back. White waves crashing over me. She hasn't left me yet. She's lying there too, right by my side, though she'll have to go soon. I don't need her to breathe for us anymore. And she can't breathe out here. She has to go back to the water. But I don't want her to go. We lie side by side in the light she hated. All her life.

But I loved you, Sunshine.

"I love you," I say to her. Beating like a heart against my heart.

Tentacles around my neck turn to white arms. The red head becoming a face I know so well. That smiles at me now.

"I'm sorry, Mother," I say to the face. Tears of salt spill from my eyes.

They spill from her eyes too. *I'm sorry*, they say, even though she does not speak, cannot speak. I hear the words in my heart. I hear them all through me like waves.

She kisses my forehead.

And then a light fills me. A warmth. A remembering that branches. Of you and me, Mother.

Of you and me, Sunshine. Of us. Standing in an orchard. A sea of trees and September light. You're handing me an apple you picked yourself. For you, Mother, you say. You say it matches my Chanel lipstick, my best red. And your face is so full of sunshine. No shadows yet. You reach out to hand it to me. And I'm afraid of how beautiful you are. How much I love you. How I won't be able to protect you from this place. From me. My places that I go. One is locked away in the closet. Cracked and turned to the wall, but one day you'll find it. You'll stand in front of its shining face, not knowing why I turned it away. That I'm only protecting you from myself. The things I can't change. The things I wish I could. I'll try to stop it in my clumsy ways that are out of love, that won't work. But my places will soon be your places. And everything will shatter like glass. Terribly. Both broken for years. I'm in a blackness that knows no end even among the palm trees and the light that melts me like a witch. My smile is a ghost. My heart is in a beige guest room on the other side of the continent, on an island by a slushy river, covered in bandages. Years later, I'm turning circles in arrivals at the San Diego airport. September sun streaming into the windows. The board says your flight's landed and I have no idea. No idea how I'm going to do this. If I even should. Should I save you from me? Keep you miles away in that awful woman's moldering apartment? But I hate to think of you in that beige prison. Don't know what's better in the end: me or the beige prison. Also I miss you. Now I see you at the top of the escalator making your slow way down. Some predator is talking to you—they'll do that for the rest of your young life. You're looking at me. When I see your face, I'm so happy, and then I feel such pain. How much you've grown. How many years. I'm back in the orchard, afraid all over again. How beautiful you are. How much I love you. That I can't protect you from my terrible places that I still go, can't help but go because no one protected me, no one saved me, no one ever held out their hand and walked me away. But I'm trying to save you, Sunshine. I'm trying in my broken way. I'm holding out my arms. I'm taking the apple you're handing me. I'm looking into your eyes and saying it's the most perfect thing. Even though you're not hearing me. You're already skipping away. Still I call after. I love you.

A warming of the light all around us. I feel it, just as I feel Mother's voice all around me. Telling me its last story. The story of her and me and a piece of glass. The glass is gone at last. Shattered and returned to sand. I close my eyes in the warmth of it. And my throat opens like a rose.

I love you too.

And the kiss is over. She's gone from me. Nothing but air on my skin. When I open my eyes, she's water. White foaming waves lapping against the shore, against my breathing body. The sun on my face. And my heart beating all by itself.

32

Something is licking my face. A great, panting tongue. I feel a very cold nose sniffing me tenderly. *Mother?* I open my eyes. A dog. Looking at me with large liquid eyes, one blue, one brown. When it sees I'm awake, it barks its face off very happily. Then it goes galloping away.

I'm lying in the wet sand. Shivering though overhead the sky is a bright blue. Early morning sun on my face. Mother's not with me anymore. I'm alone except for the dog. Where am I? At first, a blank. Then slowly words come to me. California shore. The cove near home. The children's beach that the seals took over long ago. Look, there are seals over there on a rock in a stinking huddle, tilting their bodies backward so gracefully. Exposing their necks and bellies to the sun. Mother used to take me here, remember? *Look how sweet*, she'd say, pointing to them lying there. *Look at the little one thumping his way toward the shore*. Home's not too far at all from here. A walk if I could walk. But I can't seem to move just now. Can't even cover my ears against the sound of the still-barking dog, getting louder again. *Mother's gone* is a fact coursing through me. Turned to foam. And somehow I'm alive still. Though my breath is quick, my heart beats slow. Cold skin and getting colder. Shivering in the sun. Then I hear a name being called.

"Belle! Belle!" My name, I know.

With all my strength, I look in the direction of the sound. A little blond woman in activewear, running toward me with the golden-haired dog that happily licked my face running along beside her. The dog's leading her to me. *I found her, I found her*, its face says. *Look!* And the woman is looking. Very worriedly. Her face is creased with it. Sylvia's her name. Because she knows Mother and me very well, I remember. Because she's a friend.

"Where were you?" she's saying to me. "I was looking everywhere, everywhere. Thank god. Thank god we found you."

"Mother's gone," I tell her. My voice is an empty shell. My teeth chatter through my words. "She was right here a minute ago and now she's gone."

Sylvia looks at me lying in the sand. My bare legs in the cold, lapping water. My shivering wet body in ripped silk. How I'm gripping the shore in my hands. My fists clutching crystals of sand.

She nods. "I know," she says in a lower voice. "I'm so sorry."

"I'm sorry," I say. They are the only words I have breath to speak.

"Let's get you home," she says. She picks up her phone. "Emergency? Hi, yes, I need help at . . ."

Help, I think. And I'm nodding, my cheek in the shining sand crystals.

33

After they drag me up from the beach, I sleep for a week at Sylvia's place across from Mother's. Her guest bedroom is entirely blue. Blue walls, blue pillows, blue bed. Glass seashells and starfish everywhere you look. *Peaceful*, Sylvia said. *I hope you'll be comfortable here.* There's a little placard on the nightstand that reads MERMAID KISSES STARFISH WISHES. I look at that whenever I open my eyes. The mermaid kiss and the starfish wish. Mostly, though, I keep my eyes closed. Sometimes I dream of black veils and red jellyfish. I wake up screaming. Sylvia's there in an instant. *Shhhh*, she says like I'm a child. *It's all right. You're safe. Only a dream.* She does not say *tell me your dreams.* She does not say *what's this about black veils and red fish?* She does not ask what the hell were you doing in a torn dress, washed up by the waves, anyway?

A doctor comes and takes my pulse and shines a light into my eyes. He listens to my heart and lungs and he says Yup. Just fine. Unbelievably. "No hypothermia. No concussion. No psychosis," he whispers to Sylvia, who blushes. "Of sound body and mind," he declares, like he could declare such a thing in five minutes. I'm a very lucky young lady. Especially given how long I seem to have been lying there half-naked, submerged in ocean water. Who knows? Maybe I'm part fish. A mermaid. Is that my secret? And he winks at us.

We stare at him.

"No more evening swims, okay?" he says, not smiling anymore.

And Sylvia says, "Thank you, Doctor." Her voice is a door banging shut in his face.

More than the black veils and jellyfish, I dream of other things.

Lake looking at herself in the tray mirror and whispering, *Beautiful*. Her house on a hill with thirteen windows, I was supposed to help her find it. Dancing with Hud Hudson, beautiful detective. Gray eyes full of tenderness, full of wanting to save me. Who needed to be saved himself in the end. I can only pray he was. Sometimes I dream of Tom. *Seth*. The breeze of his blown kiss on my forehead. The twin black holes of his true eyes. Mostly, I dream of her. Swimming me up through the dark night of water. Lying side by side with me in the white sand. Watching her red tentacles turn to white arms. Watching her white arms turn to foam on the waves.

"A terrible accident at the house on the cliff," Sylvia says to me one morning, bringing me coffee. "A flood, can you believe that?"

"A flood?" I picture the veiled ones thrashing in dark water. Their long table of rose petals and black candles floating.

"Terrible," she says. Her golden retriever comes trotting in after her. The one who found me on the beach. He jumps on the bed beside Mother's cat and they lie together. They actually get along, Sylvia told me. They've been around each other enough in their lives that they're just fine. Anyway, quite the story about this house on the cliff. There was some sort of giant tank in the middle of the house like an aquarium? It shattered and the whole place flooded. Top to bottom.

"Top to bottom?"

"Yup. People drowned. In a house!"

And now I see everyone floating. The Queen of Snow with her carving knife. The Statues of Cold with their nets, the moonbright ones with their silver mirror trays. All of them drifting lifelessly under black water. Their silk gowns billowing around them, making them look like ghosts. The red chandelier of fire finally out. I think of Hud Hudson again and my chest tightens. The last time I saw him we were dancing beneath it. *Dance with me, follow me*, his eyes on my eyes, and something in him breaking when I wouldn't follow. My heart swells.

"Did they find anyone?"

Sylvia looks at me, suddenly curious. "Everyone else must have fled, apparently. No one found. No one taking responsibility, can you believe it? Just typical." She shakes her head of spikes. That's the world for you. Right there.

She walks around the blue room, drawing back the pale curtains, opening the windows. "You need air," she says to me. Every morning when she draws back the curtains, I think they're going to reveal a tank of blue-green water, a swarm of red tentacles, and I brace myself. But it's only ever blue sky. A high pale sun. Palm trees, their frondy fingers swaying in the breeze. Sylvia smiling. *There you go.* She thinks I need more light these days too.

"That house will be condemned now, of course," she says. "Far too much damage to the foundation. It might even fall into the sea, who knows. Good riddance, I say." She walks over to the bed and pats the dog's head. Mother's cat, Anjelica—my cat now, I guess—just looks at me. "I never liked that place. Creepy, you know the one. You'll have seen it if you went for a walk on the path along the cliffs?"

"I never walked along the cliff," I lie, staring at Anjelica.

She doesn't say, *I could have sworn I saw you.* Instead, she keeps petting the dog, whose eyes close and open. "Well, it's a pretty walk, anyway. Pretty walk, weird house. A mansion, really. Right at the edge of the cliff. I always wondered who the hell lived there. I guess now we'll never know, will we?"

She's asking me. I feel her asking me.

"I guess not."

"I always wondered if it might tip into the water. I was even going to warn them about that. In case they didn't realize. Sometimes it takes an outside eye to see things."

"Yeah."

"But they didn't seem very approachable. Living behind those tall black gates."

"Right." I picture Sylvia knocking primly on the door to tell them, to do her neighborly duty. The look on their pale faces when she explained herself.

"For a while I thought it was abandoned," she says. "But it had the most beautiful roses in the front yard. Those take cultivation, you know. Care. Roses like that."

"Yes."

"And I think they had some sort of spa in there?" Sylvia says. "Something like that, anyway. French. Very exclusive. To do with beauty," she presses.

"Beauty," I repeat.

"Skincare," Sylvia says, frowning a little. The concept is far too suspect and mysterious for her. "I think your mother used to go there."

"Did she?"

"You know your mother. Always into the treatments and such. The weirder the better for her." And she laughs. But I know Sylvia's laugh now. Not cruel. Mostly just embarrassed by the want she observes in the world. Even her own. "You like that stuff too, don't you?"

"I used to."

"You know that flooding happened the same morning we found you on the beach. Not very far away."

"Huh," I say. And that is all I say. Even though Sylvia sits there for a very long while. After she leaves me at last, I go online and try to find a woman called Lake. I want to do something for her. To let her family know. To find the house with the thirteen windows. To tell whoever lives in that house what happened. No woman called Lake in La Jolla that looks like Lake. Though I remind myself Lake didn't look like herself. And probably she wasn't called Lake. Probably she was just like me, like Hud's brother. With her own dark mirror, her own story of envy and longing that made her the Perfect Candidate and then the perfect feed. What was your mirror like, Lake? What did you see when you looked into its shining face? Did you ever see how beautiful you were? Did you ever see your own face as it truly was? Or was it another face you saw there? The name and shape of some childish dream. Did he dance with you in the bedroom dark? Whisper poison into your young ear, his breath on your neck like a cold, cold breeze? Did yours look like a famous movie star? Someone that as a child you might have recognized, already learned to love, trust, find beautiful. Face like the sun, eyes like the sea. And yet something about the cold sticking of his touch, the endless deep in his eyes, the poison words on his red lips told you he was also something else. Something awful you couldn't name. Where did it come from? Your soul or the glass or something else between? What did it make you destroy? *I was only ever a mirror for your darkness, seedling*, Seth said, his eyes going from blue-green to red to blue-green.

I wish I could ask her.

I find a phone number for Hud Hudson, try it. Not available. I call the pink hotel. He's still checked in there, but they haven't seen him, they say. They put me through to his room and the phone rings and rings, and then it's the front desk clerk I'm speaking to again.

"Would you like to leave a message?"

"No message. I'll try again later."

Sylvia never asks me about the house directly again. She never asks why I washed up in a torn white-and-red silk dress on the shore like I did. She never asks why I went insane in her clothing store. She never asks and I never tell her that I did indeed walk the path along the cliff. In a pair of Mother's red shoes, shoes I seem to have lost in the night of water. Shoes that led me down the very same path she must have walked, that led me right to her in the end. Maybe she is where they were always leading me in the end. I never tell Sylvia about going the Way of Roses, where I very nearly became my Most Magnificent Self. I never tell her about the Treatment Room, where the black box of my mind was opened and I came face-to-face with my deepest secret, almost lost my soul in the shape of a red jelly-fish. She doesn't ask, though I know she's suspicious, and I don't tell, though it doesn't feel like such a secret anymore. Not like Seth was.

Seth in the black box that Rouge opened. In some ways, it feels like Sylvia knows anyway.

If she did ask, I would say it was grief. The deepest grief. I know she would accept that as an answer. No one knows what's inside grief.

Anything at all can be there.

I call the funeral director and arrange to pick up the ashes. I call Persephone and tell her I won't be back to Montreal for a while. I call Monsieur Lam and he says Lucifer is doing beautifully, not to worry. *Do what you have to do.* I lie in Sylvia's blue guest bedroom and through the wall, I hear her sitting in her beige living room alone watching *Wheel of Fortune* and then *Jeopardy!* in the evenings. I remember Grand-Maman rocking alone in the dark. The sound of the rocking and the sound of the television and the sound of her silence. Her fist of gold and stones. How she pressed it to her heart when she taught me about forgetting, though she herself never forgot. *Now is the time to bury.* The gold bracelet winks on my wrist, thin as thread. I look down at the eye that kept me watchful that terrible final night. *Father's eye,* Mother said. *Always open.* There are some stones that close and some stones that open.

One night, I join Sylvia in the living room.

She looks at me standing in the doorway and smiles. There's her cup of tea on the coffee table. "Not watching your beauty videos tonight?" she says as I take a seat beside her on the crinkly couch.

"Not tonight," I say. When I first got my laptop back, I immediately opened YouTube and tried. But just one look at Marva's pale, expressionless face and all I saw was the Queen of Snow covered in Lake's blood spray. All I heard was her fake motherly voice. All I saw in the vial of serum Marva was holding up was a white pulsing fish. I snapped the laptop shut.

"You know I could use someone at our little shop," she says.

"Really?"

She nods, flipping channels. "Someone to buy and manage the stock. Do the displays. That was never my forte, as I know you know. I'm really more of a numbers person. And Esther's sweet, but she's hopeless. Your mother was the one with the eye, the style. Always so sharp. We really miss her." She looks at the TV screen. "Do you know anyone who might be—?"

"Yes." I say it before I can even think.

Sylvia smiles at the television. "Wonderful."

We watch *Jeopardy!* like I used to do with Grand-Maman. Except I don't lie upside down, and unlike Grand-Maman, Sylvia isn't silent. She blurts out her guesses. Blurts them out even if she's wrong. She doesn't care. "I'll always say the answers," she says. *Not the answers, dear. The questions*, Mother would say if she were here. "I can't contain myself," Sylvia says. "Sorry."

"I like it," I say.

I feel her looking at me instead of the screen, smiling. "What?"

"Just, you're looking better these days."

"Am I?" I haven't looked in a mirror since I arrived. Can't bring myself to face a glass. Not yet. Don't know what face I'll see there. Mother's. Seth's. Some moonbright monster.

"How?" I ask Sylvia, and I remember Lake and me in the After Place, the room of white faces. Lake asking me how she looked, *If it's beautiful*. Me telling her it was, though I was afraid for her, though the word *dead* was swimming in me like a small gray fish. I said, *Beautiful*. Her giving me the same word back.

Sylvia doesn't look at me like she's afraid for me. She's smiling. Like there is someone there she recognizes, in my eyes. A friend.

"Like you," she says.

34

When I go back to Mother's apartment—my apartment now, Chaz says—the roses are still blooming redly under her windows. Her door is still flanked with spiky, pretty plants. *Wipe Your Paws* it says on the welcome mat, the lettering faded. Anjelica is wriggling in my arms as we approach. *Home*, I can feel her thinking.

I'll admit I'm afraid to go in. What will I find? Evidence of my insanity? Evidence of hers? Evidence of all the thorns between us?

When I open the door, it looks both the same and different. Cleaner and brighter, more open somehow. Filled with air and light. There are two mannequins sitting at the dining room table by the window like they're having tea by the sea. I flash to the moment when I took them from the shop, believing they were my sisters. Didn't I have three?

And then I hear a voice from the kitchen. "Hey."

He's standing by the table. Wearing an actual shirt. His hair is tucked neatly behind his ears. No squeegee in sight.

"Tad." I can't believe how happy I am to see him. "You're still here."

He smiles a little. "I just stayed so I could say goodbye," he says.

"You're leaving?"

"I should get out of your hair. Let you get your bearings. Anyway, it's all done."

"Done?"

"Everything's fixed. Patched it all up, too. Pipes, walls. Even cleaned the windows again."

I look around the place. Now the difference, the openness, the new quality of light and air, makes sense. "I don't know what to say. Thank you."

He shrugs like it was nothing. "It's in the best shape it can be now. Whatever you decide to do with it." He doesn't ask what I'll decide to do with it.

"What do I owe you?"

"Just take care of yourself, okay?"

"Surely I owe you—"

He shakes his head. "I did it for your mom. She was good to me. Probably too good. This is the least I could do." He turns away from me to face the kitchen cupboards. Silent for a while. "I did some grocery shopping for you too," he says at last to the cupboards. "Just so you wouldn't have to think about it for a while."

I stare at his back, thinking of that awful moment in the bedroom with him. How I made him white with fear. Kissed him until he left me, mumbling about how he had to go buy some fruit.

"You bought the fruit."

He's still turned away from me, staring at the cupboards. "Yup."

"Tad, I'm really sorry I was behaving so strangely before. I wasn't . . . myself."

"It's all good," he mutters.

But I know he's red in the face. I am too. I look at the kitchen floor, which Tad has swept and cleaned in my absence, like he's swept and cleaned everything else.

"It isn't good. I'm sorry if I did anything to make you—"

"Hey," Tad says, turning around at last to face me. His eyes are rimmed red, shining with tears. He walks over and hugs me then. In the warmth of his arms, I feel his love for her. I smell her happiness in his scent of beach and bright days.

"Grief is a journey," he says. "And everyone has their own way, you know?"

"Still," I say, shaking my head. "That wasn't the way I ever meant to go."

He pulls away a little so we're face-to-face. He brushes my hair away from my eyes. "There's no one right way to ride a wave, Belle."

"Thank you for being good to my mother. Thank you for loving her. I'm glad you were in her life."

"I'm glad she was in mine. I'm only sorry I wasn't there that night she . . ."

He looks away.

"Me too," I say, tears in my own eyes now.

"The truth?" he whispers. "Is that I really didn't know what was going on with her. She wouldn't see me much toward the end. At all. She'd taken up with this . . . crowd. Fucking weird rich people. Really into skincare, I guess it was?" He laughs darkly, but his eyes look pained, helpless. "I wasn't sure. She didn't really let me in. Your mother was pretty secretive about that stuff. About a lot of stuff, honestly."

I stare into his kind eyes, where once I thought I saw darkness. What was it I really saw there? Sorrow. Loss. Denial. A sunny attempt to sweep it all away.

It's on the tip of my tongue to tell Tad everything. Whisper it all into the shell of his ear.

Instead I say, "I hope you'll come back. For the windows."

He smiles. "Of course. I'll come back anytime. I'll be around. For the windows or not the windows."

He leans in, and for a moment I feel a thrum of panic. Then he kisses my cheek. Ruffles my hair. No cold. Not a trace of cold do I feel from his touch. It feels like being warmed through. And then we're parted.

"Oh hey, I didn't know what to do with those." He points to the two mannequins sitting at the table. "I guess they're new?"

I stare at their white smiling faces. Red lips and hair. Golden eyes. One in a dress of starry midnight. One in a dress of gold.

"Oh no, not new. Old friends. Sisters, you might say."

Tad looks at me. *Sisters?*

"You didn't see a third one, did you?"

"A third one? No. There was a broken window though. I think

someone might have tried to break in while you were gone. I fixed it for you. Reinforced them all too so you won't have trouble like that again."

He smiles at me. Taking me back to the child I once was, standing in Mother's hallway. I picture him waving at me in the dark. A waver, he would have been for sure.

"Thank you."

Through the window, I watch him leave the apartment. Get on his bike and drive away in a cloud of smoke and "God Only Knows."

Hard not to tell him to come back. But I just stand there watching him disappear into the sun from the glass. So clear, you can't even tell there's a glass there. So clear, you would never believe there was anything at all between you and the sea.

At the windows, I sit looking out at the crashing water for a long time. I'm not afraid to look out at the water anymore. Above the waves, the sun is setting. The sunset is really a story all its own. *A movie*, Mother used to say when I'd first arrived here. *The best one ever made*, she said, taking my hand. *It goes on and on, see?* Many twists and turns of color. Magic, really. Like a fairy tale. It begins with a pinkening of the clouds. Then a reddening, so that they look like the underbellies of some great fish. Then a bluing, which can go on awhile, giving way at last to starry black. Then you can hear the water but can't see it. You can only see yourself in the glass, looking out.

I pour myself some prosecco in one of Mother's cappuccino cups. I light one of her cigarettes, the second-to-last one. I'll keep the very last one. I watch the sunset with my sisters and Anjelica, her furry white body at my side, her pale eyes closing.

I think of Mother watching the sunset here. Alone, with a cigarette and a drink, just like this. She'd call me up some nights. I'd hear the waves crashing around behind her voice. I'd hear the wind and the gulls. I'd know she was looking at something other than herself by her voice. I'd hear all the sharp edges of it softened by what she saw happening through the glass, what I'm seeing now. Wind moving through blackening trees. White waves. That's when she'd ask me, *Are you happy?* That's when she'd say, *I do love you.* That's when she'd say, *Do you think you'll be coming to visit soon?*

Yes. I love you too. Soon, I'd answer, not even knowing if I meant it. But Mother pretended I did.

I'm glad.

The light changes and the moon and sun are in the sky together now. One falling light, one rising. *They can be together like that in the sky?* I asked Mother once. *The moon and the sun? Of course*, she said.

Of course they can be together like that. It doesn't happen often. Most of the time they're far apart. Sometimes at opposite ends of the earth. But sometimes—

Like tonight?

Like tonight. And she put her arm around my shoulders. *They're close.*

From where I sit now by the window, I can see where I lay with her on the rocky shore. The morning after our night of water. Where we saved each other from the nightmare of our Most Magnificent Selves. Where I watched her turn from a tangle of red tentacles into the face I knew all my life, into sea-foam. Just sand and water and rocks now.

In my mind, I answer her questions again.

Yes. I love you too. Soon.

My face begins to appear in the window glass. No Glow. No Moonbright. Just my old self. My familiar skin with its shade and texture and age. Only my forehead scar seems to have gone for good. Not even a shadow of a shadow remains. My eyes seem open in a new way. Like a fist, long closed, finally opens. Or like a flower opens for the sun. I smile at what I see.

And then just beyond my reflection, there's suddenly something else.

Someone else.

A man. Out there on the beach. Dark suit and hat. Walking barefoot along the lapping shore, his pant legs rolled. I stand up from my chair, looking closer. He seems to be dragging something behind him. Some sort of female figurine. Like a doll, but much bigger. Stiffer-looking.

I look at my sisters, who are watching him with interest. *Who is that?*

And then I'm running to the darkening beach.

When I get to the shore, he's shin-deep in the water. No disguise tonight. He's dancing with the third mannequin, my missing sister. Turning her around and around like they're doing a waltz in the water. Her silver dress is drenched. His dark suit is also drenched. But he doesn't seem to mind at all. Or even notice. He's too busy dancing, just like he and I danced in the grand hall. Like the waves are the music. Like the setting sun and the rising moon are a chandelier of fire above their heads. He's holding her like he held me. Close. Whispering tenderly into her ear. Words I can't hear in the waves. She just stares into space with her painted eyes.

"Hi," I call to him over the waves.

He looks at me. He knows me and doesn't know me, I can tell by his eyes. Searching mine. There's a Glow to his skin I recognize. A Brightening. But the scar is still there like a slash over one brow and down his cheek. Whatever they took from him, they didn't take everything.

"Can I cut in?" I ask him. "Do you mind?"

He looks from me to the mannequin. He's reluctant, I can tell. Doesn't want to leave her. He's gripping her hand so tightly in his fist. The fist is bloody, I see, speckled with small cuts, like he might have punched it through glass. He was the one who broke into Mother's apartment. Took her with him. *I'm saving you*, he probably told her.

"She'll be all right," I tell him. "We'll just put her right here on this chair," I say, pointing to a rock behind me. I remember him trying to soothe me like this not so very long ago. "She's been dancing for a while. I'm sure she'd love to rest."

I take her from him and sit her down on the rock. When I turn to him, he's still dancing with the shape of her, still dancing with air. He's moved farther away from the shore, deeper into the water.

So I take off my shoes. So I walk deeper into the cold waves that take my breath away. I wade out to where he's turning and turning with air, lost in the ocean's music. Hip-deep in the water. He looks at me and I take his hand. I wade into the empty space between his arms. Slip his hand on my back, my arm on his cold wet shoulder. I become the shape of her. His body visibly relaxes. I feel it relax in my embrace. He smiles for a moment, then looks serious again.

"We have to get you out of here," he whispers.

I stare at his moonbright face. Glowing, glowing in the light of the bloody sun and the high pale moon. The waves are gentle tonight, but they're rising. "We do?"

"It'll be dangerous. You'll have to fall for me. *Follow* me. Like I fell for—followed you. Didn't intend to love—to lose you there like that."

I trace the scar's curve along his cheek. "Me neither."

"Just keep dancing with me. Don't let anyone else cut in. Ever, okay?"

"I won't," I say. "Promise."

He sighs with relief. Looks at me, his eyes clear and deep as the first mirror. Beautifully broken. "I'm saving you, you know," he says as we turn in the waves.

"I know."

Above us, the blue sky begins to blacken. Though the sun's fading now, there's still some light on the waves. It's nearly the end of its story, the fairy tale of the setting sun. Time for the moon's full rising. We're still deep in the dark, shining water, but I'm dancing us slowly, surely, to shore.

Acknowledgments

To my parents, Nina Milosevic and James Awad, for everything.

To my uncle Michael O'Brien-Milosevic, who recently passed, but whose influence on me and my way of seeing the world lives on in my heart and in these pages.

To my grandmother Ruth O'Brien, who is (and isn't at all) the grandmother in this book. Part of the joy of writing *Rouge* was getting to spend time with you again in this other world.

To the dear friends and family who read drafts and who supported me (endlessly) during the writing of this book: Ken Calhoun, Jess Riley, Alexandra Dimou, Rex Baker, Laura Sims, Laura Zigman, Teresa Carmody, Emily Culliton, Lauren Acampora, McCormick Templeman, and Lynn Crosbie.

To Ken Calhoun, who read more drafts than I can count, for the magical plot talks and the unwavering faith.

To Bill Clegg for being the best reader and champion I could hope for. To Simon Toop and to everyone at the Clegg Agency (Nikolas Slackman, Marion Duvert, and MC Connors) for everything you do and for the invaluable early reads and support.To Anna Webber at United Agents.

To my wonderful editors, Marysue Rucci, Nicole Winstanley, and Chris White, and to the publishing teams at Simon & Schuster, Penguin Canada, and Scribner in the UK: Andy Tang, Katie Freeman, Clare Maurer, Jessica Preeg, Ingrid Carabulea, Zach Polendo, Laura Jarrett, Erica Stahler, Georgia Brainard, Wendy Sheanin, Elizabeth Breeden, Stephen Myers, Dan French, Beth Cockeram, Kate Sinclair, and Meredith Pal. To the amazing sales and marketing teams who get books into the hands of readers.

To the brilliant Oliver Munday and Patrick Sullivan for their incredible work on the dreamy jacket design. If ever the soul of a book could be captured in a jacket, this is it.

To my amazing students and colleagues at Syracuse University for their support throughout the writing process.

To Margaret Atwood for the wise and eerily prescient advice.

To Tom Cruise, who is not in this book, despite appearances.

Music has always been important to my writing, but this book was especially helped along by certain songs and albums, many of which are mentioned or featured in the story. I'm grateful to all the musicians who made this story come alive for me, particularly Cavern of Anti-Matter and Tangerine Dream. And of course, Berlin.

Lastly, once more to my mother, Nina Milosevic, who was nothing like Noelle, but who undoubtedly informed the relationship between mother and daughter in this book, both its petals and its thorns. I still miss you dearly.

About the Author

Mona Awad is the author of *All's Well*, *Bunny*, and *13 Ways of Looking at a Fat Girl*. *Bunny* was a finalist for a Goodreads Choice Award and the New England Book Award. It was named a Best Book of 2019 by *Time*, *Vogue*, and the New York Public Library. It is currently under option for film with Bad Robot Productions. *All's Well* was a finalist for a Goodreads Choice Award and long-listed for the International Dublin Award. *13 Ways* won the Amazon Best First Novel Award and was short-listed for the Giller Prize. *Rouge* is optioned for film with Fremantle. Awad currently teaches fiction in the creative writing program at Syracuse University. She is based in Boston.